Two Songs This Archangel Sings

The Mongo Mysteries

Shadow of a Broken Man
City of Whispering Stone
An Affair of Sorcerers
The Beasts of Valhalla
Two Songs This Archangel Sings

Two Songs This Archangel Sings

George C. Chesbro

A DELL BOOK

Published by
Dell Publishing
a division of
The Bantam Doubleday Dell Publishing Group, Inc.
1 Dag Hammarskjold Plaza
New York, New York 10017

ISBN: 0-440-20105-5

Reprinted by arrangement with Atheneum Publishers

Printed in the United States of America

April 1988

10 9 8 7 6 5 4 3 2 1

KRI

Two Songs This Archangel Sings

1

The man I was on my way to see had the odd but curiously appropriate first name of Veil. For the past six years he'd been one of the hottest painters on the fickle and volatile New York art scene and could presumably afford much better quarters than the loft he rented in a rotting, otherwise empty factory building in one of the roughest sections on the city's Lower East Side, but apparently simply preferred not to.

I'd known Veil Kendry for slightly more than eleven years, since a summer Sunday in 1977 when I'd been the first person to purchase one of his paintings from a sidewalk display at a Greenwich Village art fair; he'd looked exhausted and hungry, and had accepted my invitation to celebrate his first sale and the launching of his career as a professional artist with dinner later in the day. He'd come a long way since then, and I assumed that the painting I'd bought, now hanging on a wall in the living room of my apartment, had become quite valuable; I certainly couldn't afford anything he did now.

In addition to his career as an artist, Veil was also a kind of benign warlord and protector of his neighborhood, a roughly eight-square-block area he had transformed into an island of relative calm and safety within a surrounding polluted sea of street crime and violence. He spent a good deal of time walking night streets, and a few years before, during the course of a particularly hot and ugly summer, a grand total of nineteen unfortunates armed with assorted chains, knives, steel pipes, and guns had attempted to mug the solitary walker. Score: Veil Kendry—armed only with the fastest hands and feet I'd ever seen and awesome talents in the martial arts—nineteen, muggers zip. He'd pretty thoroughly maimed eighteen of the unfortunates, and the nineteenth had died when, running in a blind panic to escape Veil, he had collided with an equally unforgiving lamppost and crushed his skull.

Veil had the habit of unexpectedly emerging from the night when others, as well, were being mugged, or when a drug deal was being made, or when an abandoned building was being set up as a shooting gallery. Score, according to NYPD statistics: Veil Kendry twenty-seven; drug dealers, junkies, and muggers zip. Word gets

around. Veil was a hero to his neighbors, not so beloved by the
police, including my detective brother, who considered Veil a kind
of pesky, unlicensed "street detective" and vigilante who'd managed to stay just beyond the reach of the law because his victims
kept displaying the poor judgment to come at him with weapons,
while he had never been known to use anything but his hands and
feet. But then, Veil was utterly indifferent to what anyone thought
of him; it showed in his style of painting, and in the way he lived
his life. He was a man who sang his own songs, and I liked him
very much.

In addition to being my friend, Veil was also my informal martial arts instructor—the best I had ever had—and workout partner.
I held a black belt in karate—the result of excellent reflexes and
coordination, countless hours of practice, and what Garth, with a
malicious grin, always insisted was an insufferable tendency to
overcompensate in virtually every area of my life. He was probably
right. I'd enjoyed a full and most satisfying career as a circus head-
liner, and was now a criminology professor and private investigator. I liked to think that I had a few ditties of my own to sing.

Veil Kendry, to my knowledge, held no belts in any of the martial arts disciplines in which he was a consummate master. He
never competed, and I had no idea where, or by whom, he had
been trained. Indeed, by mutual agreement his life before he came
to New York City was closed to me—and, I assumed, to anyone
else who had not been a part of it. While Veil was a sensitive and
gifted artist with a soft-spoken and gentle manner, he was also the
most potentially lethal human being I had ever met, or heard of.
The people who steered clear of his neighborhood agreed.

Still, even the toughest kid on a block doesn't leave the door to
his building open when he lives in that part of New York, and I
was filled with a vague sense of foreboding when I found it that
way. Veil Kendry might be fearless, but he was neither stupid nor
careless.

Our appointment had been for seven thirty, and I'd been ten
minutes early. I'd rung the bell, waited. The intercom beside the
bell had remained silent, and there had been no loud electronic
buzz signaling that I should push open the door and go up. I'd
rung again, keeping my finger on the button for a good ten seconds, then stepped back on the sidewalk and looked up. In the
windows of the loft on the fourth floor of the otherwise gutted

building the bright mix of fluorescent and mercury vapor lamps Veil used to light his huge loft when he was working burned like a blue-white luminescent banner of defiance in this dark, wounded block of abandoned and boarded-up storefronts and warehouses. Thinking that the bell might not be working, I'd shouted his name a couple of times, but the only response had been a slight, hollow echo of my voice in the long metal and stone canyon that was the street. Finally, in a casual gesture of frustration, I'd stepped forward and slapped the heel of my hand against the steel plate of the door. It had swung open on its well-oiled hinges. Not good.

The door opened into a small vestibule at the bottom of an elevator shaft. Here, too, the lights were on, and the large, rickety freight elevator was on the ground floor, its wooden gate raised. Four floors above, clearly visible through the steel and wood latticework that comprised the elevator shaft, the sliding steel door at the entrance to Veil's loft was wide open, bleeding heat into the winter that filled the rest of the building. The mercury vapor glow from inside the loft mixed with the paler light in the elevator shaft to create a kind of eerie aura similar to the ghostly white on white shadings that had become the signature effects in Veil's latest paintings.

"Veil?! It's Mongo! You up there?!"

There was no answer. I closed the door behind me, stepped into the elevator, and pulled down the gate. I pushed the UP button, rode the elevator to the open door of Veil's loft, and stepped in.

"Veil? You here?"

A quick check of his living quarters, behind a partition to the right of the entrance, showed me he wasn't there, and I went back out to the much larger work area. There was no sign of disturbance; the loft looked the way it always did, except for the fact that there was nobody in it.

The entire wall at the far end of the loft consisted of windows, approximately two feet square, rising to merge with a great skylight. Heavy drapes that Veil had installed and that were usually closed at night were open, and the light pushed back the night outside far enough for me to see the pitted bricks of the wall of the abandoned warehouse fifteen yards away, across a weed and refuse-choked alley.

To the left of the panel of windows was an area covered with mats where Veil and I worked out together. In addition, there were two punching and kicking bags suspended from the ceiling, a wooden box filled with martial arts weapons, and a target board used for practicing with throwing knives and the small razor-sharp, star-shaped blades called *shuriken*.

The rest of the loft was given over to the business of painting, and it looked like a scarred battlefield strewn with the multihued blood of alien creatures on some distant planet. A paint-spackled telephone was mounted on one of the three support columns rising from a turbulent sea of covered or coagulated paint pots, assorted palettes scattered over paint-encrusted tarpaulins, brushes of every size and shape soaking in jars of turpentine, hundreds of mauled tubes of oil paint, dozens of palette knives of various sizes. This tortured mess covered every square inch of space in the loft outside the workout and living quarters, and one wandered through it all carefully stepping—or jumping—from one dry area to what appeared to be another dry area, and hoping one guessed correctly.

What arose from this chaos was neatly arranged on one wall running the length of the loft, a sight that reminded me of nothing so much as tranquil clouds of mist floating out of, and over, the mouth of a live volcano. Like many artists in the eighties, Veil Kendry worked on a large scale; however, only a handful of people appreciated just how large a scale that was. I had never read nor heard of any other painter who worked the way Veil did, and only a privileged few who had been invited up to his loft had ever seen a "mother work," the overall conception of one of Veil's ideas, before the individual canvases that comprised it, sometimes as many as fifty, were removed at random from the wall, like pieces from a jigsaw puzzle, and sold individually, often over an extended period of time, by Viktor Raskolnikov, Veil's dealer.

The work-in-progress, an eerie seascape, was almost finished. Made up of thirty-six separate canvases, arranged nine across and four down, I found it hauntingly beautiful but also frightening, with suggestions of strange, toothy shapes lurking just beneath the surface of a too-calm sea. Thunderheads gathered on the horizon.

The art world considered Veil an abstract painter, and it was not surprising; while each canvas, each piece of the puzzle, was beautiful and seemed complete in itself, it gave no clue to the overall nature of the larger work. I found Veil's method fascinating.

Sliding the door closed behind me, I walked across the loft, set my gym bag down on the floor, and sat down on the mat to wait.

My sense of unease, the conviction that something was wrong, was steadily increasing. It was, of course, possible that my friend had stepped out for a few minutes to get a quart of milk or something; the problem was that the nearest store open at this hour was six blocks away. I'd passed that store on my way, had not seen Veil in it, and had not passed him on my way. For six years, except when Veil or I was out of town, we had always met at seven thirty on Wednesday evening to work out together. I'd spoken to him on the phone the day before, and he had not indicated there had been any change in his plans. In any case, he would not have gone away and left his loft open with all the lights on.

Those burning lights were another problem. The complex system of mercury vapor and regular lighting in the loft was controlled by six different rheostats, and was varied depending upon what area of the loft Veil was working in at any particular time; I had never known him to have all the lights on at one time, since it would be inefficient and prohibitively expensive.

My watch read eight o'clock. Increasingly nervous, I rose from the mat, went to the central control box on the opposite wall, and shut off all the mercury vapor lamps. I forced myself to wait another half hour, then went to the telephone and the city directory hanging on a nail beside it. It took me fifteen minutes to call all the hospital emergency rooms in New York's five boroughs; Veil was not in any of them. Next I called Garth's apartment, but got no answer. Finally I called his precinct station house. I'd expected to get one of his colleagues and was surprised when Garth answered the phone himself.

"Hey, brother."

"Hi, Mongo. What's up?" He sounded tired and out of sorts, as he had for some time. Things didn't seem to be right with Garth, either, and I was beginning to worry about him.

"How are you feeling, Garth?"

"About half."

"How come you're working? I thought you were off for a couple of days."

"Big political doings, which means lots of forced overtime."

"What big political doings?"

"Where have you been for the past two days? Don't you read or listen to the news?"

"Uh-uh—at least not for the past week. With exam papers to

grade and this lecture tomorrow to prepare for, I haven't had time
to keep up with the outside world. What's cooking?"

"Shannon held a surprise press conference yesterday to announce that he's introducing the choices for his cabinet at a dinner
at the Waldorf tonight. Coming to New York to do it, he says, is
his way of showing his concern for the cities." Garth paused,
laughed harshly. "Some concern. I wonder if the idiot realizes that
his showing up here costs the city millions for police overtime and
extra security precautions, not to mention traffic jams that take
hours to unsnarl. I got called in to work the switchboard."

"I like Shannon," I said. "He's tough and realistic, and I think
his head and heart are in the right place. He's not your average
liberal, and I'll be interested in seeing what he does as president. I
think he'll be the best we've had since Roosevelt, and I think he
has the potential to be great."

"All politicians are worthless pricks," Garth said with unexpected vehemence and bitterness that surprised me and made me
uncomfortable. "They're worse than useless, and you know it.
They're eventually going to kill us all, and it doesn't make any
difference whether it's the president of the United States or that
new KGB creep in the Kremlin who starts the ball rolling for the
last time. If Kevin Shannon, or any other politician, gives you a
happy heart, it means you have a short memory."

"I don't have a short memory, Garth," I said quietly. "No matter what, you have to keep going."

"As if Valhalla had never happened? As if we didn't know what
we know?"

"Yes. You have to have hope. Kevin Shannon gives me hope."

Another harsh laugh. "You'd have a different opinion of the man
if you were trapped in a car anywhere in midtown Manhattan right
now. Traffic's a nightmare."

"I didn't notice; I was on the subway. Who's in his cabinet?"

"Turn on the television at nine tonight and you'll find out the
same time as everybody else in the nation. You know how Shannon
likes his little dramas and surprises; he's worse than Johnson."
Garth grunted, and then his voice became more mellow. "So much
for my problems. What's your problem, Mongo?"

"I need a favor."

"That doesn't surprise me at all," Garth said dryly.

"I'm at Veil Kendry's place." I paused to allow Garth his obligatory, hostile grunt that came whenever I mentioned Veil, then continued: "I was supposed to meet him here at seven thirty for a karate workout; we do it every Wednesday night. He's not here."

Garth laughed without humor. "So? What do you want to do, file a complaint? He probably forgot."

"No. There's something wrong, Garth. When I got here, I found the loft open and all the lights on."

"Maybe he stepped out for a minute to get something."

"It's almost nine. I've been here an hour and a half, and I don't know how long he was gone before that. Besides, there's nothing around here to step out to."

"Kendry's a very spooky man, Mongo. What can I tell you?"

"You can tell me if his name's on any of the arrest sheets. I've checked with the hospital emergency rooms, but he's not in any of those. I thought maybe he got into some law trouble."

"It wouldn't be the first time, and it wouldn't surprise me."

"It also wouldn't be the first time you guys rousted him."

" 'Roust' is a pretty strong word, Mongo. Your buddy has a nasty habit of taking the law into his own hands."

"Only when the cop's hands are busy elsewhere, which is most of the time in this neighborhood. Just check it for me, will you, Garth? I know you're busy. I'll wait here, and you get back to me whenever you can."

"It's all right," Garth said grudgingly. "I've got a computer terminal here, and it won't take me that long. Hang on." Garth put me on hold, came back on the line a couple of minutes later. "Nothing, Mongo. Wherever Kendry is, it's not with cops."

"What about the other boroughs?"

"I checked the other boroughs."

"Thanks, brother."

"Yeah. Now go home and polish your lecture. I wouldn't want you to embarrass me tomorrow."

I hung up the receiver, then walked back to the windows. I pulled the drapes shut over the huge expanse of glass, then once again went back to the phone and called my answering service. There were no messages. There was a pad and pencil hanging next to the directory, and I wrote Veil a brief note explaining that it was me who had shut off the lights and pulled the drapes, and asking him to call me whenever he got in. Then I picked up my gym bag and walked to the exit. I pulled open the sliding door, started to step into the elevator—and stopped. I knew that even if I went home, it was doubtful whether I would sleep; I would be up all night worrying about Veil, waiting for the phone to ring, searching for answers to the questions that filled the loft.

Even if Veil had been in such a rush that he had neglected to check to make certain the downstairs door was locked, it still did not explain why the loft door had been left open, or why every light in the place had been turned on full blast and left burning.

Unless the open doors and burning lights had been meant as some kind of a message to me. An invitation? A warning? Was it conceivable, I wondered, that Veil had literally meant to "shed light" on something? If so, what? His absence?

I decided it was an absurd notion, considering the fact that it would have been far simpler and more logical, not to mention cheaper, simply to call me, or at least to leave a note. But Veil had to be in some kind of trouble and, whether or not he had meant to send me some kind of message, there seemed to be absolutely nothing I could do about it.

Except hang around and wait to see what might happen.

I slid the door shut, then turned the rest of the lights down to a dim glow. I went over to the mats, lay down, and rested my head on my gym bag. And I waited.

2

I awoke tired and stiff, with a milky, blurred January dawn seeping into my face through the skylight over my head. I knew Veil was not there; even if I had missed the opening and closing of the steel door, he would certainly have covered me with something, if not woken me up. It was cold in the loft, and I was shivering. Wishing I had worn my parka, I zipped up the jacket of my warm-up suit, pulled the hood over my head, then jogged in place a few minutes to get my circulation going before pulling back the drapes on a gray, cheerless morning that looked pregnant with snow.

In the early morning light Veil Kendry's vaguely menacing sea-scape seemed even eerier and more otherworldly, like some great sign posted to warn me that I was in a place where I did not belong.

There was zone heating in the loft, and the living quarters turned out to be warmer than the work area. In the kitchen, I went to the stove and put on a kettle of water to boil. After making myself a large mug of instant coffee, I unzipped my jacket and went to the telephone extension next to the sink. Once again I called all the hospital emergency rooms, and once again found that Veil wasn't in any of them; I hadn't expected that he would be, but thought it a necessary base to touch. Next, I called my service, but the only message that had been left was from a panicky student who feared—with good cause—that he'd failed my course. I didn't bother calling Garth. I assumed Garth would have gotten back to me if Veil's name had turned up on an arrest sheet, and I no longer considered it probable that Veil's trouble was with the police; it wouldn't explain the open loft and burning lights. Veil's problem, whatever it was, had to be more serious than one of his periodic run-ins with the cops, and his absence was beginning to feel like an oppressive weight growing ever heavier on me. Uninvited, I had entered more than a painter's loft; I had walked into a situation I was not certain how to walk away from.

Picking up my coffee mug, I went back out into the work area, went to the wooden equipment box next to the mats, and opened the lid. A chill that had nothing to do with the cold in this part of the loft went through me as I looked down into the box. Veil's oversize gym bag was missing, along with the half dozen *shuriken* he kept there, two throwing knives, and his *nunchaku*—two polished, rock-hard sticks of mahogany joined by a six-inch chain, a fearsome and deadly bonecrusher in the hands of a martial arts master like Veil Kendry.

Closing the lid, I leaned back against the box, sipped at my coffee, and tried to think. Wherever Veil was and whatever he was doing was his business, I thought, not mine. The missing weapons indicated that Veil was taking care of that business, and my chief concern should be for whoever it was Veil had gone to do business with. It had nothing to do with me. Veil would have asked for my help if he needed it, and he hadn't.

Or had he . . . ?

Aside from locking up his loft and turning off his lights, what the hell did he expect me to do?

My coffee had gone cold. I set the mug down on top of the equipment box, glanced nervously at my watch, then went across the loft to the wall where the seascape hung. Walking slowly toward the opposite end, I carefully examined each canvas in the mosaic, thinking there might be some answer hidden in one of them. There wasn't—at least none that I could find. Viewed individually and at close range, each canvas indeed became "abstract," and even the menacing figures beneath the surface of the sea sank from sight. I could find no indication of anything in the individual canvases except for the fact that Veil Kendry's imagination and artistic talent seemed as unique to him as his almost superhuman fighting skills. Searching for my friend in the loft he had vacated was getting to be most frustrating, and it seemed increasingly apparent that I was on the errand of a fool.

Adding to my frustration was a sense of mounting time pressure. In slightly less than an hour and a half I was supposed to deliver a lecture—and not just any lecture, and not to students. As far as my career in academia was concerned, it was probably the most important speech I would ever make. There were police chiefs and criminologists in town from all over the world to attend a four-day symposium on serial murderers under the auspices of the John Jay College of Criminal Justice. The keynote address was being delivered at my university because it had the only auditorium large enough to accommodate all of the people expected to attend. In ninety minutes a few hundred people, including the university chancellor and the head of my department, were going to be sitting in their seats in the huge lecture hall, staring up at the lectern and expecting to see—me.

Some research I'd done on the minds and motives of serial murderers, published in a half dozen monographs in various professional journals, was now considered seminal, and possibly even predictive. As a result of those papers, I'd been invited to deliver the keynote address and was expected to discuss my most recent work. It was a signal honor, the kind of thing that allows one to advance rapidly in the academic world, an intense focus of attention on one's self and work for which most professors would sacrifice a year's sabbatical. I should have been home eating a good breakfast, studying my lecture notes, and trying to relax. Instead I was unshaven and grungy from spending the night on a gym mat, dressed in old, patched sweats and worn, dirty sneakers. If I got lucky and found a cab at this hour of the morning, or if I left immediately and sprinted to the subway, I might just make it to my apartment in time to shave, shower, put on my one good suit, and get to the university with a minute or two to spare before I was scheduled to begin speaking.

Turning back toward the far end of the loft, I caught a wink of light high up on the bank of windows. Puzzled, I moved a few feet to my left, keeping my eye on the spot, then realized with a start that what I was looking at was a bullet hole. I had not seen it the night before because of the darkness and would probably not have seen it at all if I had not been standing in the right place and looking up at the right angle. The fact that the glass had not been shattered indicated to me that the weapon used had been small bore, high velocity. I could now see that the glass was thicker than it first appeared and optically distorting. It could explain why the bullet had missed its mark.

If it had missed its mark.

The bullet had to have been fired from the roof of the factory building across the alley, which was some two stories higher that the loft. That gave me an approximate downward angle, but it wasn't much help in allowing me to determine the exact trajectory of the bullet into the loft.

The canvases on the one wall hadn't been damaged, which meant that the bullet hadn't entered there. Slowly, eyes on the floor, I began to walk back and forth across the work area, looking for a bullet hole or bloodstain. I gave up after a couple of minutes; if there were bloodstains on the wrinkled tarpaulins that covered the floor, they would be indistinguishable from the innumerable splotches of red paint.

The good news, I thought, was that there had been no bloodstains in the elevator; but then, Veil, if he had been hurt, could always have bandaged the wound. Whatever had happened to Veil, the answer to where he had gone, and why, did not seem to be in this part of the loft.

Which did not mean that there might not be answers somewhere else in the loft.

I went back into the living quarters, through the kitchen into the area where Veil slept. I'd been in this area before, but only now did it strike me how very little there was to see. After the vast expanse of the work area, the living quarters seemed excessively cramped and ascetic, like a monk's cell. It was all strictly functional. Just to the right of the kitchen entrance was a neatly made bed covered by a thick brown quilt that matched the color of the walls and ceiling. There was a bathroom with toilet and shower, and next to the bed a leather reclining chair with a reading lamp behind it. There was a bookshelf filled with books that looked well worn. Judging from the titles of the books, his reading was thoroughly eclectic, from Carlos Castaneda to Proust to Melville to Ross Macdonald, in addition to lots of history, philosophy, and science. A separate bookcase held dozens of back issues of magazines and newspapers —*Scientific American, Newsweek, Time, The New York Review of Books,* and various martial arts journals. Next to the wall on the opposite side of the kitchen entrance was a writing desk—bare except for a lead paperweight and a letter opener. There was also a small television set and stacked stereo components. His record collection, like his books, was eclectic, and his tastes ranged from classical to rock, from folk to vintage blues and jazz. There was a dresser and mirror flanked by two wardrobes, both filled with clothes.

Wherever Veil had gone, he was traveling light.

It struck me that, aside from the shards of personality that can always be extracted from a person's book and record collections, there was absolutely nothing *personal* in the living quarters—no pictures, no photographs, no mementos of any kind. The walls, like the surfaces of the desk and dresser, were bare of personal statement or reflection, making the living quarters as silent about Veil Kendry as the man himself. It was as if Veil had gone to great lengths to erase all traces of his past.

Once, soon after I'd met the painter, I'd asked him where he had been and what he had done before coming to New York City. His reply had been flat and simple; there was no offense intended, but his past, all of it, was something he preferred not to discuss. That had been fine with me. I'd liked Veil Kendry for who and what he was, and who and what he might once have been had been irrelevant to me. Indeed, after that initial conversation I hadn't given the matter further thought—until now, eleven years later, standing in this spiritually stripped cell.

Not bothering to glance at my watch because I knew it would only make me nauseated, I walked quickly to the desk and opened the middle drawer. Inside were invoices and receipts for art supplies, a checkbook, a few pens and pencils. There were no entries in the checkbook that seemed unusual, and there were no personal letters.

I closed that drawer, opened the single, deep drawer to the left. There was nothing in the front of the drawer, and as I bent over to look in the back my eye caught something mounted beneath the desk, high on a back leg: a switch. I hesitated just a moment, then reached back and flipped it. I heard a sharp click behind me, spun around, and saw that a section of the floor about the size of a door had popped up an inch or so.

At once excited by my discovery and embarrassed at just how far I was intruding into a very private man's private space and affairs, I walked quickly over to the raised section of floor, got down on my hands and knees. I pushed the panel back off its spring-loaded supports, grunted with surprise when I looked down into the hidden compartment, which was perhaps a foot and a half deep. There was a sharp odor of machine oil, and in one corner were bottles of gun oil, gun cleaning equipment, and a number of soft, oil-soaked rags. Around the edges of the compartment were brackets—now ominously empty—obviously intended to hold guns; judging from the configuration of the brackets, one of those weapons could well be a submachine gun.

At the bottom of the compartment, directly in the center, was a fairly large oil painting, obviously by Veil but painted in the kind of dark, rich, vibrant colors he had employed at the beginning of his career, but which he hadn't used for years. The style, the brush-strokes, were undeniably Veil's, but this painting was unlike any of his other work I had ever seen. To begin with, the single canvas was complete in itself and painted in a totally realistic style.

It was also jarring. In the painting, black-pajama-clad and uniformed Asiatics armed with carbines and semiautomatic weapons moved stealthily along a narrow trail winding through thick jungle growing over the foothills of a cloud-shrouded mountain range that rose in the distance. Hovering over the entire scene, rising over the misted mountains and suspended above the armed figures, was what could only be described as an angel, albeit a most unusual one. The suggestion of wings on its back and a halo around its head were composed of fire and dark smoke. The angel wore a long, flowing white robe covered with strange, mystical symbols colored magenta, crimson, and brown. Bullet-choked bandolieros crisscrossed the angel's chest, and he brandished a submachine gun. Long, thick yellow hair was whipped by a fierce wind that apparently affected nothing and nobody else in the painting. The angel had pale blue eyes, handsome features, unusually high cheekbones, and a strong chin. His lips were drawn back in a grimace of pain or rage, or both.

That long, yellow hair of the figure in the painting was now liberally streaked with gray, and the flesh over the high cheekbones was no longer stretched quite so taut; there were more shadows under the eyes that remained a kind of glacial blue, but the face was nevertheless unmistakably that of Veil Kendry as he must have looked more than twenty years before.

When I lightly touched the surface of the painting, I found it still tacky; it had been painted recently, within the past twenty-four hours. I gripped the canvas by the edges of its wooden stretch frame, carefully lifted it up and out. As I did so, I was startled to find a large, bulky manila envelope beneath it. My name, in black oil paint and written in Veil's familiar hand, was printed in large block letters across the face of the envelope.

Setting down the painting, I picked up the envelope, ripped open one end, and dumped the contents on the floor. A quick count with trembling fingers told me there was ten thousand dollars, in hundreds and fifties, spread out before me. I shook the envelope, but nothing else came out, and a look inside confirmed that the envelope was empty. There was no note.

After stuffing the money back into the envelope, I rose and hurried to the phone extension in the kitchen. This time I reached Garth at his apartment.

"Yo, brother."

"Mongo, where the hell are you?"

"Veil's place."

"What the hell are you doing there? You know, you just caught me; I was on my way out the door. Want to try and guess where I was going?"

"Garth, listen—"

"As a matter of fact, I was afraid *I* was going to be late for a very heavy lecture my brother is giving this morning to law enforcement people from all over the world. This brother of mine is supposed to be some kind of expert on serial murderers, which doesn't surprise me at all; loonies love him. Anyway, I'm very proud of this brother. There are a lot of cops from a lot of different places who arrived in town a few days early to see the sights, and I've been spending a lot of time getting drunk with them, bragging about my brother and telling them what a great speaker he is. By the way, do you plan to show up?"

"Just shut up and listen to me, Garth. This is more important."

"I'm listening," Garth said seriously. "Are you all right?"

"I'm all right, but I've been here all night and Veil hasn't shown up. I'm almost certain he took off after someone winged a shot at him; there's a bullet hole in one of his windows."

I paused for a moment, debating whether or not I should tell Garth now about the weapons Veil was undoubtedly carrying, decided that it would only cloud the more important issue. "I told you that he left his loft open, with all the lights on. It felt all wrong, and that's why I stuck around. I found the bullet hole this morning."

There was a pause, then: "Explain to me the connection."

"After I found the bullet hole, I started poking around the place. I got lucky and found a secret compartment. Inside, I found an oil painting and an envelope, addressed to me, with ten grand in cash inside."

This time there was a much longer pause. "Very strange, Mongo," Garth said at last. "Just like your friend."

"I want you to forget about the lecture; I'll give you a blow-by-blow description tonight, over steak and whiskey sours. I'll take care of that business, but I'd like you to go down to the station house and file a missing persons report on Veil Kendry. Now."

Garth thought about it. "It's too soon," he finally said. "And you're not a relative. You have no legal standing to—"

"I'm his friend. He's in trouble, Garth."

"Any signs of a struggle in the loft? Blood? Overturned furniture?"

"No," I replied reluctantly.

"Then what's the problem? It wouldn't be the first time somebody went out, left the lights on, and forgot to lock the door."

"You don't understand; you have to be here. I know he's in trouble."

"You say. Kendry doesn't get in trouble; he gives it to other people."

"I told you somebody took a shot at him. You don't seem to be taking that very seriously."

"Wrong. The problem is that you don't know for certain that somebody took a shot at *him* because you don't know how long that bullet hole has been there. Am I right?"

"Garth—!"

"Did you find the bullet, or another hole where it hit?"

"Garth, the loft's big as a Goddamn football field."

"The hole could have been plastered over, or covered with something. I take bullets most seriously—but remember that this is New York, and that area where Kendry lives is zooier than most. That bullet hole could have been there for months, even years. Now, do you want me to send a car to pick you up?"

"No," I answered curtly. I thought Garth was being totally unreasonable, not to mention callous, and it was beginning to make me angry. "I'm already downtown, and I can probably get there faster on my own. The shot had to have been fired sometime yesterday; it's why Veil left. Why don't you come down here? Maybe if you see—"

"Whoa, brother," Garth interrupted, impatience creeping into his voice. "You may think I'm turning off on this thing because I don't like Kendry."

"Are you, Garth?"

"Just stop and think a moment. You tell me nothing in the loft has been disturbed. The police can't go in there, and I can't file a missing persons report, just because your buddy didn't keep an appointment. As a matter of fact, *you* shouldn't be up there right now."

"What about the money, Garth? And the painting? I know this sounds crazy, but it occurs to me that it's almost as if he couldn't decide whether or not to ask for my help, so he left it all up to chance—first, whether I'd even notice that the door was open and come up to the loft, and then whether I'd find the things he left for me."

"You're right. It sounds crazy."

"Well, I *did* find those things."

"Only because you're outrageously nosy."

"The painting has to be some kind of clue."

"A clue to what?"

"Maybe to where he's gone, and why."

"And what is it that you think he wants you to do?" Garth sounded as if he were talking to a child.

"I don't *know*, Garth," I said, time pressure and frustration combining to squeeze my voice into a kind of plaintive whine. Garth thought I was being absurd, and in a way I could see his point. But he hadn't looked down into the secret compartment beneath the floor and seen the painting, or found the envelope with my name on it and ten thousand dollars inside; he hadn't seen the empty brackets or smelled the machine oil. "The only thing I can figure is that he may want me to search for him."

"Ah, yes, a little game of hide and seek. Are you listening to yourself? If Kendry wanted something from you, why wouldn't he just say so? Why play games?"

Of course, I didn't have an answer. "Garth, I just have this feeling."

"Get rid of it," Garth replied in a low, very serious tone. He paused, sighed heavily. "Mongo, my beloved brother, you think somebody snatched Kendry?"

"I didn't say that."

"Good, because it would take a battalion of men to do that, and that place would be torn apart. You listen to me carefully. Kendry never got in touch with you, and you haven't been hired to do anything. The university, on the other hand, pays you good money to play professor, and in a very short time you're supposed to deliver a very important lecture. Get your ass out of there."

"Garth, the envelope with the cash was addressed to me!"

"I don't care if it was addressed to Mary Poppins. It sounds to me like *you* just about had to tear the place apart to find it, which means that it doesn't belong to you. You're already trespassing; if you take anything out of there, some people might call you a burglar and a thief. Besides, you're the one who once told me that Kendry often drops out of sight for long periods of time."

"That's true, but he'd always let me know when he was leaving so that I wouldn't count on our Wednesday night workouts."

"So? This time he forgot."

"Garth—"

"Did he ever tell you where he was going?"

"No."

"You never asked?"

"Veil's a very private man."

"Right. This is the private man whose loft you're tearing up and looting while he's away taking care of some private business."

"Come on, Garth, be serious. At least stop being ridiculous. Why the hell would he leave without turning off the lights and locking the door?"

"You be serious. Kendry's a loony, Mongo. In fact, he's even loonier than you think he is."

The smell of machine oil was still in my nostrils, and something in Garth's voice—perhaps a warning—gave me pause. "Meaning what? Why is Veil even loonier than I think he is?"

"Never mind; he just is. Now turn off the lights and lock up that loft, brother, after you've put everything back exactly the way you found it. Later, after you've taken care of the other little item on your agenda for today, I want you to go home and write 'I will mind my own business' one hundred times on your blackboard."

"Veil's in serious trouble, Garth, and he needs my help. I know it."

"Shit. You're going to go looking for him, aren't you?"

"Well, not right now. I've got a lecture to deliver, remember? See you later, brother."

3

The university was a lot closer than my apartment, so I went directly there and managed to be only twenty minutes late. From the looks of the packed auditorium, just about everyone had hung around considerably longer that any of my graduate students would have if I'd been late for a lecture. Walking through the building to the appropriate backstage entrance would have taken another three or four minutes, so I made a grand entrance from the rear of the auditorium. Holding a still-wet oil painting by the frame in one hand and a gym bag containing two towels, a change of socks, and ten thousand dollars in cash in the other, one unshaven and thoroughly grimy dwarf dressed in an orange sweat suit and dirty sneakers marched briskly down the center aisle and up onto the stage. There was scattered, uncertain applause as I set down the gym bag and painting, then stepped behind the lectern and up on the stool placed there for my convenience. I found myself looking out over a sea of puzzled and disapproving police-officer-type faces. To my right, ten rows back, I spotted the university chancellor; he did not look pleased. Next to the chancellor sat the head of my department; she did not look pleased, either. Garth had obviously arrived too late to get a seat, because he was standing up at the back, leaning against a windowsill. His arms were crossed over his chest, and he was shaking his head as he rolled his eyes heavenward.

Showtime.

There was nothing to do but apologize for being late, leave the matter of my somewhat unconventional appearance a mystery, and get on with it—which is what I did. Fortunately, lurid tales of sex and violence, however professionally and flatly offered, are always crowd pleasers, and sex and violence were what this talk was all about; the crowd of cops and academicians seemed pleased. I thought I had a few valuable things to say to them, and they seemed to agree. My audience sat attentively through a dry presentation of charts, statistical tables, graphs, and maps as they listened to stories of the grisly, blood-soaked scenes and episodes that had spawned the data. This was the stuff of nightmares in which I had been immersed for the better part of a year and a half, since what I thought of as my return to the real world from our parents' farm, where Garth and I had spent six months recuperating from our mind-bending and body-breaking excursion into a terrifying world of criminals, fools, and madmen.

Garth and I, with a lot of help from a decidedly odd assortment of friends, had managed to survive the Valhalla Project, and the experience had brought two close brothers even closer together. However, what could very well have been a sneak preview of the end of the world as we know it had changed both of us forever, initially plummeting us into a deep depression. We'd emerged from that bone-deep melancholy when we'd finally realized, and accepted, the fact that there was nothing to do but go on with our lives, immerse ourselves in our work, and try to be decent and just men.

For me, immersing myself in work had meant attacking the riddle posed by the mind of the so-called serial murderer: the rogue individual who roams across the face of the nation killing dozens of faceless strangers—men, women, and children—at random and without warning, with no more motivation than an ephemeral sexual thrill associated with the torture and murder of others. Financed by a number of generous grants awarded to me on the basis of past performance, I'd crisscrossed the country, visiting scenes of violence and then prisons, logging more than a thousand hours of taped conversation with convicted serial murderers who'd agreed to talk with me. What I hoped were a few fresh insights garnered from this research was what I shared with this audience, and they rewarded me at the end with a standing ovation that lasted almost five minutes.

If I was getting a bit gamy, and I was certain I was, no one at the sumptuous buffet and reception following the lecture seemed to notice—or at least they didn't mention it as I stood in a corner of the reception hall shaking hands and chatting with the many people who came up to wish me well, congratulate me, offer their own opinions, or simply ask questions. To my surprise, quite a few people had seen me perform in the circus years before, or they had heard about it, and they wanted to talk about this. Others were curious about my dual career as a private investigator, had read about some of the bizarre cases in which I'd been involved, and wanted to talk about that. I wanted to talk about neither and always steered the conversation quickly back to serial murderers. Since my involvement with the beasts of Valhalla, my past was something I preferred not to discuss.

Not until that moment had I realized this was a trait I shared with Veil Kendry. It occurred to me that he had suffered his own Valhalla Project, and I wondered what it could have been. The answer, I thought, could be in the painting.

After a half hour or so the well-wishers started to drift away toward the food and drinks, leaving me alone for a few moments. Garth emerged from a crowd of cops at the other end of the hall and came over to me.

"Great job, brother," Garth said as he gripped both my arms. His dark brown eyes glowed with pride. "God, you're such a ham."

"Is that a compliment or a complaint?"

"It's an opinion formed from careful, lifelong observation."

"Thanks. I think."

Garth pointed down at the painting propped against the gym

bag at my feet. "This is the painting you talked about?" he asked in
a low voice.

"Yeah."

"Then you did take it out of the apartment." There was a distinct scowl in his voice.

"Obviously."

"Not a good idea at all, Mongo. What about the money?"

"It's in the gym bag."

"Even a worse idea."

"You're probably right."

"What the hell's the matter with you?"

"I took the painting because I'm convinced Veil left it for me,
and because I think it could provide answers to why Veil did what
he did, what his problem is, and maybe what he wants me to do for
him. I think the cash was meant to be a retainer."

"Thinking that doesn't make it yours, Mongo."

"I'm aware of that. I took the money because it's probably safer
with me than it was up in the loft. I'm putting it in the bank for
him."

"Damn it, Mongo, this is none of your business. You're leaving
yourself open to a lot of grief—legal and otherwise."

"I don't think I'm needed here anymore," I said, picking up the
painting and gym bag and turning toward the door behind us.
"Let's go someplace where we can talk."

Garth held the door open for me, then followed me out into the
curved corridor that arced around the reception hall. I walked to
my left, kept going until we found an empty office.

"There's something else you should know," I said as we entered
the office and Garth closed the door behind us.

"What's that?" Garth asked in a flat voice as I set the painting
and gym bag down against the wall.

"Veil's armed. He has *nunchaku*—"

"*Nunchaku* are illegal in New York State," Garth said in the
same flat tone.

"Yeah, but he's also got guns. I should have mentioned it when
we talked on the phone. I'm sorry."

Garth sighed heavily, bowed his head slightly, and ran the fingers of his right hand through his thinning, wheat-colored hair.
"You're damn right you should have mentioned it to me before,"
he said, anger in his eyes and voice. "Veil Kendry may be a friend

of yours, but armed like that he's breaking the law and poses a threat to the public. You had no right to withhold that information."

"I know. What can I say? When you're right, you're right. I was concerned that—"

"How many guns?"

"At least two, maybe three."

"Any idea what kinds of guns we're talking about?"

"At least one handgun, maybe two. I think he's also carrying a semiautomatic rifle or submachine gun with a collapsible stock."

"How the hell do you know what he's carrying if you didn't see him?"

I told Garth about the empty brackets and gun oil in the hidden compartment. My brother listened in silence, staring at a spot just above my head. When I'd finished, he hunched the broad shoulders on his six-foot-three-inch frame, shoved his hands into his pockets, and proceeded to pace. Finally he came to a stop in front of me again.

"Except for the mountains, that looks like Viet Nam," he said, nodding toward the painting.

"There aren't mountains in Viet Nam?" I asked. Garth would know; he'd spent time there during the war as an MP stationed in and around Saigon.

"Not like those."

"Still, he must have been somewhere over there. The soldiers are definitely Asian—Viet Cong and North Vietnamese regulars, I'd say."

"Veil Kendry as an angel," Garth said with a sardonic smile. "Not likely."

"It means something."

"And I come back to the same question I asked earlier: If Kendry wanted to tell you something, why not just pick up the phone? Or leave a note?"

"The painting is the answer to that, and I'll let you know when I figure it out. Incidentally, that picture's interesting for other reasons. As far as I know, he's never painted anything else this realistically. Also, I've never seen anything else of his that had people in it."

Garth's response was an indifferent shrug; his mind seemed to be elsewhere—undoubtedly on the man himself, not his painting.

"What are you going to do now?" I asked.

"Officially or unofficially?"

"Let's hear the official part first."

"I'm not sure, Mongo. You're the one who opened the can, but I get responsibility for the Goddamn worms. *I* have no doubt that Kendry's carrying all the stuff you say he is. The problem is that you haven't even *seen* him, much less witnessed him carrying weapons. As far as the law is concerned, Kendry has committed no crime; *you* have. Still, if I spread the word that Veil Kendry is wandering around loaded for bear, every cop in the city is going to be looking for him, and those cops are going to have itchy trigger fingers. That could lead to somebody unnecessarily getting hurt. On the other hand, if I *don't* spread the word, some unsuspecting cop is likely to get blown away."

"That's not going to happen, Garth."

"Oh, isn't it? Can you guarantee me that? Can you tell me what's on Veil Kendry's mind?"

"You know I can't."

"Then don't try to tell me what's not going to happen."

"I hear what you're saying," I said quietly, "and I appreciate the dilemma. It's one reason I didn't mention the guns over the phone; I wasn't sure how the cops would react."

"You mean, you weren't sure how I'd react."

"It's the same thing. I didn't want him killed by some nervous cop while all he was trying to do was defend himself against somebody else who was trying to kill him. Christ, Garth, I'm just following my nose on this thing, playing it by ear."

"A long nose in this case, Mongo. And maybe a tin ear."

"You still haven't told me what you're going to do officially."

Garth sighed, shook his head. "I'm going to have to put out the word, Mongo, but I'll have to give some thought to what that word is going to be. I damn well don't want either Kendry or some cop blown away just because you can't mind your own business."

"Jesus Christ! You—!" I paused, swallowed my anger. "What the hell is it between Veil and the NYPD? He keeps putting away muggers and dope dealers, and you keep putting him away. Talk about overreaction! He's never hurt anybody who wasn't trying to hurt him or somebody else. I can see some of the other guys on the force getting jealous because they think Veil makes them look bad, but not you. What's your problem?"

"You don't know what you're talking about, Mongo," Garth said tightly. "That's *your* problem."

"Why don't I know what I'm talking about?"

"You just don't."

Whatever it was Garth knew about Veil, or thought he knew, he obviously wasn't ready to share it with me. That only served to arouse my curiosity further, but I knew better than to push. I shrugged my shoulders, asked, "So, what are you going to do unofficially?"

"Keep an eye on you."

"I don't need anybody keeping an eye on me," I replied tersely.

"Bullshit," Garth said, and laughed. "Never in the history of the world has anyone needed a keeper more than you." The laughter and his broad smile abruptly vanished. "Here it is up front, Mongo. I want you to back right away from this thing. Whatever may be going on, back off. Why the hell do you want to get involved in Kendry's miseries, anyway?"

The question both puzzled and troubled me, and I searched Garth's face for some answer as to why he had asked it. He stared back at me impassively. "Because he's my friend," I replied at last. "I don't understand what you're saying. Wouldn't you do as much for a friend you thought was in trouble and needed help?"

Garth abruptly turned away and walked to the one window in the office. When he finally spoke, his deep voice sounded strange, muffled by the glass. "You're the only friend I have, Mongo. Except for Mom and Dad, and a few of the relatives, other people are just ghosts. You've already used up more lives than a litter of cats, and there's no reason for you to take any more chances. The lesson we learned from those nice people who ran Valhalla was that almost nothing we do really matters, not in the long run. Well, you matter to me. I don't want you hurt, and I certainly don't want you hurt because of a creep like Veil Kendry—and he is a creep, as far as I'm concerned. We've both dealt with enough crazies to last us a lifetime, so to hell with Kendry and the rest of the crazies."

Garth's words and manner deeply distressed me. For some time it had seemed to me that a shadow hung over my brother—now I knew I'd been right, and I recognized the face of the shadow. When Garth and I had left our parents' farm, I'd thought both of us were sufficiently healed to get on with our lives. Now I realized that I'd been wrong. Garth wasn't immersed in work, or anything else; he was just floating on the surface under a rotting sun of memory and despair that was eating him away. He wasn't living a life, I thought, but just going through the motions. I wondered if the serum we'd both been repeatedly injected with had done it to him; it was hard for me to imagine Garth being beaten by his own mind.

"Garth," I said, trying to fight my own despair with words, "I can't just walk away from this until I at least find out what's going on. You almost act as if there's nothing to it, and—"

"I never said there was nothing to it!" Garth snapped, wheeling back to face me. "I'm not a fool! If you tell me he's carting around a submachine gun, then he almost certainly is. What I said is that it's none of your business. Wherever he's gone, it's fine with me. I just don't want you sucked away with him. Veil Kendry stinks of madness and death."

"What the hell's the matter with you, Garth?" I asked softly. "You talk like a stranger. Just because you don't like—"

"How long have you known Kendry, wise-ass?!"

Taken aback by the anger in his voice, I blinked in surprise. "About eleven years," I answered warily. "I met him when I bought one of his paintings at—"

"I know how you met him," Garth said curtly. "What do you suppose Kendry was doing before he started all this painting bullshit?"

"Bullshit?"

"What's his background?"

"I don't know."

"What the hell do you mean, you 'don't know,' wise-ass? I thought this guy was a great friend of yours. After all, you felt close enough to him to walk into his place uninvited and spend the night. You felt close enough to him to walk out with one of his paintings and ten grand in cash."

The effect of Garth's scornful sarcasm was to make me feel more distant from him than I could ever remember feeling in my life. "Why don't you get to the point?" I said coldly. "That's assuming you have one."

"The point is that I've known Kendry longer than you have, and he had a police record longer than both our arms put together *before* you met him."

Ah.

"The reason the cops keep such close tabs on him," Garth continued in a much softer tone, "is because, unlike some criminologists and other professorial types, we don't believe any man can change as completely as Kendry appears to have changed. The rot's still there, just waiting to eat its way back up to the surface. That's what I think probably happened."

"What rot?"

"According to his police record, Kendry blew into New York about four years before you met him, probably in the summer of 'seventy-three."

"Where'd he come from?"

"Military stockades—first in Saigon, then in Leavenworth. Needless to say, he'd been dishonorably discharged."

"How do you know that?"

Garth shrugged. "A quick call to connections in the military justice system. Standard operating procedure. Anyway, at that time he was living in a series of flea traps on the Bowery, along with the other bums. He was a drunk and a junkie himself. He'd work as a bouncer in some of New York's less glamorous night spots until he had some cash in his pocket, then he'd quit."

"What was he busted for?"

"Drunk and disorderly."

"That doesn't sound very serious to me."

"It is when it keeps happening, and it's even more serious when it keeps happening and you bust up some police officers resisting arrest."

"Okay, agreed. But—"

"He was a brawler."

"Did he ever kill anyone in any of these brawls?"

"No. He just kept making good business for the hospitals. The only reason he never did any serious time was because most of the people he brawled with had longer records of violent behavior than he did."

"He could have, you know."

"Could have what?"

"Killed somebody. I'm betting he could have killed anyone he went up against."

"You're missing the point. The man was committed to Bellevue for observation twice; for some reason, the shrinks there let him out both times. When I say he's crazy, Mongo, I'm not exaggerating. He was a man bent on self-destruction, and that's the rot I was referring to."

Garth's description of Veil upset me, as my brother had known it would, and I took some time to think about it. There was no doubt in my mind that what Garth had said was true, but I could not make the description of a drunk and a junkie and a bar brawler match the strong-willed and controlled man I had known for over eleven years. "People *do* change," was all I could think of to say. "Veil Kendry did."

"Maybe."

"*Maybe?* That was more than eleven years ago. For Christ's sake, Garth, give the man a break."

"I grant you that he cleaned up his act for eleven years, but now he's wandering around with martial arts weapons, handguns, and a submachine gun. It's also possible that for all that time he was nothing more than a time bomb waiting to go off. You interpret the lights and the open loft as the actions of a rational man trying to send you some kind of signal. Judging from his past record, I say it's possible he wasn't thinking of you at all; he wasn't thinking of anything. He just went off, and when he did there wasn't a rational thought left in his head."

"Which explains why you've been trying to downplay everything I've been telling you."

"Right. You're incredibly loyal to your friends, and you can get a bit myopic where they're concerned. When a friend is involved, you walk into a wide open loft with burning lights and missing guns and smell a mystery. I smell a potential mass murderer. If that's true, there's no reason for you to be in his line of fire when he goes nova. The fact that he had that kind of armory squirreled away in the first place indicates that he's been thinking some very heavy thoughts for a long time."

"Maybe he was thinking of defending himself."

"Against what? A fucking army?"

"Against whoever it was who winged a shot at him."

"You can't be certain that's what happened. If he did go buggy, and that's what *I* think happened, he could have put that bullet hole in the window himself, as a kind of warm-up. If you go looking for him, you may not find what you think you will; it's even conceivable that you could trigger him into killing you, and a lot of other people. You let us handle Veil Kendry. He's a loony."

"What about the painting and the cash?"

"It could be that he expects to die, and that he wanted to leave something for you. He didn't expect you, or anyone else, to find it so soon."

"All of this occurred to you even before I mentioned the weapons, didn't it?"

Garth nodded. "It occurred to me during our second telephone conversation."

"You should have told me about his background then."

"You had an important lecture to deliver, and you already had enough things on your mind. There wasn't time to go into gory detail, and I was hoping I could talk some sense into you." He paused, smiled thinly. "That's still my hope."

"Why didn't you tell me about Veil before?"

"Because he'd been clean for almost a year at the time you met him. Under those circumstances, I would have considered it an abuse of my authority to discuss his record with you, or anyone else, who didn't have an official need to know. I'm a police officer, not a gossip, and Kendry's record was strictly police business. In any case, you'd have accused me of gratuitously badmouthing one of your friends—and you'd have been right."

"That was very honorable of you, Garth," I said simply. "It's exactly what I would expect."

"Now it's a different situation, because you've been toying with the idea of becoming involved in a search for a very dangerous man who isn't playing with a full deck."

"Thanks, Garth," I said as I picked up the painting and my gym bag. "I appreciate it. And don't worry; I'm not going to do anything foolish."

"You already have."

4

After leaving Garth I walked across campus to my office, where I typed up a letter to Veil explaining in detail everything I had done and planned to do, and giving my reasons. I made two copies of the original, then, after locking up the painting and gym bag in the office, walked the four blocks to my bank, where I opened a new savings account in Veil's name and mine and deposited the ten thousand in it. I added the account number to the letters, then went next door to the post office. I sent the original, by certified mail with no signature required, to Veil's address. The two copies I sent by registered mail to Garth and myself.

I debated going back to my apartment to clean up, decided that it would just be a waste of time. I still had a load of examination papers to grade, so after picking up a couple of sandwiches and some coffee from a deli, I went back to my campus office. After turning Veil's painting to the wall so as not to be distracted, I tuned my small desk radio to an all-news station and proceeded to attack the mountain of papers piled all over my desk.

Grading papers kept me busy until seven thirty in the evening. I went home, soaked myself under a hot shower, put on pajamas and a light robe. I poured myself a liberal Scotch over ice, then proceeded once again with my telephone ritual—Veil's loft, my answering service, the hospital emergency rooms. Nothing. The first Scotch felt warm and pleasantly heavy on my stomach, so I poured myself another. I put a TV dinner in the oven, made myself a salad, then went and sat down in the leather reclining chair in my den to study Veil's painting, which I had propped up on my desk, beneath a small spotlight.

A sulphurous, gun-toting angel—a lone American—draped in a strange robe and hovering over a jungle filled with soldiers in a country that might or might not be Viet Nam, but was almost certainly in Southeast Asia.

A close examination with a magnifying glass revealed no hidden messages or symbols, at least none that I could detect, and when I scraped paint from one corner I found nothing beneath but canvas. Garth could be right about an insane Veil Kendry going over the edge and falling into some black abyss in his admittedly complex and problematical mind, but I didn't think so. Wherever he was, I was still convinced he'd been pushed there and that, with time, the painting would tell me where and why. The problem was that I didn't know how much time I had.

The smell of burning TV dinner sent me padding into the kitchen. I managed to salvage most of my meal, ate it in front of the television set while I watched the Cable News Network. I'd hoped to pick up some news item that I could possibly link to Veil's disappearance, but the vast majority of the coverage was given over to background reports on, and interviews with, Kevin Shannon's cabinet nominees, which didn't interest me at all. My time with the people involved in the Valhalla Project had convinced me that nations were neither moral nor immoral; only individuals could make those kinds of choices, and only time, not television appearances, would determine in which camp Kevin Shannon and his new crew on the Potomac belonged.

When I began to doze, I turned off the TV, threw away the rest of my dinner, worked up enough energy to brush my teeth, then fell into bed, exhausted. I fell asleep almost immediately.

I exploded awake, jackknifing forward in bed as the air exploded from my lungs. Then, writhing and rocking back and forth helplessly, I imploded into a small, airless world of throbbing agony centered in the pit of my stomach. Doubled up in a fetal position tighter than a clenched fist, I kept gasping—but air wouldn't come, and the veins and arteries in my neck and head felt about to burst from the pressure of effort and need. Gasping in my universe of pain, I vaguely realized that the lights in my bedroom were on. Two men in business suits were standing at the left side of the bed, staring impassively down at me. Just before I got my head over the edge of the bed and threw up on their polished surfaces, I found myself looking down on two pairs of expensive, wing-tipped shoes, one brown and one black.

I was just managing to drag some air into my lungs when two sets of hands with strong fingers gripped my arms and legs and pushed me back on the bed. Ropes were quickly looped around my wrists and ankles, pulled taut, and secured to the four corners of the bedframe. Thus spread-eagled, the joints in my shoulders, arms, and legs immediately began to ache. I was still unable to breathe right, much less scream for help, and so I concentrated on getting air into my lungs while I studied my uninvited guests and fought against rising panic.

The brown-suited night visitor standing at the foot of the bed looked to be in his late twenties or early thirties. He was clean-cut, with short brown hair that matched his cold eyes, and a neatly trimmed mustache. Despite the fact that it was the middle of the night, he, like his partner, appeared to be freshly shaven and smelled of cologne. He could have been an up-and-coming stockbroker, except that instead of an attaché case he held the blackjack that had served as my alarm clock in his right hand. In his left hand he held Veil's painting.

The second man wore a charcoal-striped suit. He was middle-aged, with thinning gray hair and thick eyeglass lenses. Standing to my left, he suddenly bent down, and when he straightened up I could see that he was holding one of my bath towels, which was sopping wet.

They were top-of-the-line professionals, I thought, tough-minded and cold-blooded. They were also obviously well equipped, since by breaking into my apartment without a sound they had managed to bypass not only a most suspicious concierge in the lobby, but my own alarm system and a double lock as well. I was impressed. It occurred to me to ask what they wanted, but I was fairly certain they'd get around to that in time, and I wanted to conserve what little breath and energy I had.

"I'm sorry for your discomfort, Dr. Frederickson," the older man said in a soft voice that was just above a whisper. There were no chairs in the small room, and so he eased himself down on the edge of the bed, a foot or so from my head, and casually crossed one leg over the other. Then he snaked the wet towel out across the floor, like a whip. "I hope we won't have to hurt you again. Experience has taught us that it is often best to begin with an intense, sudden burst of great pain, so as to save a person even greater agony over a prolonged period of time." He paused, gently rubbed my diaphragm, helping me to breathe. "See? I think you're feeling better already, no? Please answer all our questions fully, without raising your voice. We certainly don't want to wake up any of your neighbors, and everyone knows that even the best buildings in New York have walls that are notoriously thin."

I most certainly did want to wake any and all of my neighbors, whether those on either side of me or those across the hall. I sucked in a deep breath and was just about to let loose with what I hoped would be a blood-curdling scream when the thick, wet towel snapped through the air and slapped across my face. A fraction of a second later the blackjack thudded into the bare sole of my left foot. A pain with a quality quite unlike anything I'd experienced before shot up through my left leg, slammed into my groin and belly, then traveled in a shock wave up my spine into my skull, where it seemed to expand to the point where it felt as if my eyeballs were being pushed from my head. It got a blood-curdling scream out of me all right, but, with the wet towel over my face, I was the only one who heard it.

No sooner had the shock waves from the first blow begun to subside—gradually, like water sloshing in a pail—than the blackjack slammed into the sole of my right foot, starting the process all over again. Another smothered scream.

Just as it seemed I would pass out from pain or lack of air, or both, the towel was removed from by face. Sucking air, my chest and stomach heaving, I turned my head as far as I was able and vomited again. When I was finished, the man with the thick glasses used a corner of the wet towel to wipe my face clean, then heaved a deep sigh and slowly shook his head. With a flick of his wrist, the towel was snaked back into snapping position.

The younger man at the foot of the bed who had hit me held up Veil's painting.

"Please, Dr. Frederickson," the man sitting on the side of my bed said in the same, soft voice. "Save yourself needless suffering; no more nonsense. Tell us about the painting."

"What the hell do you want to know that you don't already know?" I sobbed, gasping for breath. My joints felt locked, welded together with pain. "You wouldn't even know about me or be here unless you'd had Kendry's phone tapped. You've already heard everything there is for me to tell."

"Who else have you discussed this matter with besides your brother?"

"Nobody."

"Are you sure? We don't want to have to hurt you again."

"I'm sure."

"We wish to know every place you've been since leaving Mr. Kendry's loft this morning."

"If you know when I left the loft, then you must know where I went. Weren't you following me?"

The younger man let his right hand drop, and the cold black leather cover of the sap brushed my sole. I cringed and closed my eyes, but no blow came. When I opened my eyes, I found my interrogator looking at the younger man with a distinct air of disapproval. "You were just a bit too quick for us in the subway," he said, turning his thick lenses back on me. "I'm afraid that lapse on our part is what necessitates this conversation. We have quite a few lost hours to account for."

"In that case, you can pick up Blackjack Barney down there and go home. From the time I left the loft, I didn't have time for anything but business. I ran in the subway because I was late. Unless you've got wax in your ears, you heard my brother and me discussing the lecture I was sup—"

"Did you give the lecture?"

"Yes."

"That's the kind of response we like. Don't concern yourself with what you think we must have heard. Just answer the questions."

"How did you know who I was, and where I live?"

"You're much too modest, Dr. Frederickson. How many noted criminology professors of your stature, so to speak, are nicknamed 'Mongo'? As a result of some of your past exploits, you enjoy a measure of fame."

"Lucky me."

"And, of course, you're listed in the directory. Where did you go after your lecture?"

"To my office."

"Which office? You have two."

"My campus office. When I said I was involved in business all that time, I meant university business. I didn't do any investigating. I had examination papers to grade. I finished up around a half past seven and came home. Who do you guys work for?"

"Where is the money you mentioned, Dr. Frederickson?"

"In the bank."

"Really?" The thick gray brows above the thick lenses lifted slightly. "I don't recall you mentioning that you'd been to the bank when I asked where you'd been."

"I forgot." The blackjack brushed the sole of my right foot. "It wasn't a big deal," I added quickly. "The bank is just off campus. I also went to the post office."

"Why?"

"I sent Kendry a letter explaining why I'd taken the painting and the money, just to cover myself. I also mailed a copy to myself."

"You should have minded your own business, Frederickson."

"You're telling me! You see, I had this peculiar idea that he

might be having trouble with some nasty people. Now that I see
how wrong I was, I have a good mind to put those things back
where I found them and forget about the whole thing."

He was a tough audience, and he didn't even smile. "Did you
send copies of this letter to anyone else?"

"No." Garth didn't need these two jokers showing up on his
doorstep. "From the post office, I went back to my office."

"You'd best be careful not to forget anything else, Dr. Frederickson," the older man said evenly. "It would be a shame for you to
suffer any more agony just because you can't remember events that
happened only a few hours ago. Now, has your brother seen this
painting?"

"No. Even if I'd had time to show it to him, which I didn't, he
wouldn't have been interested; you heard him on the phone. Why
don't you just tell me what this is all about? If you do, maybe we
can save time. What do you want?"

"Just continue to answer our questions truthfully, Dr. Frederickson."

"Why is the painting so important? What does it mean?"

"That's not your concern."

"Where's Veil Kendry?"

"Besides yourself, who else has seen this painting?"

"A few hundred cops, most of them police chiefs."

The man with the blackjack started to swing, then stopped when
my interrogator held up his hand. But the sap remained cocked,
ready to strike. The face of the younger torturer at the foot of my
bed revealed nothing; he was just a man doing his job.

"You must not try to be amusing, Frederickson," the older man
said.

"It's the Goddamn truth," I breathed, wriggling my body in an
unsuccessful attempt to relieve the cramps in my stomach. "The
lecture I gave was to a group of police chiefs and criminologists."

"You took the painting with you to the lecture?"

"I didn't have time to go home. Everyone in the lecture hall
must have seen me carrying it, but it couldn't have meant anything
to anybody. I'm considered eccentric in some circles." I paused,
tried to suck in a deep breath. "I'm answering your questions; I
don't have any reason not to. Why don't you loosen the ropes so I
can breathe a little?"

"Just a few more questions, Dr. Frederickson; you're tied to make certain we have your undivided attention. You claim that your brother hasn't seen this painting, and that you haven't discussed it with him. Wasn't he at the lecture?"

"No."

I groaned when the sap tapped harder against my left sole, but not too loudly; I didn't want the wet towel over my face again.

"But he said that he was going. Indeed, he seemed quite anxious to see and hear you."

"Some emergency came up at his precinct station, and Garth had to handle it. Look, I'm really sorry you lost me in the subway. If you'd been able to follow me around all day, you'd see that everything I'm telling you is the truth. Aside from what I've told you, I don't know anything. *You're* the ones who know all the important questions and answers, so I don't understand why you're hassling me. You've got the painting. I've got nothing left to give you, except the money, and if you'll be patient and wait a few hours without driving my feet up into my chest, I'll get that for you."

My interrogator nodded to his colleague, who raised Veil's painting to shoulder level for me to look at.

"What does the painting suggest to you, Dr. Frederickson?"

"I don't know what you want from me, pal," I replied with a rising anger that was thoroughly absurd for someone in my position. "For Christ's sake, it's not a Goddamn Rorschach blot. We're all looking at the same fucking painting; what you see is what I see. What the hell do you expect me to say?!"

"If you don't wish to be hurt again, keep your voice down," the older man said politely but firmly. "Just answer the question."

"It's Veil Kendry as some kind of armed angel floating over a jungle filled with soldiers and guerrillas. It's probably Viet Nam. Is that what you want me to say?"

"What associations to Veil Kendry does it call to mind, Dr. Frederickson?"

"None."

"What does the painting mean to you?"

"Nothing."

"Why do you suppose Mr. Kendry left this for you?"

"I've already answered that—"

"Why you, and not someone else?"

"Probably because he overestimated my intuitive abilities, not to mention my tolerance for pain."

"Ah, you're trying to be amusing again."

"I'm a private investigator as well as a criminologist, pal. You know that. It looks like he was trying to throw some business my way. I don't understand what you're trying to get at."

"The envelope with the money that was with the painting was clearly addressed to you, a point you repeatedly sought to make with your brother. I am suggesting that in the past Mr. Kendry may have said something to you, and only you, that would help you to understand the meaning of the painting. Furthermore, I am suggesting that in the past few hours you could have shared that information with one or more persons."

"That's one wrong from column A, and one wrong from column B."

"The connection could have come to you since your last phone conversation with your brother."

"Nope. You know, if you keep this shit up you're likely to make me angry."

"What do you know of Mr. Kendry's past?"

"When he first came to New York, he was apparently a very disturbed man. A few months before I met him, he'd started painting. It didn't quite keep him off the streets and out of trouble, but it apparently did help him keep his head straight. Now he's a big man on the art scene. He's also the best unarmed fighter I've ever met. Aside from that, *nada*. Zip."

"He never talked to you about his experiences in the years before he came to New York?"

"Never."

"Did he ever make insinuations?"

"About who or what?"

"About anyone or anything."

"Veil Kendry never makes insinuations of any kind. If he had something to say, about you or anybody else, he'd say it right in your face."

"You claim this man you call a friend never told you anything about his past?"

"It's the truth."

"And you never inquired?"

"I'm not the inquisitive sort. Was it one of you guys who winged a shot at him?"

"You most certainly are the inquisitive sort, Dr. Frederickson. If you weren't, the three of us wouldn't be in this unfortunate situation."

"When a friend asks me not to be inquisitive, I'm not inquisitive. Everything I've told you is the truth."

The man sitting on the edge of my bed stared at me for some time in silence. I stared back, reflecting on the fact that I had never felt more alone or helpless than at this moment, in my own bed in my own apartment, surrounded by neighbors around, above, and below me. I was cut off from everyone by pain, the threat of pain, and a wet towel.

Finally the older man stood up, turned to his partner. "I believe him," he said easily. "What do you think?"

The younger man nodded, spoke for the first time. "I think he's telling the truth. Apparently, Kendry never shared information with anybody, and he's still keeping his own council; executing this painting is as far as he would go. It's curious, but it does seem to be the case."

"Good," I said. "Now that you've got that right, let's close down this show. I'd appreciate it if you'd take these ropes off me and get the fuck out of my apartment. Go out and play in the traffic."

The man with the thick glasses looked down at me. "Do you smoke, Dr. Frederickson?"

"No," I replied quickly, glancing back and forth between the two men. I found the question decidedly ominous. "I was told it's unhealthy."

The younger man dropped the sap in his pocket and took out a can of lighter fluid. I started to yell, but the towel slapped down over my mouth. Then the older man wrapped it around the back of my head, tied it. I could no nothing but squirm and watch helplessly as the man with the cold brown eyes removed the top from the can, then thoroughly soaked the painting. This done, he walked slowly around the bed, soaking the edges of the bedclothes. He screwed the top back on the can, put it back in his pocket, and took out an expensive-looking silver lighter. He opened the cap, then flicked the lighter to produce a long blue and white flame, which he touched to a corner of the painting. The fluid-soaked painting instantly burst into flame. The younger man tossed the burning painting beneath the bed, and then, without a backward glance, the two men turned and walked quickly from the bedroom. A few seconds later I heard the apartment door open and close.

I immediately began tugging at the ropes, to no avail. Smoke was beginning to billow out from beneath the bed, and I struggled against the oxygen-greedy panic rising within me. Breathing deeply through my nose, trying not even to think of what it would feel like when the black smoke began to fill my lungs and the flames to touch my flesh, I groped with my fingers for the knots around my wrists. It was no use; the ropes were taut, and the knots expertly tied. Again, I thrashed my body and yanked with my arms and legs, trying desperately to get one limb, any limb, free. But it was not to be. The only way the ropes were going to disappear was to burn along with me, which they would, obliterating any evidence to suggest that my death was anything more than the result of a freak accident, perhaps a fire caused by a short circuit in the reading lamp beside my bed.

Smoke was filling the bedroom now, almost totally obscuring my vision. Soon, I thought, one of my neighbors was going to smell it, if that hadn't happened already, and call the fire department. Unfortunately, I'd be long gone by the time anybody reached me. Ironically, the burning bed beneath me formed a kind of baffle for the thick smoke, affording me a pocket of relatively clean air. But it was only prolonging the agony; flames were shooting up all around me, and the mattress on which I lay was growing very hot.

Sayonara, I thought with something approaching an air of resignation. I'd read somewhere that people who'd been burned at the stake usually died of suffocation before the flames finally reached them. I fervently hoped that was true, and that the same principle applied in bed as at stake. The litter of lives Garth had mentioned had finally been used up. My night visitors had nailed me quickly, and they'd nailed me good. I was going to die, and I would never know the reasons for it.

It was the last thing I thought before finally passing out from heat and lack of air.

5

I woke up coughing. To my considerable surprise it appeared that I wasn't dead—only slightly singed and short of breath, with lungs that felt as if they'd been painted with the drippings at the bottom of a barbecue pit and a mouth that tasted the same. There was a soft hissing sound that seemed to come from all around me, and after a few moments I realized that what I thought was badly blurred vision was due to the fact that I was looking at the walls of an oxygen tent. I started hacking again, brought up dark phlegm. As if on cue, a flap of the tent was pulled back and a reasonably attractive nurse appeared with a metal bowl to contain my own drippings. The large, familiar, and comforting figure of my brother loomed up behind the nurse, peered down at me over her shoulder. When I tried to speak and could only manage a huge yawn, I realized I was pretty well doped up on analgesics, expectorants, whatever. I finished hacking and spitting, then lazily waved to Garth and drifted back to sleep.

When I did finally come around for an extended stay, I had a splitting headache. My mouth still tasted like a furnace, and my lungs felt like leather, but it was considerably easier to breathe. When I took a physical inventory, I found that I was burned on various parts of my body, primarily the lower parts of my arms and legs. However, even though the burns were covered with light gauze, I was fairly certain that they weren't severe. My feet and legs, and particularly my knees, throbbed from the pounding the younger man had given my soles, but he hadn't broken anything. Incredibly, I was not only alive, but not even seriously hurt. Considering the fact that the last thing I remembered was passing out on a bed that was going up in flames, I considered my present condition most peculiar, if not downright miraculous. Try as hard as I might, I could not come up with any kind of plausible scenario that could explain my survival.

I pushed back the flap on the oxygen tent, pushed myself up into a sitting position and swung my legs over the side of the bed, groaned when pain shot through my body and pounded in my skull. Garth, who had been sitting in a chair near the foot of the bed, quickly rose, came to me, and very gently wrapped me in his arms.

"Thank God," Garth said quietly, then tried to push me back under the oxygen tent.

"I'm all right," I said, pushing back. "Just let me sit up for a time. How the hell did I get here?"

Garth pulled the chair up to the side of the bed, sat down, and lightly rested his hand on my arm. "What do you remember?" he asked quietly.

A very dangerous question, I thought as I looked at Garth. I thought I was beginning to understand at least a few of the reasons why Veil had reached out for my help in such a maddeningly problematic and circuitous manner, and now *I* was in a position where I had to be very cautious about how I did things. I believed I had convinced my torturers that Garth was a totally disinterested party who hadn't even seen Veil's mysterious painting, and that we hadn't had any discussions about the matter other than those the men had monitored on the telephone. If the men hadn't been convinced of this, I was convinced that I would have survived the fire only to be told that my brother was dead. I had myself a dilemma with no means to resolve it, no loft to leave open and no lights to leave burning. The circumstances surrounding Veil's disappearance were now most definitely a matter for the police to investigate, but the price of telling Garth what had happened could well be his life. I wasn't certain what I should do, and I wanted time to think about it.

"At the moment, all I remember is a lot of smoke and flame," I said carefully, watching my brother's face. "Who got me out?"

"It must have been a fireman, although I was never able to find out which one," Garth said in an odd tone of voice that went with the odd way he was looking at me. "I responded to the original call when I heard the fire was in your apartment building. As a matter of fact, I was the one who found you unconscious on the sidewalk where somebody had dropped you. You were wrapped in soaked drapes from your living room. Whoever got to you first had a lot of presence of mind; he was cool, quick, and gutsy."

Indeed, I thought. Also, whoever had broken through the apartment door, assessed the situation, torn down the living room drapes and soaked them in the kitchen sink, then waded under that lifesaving shroud through a sea of flame to cut me free and carry me out, had to have been very close by—like virtually in the hallway outside my apartment. Even so, I considered it quite possible that my rescuer had been more badly burned than I was.

"What about the other people in the building?" I asked.

"The whole floor was gutted. Five people died—two of them children."

"Oh, my God," I whispered.

"You'll stay at my place until you find another one of your own," Garth said. His tone had gone from merely odd to almost cold. He turned slightly, nodded toward a stack of boxes piled up next to the window. "I brought you a few changes of clothes."

"Thank you."

"I've got a couple of other items for you, as well," Garth said, rising from the chair and walking to the window. He selected a box, came back and sat down again. Resting the box on his knees, he took off the top and brought out two handguns—a nickel-plated Beretta in a shoulder holster and a palm-sized Seecamp with an ankle holster. He placed the guns, along with a box of cartridges for each, on the bed next to me. "These will replace the ones you lost. You'll find copies of your city and state carry permits in the shoulder holster. It makes me very nervous to think of you going around unarmed, even in a hospital room."

I checked the magazine and trigger action of the Beretta, shoved it back into its holster. The weapons of death looked out of place in this room inside a house of healing. "Thanks again, Garth. You've really been taking care of business."

"Yeah. You say all you remember is waking up and finding yourself surrounded by smoke and flame?"

"Uh . . . something like that." I was beginning to feel decidedly uncomfortable.

"Something like that? Let me see if I can refresh your memory." Once again he reached into the box. This time he brought out four lengths of rope, each frayed at one end and sliced cleanly with a knife at the other. He tossed the ropes into my lap. "I'll bet a month's salary that the widths of those ropes match the friction burns on your wrists and ankles," Garth continued coldly. "They should, because that's where I found them tied. God knows how you got those bruises on your heels and soles; they're black. Do you always beat the soles of your feet and tie yourself up before you go to sleep?"

I'd run out of thinking time. "Garth, I—"

"What the fuck's the matter with you?!" Garth snapped, his brown eyes flashing with anger. "Five people died in that fire! Why the hell are you playing games with me?!"

"I'm sorry, Garth. I thought maybe I had a good reason for keeping my mouth shut. I can see now that I didn't."

"The fire that destroyed that floor started in your apartment, didn't it?"

"Yes."

"Very good. It sounds like your memory is improving."

I proceeded to tell Garth what had happened, finished by explaining why I had considered keeping the story to myself.

"Dumb, Mongo," Garth said, shaking his head in exasperation. However, his face had softened, and the chill was gone from his voice. "I appreciate your concern for me, as misplaced as it was, but don't really understand what you thought you were going to do next. Did you plan to try to find and take on these two guys by yourself?"

"I wasn't sure what I was going to do, Garth," I replied, thoroughly chastened. "I was thinking about it."

"Hell, all they did was tie you on your bed and light a fire under you."

"True; but they tried to kill me only *after* they'd asked me a lot of questions, which I think is important to consider. There's no doubt in my mind that if those guys had thought they already had the answers to the questions, if Veil had left me any kind of message clearly outlining what was going on, I'd have been blown away the moment I stepped out of Veil's loft onto the sidewalk. The men weren't certain of what I knew, or what others might know, and so they followed me instead of killing me right away. Now, if they find out I'm alive, they'll kill me on sight—and I believe they'll do the same to you if they find out we've talked. Doubt in the minds of Veil's enemies—doubt about what he's done, and plans to do—is the only reason I'm alive. That's one of the things I believe I learned from my visitors."

"One of the things? I thought you said they didn't tell you a damn thing."

"They didn't, but I think we know a little more now than we did before they popped in on me. I found the questions they asked and the situation itself instructive."

"Instruct me."

"We have confirmation that Veil is the guardian of a secret that profoundly threatens a very powerful person or persons unknown. The importance the men attached to the painting confirms that it contained a clue, or clues, to what that secret is; the secret involves events that took place a lot of years ago, sometime during the decade that the United States was involved in the war in Viet Nam."

Garth thought about it. "It's hard to imagine anything about that miserable period of history coming out now that would be worse than the stuff that's already been exposed."

"That's arguable. In any case, let's pose the question differently. It may not be a matter of how bad the shit is compared to things that have already been reported, but who this particular pile of shit belongs to. The torturer-assassins who worked me over were top-of-the-line professionals. Talent like that, whether working free-lance or on a salaried basis, doesn't come cheap. That's why I smell a lot of money and power behind them. Whatever Veil knows could seriously embarrass that money and power."

"You think Kendry may have been blackmailing somebody?"

"No. Veil isn't the blackmailing type. But even if I were wrong about his character, I could still point out that he never had the proverbial pissing pot until he started to make it with his art. Yet whatever he knows, he's known it a long time, and all indications are that he assiduously kept his mouth shut. Christ, he's *still* keeping it shut, for all intents and purposes."

"Then why come after him now?"

"An excellent question. Whatever it is Veil knows, he was left in peace for close to two decades—until Wednesday. By the way, what day is it?"

"Sunday. You've been out for a while. Just because Kendry never said anything to you doesn't mean that he didn't start whispering in somebody else's ear."

"Granted that's possible. Whatever Veil did or didn't do, it now seems almost certain that money and power sent an assassin after him. But the rifleman misses, and now money and power *really* has a problem. The truce, if that's the proper word for it, is broken. Not only is a live, hidden Veil Kendry one hell of a formidable opponent, but he no longer has any reason—maybe—to keep quiet. Enter my two visitors with some difficult marching orders—track Veil Kendry; assess any damage Veil may already have done; erase possible trouble spots, like me."

"According to you, and I have no doubt you're right, he's carrying *nunchaku*, at least one knife, two handguns, and a submachine gun. That sounds like somebody bent more on killing an enemy that talking about him."

"I'm not so sure. Always, we come back to his signals to me—the open loft, the lights, the painting, the money. Why all that business, unless he wants something brought out, and is willing to pay me a lot of money to bring it out? Believe me, if all Veil wanted was to kill somebody, that person would be dead."

"Maybe the guy is heavily guarded; money and power usually are."

"He'd still be dead. You tend to underestimate Veil's skills; he's one hell of a lot more than just a street fighter. No; he wants something brought out. He can't just come out and say it himself because . . . because . . ."

Garth supplied the answer I was looking for. "Because he wouldn't be believed," my brother said distantly. "He's got a long police record, and God knows what his military file would show."

"Thank you, Sherlock. That's it. He needs proof, some form of corroboration from an outside party, for the story he has to tell. He has a friend who's a private investigator, but he just couldn't bring himself to hire a friend to do a job that could get him killed in the blink of an eye, so he—"

"That's bullshit," Garth interrupted, his voice thick with soft, subdued fury. "That fucker set you up."

"No. He left it all up to one roll of the dice. You're the one who pointed out that I practically had to rip up the floorboards to find the painting and the money."

Garth dismissed the thought with a gesture of disdain and disgust. "Anyone who knows you would have made you an overwhelming odds-on favorite to do exactly what you did under those circumstances, in that situation. He set you up."

"I'll take responsibility for my own behavior, thank you very much."

"If he'd been up front with you from the beginning, you'd at least have known what it was you were getting involved in. You'd have had some kind of warning of the kind of people you were up against and could have taken appropriate steps to defend yourself. His stupid little game almost cost you your life, and now you're a marked man until this thing is resolved. I may kill the son-of-a-bitch if I find him."

"Take it easy, Garth," I said, and eased myself off the side of the bed onto the floor. Instantly, pain shot up from my heels into my shinbones and knees, and I promptly collapsed.

"You're not going anywhere for a while on those feet," Garth said as he gently lifted me off the floor and deposited me back on the bed. "What'd they use, a blackjack?"

"Yeah," I said through clenched teeth as I waited for the pain to subside. "I've got to get on the move, Garth. If those guys find out I'm alive, and they probably will, I'll be a sitting duck here. It won't take a bloodhound to find me."

"That's why I brought you your two little friends there to keep you company. Also, there'll be an armed guard outside your door for as long as you're here."

"Who the hell's paying for that?"

"The city of New York. You're a material witness in crimes including arson and murder. In fact, this little chat may be considered an official police interrogation. As for the rest of it, I don't give a damn what Kendry did or didn't want you to do. This has become a police matter, and you're out of it. I greatly appreciate your thoughts, but thinking is all you're going to be doing from now on. You can talk to me all you want; I happen to be assigned to the case."

"You? What happened to the big industrial espionage case you were working on?"

"I asked to be transferred to this case, and they gave it to me. I have more than a passing interest in finding that prick Kendry, as well as the two men who beat on you and started that fire under your ass."

"Garth, isn't it a bit unusual to assign a case to a cop who has blood in his eye because of a personal interest?"

"Who cares if it's unusual? I've got it. You wanted the police involved, you've got it. A police artist will be around in an hour or so to talk with you and try to develop some sketches."

"Garth, you're not going to find Veil unless he wants to be found."

"We'll see about that. He's also considered a material witness. You let me worry about him. When you've coughed up the rest of the crap in your lungs and can walk, you're literally going to hole up in my apartment until we crack this thing. I'm going to booby-trap the place so that nobody but the Frederickson brothers can walk through the door and stay in one piece."

"I'm not going to 'hole up' anywhere, Garth, and you know it. I've got things to do."

"No, you don't. You carried close to a double teaching load last semester so you'd be free this semester to talk to some more loonies. So you put off your research for a time. You have to keep a low profile for a while. Make a joke about your naturally low profile, I'll swat the bottoms of your feet. I'm not kidding."

"Neither am I. You let me take care of my own business, Garth. You don't know how long solving this is going to take. It was my feet they beat on, and my ass they tried to burn. *I* take things like that personally, too. Also, Veil is still my friend, and I'd become personally involved even before my visitors came. I'd taken Veil's money."

"You took shit. You just put his money in a safer place, remember? Besides, the painting is gone. You've got nothing left to go on."

"I've got more than you do. I remember the painting, and in particular I remember the symbols on the robe the figure wore."

"Maybe they were just put there for decoration."

"Nothing in that painting was put there just 'for decoration.' They were some kind of symbols, and I'm going to find out what they mean."

Garth slowly shook his head. "You're not thinking clearly, Mongo. You make sketches of whatever markings you remember, and I'll have them checked out. You don't exactly blend into the scenery, which means you can't just go walking around the streets. You want those guys to finish what they started?"

"Indeed not. But I don't think I'm alone; I do believe I've picked up some heavy protection—a guardian angel, so to speak."

"You've got smoke on the brain. What are you talking about?"

"How many cops and firemen were on the scene when you got there?"

"They were all over the place."

"Ambulances?"

"Two or three. What are you getting at?"

"You said you found me on the sidewalk, wrapped in wet drapes. Let me tell you something; whoever cut me off that bed and carried me outside was no fireman. When I passed out, I was surrounded by flame and just this side of Barbecue City—a minute, probably less. Now, I never heard any sirens—and believe me, I was listening with keen interest. I would have been ashes by the time firemen pulled up to the front of the building, much less got up to my apartment. No way. Five people died in a fire that started under *my* bed."

Garth considered it, and I could see in his eyes that he was reaching the same conclusion I had. But then he backed away from it. "Fires are tricky things, Mongo. I'm not sure you would have heard sirens over the noise of the fire itself. The firemen could have been a lot closer than you think."

"A cop or fireman would have taken me directly to an ambulance, not dropped me on the sidewalk. It had to be Veil who got to me, cut me loose, and carried me out. He'd known what was likely to happen to me if I got involved, and he'd been keeping an eye on me from the time I pushed open his door and went up to his loft. He must have broken through the door of my apartment almost as soon as the two men left. It was probably Veil who turned in the first alarm. After he got me out, he would have gone back up to try and help others; it was too late for five of them."

Garth was silent for some time, thinking. "Just for the sake of argument," he said at last, "let's assume that you're right. One question: If it was Kendry who brought you out, and he was that close all the time, why didn't he make an earlier entrance and blow away those two guys *before* they started thumping on your feet and toasting your ass?"

"I don't know. I'll ask him when I find him."

Garth reached out, took the Beretta and the Seecamp out of their holsters, and emptied both boxes of cartridges on the bed. He put a bullet in the chamber of each gun, filled both magazines. When he had finished he shoved the Seecamp under my pillow, put the Beretta, the holsters, and the remaining cartridges into a drawer of the stand next to the bed. "If any hospital personnel try to give you a hard time about the guns, you have them call me."

"I'll keep them out of sight."

"Just as long as you keep them close at hand." Garth gave me a smile and a thumbs-up sign before rising from the chair and heading for the door. He paused with his hand on the knob, turned back. His smile had vanished. *"I'll* be the one asking Kendry why he sent you out on a paper raft into a sea of sharks," my brother said in a low voice that carried more than a hint of menace. "As a matter of fact, I have quite a few questions to ask Mr. Kendry, and I plan to have his ass in custody by the time you get out of here."

"Garth, you be very careful how you handle Veil Kendry," I said quickly, but my brother was already gone from the room.

6

My hospital stay lasted three more days, and I was out on Wednesday—the one-week anniversary of Veil's disappearance. I hadn't expected Garth and the rest of the NYPD to find Veil, and they hadn't. Nor had they found my two torturers, although, working from my descriptions, a police artist had come up with excellent sketches. In fact, neither the NYPD nor the F.B.I. could even come up with mug shots, police records, or anything else that matched the faces and the MO of the two men. *That,* I thought, was what you'd call a low profile.

Fortunately for my feet, I was able to use the telephone to take care of a lot of business involving insurance coverage, credit cards, and so on—all the pieces of paper and plastic without which you feel *really* naked after you've lost everything but your living room drapes.

I'd feared I would need crutches to get around, but by the time I checked out of the hospital I was able to hobble along pretty well with only a cane. Carrying the loaded Seecamp strapped to my right ankle and the heftier Beretta in its shoulder holster under a jacket, wearing dark glasses and a broad-brimmed fedora low on my forehead, keeping a very wary eye on everyone who passed within ten yards of me, I spent the morning filing for replacements for the documents I had lost, including my P.I. and driver's licenses. I bought two skewers of shish kebob and a can of Pepsi from a sidewalk vendor, ate a leisurely lunch on a bench in a small plaza with my back to a stone wall, peering out from under the brim of my fedora to see if I could spot anybody who might be tailing me. Satisfied after a half hour that I wasn't being followed, I picked up a pad and pen from a stationery store, then took the subway to the 42nd Street library. During the subway ride I copied down as many of the symbols as I could remember that had appeared on the robe Veil had been wearing in the painting.

With the help of a librarian, I began ordering up from the stacks books on the peoples of Southeast Asia, Asian calligraphy and symbology, and even—on the off chance that the shape and color of the robe itself might be meaningful—a text on the Asian textile industry. Four large tomes and an hour later I found what I was looking for, in an anthropology text. The symbols were of a religious nature and were used by a Southeast Asian people called the Hmong. I canceled the rest of my order, filed a new one for three books on the Hmong.

By the time I left the library two and a half hours later, I had learned that the Hmong were a tribal people indigenous to the heavily forested, mountainous regions of Laos. Fiercely independent, the Hmong had fought not only against the Pathet Lao, that country's Communist guerrillas, but against the Viet Cong and North Vietnamese regulars who had used the Laotian jungles as sanctuaries and the trails to move men and supplies into what was then known as South Vietnam. The Hmong had fought for themselves, for their own reasons, but they had also played a crucial role in the C.I.A.'s secret war in that country. The tribespeople had been equipped with American arms, trained in their use, and often led in combat, by American Special Forces personnel, who, often as not, doubled as C.I.A. operatives. When the Americans left and the arms shipments stopped, the Pathet Lao had moved on the Hmong villages and wreaked a terrible vengeance. Thousands of Hmong were murdered, and virtually all of the remaining Hmong forced to flee. With the assistance of various American agencies, many of these Hmong refugees had emigrated to the United States. There was, according to a *New York Times* article I found on the library's microfiche machine, a large settlement of Hmong in the Pacific Northwest, particularly around Seattle.

It almost certainly meant, I thought, that Veil had been Special Forces and had spent time fighting with the Hmong in Laos. Probably, he had also been a C.I.A. operative.

It was all enough to start making me a bit nervous.

* * *

I had met Viktor Raskolnikov, Veil's patron, art dealer, and friend, through Veil some years before and had eventually become friends myself with the burly, shrewd, gentle Russian. Viktor owned a gallery on Madison Avenue, on New York's Upper East Side. Despite the fact that I was beginning to feel very tired and sore, that's where I headed next, treating myself to a cab ride over a distance I would normally have walked with pleasure.

The Raskolnikov Gallery occupied a four-story building and more closely resembled a small art museum than a gallery. Viktor had made a fortune anticipating "now" movements and "hot" artists in New York's volatile art market. His specialty was the avant-garde, but he touched all the bases and his tastes were eclectic, ranging from antique Persian miniatures to performance art, allowing artists to stage and videotape their "pieces" in a small basement theater.

Each floor of the gallery was divided into rooms of various sizes where "compatible" pieces of artwork were displayed side by side. Viktor opened at noon, stayed open until midnight, and there were always crowds of people moving through the rooms, types ranging from ragtag, struggling artists eyeing the work of their more successful contemporaries, to oil sheikhs looking for good investments.

Veil had a medium-sized room all to himself. Although I happened to know that Viktor had, at any one time, dozens of the prolific Veil's paintings stored away in a humidity-controlled vault, he very shrewdly chose to display only a very few—sometimes only one— of the paintings at a time, and always out of sequence so that it was impossible to guess that they had been spawned from a much larger work. The effect of seeing one of Veil's paintings, surreal and eerie, floating in its own cubical, monochrome sea of space bathed in soft blue or white light was striking, always intriguing, and sometimes disorienting. Viewing it in this way, whether alone in the room or with others, one might have been a passenger on a spaceship looking out a porthole over the surface of an alien world.

"Mongo?"

At the sound of the familiar, rumbling voice I turned away from the painting and found myself looking up into the round, bearded face of Viktor Raskolnikov hovering like a grizzled moon over his huge belly. As always, the Russian was dressed in a finely tailored tuxedo. He was holding a glass of white wine in each hand, and his green eyes glowed with bemused curiosity as he stared down at me.

"Hi, Viktor," I said, nodding my thanks as I took one of the glasses of wine.

"I thought it was you," the gargantuan art dealer said. "But what is with the dark glasses and big hat? I've never seen you wear a hat."

"I'm traveling incognito."

Viktor thought about it, then began to laugh. Viktor Ras-kolnikov laughing was truly a sight to hear and behold, and it served to stop traffic in the room and in the corridor outside. Viktor laughed with his whole body, which meant that his great belly heaved to and fro, and rolled, inside its vested confines, seemingly stretching the fabric to its breaking point. And he did it all without spilling a single drop of wine.

"Ah, that's a good one," Viktor said when he had finally brought his laughter under control and was able to catch his breath. "Dr. Robert Frederickson, of all people, trying to hide his identity under a big hat. Yes, that's very good. I've always loved your sense of humor."

"Yeah. Ho-ho."

Now Viktor frowned. "But I see that you are walking with a limp and using a cane. Is this part of your disguise?"

"Unfortunately, no. Actually, I have two limps. I had a little accident; something bumped into me."

"I am sorry, my friend," Viktor said, laying a huge hand on my shoulder. "I hope you are feeling better soon."

"Thanks, Viktor." I paused, trying to think of a way of sliding into asking the questions I wanted to ask without giving away too much information and putting the art dealer into any more jeopardy than I'd already placed him simply by walking into his gallery. "You know," I continued at last, "every time I see Veil's work I'm struck by its originality and freshness."

"Yes," Viktor said simply, glancing up at the painting above my head. "He's truly one of a kind."

"At first, all of his pieces look the same. But then you gradually come to realize that they're not; each painting in a series has subtle differences that make it unique."

Viktor nodded in agreement, sipped at his wine.

"And all landscapes," I continued. "No people—at least none that I've ever seen. Has he ever shown you any paintings with people in them?"

The gallery owner looked at me strangely. "No. As far as I know, Veil has never done anything but landscapes, although his use of color has changed radically over the years. You can see it most dramatically when you compare slides of his earlier work with what he does now. That's curious."

"What's curious? The change in his use of color?"

"No. It's curious that I was asked the same question just yesterday."

"Really?" I could feel the fine hairs on the back of my neck begin to rise.

"Yes. Two men came in the gallery yesterday afternoon and expressly asked to talk to me. They offered to pay for my time, and I should have accepted; I spent close to an hour with them, and they left without buying anything."

"What did they want to know?" I asked in what I hoped was a very casual tone of voice.

"A curious pair, with none of the aura of warmth and excitement people in the arts usually project. They asked questions like the one you just asked, about Veil's present and earlier work. I had the suspicion they were dealers, and I made it clear to them that Veil has an exclusive contract with this gallery for the next fifteen years."

They were dealers, all right, I thought, brokers of pain and death. The discovery that my torturers had paid Viktor a visit the day before served to magnify my own feelings of being a very dangerous pariah; everyone I talked to now became a potential target for the men who had tried to kill me. I was fairly certain I hadn't been followed, but couldn't be absolutely sure; my enemies might not even know I'd survived the fire, but I couldn't be absolutely sure of that, either. The gallery suddenly seemed very large and public, and I suddenly felt very vulnerable.

"Viktor," I said, shifting my weight heavily onto my cane, "I need a favor."

"What can I do for you, my friend?"

"I have a friend in the art department at the university who's putting together a collection of promotional material that's been used by and for various artists. I told her I'd come by here and ask you for one of Veil's publicity photos."

"Of course," the Russian replied with an easy shrug. "Let's go see what I have in my office."

With Viktor setting a slow pace, I hobbled after him out of the room, down the hallway, and into his office at the end. Grateful for the opportunity to rest my burning, throbbing feet, I slumped down on a leather couch while Viktor looked through a filing cabinet. After a minute or two he found what he was looking for—a four-page brochure from a one-man show Viktor had mounted the year before with Veil's photograph prominently displayed on the cover. I took it from Viktor, had a second glass of wine, then thanked my friend and left the gallery, going down a back stairway leading to an exit door that opened into an alley.

Now thoroughly exhausted, I took a cab back to Garth's apartment. It took me a couple of minutes to go through the procedures for defusing the explosive devices with which Garth had booby-trapped the door. After resetting the devices, I took a couple of aspirin and soaked in a tepid tub for half an hour.

The phone started to ring just as I came out of the bathroom and was headed toward the wet bar. I debated letting it ring, but since this was Garth's apartment and the call was probably for him, I answered it. It was my brother.

"Hey, brother," Garth said. "I was just about to give up on you. I've been trying to reach you all day. You can hardly walk, and you're supposed to be convalescing. Where the hell have you been?"

"Just taking care of some business. Among other things, I wanted to pick up a photograph of Veil."

"You could have saved yourself the trouble. I have mug shots."

"I didn't want mug shots. For one thing, they never look like the person."

"How are you feeling?"

"Like shit."

"Well, I want you to come and see something."

"Garth, my ass is dragging. I've got my heart set on a Scotch or three, a couple of the delicious sandwiches you were so sweet to make for me, and bed. Can it wait?"

"It could, but I don't want it to. Believe me, what I have to show you will give you a real happy heart; you'll love it. It's official business, so I'll send a squad car around to pick you up. Why don't you be down on the sidewalk in ten minutes?"

"Garth, I really—"

"See you in a few minutes."

"So?" Garth said.

"Holy shit," I replied.

"Is it them?"

"It's them."

"What about the hair color?"

"Forget the hair color. It's them."

In the dim light of the morgue chamber, I stared in something approaching disbelief at the two naked, toe-tagged bodies laid out on separate stone slabs. The faces, and only the faces, of the two men who had tortured and tried to kill me were unmarked, at least in the sense that no blows had been struck there. However, even in death, lines and shadows of unspeakable agony were left in the folds of flesh around the eyes and mouths as indelibly as if they had been etched there with acid; they still looked as if they were screaming. From the neck down, both bodies were blue-black like a single great bruise, the result of innumerable ruptured blood vessels and prolonged internal bleeding. The right thumbs of both men had been severed.

My night visitors had taken a long time to die; their hair had turned bone white.

"Somebody really did a number on these guys," Garth remarked dryly. "What we've got here are two fleshbags of broken bones and mushed guts. There'll be an autopsy, of course, but it's a waste of time. The pathologists will find that just about everything inside these men is broken; they'll also find that the men were kept alive while they were being taken apart. I've never seen anything like it."

"Neither have I," I said in a hollow voice, numbed by the horror of what I was looking at as well as by the terrible, cold-blooded, and controlled savagery the man I thought of as a friend was capable of. Suddenly I was afraid of Veil Kendry—afraid of finding him, and afraid of his secret.

"It looks like you were right about having a protector."

"Yeah. It looks that way."

"Nunchaku?"

"I'd say so. Tap-tap-tap. I told you the man was a master."

"What do you think of the missing thumbs?"

"I don't know."

"Trophies?"

"No. Not Veil's style."

"After seeing this, you still think you're an authority on Veil Kendry's style?"

"Your point is well taken. I just don't think Veil would take trophies."

"Shit. Why the hell would he cut thumbs off?"

I thought about it, said: "For the fingerprints. The faces were left unmarked so that we'd have positive identification, and the thumbprints will provide the same for somebody else."

"You think he sent them to somebody?"

"Just a guess."

"And probably a good one. It would mean that the person on the other end has access to fingerprint apparatus and a record of those men's prints."

"Yes. When and where did you find these jokers?"

Garth laughed without humor. "A patrolman found them this morning, in the alley outside the station house. They were hanging upside down with their ankles wedged into the grating of our fire escape. It seems that Kendry not only takes care of our business for us, he makes free deliveries. Very witty."

"Speaking of identification, did they have any on them?"

"Loads of it; credit cards, drivers' licenses, Social Security cards. All phony, of course, good work and untraceable. Each had over a thousand in cash in his wallet."

"I assume you ran a print check from the rest of their fingers?"

"Sure. Nothing."

"Interpol?"

"Nothing there, either."

It didn't surprise me. "So they don't have criminal records. What does that suggest to you, Garth?"

"What does it suggest to you?"

"That in somebody's perception they're good guys, not bad guys. They were thugs, but they were official thugs; not gangsters. They were trained by, and worked for, an agency of some government—probably our own."

Garth shrugged. "There are top-flight professional assassins around the world with no criminal records; that's why they're so successful and difficult to defend against. Hell, there's no way to tell if these guys were even Americans."

"I think they were."

"Almost all government agencies, at least the kinds that would use men like this, fingerprint their agents."

"Yes; precisely the reason Veil cut off the thumbs and mailed them in. Some agencies keep their own computer files, so neither Interpol nor the F.B.I. would have any record of their agents. I think there's a good chance these men were C.I.A. operatives. They were working domestic territory, which means that whatever they were involved in is a renegade operation. It wouldn't be the first time."

"What makes you think they were C.I.A.?"

I told Garth about the information I had gleaned from my trip to the library, stressing the common association between Americans fighting with the Hmong in Laos and the C.I.A. Garth listened attentively, nodded appreciatively when I'd finished.

"You've done good work, Mongo. I'm going to check out some things. For openers, I'll see if I can't get hold of an official, written copy of Kendry's complete service record."

"Good idea." Suddenly I could hardly keep my eyes open, and my legs hurt all the way up to my hips. "Can I get a ride back to the apartment?"

"You've got it. The squad car's waiting outside for you."

"Good," I said with a weary wave as I hobbled toward the door. "I need some sleep. In the morning, I've got to make some travel arrangements."

"Where you going?"

"Seattle."

"What's in Seattle?"

"A lot of Hmong, and maybe a few pieces of Veil's past."

7

Seattle seemed like a city sculpted from wet snow. The skies were leaden when I arrived and looked like they would stay that way for some time. Even more depressing than the dim winter light and biting cold was the realization that I was, in all likelihood, wasting time and money on an impossible task, trying to pick up a trail that was almost two decades cold. While it was true that there were thousands of Hmong in and around this city, I didn't know a single one. I had no way of knowing how many Hmong had known Veil and fought with him, or if any of them had escaped from Laos and made it to the United States. All I had was a recent photograph of a man the Hmong hadn't seen in half a lifetime; despite the fact that the younger Veil had been clearly recognizable to me in the painting, there was no telling how he had looked in those years, in or out of uniform, probably covered most of the time with mud and blood. I hated to think of what the odds might be against finding anyone who would recognize him.

But the symbols on the robe in the painting had been specific, and the logic of my trip still seemed inescapable; the symbols were associated with the Hmong people; there were more Hmong in Seattle than anywhere else; I was in Seattle. The fact that my feet were feeling better was at least some consolation, and I could now walk without a cane.

I learned that the Hmong had gathered together in a patchwork of interconnecting neighborhoods in the southeast sector of the city, and I found and checked into a hotel near the enclave. I knew that I could spend weeks working restaurants, bars, and other places where people gathered, and consequently needed a more systematic approach in my search for someone who might have known Veil. Figuring that I had certainly begun earning the ten thousand dollars Veil had left me, I began spending it, keeping a careful record of my expenditures in a small notebook.

I made up a short message offering a five-hundred-dollar reward to anyone who had ever known Veil and could supply information about him. Then I went looking for a pay phone booth that possessed a number of specific characteristics: it had to be fairly close to the hotel where I was staying, isolated enough so that it would be almost completely unused for one or two hours a day, out of doors but with some kind of shelter or windbreak nearby, and surrounded by enough open space so that I could monitor the movements of any people who might pass by.

I finally found what I was looking for in a small park about three-quarters of a mile from the hotel. There was a bank of three phones in the center of a small, lighted plaza circled by woods. Not too many people would be using those phones in the middle of winter, and there were more convenient phones for pedestrians to use on the sidewalks circling the park. All three phones were in working order, so I incorporated the number of the one on the right in my message, instructing anyone wishing to claim the reward to call that number between six and eight in the evening.

The next step was risky, but seemed unavoidable. I had registered at the hotel under a false name, paid cash, and made a few noises about being a salesman for a manufacturer of designer jeans. I wanted as few people as possible to see me, and none at all to be able to connect me with a search for a missing American who had fought with the Hmong in Laos. But I needed a printer, which meant that I could not avoid dangerous personal contact altogether. I found a print shop with an owner who was bilingual in English and Hmong. He translated my message into Hmong, and I left him with instructions to blow up Veil's photo to poster size, incorporate my message in both languages at the bottom, then print up a hundred copies on poster-weight paper as quickly as possible. I thought that the owner, a Hmong, reacted slightly when I gave him the brochure with Veil's photo, but I told myself that it could be my imagination and that narrowly escaping being burned alive would make anyone paranoid.

In any case, the posters were ready the next afternoon, as the man had promised. I paid for them and walked out with the bundle under my arm. The palm of my left hand, which had been resting on the butt of the Beretta in my coat pocket all the time, was sweaty, even in the cold air.

My hand stayed on the Beretta as I walked out onto the sidewalk. I had been constantly looking over my shoulder since leaving New York, and as far as I could tell I was not being followed. Still, my torturers had destroyed the painting precisely to keep hidden the link between Veil and the Hmong. If it were discovered that I was alive and had left New York, it wouldn't be all that hard for my enemies to figure out where I had gone. Also, I could not discount the possibility that there might be hostile eyes and ears among the Hmong. I planned to keep on looking over my shoulder.

I had no phony ID with me, and renting a car would have necessitated using a credit card with my real name on it, which I did not want to do. However, I did manage to find a place where I could rent a bicycle. I ate some dinner while I waited for it to get dark, then—as I did each night at six—I checked in with Garth to let him know I was all right. Nothing was happening on his end; there was still no trace of Veil or clue to his whereabouts, and the NYPD had still not been able to identify the two assassins.

It was after eight when I set out on my bike with the posters and a staple gun I had purchased in a luggage rack mounted on the rear fender. I pedaled straight into the Hmong enclave.

Most of the Hmong, I had learned, worked in the fish processing and lumber industries, the industrial backbone of the county, where they had a reputation for being hard and conscientious workers. They were a close-knit community, trying as best they could to preserve their ancient culture and customs, transplanting them from the mountains and jungles of Laos, hoping they would take root and survive on the brick and glass escarpments and concrete-paved trails of Seattle.

Pedaling through these neighborhoods of dreams, I looked for telephone or light poles outside bars, post offices, shopping centers —any site where large numbers of people might congregate or pass by. The Hmong, it seemed, ate late, and I often caught the odors of food—rice, fish, curries, strange and pungent spices. I pumped fast and furiously between stops, swerving to avoid patches of ice and piles of snow in the streets, braking to a stop at what looked like appropriate sites, stapling up the posters and moving on. By midnight, I had stapled up all one hundred posters, over a fairly wide area. Half frozen, my feet throbbing, I rode wearily back to my hotel, where I soaked my aching body in a warm tub, then went to bed and immediately fell asleep.

The next day I was at the park at five, an hour before any potential informants were scheduled to begin calling. I hung OUT OF ORDER signs and unscrewed the light bulbs in all three booths, then I looked around the area. There was certainly nothing foolproof about using a public pay phone as a blind; anyone with influence and a little time could get the location of the phone from the telephone company. However, this was the best strategy I'd been able to think of, and a quick circuit of the small park told me there was no one else there, at least not at the moment. By six, I was hidden behind a tree in the darkness a few yards from the booths.

At five minutes past six the phone began to ring. I let it ring, waited and watched; except for the ringing of the phone, the park remained absolutely still, and finally the caller hung up. Two minutes later the phone began ringing again. This time I answered it.

A nervous teenage boy wanted to talk to Jill. I told him he had the wrong number. I hung up, and the phone immediately began to ring again.

"Yeah?"

"I am calling in regard to the reward being offered for information on the man pictured in the poster." The man's voice was deep and resonant, assertive. There was also a pronounced accent, which I assumed was Hmong.

"Okay. What can you tell me?"

"Who are you?"

"Who are you? I'm the one paying out the money, so I get to ask the questions."

"But I haven't seen any money. It will be necessary for you to tell me why you want information about this man before I tell you anything."

"The man in the poster: What's his name?"

"None of us who knew him were ever told his real name. He was known to us only by a code name which was given to him by the Americans."

"What was the name?" I asked, trying to keep my growing excitement out of my voice.

"In Hmong, it translates as the name of a creature who may come from either heaven or hell. In English, I believe the word means a leader of angels—Archangel. I fought with him many years ago in Laos."

Bingo, I thought as my heart began to hammer. "Sir, I'd like very much to meet with you. I need to know everything you can remember about this man and what he did in Laos. You give me that, and you'll have your money."

"You still have not told me why you want this information," the man said warily.

"First we'll talk, and then maybe we'll get to that. In the meantime, I will pay for what you can tell me. Remember that if I can't get what I want from you, I may be able to get it from somebody else."

"All right," the man said after some hesitation. "We'll meet at—"

"I'll tell you where we'll meet." I glanced out the booth's glass at the street signs on the corner. "You know the little park at the corner of First and Grange?"

"Yes."

"How long will it take you to get there?"

"Fifteen minutes, perhaps less."

"Well, I've got a few things to do, so I can't get there for half an hour or so. What kind of car do you drive?"

"A 1982 Chevrolet. Green."

"Park it under the streetlight on Grange, by the drugstore. I drive a blue van. I'll pull up in front of you, and you come to me. I'm alone; make sure you're alone."

"Understood."

"I'll see you at the park in half an hour," I said, and hung up. After replacing the bulbs in the booths and removing the OUT OF ORDER signs, I climbed up to the top of a small wooded knoll where I had a clear view of the part of Grange Street that bordered the park. Then I waited. Ten minutes later a green Chevrolet pulled up to the curb beneath the streetlight in the middle of the block. Three men, Asians, got out. One looked to be middle-aged, and wore an expensive-looking gray overcoat with a matching hat. The other two men were younger, burlier, dressed in jeans, leather boots, and jackets. Both of the younger men carried *nunchaku,* and the weapons' mahogany and steel chains glinted in the light cast by the overhead lamp. The man in the overcoat said something to the two younger men who fanned out, then crossed the street and entered the darkness of the park. One of the men took up a position behind a tree at the foot of the knoll where I was hiding. The other disappeared behind some bushes twenty yards down the street. The man in the overcoat looked around him, then got back into his car and shut off the engine.

I waited ten minutes. When it looked like I had all the company I was likely to get, I moved down the side of the knoll using a "silent walking" technique Veil had taught me, a way of moving without noise which had made me feel foolish and awkward when I was practicing it, but which now seemed downright utilitarian. I came up behind the first of the two muscle-bound young men and cold-cocked him with the butt of my Beretta. Draping his *nunchaku* by the weapon's connecting steel chain around my neck, I backed up into the trees, then moved silently through the night to my left. When I had gone about twenty-five yards, I moved toward the street and, after a few minutes of stalking, found the second young man crouched behind a row of bushes near the sidewalk, staring intently down the street toward where the car was parked. I bounced a *nunchaku* stick off the top of his skull, and he collapsed into the bushes.

Once again I backed into the trees, then turned and sprinted back the way I had come, running all the way to the opposite end of the park. Keeping low, I ran across First Street, just below the intersection, darted into the shadows of a recessed storefront. I waited a minute to catch my breath, then, keeping to the shadows of the buildings, crossed at the intersection and made my way quickly down Grange toward where the green Chevrolet was parked.

Both the car's right rear and passenger doors were unlocked, and I could have simply opened a door and jumped into the car. But the events of the past few days had made me slightly irritable, and so I opted for another way of getting his attention. I gripped one end of the *nunchaku* I was holding, let the other stick hang down behind my back, then, as I leaped out from the shadows toward the car, I swung the free stick five or six times around my head to gain velocity, then brought it smashing down onto the windshield, shattering the glass. Again I spun the stick by its connecting chain, turned counterclockwise and stove in the window on the passenger's side. The safety glass first spider-webbed, then disintegrated into powder as it exploded in and over the man in the overcoat, who was already covered with debris from the windshield. When the thoroughly shocked, ashen-faced man finally took his hands away from his face and looked in my direction, he found himself staring down the barrel of my Beretta.

The man's mouth opened and closed as, wide-eyed, he glanced back and forth between me and the park across the street from where, obviously, he expected the young men to come rushing to his rescue. "Wh—who—?"

"Never mind who I am," I said curtly as I quickly opened the door, got into the car, and slid across a carpet of powdered glass until I was right next to him. I pressed the Beretta up under his jaw. "It's enough for you to know that I'm going to blow a hole right up through your skull if you make a move I don't like, or if you don't do exactly as I say. Now turn on the engine and get us out of here. Now!"

The middle-aged man didn't do anything except keep turning his head back and forth between me and the park across the street. The force of the exploding glass had knocked off his hat, but he had not even bothered to wipe the powdered glass from his hair and face. What I saw in the man's eyes and the lines around his mouth was not anger, but fear and self-reproach. There was dignity in the man's face, and he looked like he might be a minister, or a college professor, or some other pillar of the community; his expression was that of a member of the church board caught by the local police soliciting a hooker.

If he was surprised to find a dwarf busting up his car and shoving a gun into his face, he didn't show it. It surely meant he'd known at least a few things about me before he'd set off for our rendezvous.

"Listen," I continued, trying to sound threatening but without much enthusiasm. "This is a loaded gun I've got pressed up against your neck. The rules of the game say that puts me in charge. I told you to get this car moving."

"My sons," the man said, staring at me with large, haunted, gold-colored eyes. "Are they . . . ? Did you . . . ?"

"Your sons are in a lot better shape than I'd be in if one of them had hauled off and seriously whacked me with *nunchaku*, pal. They're just napping."

"Thank God," the man said with a sigh as he leaned his head forward on the steering wheel. Powdered glass rained off the shoulders of his overcoat. I kept my gun pressed tightly against his carotid artery. "They were only here to protect me in case . . ."

"In case of what?"

"Just . . . in case. I didn't know what you wanted, or who might be with you."

"Do you know who I am?"

"I don't know your name. I had a physical description. I received dozens of calls."

I'd been worried that no one would know, or remember, Veil; obviously, a great many people did. "Why should you suspect that I meant to harm you?"

"I was not concerned about myself. Our fear was that you might intend to harm . . . him."

"Archangel?"

"Yes."

"You say 'our' fear. Why did the people call you?"

"I am the president of our community association." The man bowed his head slightly after he raised it from the wheel. "My people honor me by considering me a leader. My name is Loan Ka. The American was my personal friend. The Hmong owe him more than can ever be repaid."

One of Loan Ka's sons, the one I'd dropped into the bushes, came staggering out into the street, holding his head with both hands.

"Tell him to stay put," I said quietly, pushing the gun hard up into the father's neck. "We have some more talking to do."

The man shouted something in what I assumed was Hmong out through the broken windshield. The young man looked up, started forward threateningly. Another command, this one sharper, and the young man stopped, turned back, and sat down dejectedly on the curb.

"Archangel was my friend, too," I continued to the Hmong. "His name is Veil Kendry, and he's still my friend."

"He is . . . in trouble?"

"Yes," I answered after some hesitation. I found that I instinctively trusted and liked the Hmong; there was no harm in his face, only concern for his sons. "He's disappeared, and some very nasty people want him dead. For that matter, they also want me dead."

The second son came out of the park, and Loan Ka shouted a warning to him without being told. He, too, sat down on the curb, although he continued to stare intently at the car.

"How can I help?" Loan Ka asked quietly as he turned back to me.

"I'm not sure. Although I consider Veil Kendry my friend, much of his life has been kept a secret from me, as well as from others. I need all the information you can give me about what Veil did in Laos, every detail you or anyone else can remember. It could provide the key to where he's gone, who's after him, and why."

"Who are you?"

"My name's Frederickson."

"I apologize for your . . . reception, Mr. Frederickson. I will tell you all I remember, and do anything else I can to help; I believe that you are Archangel's friend. But, please; you will come to my home for dinner."

The invitation caught me by surprise; I wasn't certain I should even take the gun away from the man's neck, much less agree to sit down and eat with him. Under the circumstances, specifically considering Loan Ka's smashed car windows and slightly damaged sons, it seemed a rather bizarre invitation—too bizarre to be anything but sincere. Still, I hesitated; the two youths sitting across the street represented a lot of muscle.

"I'm not sure we know each other that well," I said. "We'll talk here."

"All the things you need to know will take time to tell, Mr. Frederickson. You say you are a friend of the American's, and I believe it is true. That makes you my friend." The Hmong paused, shuddered, then looked at me with a strange expression on his face, as if he were ashamed of what he was about to say. "Also, quite frankly, I am cold. Peter and Jimmy may need medical attention, and I am concerned about their health. It is very difficult for me to speak under these circumstances."

"Peter and Jimmy?"

"We are Americans, and those are my sons' American names. Will you come to my home, Mr. Frederickson? You have nothing more to fear from me or my sons."

Loan Ka wasn't the only one who was cold; night daggers of arctic air were jabbing through the open spaces of the car which I'd just about managed to turn into a convertible. Still keeping my gun trained on Loan Ka's head, I got out, then slid into the backseat.

"Tell your boys to squeeze into the front with you," I said through chattering teeth. "And remind them that I have a gun."

"You won't need your gun, Mr. Frederickson."

"We'll see about that. It's a good thing for you people that I'm hungry."

8

"Many of the ethnic and national enmities in our part of the world go back centuries, Mongo. Not a few of these hatreds predate not only America's decision to go to war there, but even America's birth as a nation. This is a fact about Southeast Asia I find my new countrymen still find it difficult to grasp."

Sometime during the course of the evening Loan Ka, his family, and myself had gotten on a first-name basis. Although I'd kept my Beretta trained on the Hmong and his two sons during the short ride to his home, it had gone into my pocket when we had pulled into the driveway of Loan Ka's modest, two-story frame house on a quiet residential street near the perimeter of the Hmong enclave. Loan Ka's wife, Maru Tai, and an older woman I assumed was a grandmother had been waiting anxiously at the door, and the two women had reacted with some distress to the sight of the car with its shattered window, two sons with bleeding heads, and a decidedly strange stranger in the backseat. I never knew what Loan Ka told the two women, for the hurried family conference had been held in hushed tones, in Hmong. However, after the conference the two boys were led away by their grandmother to have their heads tended to, while Maru Tai began the preparation of a simple but delicious meal of fish and seasoned rice garnished with Laotian sauces and surrounded by braised vegetables. Now Loan Ka and I sat in a small den off the living room, drinking heavy Laotian liqueur and smoking cigars.

"The Pathet Lao were our enemies," the Hmong continued as he tapped the ash off his cigar into a heavy glass ashtray situated between us. "While it is true that we served the Americans' interests by fighting against the Communists, it is also true that the Americans served our interests by providing us with automatic weapons, advisers to train us in their use, and ammunition. But the American—Veil Kendry, as you call him—was always much more than just an adviser. First, he had gone to the not inconsiderable trouble of learning the rudiments of our language before coming to us, and he became very fluent during the four and a half years he stayed with us. There had been other Americans, of course, but this one was different from all others. He became our leader, not because he was an American, but because he was by far the best warrior among us. Archangel was afraid of nothing. The Pathet Lao, though, came to fear him very much, to the extent that they put a very large price on his head; any Hmong who killed him, or who helped to trap him, would be paid the bounty. Needless to say, the reward was never collected."

"I assume the Pathet Lao wanted to kill all the Americans."

"Of course, but not as badly as they wanted to kill this one. Archangel was the only American they ever put a bounty on." Loan Ka paused, studied the end of his glowing cigar as he rolled it between his thumb and index finger. "Could anything I say get the American into any more trouble than he's already in?"

"Nothing you can say to me will hurt him. And I won't repeat anything you say to anyone else who might hurt him."

The Hmong thought about it as he puffed on his cigar. "I wouldn't want anything I say to be misunderstood," he said at last.

"It won't be."

"I believe that Archangel was quite mad," Loan Ka said through a thick cloud of pungent, blue cigar smoke which lent his words a surreal, disembodied air. "He seemed to have a terrible and almost insatiable need for violence, as others have a need for food, water, and rest. I will not say that he loved to kill; it may be true, but I am not certain. I do know that he loved to fight; he seemed to need to be near death, his own or others'. If more than three or four days would go by without contact with the enemy, he would become very restless and irritable. Then he would go out alone, at night, and hunt the enemy himself, armed only with his bare hands, perhaps a knife or martial arts weapons designed for silent killing. Sometimes he would be gone for as long as a week, and we would think that he was dead. But he always returned, usually reeking and filthy, covered with dirt and caked blood. I do not know what he did to his victims and did not want to know even then. I suspect he was even more savage than the Pathet Lao, and the acts he committed led to their fear of him and the bounty they placed on his head. In any case, after these lone hunting forays he would be all right for a time—relaxed, the wildness gone from his eyes, seemingly once again at peace with himself. But then the tension in him would begin to build again if there was a prolonged period without combat. Always, if the enemy did not come down the trails or through the jungle to us, he would go out after them. Archangel was the most savage and awesome warrior I have ever known. He became a legend, Mongo, as hated and feared by the Pathet Lao as he was respected and revered by us."

"When did he first come to you?"

"In early 1968, soon after the Tet offensive."

"How did he come to you? Did he just walk into your village out of the jungle?"

Loan Ka shook his head. "No. As I said, there were Americans before him. A mile or so from the village there was a clearing which was used as a helicopter landing site. That was how our supplies were brought in, and how American personnel were shuttled in and out."

"What about communications?"

"Archangel, like the others, had a shortwave radio, but its use was always kept to a minimum. There were regularly scheduled meetings twice a month between Archangel and his superiors, and Archangel would always go to the landing site at a prearranged time, unless he'd received a radio message instructing him not to."

"Did you ever see any of the men who came to meet with Veil Kendry?"

"On occasion, but only when the helicopter was bringing in supplies; then we would go to carry back the munitions. However, we were not allowed to go along when the meetings took place; Archangel was supposed to go alone. We ignored this restriction after the Pathet Lao put a price on the American's head. After that we always accompanied him, despite his objections. Six of us would escort him to the landing site, then remain a distance away."

"Were you close enough at these times to see the landing site when the helicopter came in?"

"Yes."

"Did you ever see the faces of the people who came just to talk to him?"

"Until the last time, there was only one man—the same man—who came with the pilot. He was dressed in civilian clothes."

"You're sure it was always the same man?"

"I believe so, yes, although I never saw his face because of the long-billed cap he wore. Also, every time I saw him he was wearing a pale green raincoat that seemed too small for him. He was fat, about a foot shorter than Archangel."

"If he was wearing civilian clothes, it may have been Veil's C.I.A. controller," I said, half to myself.

"They didn't like each other."

"Veil told you that?"

"No. The American never spoke of the man or what they talked about. But they were always gesturing angrily at one another, and their loud voices carried. I did not have much English then, but I could understand the sound of anger. Archangel was always highly agitated after these meetings, and he would usually go out alone hunting afterward."

"You say there was only the pilot and this man in the green raincoat at the meetings up until the last time?"

"Yes."

"When was the last time?"

"The early fall of 1972."

"This was when Veil left your village?"

"It was when he was taken away," Loan Ka replied curtly, his voice taking on a sharp edge of emotion. His eyes had gone slightly out of focus as he stared at a spot just above my head, and his face had a haunted expression, as though he were looking into the depths of a nightmare which was very old, but which he could not forget. "I'm certain Archangel received no warning that he was being taken out, or he would have told us. We escorted him to what we assumed was just another regularly scheduled meeting, but this time there were two helicopters waiting at the landing site, One was a large troop carrier, and there were a large number of South Vietnamese soldiers inside with assault weapons. The other helicopter carried the man in the green raincoat, and . . ." Loan Ka paused, swallowed hard, then virtually spat out the last name. "Colonel Po."

The name, "Colonel Po," struck a distinctive chord—one that was very loud and dissonant. "Liu Sakh Po?" I asked.

The Hmong nodded, and I felt the muscles in my stomach and

across my chest begin to tighten. The information touched on a situation—and answered questions—that had made headlines in American newspapers for a week or more in 1972, in the fall.

Colonel Liu Sakh Po had been the most notorious officer in the South Vietnamese army. A scion of one of the wealthiest, most powerful—and, many said, most corrupt—families in South Viet Nam, Colonel Po had never, to anyone's knowledge, had a single bullet fired at him in combat. Yet he had been the most prominent spokesman for both the government and the army, in effect a flamboyant propagandist in French-tailored uniforms constantly warning that South Viet Nam would fall to the Communists if the United States did not provide ever-increasing amounts of aid. Po spent all his time in Saigon, a distance from the battlefield that did nothing to slow the numbers of large, glittering medals with which he was constantly being decorated in recognition of his "public relations" efforts.

Then a *New York Times* reporter had discovered that one Liu Sakh Po, ARVN colonel, was Saigon's most prominent crime czar, trafficking in narcotics sold to American servicemen, a thriving black market in American-supplied foodstuffs and munitions, and prostitution. Although angry denials were issued by both the South Vietnamese and American military commands, and even though the reporter was hastily expelled from the country and branded a traitor by certain United States senators and congressmen, the evidence against Po had continued to build. Then, at the height of the scandal, Colonel Po had simply disappeared from public view. Now I knew where he had gone—into the jungles of Laos, with the help of the Americans.

Ironically, within the past year the *Times* had begun another series of articles on the infamous Colonel Po, a kind of retrospective and update written by the same reporter, a winner of three Pulitzer Prizes. According to the articles, Po had been spirited out of South Viet Nam after the collapse of Saigon and helped to settle in the United States, a fact that had been well hidden for more than a decade, up until the publication of the articles. Also, according to the articles, Po had brought his old tricks with him to his new country. Operating from a well-guarded mansion in Albany, New York, he was said to control a wide empire in drugs and prostitution throughout upper New York State. Déjà vu.

"Why was Po brought into Laos, to your village?" I asked, pretty certain I knew the answer.

"He was to replace Archangel, and the soldiers in the second helicopter formed his personal bodyguard. I do not know why this decision was made; as far as I know, he was the only non-American adviser sent to work with the Hmong anywhere in Laos."

"The Americans were helping him hide from a very nosy press."

"Even from the distance where we were standing, we could see that Archangel was angrier than he had ever been before. There was another American in the helicopter with the man in the green raincoat, an officer. Po and his men just walked away while Archangel argued with the officer and the man in the raincoat. They shouted back and forth at each other for almost half an hour."

"Could you tell the officer's rank?"

"I believe he was a general; he had stars on his cap and the epaulets of his jacket. It was this man who finally ended the argument; he spoke very sharply, and then Archangel threw down his gun in disgust and climbed into the smaller helicopter."

"And you never saw Veil Kendry again?"

Loan Ka shook his head. "We saw him again."

"But you said this was the last time—"

Loan Ka held up his cigar in a gesture asking for patience. "It was the last meeting between Archangel and his superiors."

At a sound to our left, both of us turned toward the doorway where one of Loan Ka's sons stood with a girl about his own age. She was dark-eyed, with long, shimmering black hair and olive skin. I thought she was beautiful. I had not heard the young man leave the house, had not heard a car start up, but Peter had obviously gone out into the night to bring the young woman back.

"This is Kathy," Loan Ka continued quietly.

"Hello, Dr. Frederickson," the young woman said, her English delivered with a lovely, lilting accent. She stepped forward, and I stood up and took the hand she offered. "I know of you. I am a sociology major at the university here, and two of your monographs on family structure and crime are required reading in a course I'm taking. It's an honor to meet you."

"My pleasure, Kathy."

We sat, and Loan Ka's wife entered carrying a tray with hot tea and pastries. After serving us, she left, motioning for her son to go with her.

"Colonel Po and his soldiers were not interested in fighting the Communists," the Hmong continued. "They were interested only in preserving their own safety. Indeed, they didn't even trust us; they stockpiled most of the arms and ammunition in their own private compound, which they forced us to build for them.

"Then, about two weeks after Po arrived, our children began to disappear. At first we thought it was some kind of Pathet Lao terror tactic, and that individual Communists had somehow found a way to penetrate our defense perimeter and kidnap our children. But, as we were to learn, this was not the case. The most beautiful of our children, both male and female, were being stolen by Po's men, then smuggled into Viet Nam for use in Po's Saigon brothels."

The words had been softly spoken, without any effort to lend them special weight. Still, I felt as if I had been dealt a physical blow. "My God," was all I could think of to say, and I lowered my gaze.

"It was almost a month before we discovered who was responsible for the disappearance of our children," Loan Ka continued softly. "It was not in our power to bring our children back to us, but we could do our best to punish those responsible. By this time we had few arms and little ammunition, but we took Po and his men by surprise and managed to kill many of them. Po himself escaped into the jungle.

"Without arms or ammunition, we could no longer fight the Pathet Lao and Viet Cong, and so they began to move freely down the trails in our region. On the other hand, we were not attacked—probably because the Pathet Lao assumed we were still as well defended as we had always been. We waited for the Americans to contact us again, for another adviser and more arms. But no more helicopters came. For us, it was as if the war had ended—except that our children had been lost to Po's brothels, and nothing could assuage the grief of our tribe."

Now there was a prolonged silence, broken only by the muffled sound of rock music coming from a room upstairs and the clink of dishes as Maru Tai worked in the kitchen.

"I was one of the children taken," the girl called Kathy said, picking up the thread of the story. Her voice was barely audible at first and was often broken by sighs, but it gained strength as she continued to speak. It was all I could do not to reach out and take her hand, tell her that it was all right and that she did not have to relive this nightmare. But I needed to hear all of it. It was why Veil had put the symbols in the painting.

"I was caught by one of the soldiers as I was walking along a trail just outside the village," Kathy continued. "He put a hand over my mouth and jabbed my arm with a hypodermic needle. I can't remember how I was taken away, but I seem to remember the sound of a helicopter. I was taken to a . . . place, in a city, where I found some of my friends who had disappeared before me. I'm sorry, Dr. Frederickson, but it would be most difficult for me to talk about the things that were done to me there."

"It's all right, Kathy; that's not important. Just tell me what you can."

"Some time after I arrived, a pimp took a boy and myself out on the streets to look for customers. It was perhaps three or four in the morning. The boy and I were so . . . tired. The streets were empty, but still the pimp would not take us back and let us sleep. We stood in a doorway, the pimp gripping each of us by the shoulder so hard that it hurt very much. Then we heard the sound of footsteps coming along the street, just around the corner from where we stood. The man came around the corner, and the pimp pushed us out in front of him. It was the American."

Something that felt like an electric shock flashed through my chest, momentarily making it difficult for me to breathe. "You mean Veil Kendry?"

"Yes—if that is the name of the man on the posters you hung up around the neighborhood. The children just called him the American, and the adults called him Archangel. He was wearing a uniform. He was clean shaven, but his face was haggard, and he looked like he had not slept in a long time. The pimp spoke to the American, offering one or both of us for his pleasure. The American stood very still as he listened to the pimp, but all the time he was looking down at us. There was an expression on his face which is very difficult to describe. I believe I saw tears in his eyes, and he was smiling gently, as if to reassure us that everything would be all right. But behind the tears and the smile was an expression more frightening than anything I have ever seen.

"When the pimp finished his proposition, the American killed him. It was almost a casual gesture—the American just reached out with one hand, wrapped his fingers around the man's neck, and snapped it with a twist of his wrist." Kathy paused, shuddered. "Sometimes, in nightmares, I can still hear the sound of the pimp's neck breaking; it was a hollow pop almost as loud as a gunshot.

"Then the American stepped over the body of the dead pimp and picked up the boy and me in his arms. He held us close for some time, and when he set us down on our feet his face was once again filled with this terrible rage. He asked us to take him to the brothel. We couldn't remember how to get back, but the American was very patient with us. He walked with us through the streets, carrying us when he could see that we were too tired to go on, until we finally found the brothel. He held us close once again, then gently pushed us back into the shadows before he crossed the street and entered the brothel.

"I don't know what happened in there. I do know that there were always big men inside, armed with guns. I didn't hear any gunshots, nor even any shouts; still, I believe the American killed all the guards and managers inside the house, for when he came out he had the other eight children with him.

"The American, walking in the middle with his arms around us, led us through the city to a Catholic Relief Agency. I remember that it was dawn when we got there, because orange sunlight shone in the nun's face when she opened the door. The American explained the situation to her, and she promised to see that we were returned to our families. Then the American turned and walked quickly away. It was the last time I ever saw him."

Maru Tai, who had been standing and listening in the doorway, now entered with more pastries and hot tea, and a new bottle of liqueur. I opted for the liqueur; I needed it.

"Thank you, Kathy," I said. "I know how hard it must be to relive that experience. You said the American was in uniform. Could you tell his rank?"

The beautiful young Hmong woman shook her head, causing her black hair to ripple across her shoulders. "It was the only time I'd ever seen him in uniform, and I was a child. Rank wasn't something I was thinking about at the time."

"Of course. Can you remember if he was wearing any kind of decoration on his cap, or on the shoulders of his shirt?"

The girl closed her eyes and cocked her head to one side as she tried to remember. Finally she opened her eyes, nodded. "Yes. Now I remember that when he lifted me up and held me, I saw some kind of metal bird on his shoulder. It was silver. Does that tell you anything?"

"Yes, Kathy. I can't tell you how grateful I am that you were willing to come here and tell me this."

"When Peter picked me up, he said that the American had disappeared and that you were trying to help him. I'll never forget what the American did for me, and I would do anything to help him."

"Do you have any idea what the American was doing in Saigon, or how long he'd been there?"

"No, sir."

"Do you have any idea how much time had passed between this incident and the day he was forced to leave Laos?"

"I can answer that," Loan Ka said. "From information I've gathered from speaking with others since then, I would estimate that it was seven or eight weeks from the time Archangel left our village. And the attack came on the same day that Archangel dropped Kathy and the other children off at the Catholic Relief Agency."

"Attack?"

"Kathy saw the man you call Veil Kendry for the last time in Saigon; it was not the last time the rest of us saw him. He came to us in late afternoon of the day he'd killed the whoremasters and rescued the children. He came alone in a helicopter, flying in low over the jungle. He landed in the village, virtually at the edge of a cliff; it was very dangerous to attempt this, but he made it. Then he got out, leaving the helicopter running. He was still dressed in his army uniform, but now there was blood all over the front of his shirt and pants. He stayed only long enough to give us a warning. It seems Colonel Po had made it safely out of the jungle and back across the border. He'd claimed that our village had gone over to the Pathet Lao, and he argued that we should be made an example of. The South Vietnamese had been pressing the Americans for permission to launch some kind of joint offensive across the border. Now permission was granted, and our village was to be the object of the offensive. A combined force of American and South Vietnamese commandos had already crossed the border and was now very close, ready to begin the attack with rocket launchers. The entire village was to be destroyed.

"We had no choice but to flee with whatever possessions we

could carry, and that's what we did. After warning us, Archangel got back into the helicopter and flew off.

"The first rockets landed on our village perhaps a half hour later, and then the commandos rushed in after them. By this time we were all out of the village, but the women and children slowed us down so that we were not as far up into the mountains as we would have liked to be. From our position, we could look down and see them burn our village and kill our livestock. Then the Americans and South Vietnamese began to fan out into the jungle, searching for us. Three helicopters were brought in to aid in the search, and they probably would have found us if not for Archangel. Suddenly his helicopter rose from a ravine and attacked the helicopters that were searching for us. Archangel fought in the air as he had always fought on the ground—with great skill and courage, and total abandon. He bought us the time we needed to climb higher into the mountains, into caves where we could not be found. It was from these caves that we saw Archangel's helicopter crash. All these years we assumed he had died in that crash. We are sorry for the great troubles you say he has now, but the entire Hmong community is overjoyed to learn that he is alive."

For some time I sat in silence, stunned by images of Veil being forced to fight against, and probably kill, a great many of his own countrymen and allies. It would have made him a traitor in the eyes of most of his countrymen, and certainly one in the view of the United States Army.

Traitors who kill their own people are shot or locked away in a military stockade for a very long time. Instead, in a very short period of time after the incident Loan Ka had related, Veil Kendry had been set free to turn up on the streets of New York City, where he had remained unmolested by anyone but himself—until many years later, when someone had winged a shot through his window. Although the bullet had been fired from a rooftop across an alley from Veil's loft, I was absolutely certain that the shot had also been traveling through a warp of space and time, traversing thousands of miles and nearly twenty years.

"It is all I can tell you," Loan Ka finished softly. "I hope it will be of help."

"Kathy?" I said, turning to the young woman. "On the morning Veil rescued you and the other children, did he have any blood on his uniform when he came out of the brothel?"

"No, Dr. Frederickson. I'm certain that his uniform was still clean."

"Thank you," I said, wearily rising to my feet. "I'm not sure how I can use this information; I am sure Veil wanted me to have it. I'll let you know how things turn out."

"What will you do now?" Loan Ka asked as his wife, two sons, and the grandmother came into the room.

"Go back to New York, think about the things you've told me, and try to sort some things out."

"You said that these men wish to kill you, too. You're in a great deal of danger yourself, aren't you?"

"Some."

"Then you must be doubly careful. You're being followed."

I turned quickly toward Loan Ka, swallowed hard. "How do you know that?" I asked, trying to keep my sudden attack of panic out of my voice. If it were true, I didn't even want to think about the possible consequences to this man and his family, and to Kathy.

"You've attracted a great deal of attention from the time you rode your bike into our neighborhood and tacked up the first poster. Many eyes have been watching you. Those same eyes watched what was going on around you; it was observed that a car was following you on your rounds—a late model Ford, dark blue or black."

My mouth was very dry, and I swallowed again. It didn't help. "Loan Ka, I could have sworn I wasn't being followed. I kept looking back—"

"You wouldn't have seen him. He took care to keep a safe distance behind you, and he was driving with his lights out." The Hmong took a slip of paper out of his pocket, handed it to me. "This is the license plate number of the car, written down when the car passed under a streetlight. People who caught a glimpse of his silhouette described him as a very big man. One caller said he thought the man might be Oriental, but not Hmong—perhaps Chinese or Vietnamese. I thought the information might be useful to you, and I'm sorry I don't have a better description."

"Thank you, Loan Ka," I said quietly as I put the slip of paper into my pocket.

"Would you like us to do something about this man, Mongo? The enemy of you and Archangel becomes our enemy, and there are many good warriors in this neighborhood. We have long memories and have not forgotten or lost our fighting skills."

It was certainly a tempting thought. My enemies knew I was alive and, despite all the precautions I had taken, I'd been followed, not only to Seattle but through its streets. Still, it would have been an easy matter to shoot me or simply to run me down while I was pedaling merrily along on the bike. It seemed that the word had gone out that there'd been a change of strategy and the quarry was not to be damaged—at least for the time being.

"No, Loan Ka. If this one disappears, whoever's behind him will just send someone else. It's probably better to leave him in place; it's enough for me to know that he's there."

"As you wish, Mongo. Just let me know if you change your mind. The big Oriental can be made to disappear very quickly."

"Loan Ka," I murmured, hoping the others could not hear. "I believe you and your family may be in danger now. Just the fact that you've talked to me could make you a target. I was careless; I shouldn't have come here. It might be best if you all went away for a while."

The Hmong dismissed the suggestion with a casual wave of his hand, spoke in a normal tone of voice. "As I said, Archangel's and your enemies are mine. After the Pathet Lao and Colonel Po, there are few things we fear. This man in the car is not one of them. We'll be careful, but we're safer here than we would be anywhere else."

"It's not just the man in the car, Loan Ka. There are others. These men are very dangerous. I'm concerned for you—for all of you."

"Don't be, my friend. There's nothing to worry about. In the meantime, I'm gratified that we could be of some small help. You must be very tired. Jimmy will take you back to your hotel now, or wherever else you wish to go."

"Loan Ka—"

"We'll be safe, Mongo. Don't worry. Just make certain that you protect yourself."

"I have to go back to the hotel to pick up some clothes," I said with a sigh. "Then I could use a lift to the airport. There's a late flight to New York."

"As you wish," the Hmong said, nodding to the boy named Jimmy.

"Sorry about your car, Loan Ka," I said, heading toward the door.

"It's not a problem; the insurance company will pay for it. If only all things could be as easy to repair as broken windows."

"Yes."

"When you find Archangel, tell him that the Hmong have not forgotten."

"I'll tell him, but it won't be necessary. He knew you wouldn't forget."

9

Loan Ka's son and I were alone on the highway—until a car, traveling at high speed, shot by us and quickly disappeared into the darkness up ahead. The car had sped by too fast for me even to identify the make, much less note the license plate number, but it was enough to make me suspicious—and sufficiently nervous to ease the Beretta surreptitiously out of its shoulder holster and hold it in my hand, next to my right leg.

We reached the airport without incident, but I was still suspicious. I asked Jimmy to take a turn through the parking area collectively used by the car rental agencies for returns, and almost immediately spotted a dark blue, late model Ford; the license plate number matched the one on the slip of paper Loan Ka had handed to me. Whatever else my shadow might be, he was a clever fellow; after seeing me leave the hotel with my bags, he'd preceded me to the airport and would be accompanying me on my flight back to New York. Cute. At the least, I hoped it meant Loan Ka and his family would be safe.

The "red eye" flight from Seattle to New York was less than half full, and I was the last passenger to get on. The best candidate for the man who was tracking me was sitting by himself in the window seat over the left wing. He was big, all right, and even though he was seated and slumped forward slightly as he read a magazine, I estimated his height to be at least six feet five or six inches. Not certain what, if anything, I wanted to do next, I squatted down in the aisle and pretended to tie my shoelace while I thought about it.

I decided that there was no way the man could know that I was aware he was following me. It was some advantage, but so minuscule as to be virtually worthless. Since I couldn't very well follow him while he was supposed to be following me, I was left in an almost totally passive position while he controlled all the options—including that of perfunctorily blowing me away if his marching orders were abruptly changed. I'd never liked passive positions and, as risky and uncertain a move as it might be, I decided to gamble for more while I had the opportunity, to see what would happen, or what I might discover, if I put a sharper edge on the situation.

"Mind if I sit here?" I asked as I dropped into the empty seat next to the big man. "I get airsick if I don't sit over the wing."

The man lowered his magazine and casually studied me with khaki-colored eyes that were so pale as to seem almost white; they were cold eyes, startling and chilling, and I had the distinct impression that they were mocking this feeble effort on my part to challenge and outwit him. Now that I was actually sitting next to him, I could see that he was more than just big—as a premiere NFL running back is more than just big, with enormous shoulders and torso narrowing down to a slim waist and hips, heavily muscled thighs that seemed to bulge even inside the pants of the finely tailored gray, three-piece suit he was wearing. He would be enormously strong, I thought, and—even more dangerous for me, since it would negate the one real physical advantage I had—quick, despite his looming size. He was certainly capable of much more than just following a man; if he was a killer, he would be a good one, and his body would be all the weapon he needed.

"Not at all," the pale-eyed man replied easily. "Would you prefer to sit here by the window?"

"No, thanks," I answered, managing what I hoped was a smile on a face that felt like rapidly setting concrete. "I also get airsick if I can see the ground."

The man grunted amiably, then turned his attention back to his magazine—a month-old issue of *Sports Illustrated*.

I didn't like anything I saw or sensed. It's sometimes possible, I'd learned from past experience, to extract a surprising amount of information about a person in a brief period of time just by being in close physical proximity and engaging the person in some light conversation—the reason I was sitting where I was. Hands, clothes, mannerisms, reactions, choice of reading material, a piece of paper sticking out of a pocket, an accent, choice of words or topics of conversation, even odors—all can merge together to form a composite picture of a person which, while blurry and incomplete at best, can nonetheless provide valuable clues to character and, sometimes, be a predictor of behavior. Not this time.

What I was getting from this man was nothing; too much of nothing.

He had not reacted at all to my sudden appearance. The winter eyes had revealed nothing but keen intelligence and—perhaps—a hint of bemusement behind a thick scrim of control. I put his age at around thirty-five. His hair was a light brown, cut short. To me he looked more European or American than Oriental—but then, only one of Loan Ka's informants had suggested that the man might be Asiatic. He had a rather triangular face, with a high, broad forehead tapering into shallow cheekbones, thin lips, and a surprisingly narrow chin for such a big man.

He was slumped in his seat, leaning to his left at an awkward angle, as if favoring a stiff neck or sore back. He held the magazine with his fingertips, and when he turned the pages it was with quick, nervous movements. His legs were crossed, and he would occasionally tap his right foot nervously against a brown cowhide attaché case he had placed on the floor by his seat. The image he projected was of a well-dressed and, despite his size, slightly effeminate businessman or accountant.

But "projected" was the key word, and I had the distinctly unnerving feeling that the man was playing games with me, enjoying a private joke at my expense. Of course, I had to take into account the possibility that he *was* a slightly effeminate businessman or accountant, and not the man who had been following me. But the blue Ford had been parked at the airport, and my seatmate was the only fellow passenger who came even close to fitting the description Loan Ka had given me.

I recalled the many conversations Veil and I had had regarding the *ninja* art of "psychological disguise"—meaning, in the case of the *ninja,* that a person did not have to be truly terrible to be truly terrifying, and vice versa. The point, always, was to lull and coax your enemy, or quarry, into perceiving you as *you* wanted him to perceive you. What and who you really are, Veil had always said, was nowhere nearly as important as what others thought you were.

This was the axiom that the *ninja* used to create a desired reality from illusion.

It was a set of skills I had, of necessity, used all my life, without ever having a label for what I was doing. Now I suspected that these same skills were being used against me in an attempt to disarm and beguile.

I knew I had made a mistake in confronting this man. I had hoped at least to shake him, to gauge him as an opponent, and, if I got lucky, perhaps to learn something that would be useful to me in my search for Veil. But in trying to inflate my small advantage, I had seen it blow up in my face; I was the one who was shaken, thoroughly intimidated by the man's physical size and psychological control. All I had accomplished with my stunt was to drive my tracker even deeper into the deadly shadows at my back.

Responding to a very real sensation of queasiness in the pit of my stomach, I indulged in a little psychological disguise of my own; I removed the airsickness bag from the pouch on the back of the seat in front of me and cradled it in my lap, then closed my eyes and pretended to fall asleep. I felt like the village idiot.

10

Garth heartily concurred.

"What are you, the fucking village idiot?!"

"It seemed like a good idea at the time," I replied lamely, reaching across the kitchen table for another doughnut. Garth's shift didn't begin until one in the afternoon, and we were enjoying a late breakfast while we considered together what I had—and hadn't—learned from the Hmong in Seattle. "I wanted to see if I could get some kind of line on the guy."

"You got a line on him, all right. Now he knows you're on to him."

"Not necessarily," I said without conviction. "There were enough people on the plane to make it seem reasonable for me to choose to sit next to him purely by chance."

"You still acted like the village idiot. You should have taken up the Hmong on his offer to have the man taken out."

"No. They'd just have sent somebody else."

"Yeah, but probably a smaller edition. This big guy sounds really spooky."

"That's a pretty good description."

"And we still don't know who's behind him."

"True, but it's interesting that they've decided to follow instead of kill me. These people aren't stupid."

Garth nodded in agreement as he took a bite out of a doughnut and washed it down with black coffee. In the morning light his skin seemed to have a greenish pallor, which I didn't like. He'd lost weight, and it occurred to me that he hadn't looked well for weeks. It bothered me.

"They tried to kill you in the beginning because they figured you as a loose end that could be chopped off quickly," Garth said when he had finished chewing. "Their main concern was in catching up with Kendry, but they quickly learned that finding Kendry wasn't going to be as easy as they'd thought. He was playing games with them, mostly hide and seek. Then two of the front-line players lost their lives and their right thumbs, so they decided that it might be easier to let you find Kendry for them. They're using you as a stalking horse." Garth paused, smiled thinly. "After all, you're the one whom Kendry's considerate enough to leave clues for."

"Yeah."

"Your friend Kendry is a real prick, Mongo. He's tied you across the mouth of a cannon. He's using you as a stalking horse, too."

"It does look that way. It seems like he needs me to gather evidence that will indict a person or persons unknown."

"Damn it, *he's* the evidence!"

"No, not evidence; he's the story, and it has to be corroborated."

"Well, he should have told *you* the story. *Kendry* damn well knows who wants to kill him, and it would have been nice for him to share the information with you before he sucked you into a situation where you almost got your ass cooked and could still end up with bullets where your brains used to be. Nobody else might have believed him, but you would have. He not only put you out in front of him, the son-of-a-bitch left you blindfolded on a killing ground."

"We've played this number, Garth, and there's no sense in doing it again," I said with some impatience. "Before we can pass judgment on Veil's methods, we have to find out who's trying to kill him, and why. When I found out that Liu Sakh Po was involved in this thing, it crossed my mind that he was the man we were after; after that last series of articles on him appeared in the *Times,* he could have started worrying about the loss of his low profile and wanted to erase links to his past. Or he could have feared that Veil would find out where he was and come gunning for him."

Garth looked skeptical. "You said the articles appeared six months ago."

"Precisely; too much time between events. If it is Po who's gunning for Veil, it wasn't the articles that triggered him. But I don't think it is Po. The men who tried to cremate me and the big guy on the plane aren't Po's type of people. Po's a low-class thug, and he uses other low-class thugs. The thugs I keep bumping into are nothing if not high-class. Still, the good colonel most certainly knows things we want to know, which is why I'm going to take a spin up the Thruway to see him."

"Dumb idea, Mongo; seriously dumb. There's no way he's going to talk to you about anything, much less about things he wants kept hidden. You'll just end up with low-class thugs chasing you along with the high-class ones."

"You're probably right. But I have to follow the bread crumbs wherever they lead, and right now Colonel Po is standing right in the middle of the trail. How can I go around him? He was one of the three men in the helicopter that came to take Veil away from the Hmong village, and he'll know the names and functions of the other two. He may know who wants Veil dead; it could be the man whose blood was on Veil's uniform."

"What blood?"

"Loan Ka told me that Veil had blood all over the front of his uniform when he came to warn the village of the attack."

"It was probably Kendry's blood."

"That's possible. But if it was Veil's own blood, it means he was wounded *after* he cleaned out the brothel and took the children to the Catholic Relief Agency. Kathy, the Hmong girl, was very clear on the point that Veil's uniform was clean when he walked out of the brothel, so the blood got there sometime between early morning, when he dropped off the children, and the afternoon, before he got into the helicopter. It was sometime during those hours when he found out about the plan to attack Loan Ka's village."

"You said the girl told you Kendry looked like hell. Maybe he already knew about the operation and had been brooding about it."

"Veil would have flown to warn the village as soon as he learned of the plan. If he'd known earlier, he could have avoided a situation where he had to shoot at his own people. No. He learned about it that same day, with only hours to go before the American and South Vietnamese commandos were scheduled to reach the village."

"Who did he learn it from?"

"The person or persons he went to see right after dropping off the children. Veil was enraged, so he would logically go to see the person he held responsible for the children ending up in a brothel —the man who'd made the decision to replace Veil with Colonel Po."

"One or both of the other two men in the helicopter."

"Right. Po was a monster, and everyone in the American and South Vietnamese command structure knew he was a monster. But not the Hmong. The Hmong finally unmasked him and drove him and his men out of the village, but not before they'd done irreparable damage to the children. This was the account Veil went to settle. There could have been a fight, with fists or guns, and Veil wound up with blood all over him. During the course of the confrontation, he learned about the plans for the attack. He just had time to abort it, but not to avoid actions that would brand him a traitor. It's doubtful that Veil would have known where to find Po so quickly; it was an American he went to see."

Garth absently sipped at his cold coffee, finally looked up at me and nodded in approval. "I like it, brother," he said simply. "It could very well have gone down that way."

"But it's still conjecture, without a shred of proof. And all the big pieces of the puzzle are still missing. That's why going upstate to at least try to talk to Po has to be the next step."

"Why don't I pick up the big guy who's tailing you and sweat him? It would be a hell of a lot safer."

I shook my head. "He won't sweat. Besides, he's nothing more than a hired hand who won't necessarily be able to tell us what we need to know. He was just told what to do, not given a look at the skeletons in the closet."

"He'll know who hired him."

"He was probably hired by some flunky way down the chain of

command. Snatching him won't get me any closer to Veil, and it will only tip my hand. First, let me try to get next to Po. If that doesn't work and there are no other leads, then we can always try sweating the big guy."

My brother grimaced. "I don't like it, Mongo. I've got no jurisdiction in Albany, and no close contacts with any Albany cops. In fact, they might well resent me poking my nose into what they consider their business."

"I'll go alone. In fact, Po might be more willing to talk to me if I go alone."

"Bullshit. Even if I weren't specifically assigned to the arson and murder aspects of this case by the NYPD, I most definitely would be assigned to *you* by me. No heavy moves without checking with me first. Agreed?"

"Agreed. Garth, you don't look good."

"I don't feel good," Garth said, with what for him was remarkable candor in regard to his health.

"What's the matter?"

"I don't know. I've got headaches, nausea, loss of appetite, and general all-around crankiness, but those are just symptoms."

"Why don't you go see a doctor?"

"I did—while you were in Seattle."

"And?"

"He couldn't find anything wrong. He suggested it might be psychosomatic." Garth paused, laughed without humor. "He wanted to know if I'd been under any unusual kinds of stress during the past year or two."

That got me to laughing too, and we ended by slapping each other's arms. But Garth's pallor wasn't funny, and the bittersweet laughter died in my throat. "What kinds of tests did he run?"

Garth shrugged disinterestedly. "How the hell do I know?"

"You should check into a hospital."

"That's a great idea. Hell, we'll just ask the nice men who are after you and Kendry for a truce."

"Garth—"

"I'll be all right, Mongo. Right now, we've got business to take care of. Before you go merrily on your way into Po's nest of vipers to ask him pretty please to tell you the details of his dirty past, I think it would behoove us to sum up what we know, or can reasonably assume, to this point."

"Okay. We know that Veil was part of the C.I.A.'s secret war in Laos for better than four years, almost to the end of the war. If Kathy remembered correctly about the insignia on his uniform when she saw him in Saigon, he was a full colonel in 1972. He wasn't thirty yet, which means he had to be the youngest bird colonel in the whole damn army. And that means he was one hell of a soldier *before* he was sent into Laos.

"He was Special Forces. Because of the nature of his assignment, it's almost a sure bet that he was also a C.I.A. operative, possibly also highly ranked in that organization. We can reasonably assume that the man in the green raincoat who came to see him was his controller. They didn't get along.

"For whatever their reasons, the C.I.A. agreed to help the South Vietnamese solve the embarrassing problem of what to do with Colonel Po after his extracurricular activities were exposed. We don't know why Veil's sector was chosen, only that it was—despite the fact that the move didn't make any sense from a military point of view, since Veil was obviously very effective doing what he was doing, harassing the Pathet Lao and Viet Cong. To try to explain it, we have to start doing some heavy speculation."

"You're just the man to handle heavy speculation," Garth said dryly. "Let's hear it."

"The army and the C.I.A. had a new assignment for Veil, one that they considered even more important."

"At the end of the war?"

"Hey, c'mon: Don't you remember all those lights at the ends of tunnels? The generals didn't know it was the end of the war."

"Good point. Go ahead."

"Veil took strong exception, certainly to being taken out of Laos —and maybe to this hypothetical new assignment. Both the army and the C.I.A. *knew* Veil was going to resist, so the controller brought along Veil's commanding officer—the man in uniform—to back him up and enforce discipline."

Garth cocked his head to one side and scratched behind his left ear—a sign I was being less than convincing. "Four years in the jungles of Laos is a *long* time, brother, especially in view of the fact that the average tour of duty for officers in Viet Nam was *one* year. Maybe Kendry's tour was simply up; it was time to give him a rest, whether he wanted it or not."

"There was nothing average about Veil, or his assignment. Besides, if it were just a matter of Veil's tour being over, he almost certainly would have been back in the United States six to eight weeks later, not wandering the streets of Saigon in the middle of the night. But he *was* in Saigon—and he may have had something very heavy on his mind.

"After rescuing the Hmong children and cleaning out the brothel, he probably went to see the big honcho who'd reassigned him and put Po in his place. He probably found out about the impending commando attack from this man, and may or may not have physically fought him. He most certainly *did* fly into Laos to warn the village and ended up shooting at his own countrymen. His helicopter was shot down, but he survived the crash. He must have made it through the jungle back to Viet Nam, where he either turned himself in or was captured. A relatively short time later he was a civilian, newly arrived in New York City."

Garth rose from the table, took the coffeepot off the stove, and refilled both our cups. He took his cup to the window, where he stared out into another wet, gray winter day. "The last part doesn't make any sense at all," he said quietly.

"Indeed."

"So we get to what we don't know. We don't know why he was abruptly yanked out of Laos; we don't know where he was or what he was doing for six to eight weeks afterward; we don't know who he went to see after dropping off the children—if he went to see anyone; we don't know why the military simply cut him loose instead of throwing him in prison or shooting him. Finally, we don't know why some very heavy people who were probably involved in those incidents and decisions decided to come after him now, a lot of years after the fact."

"If we could find out the name of the officer who came in the helicopter, or that of the man in the green raincoat, we could probably get all of the information we want, without having to try to play footsie with Po."

"We may have one of the names."

"Oh?"

"Hey, I haven't exactly been sitting on my ass while you were away. Hang on a minute." Garth went into the other room, and I heard a drawer in his desk in the den open and close. He reappeared holding a thin manila file folder, which he tossed on the table in front of me. "Check out this masterpiece. It came through yesterday."

I opened the file, found myself looking at an official, stamped photostat of Veil Kendry's service record. It consisted of two pages, and took me less than a minute to read. "It's bullshit," I said, closing the file and pushing it away from me.

"Sure," Garth replied evenly. "But the fact that the Pentagon would go to so much trouble not only to expunge facts, but to create new ones, makes it interesting bullshit."

"I love it. The army claims Veil was a supply clerk in Saigon from 'sixty-four to 'sixty-nine, and never saw combat. Highest rank: corporal. Committed to a mental hospital for four years, diagnosed by the military shrinks as a paranoid schizophrenic with a borderline personality. Finally discharged in 'seventy-three as stabilized with chemotherapy, but still hopelessly psychotic. This is what would have surfaced if Veil had tried to go public with whatever it is he knows."

"Right," Garth said curtly. "Jesus, Mongo, that's an official photostat, and the damn thing's a phony. A lot of high-ranking people conspired to break a lot of laws in order to produce that thing."

"And Veil went along because that was the price for his life and freedom. Now somebody wants to cancel that contract." I retrieved the file, glanced again at the last page. "Here's the name you mentioned: General Robert Warren is listed as Veil's C.O. He signed the discharge papers. You think he's real?"

"He's dead. He was killed in an automobile accident in Saigon three days after those papers were signed. I double-checked it."

"They could have picked the name of somebody they knew was dead, forged it on the paper."

"It's possible," Garth said with a shrug. "We have no way of knowing."

"Po would know. What about the personal data on Veil? Did you check that?"

"I did, and that much is accurate. He did grow up in Colletville. I called the high school; he went there, and he came up through the school system."

"What about the home address?"

"Accurate. The problem is that the Kendrys moved away ten

years ago, forwarding address unknown. The people living there now don't know anything about them."

"Where the hell is Colletville?"

"It's a farming community in a depressed economic area about a hundred and thirty-five miles northwest of here, in the Catskills."

"If those are the only accurate things in this record, it's probably because the people who phonied up everything else considered the information useless. Veil didn't go home when he left the service, he came to New York. He probably doesn't have anyone, friends or relatives, left there."

"Arguable. He lived there a long time. What about the times when he dropped out of sight for two or three weeks at a clip? He could have gone back home then."

"Maybe, maybe not. If the Pentagon doesn't care if people know where he grew up, it probably means there's nothing there worth finding out. Besides, why clump around up in the Catskills when we have Colonel Po? I say we go to Albany first and save Colletville for another day. If Po will talk, we probably won't have to go anywhere else."

Garth stared into the bottom of his coffee cup while he thought about it. "All right," he said at last. "But hold off for a while."

"Why wait?"

"To give me time to check out some things and talk to a few people. We know the Albany cops and State Police are on Po's ass, so let me find out what stage their investigation is in now. It's just possible that the Albany D.A. or the state cops will give us a bone or two to throw to Po in exchange for him giving us the information we want. Po isn't going to give us anything for free. On the other hand, what happened in Viet Nam and Laos was a long time ago, and doesn't have anything to do with his current problems. He'll probably be more than happy to talk to us *if* we can offer him, say, a reduced charge or two. At the least, we'll be showing the authorities upstate that we're properly humble where their jurisdiction is concerned, and I should be able to get a good line on Po's operations. Without some kind of leverage to use on him, we'll be wasting our time and gas going up there."

"Okay. I've got some things to do, anyway. How long do you think all this humble maneuvering is going to take you?"

"It depends on who's available to talk to me, and how much negotiating I have to do. Maybe two or three days."

"Two or three days?! You've got to be kidding me!"

"Don't be so Goddamn impatient. These things take time." Garth paused, narrowed his eyes. "Just what 'things' do you have to do?"

"Just minor errands."

"With you, a 'minor errand' is likely as not to end with you hanging by your heels from the top of the Empire State Building. I hate to let you out of my sight, brother. Tell me what you're going to do."

"First, Mother, I'm going to use your phone to take care of some personal matters. Then I'm going downtown to the Federal Building."

"Why the hell are you going to the Federal Building?"

"I'm going to file a request under the Freedom of Information Act for any and all information concerning Colonel Veil Kendry, code name Archangel, specifically the nature of his assignments for the United States Army and the Central Intelligence Agency during the time he was in Southeast Asia."

Garth winced. "I don't like it, Mongo. It could get you in trouble."

"You're making a joke, right?"

"Why bother? Do you seriously think the people in Washington are going to give you anything that contradicts the service record they manufactured? Freedom of Information Act or not, you'll get diddly-squat."

"That's probably true, but it still might be interesting to see what kind of diddly-squat they try to hand me."

"You want to throw a piece of paper at these guys? At least Kendry throws thumbs. Now *there's* an attention-getting mechanism."

"I'm short on thumbs. Granted, it's a shot in the dark; but it could be a noisy one, and there's no telling who might hear it. Not everyone in Washington is necessarily our enemy. Also, I'm going to try to make an end run around the bureaucracy. I'm going to call Lippitt at the Pentagon. What's the use of being a personal friend of the Director of the Defense Intelligence Agency if you don't use the contact from time to time?"

"I already thought of that," Garth said in what seemed to me an oddly bitter tone of voice. "I put in a call to him on his private line right after I received the phony service record. He's supposedly out of the country for an indeterminate length of time."

"Supposedly?"

"I called him two days ago, Mongo."

"You think he's ducking us?"

"Not us; he's ducking this Archangel business."

"It amounts to the same thing. Lippitt wouldn't do that, Garth."

"Wouldn't he? As I recall, the last time we spoke with him was after he'd spent six months with us on Mom's and Dad's farm. Before we went there, we were all marked for death; by the time we left, he'd been appointed Director of the Defense Intelligence Agency. He was the one who personally gave us that number I called, along with a code word to use in case we ever needed him in an emergency and he wasn't there. According to him, his people would immediately patch him in to us, no matter where he was in the world. If that wasn't possible, he'd get back to us within an hour or two. It's been two days."

"Who answered the phone?"

"How the hell do I know? A woman; probably his secretary."

"You told her who was calling, and mentioned Valhalla?"

"I did. Not a peep from our dear friend, Mr. Lippitt."

It disturbed me, too. The ageless old man had shared two of the most dangerous times in my brother's life and mine, had suffered many of the same emotional scars in the aftermath of the deadly Valhalla Project. It was from our parents' farm that he had directed the cleanup of the operation but, like us, he was there to decompress, to let the memories of the horrors we had witnessed fade away. We owed the old man our lives, and he owed us his, many times over. After all we had been through together, it was incomprehensible to me that he would ignore our call for help. That was what I told Garth.

My brother shook his head. "Remember what concerned Lippitt most about the Valhalla Project? He couldn't accept that the government of the United States could be involved in something like that. Well, he turned out to be about half right on that one. But not this time. Now he's part of the establishment, and his own people are involved in this Archangel shit right up to their eyeballs."

"He was always part of the establishment, and he was never one of your favorite people."

"Christ, Mongo, he's the head of one of the most important

agencies of the Pentagon. When it's a choice between helping us and doing all he can to protect his outfit, the outfit comes first. That's how I read his silence. This gives you some idea of just how isolated we are on this thing, and what we have to look forward to. If you want my opinion on something else, I'm beginning to smell something bad about the way I was so quickly transferred over to this case. You remarked on it. It could be that strings were pulled. Somebody knew that I'd be making moves to protect my brother in any case; by officially putting me next to you, they're getting written reports on everything we turn up. It's a good way to keep an eye on you, courtesy of the NYPD."

"It sounds a little paranoid, Garth," I said, chilled by the thought that he could be dead on the mark. "And I still believe Lippitt will have a good explanation."

"Good. When Lippitt calls, you let me know what it is." Garth rose from the table, removed his coat from a rack in the corner of the kitchen, shrugged it over his broad shoulders. "In the meantime, I'm going down to the station house and see if I can get a line on the best way to approach Po." He started to leave, turned in the doorway and pointed his index finger at me. "Remember, no heavy errands on your own. I want you in one piece when I get back."

"Lippitt will call."

11

"Nine-six-seven-forty."

"May I speak with Mr. Lippitt, please?"

"May I ask who's calling?"

"Robert Frederickson."

"Your name is familiar to me, Dr. Frederickson. Mr. Lippitt has spoken of you and your brother often."

"I'd like to talk to him."

"I'm afraid he's unavailable, Dr. Frederickson. He's out of the country for an indeterminate length of time."

"Is he all right?"

"I'm sorry, but I can't divulge any information other than what I've told you."

"Will you patch me through to him? This matter has Valhalla priority."

"I understand. But it's not possible for him to speak with you now. He'll return your call when he has an opportunity."

"Will you be speaking to him soon?"

"I'm sorry, but I can't—"

"When you do get in touch with him, tell him I want to talk to him about a certain Archangel by the name of Veil Kendry. I think he'll know what I'm talking about; if he doesn't, he should take steps to find out."

"I have the message noted, Dr. Frederickson."

When I hung up, I had the unpleasant feeling that Garth could be right. My feet burned, and suddenly I felt thoroughly exhausted. I decided that my other business could wait, and I spent the rest of the day resting and thinking, and waiting for Lippitt to call. The phone remained silent.

The next day I called a local florist and made arrangements to wire flowers and a thank-you note to Loan Ka and his family, the order to be delivered by a Hmong-owned florist shop in Seattle. Next I touched base with my insurance company to see what they were doing about my claims for personal possessions lost in the fire, and then called a rental agent I was using. The woman had three apartments for me to look at, and I told her I'd get back to her to arrange appointments. Then I put on my parka and went out into the day.

The Federal Building was slightly less than forty blocks downtown, and I decided to walk at least part of the distance and try to find out who, if anyone, was playing tail-of-the-day. The people interested in my comings and goings were obviously serious, and I assumed that the big man with the white eyes had at least one backup.

The noon streets and sidewalks around midtown were clogged with cars and pedestrians, which made if difficult for me to tag anyone who might be following along behind me. I decided to try to clear the picture a little. I abruptly turned left and crossed the avenue against the light, hopping and skipping my way through an obstacle course of speeding, honking cars. The next block of the cross street was closed to traffic due to a construction project utilizing two monstrous cranes. The sidewalks on both sides of the street were shielded by narrow, wooden walkways in which people could only walk two or three abreast. I waited for a crowd of people to come across the avenue, then cut in front of those heading for the walkway on the right side of the street. Screened from anyone who might have been following me, I sprinted to the end of the wooden tunnel, turned right at the corner, and stepped behind a newsstand.

The people who'd been behind me in the walkway emerged, parted at the corner. I waited, and more people came out; there was no one who seemed in any great hurry or who stopped to look around. I decided that if I'd had anyone tailing me, I'd lost him, and I stepped out from behind the newsstand.

As I reached into my pocket for change to buy a *Times,* I scanned the day's headlines; one story leaped out at me, and I sucked in my breath and involuntarily took a little step backward.

The *Times* had the story halfway down the front page, in the third column. However, both the *Daily News* and the *Post* carried the item as their sole lead story, complete with large, grisly photographs. Liu Sakh Po, notorious ARVN colonel and alleged unreformed whoremaster and gangster, would not be answering my questions, or anyone else's, since he was quite dead, his brain having been mashed inside his crushed skull sometime during the previous evening. I felt lightheaded and slightly nauseated; it was an eerie feeling to be standing on a windy, snow-blown corner in New York City looking at headlines announcing a man's death in a city a hundred and fifty miles away and knowing you are responsible. There was no doubt in my mind that it was my trip to Seattle that had killed him.

I bought copies of all three newspapers. I had a strong urge to stop in some warm coffee shop and start reading at once, but I had an even stronger urge to get my Freedom of Information Act request on Veil filed. I folded the newspapers under my arm, turned to my left, and started to cross the street. I glanced up, stopped so suddenly that the man behind me had to do a little pirouette in order to avoid tripping over me.

On the opposite corner, casually leaning against the side of a building, was the big man with the triangular face and cold, pale eyes. I had no idea where the man had come from, but he was unmistakably there, staring directly back at me with a slight, mocking smile on his face. Game time was over. He had appeared out of nowhere, like a ghost; his lack of pretense and his smile were a challenge, a blunt statement that I belonged to him, no matter what I did. He could hide or not hide, as it suited him, leave me be or kill me. He was saying that he would be with me each step of the way as I tried to piece together the pieces of the puzzle that would help me find my friend; if I finally found Veil, he would have found him too. And there was nothing I could do about it.

I found the man's skill unnerving, his arrogance enraging. My face flushed and hot, I started toward him—then abruptly stopped. He hadn't moved; he remained leaning against the side of the building, hands jammed into the pockets of his sheepskin coat, the same mocking smile on his face. He was in charge of the situation, I thought, not me. I had been startled, was now frustrated and upset, and I could think of absolutely nothing I could say to the big man that would make me feel any better. He had already made a fool out of me; by crossing the street and confronting him, I would only run the risk of making a fool out of myself. The only way for me to seize the initiative from this man and his employers was to gain the information I needed.

I stepped out into the street and hailed a cab, told the driver to take me to the Federal Building. When I looked back through the window the big man was gone, but I was certain he was in one of the dozen of so cabs behind.

When I got back to Garth's apartment building, I took a long look up and down the block. The man tailing me had special skills, to be sure, but he was no ghost; he had to have access to food, warmth, and shelter someplace close by, and he had to have help.

Directly across the street from the apartment building an over-sized Consolidated Edison van was parked beside an open manhole cover inside a barricaded work area. There was also a lot of digging and electrical equipment. It was the kind of scene one passes a dozen times a day in New York City. However, what was curious about this setup was the fact that there were no utility workers on the work site—unless the entire crew was down in the manhole, which I seriously doubted. Also, there was no driver behind the wheel of the van.

Now that I thought about it, it occurred to me that the van, barricades, and digging equipment had appeared across the street the day after I'd moved in with Garth, and I had never seen anyone working on the site. I noted the plate number of the van, then went up to Garth's apartment.

The flag on Garth's telephone answering machine had fallen, indicating that at least one call had come in while I was out. However, at the moment I was far more interested in the information in the newspapers I was carrying. I poured myself a cup of coffee, spread the *Times* out over the kitchen table, and began to read.

The lead story and accompanying obituary were rich in details concerning Po's background—the scandal surrounding his activities in Saigon during the war, his mysterious disappearance at the height of the scandal, and his unexplained—and, at the time, unnoticed—entry into the United States after the fall of Saigon. No one questioned the legality of his immigration, but there was no record of which American official or officials had sponsored him. A long sidebar detailed Po's alleged criminal activities since his entry into the United States and mentioned the investigations that had been cut short by his death.

The background pieces were interesting, but I could find nothing relevant to my interests in them that I had not already learned from Loan Ka and Kathy.

Po's death had been quick, brutal, and mysterious. Despite the fact that his Albany mansion had an intricate alarm system and a half dozen live-in bodyguards, somebody—the police theorized one man—had managed to penetrate that tight security and kill Po without leaving a trace. Po's skull had been crushed and his neck broken by a single, powerful blow—possibly delivered with a bare fist—to the top of the skull. Although a window in the third-story study where he had been killed was found open, the authorities did not believe it possible that the killer could have scaled the outside of the building and entered that way. Suspicion now centered on Po's bodyguards, and each was being questioned extensively. The police had issued a statement to the effect that they believed Po had been killed by another gangster and that it was probably an "inside" job.

There was no mention of a severed and missing right thumb, but that was the kind of detail police might keep secret. I knew damn well Po hadn't been killed by a business rival, and I seriously doubted that any of his bodyguards had been involved. I knew a man who was capable of scaling the mansion wall and killing with a single blow of his fist, and I suspected that I might have met another.

The *Times*, as usual, was long on information, short on sensationalism. For sensationalism—and the photographs I wanted to see—I turned to the *Daily News* and *Post*.

The main photo in both papers, attributed to a UPI photographer, showed Po in his dressing gown sitting at a massive desk in his study. His head was tilted forward at an impossibly acute angle, and it looked like it had literally caved in. Blood which had seeped from his skull and burst from his nostrils and mouth had puddled on the desk in front of him and stained much of the newspaper he was clutching with both hands. Behind the desk, slightly to his left, was the open window mentioned in the *Times* report.

Something about the photo struck me as odd, but I couldn't immediately identify just what it was. The picture in the *Post* was large and slightly clearer than the one in the *Daily News*, and I spent some time studying it; I still could not tell what it was in the picture that was not as it should be. I folded the newspapers, rose, and went to the answering machine in Garth's study.

The counter on the machine indicated one message. I rewound the cassette, listened to it. It was from the New York florist through whom I had placed the order for flowers; she was asking me to call her to provide "clarification" on the instructions I had given her. I thought my instructions had been quite clear, and I experienced a growing sense of unease as I picked up the phone and dialed the number.

"Haley Florists." It was the woman who'd taken my order.

"This is Robert Frederickson. I placed an order earlier for—"

"Yes, Dr. Frederickson. There seems to be some confusion in Seattle over just what you want done with the flowers. I recall that you specifically requested that the flowers be sent to the residence of Mr. Loan Ka, but the florist in Seattle insists that you must want them delivered to the funeral home."

"What funeral home?"

There was prolonged silence on the other end of the line. When the woman finally spoke again, her voice was halting, distinctly uncomfortable. "Was Mr. Loan Ka a close personal friend of yours, Dr. Frederickson?"

"Yes," I managed to say.

"Sir, I don't know quite how to say this. There . . . is no

longer any residence to send your flowers to. According to the florist in Seattle, it was destroyed two nights ago in some kind of explosion the police think may have been caused by a defective boiler in the basement."

"And the . . . family?"

"All dead, sir," the woman said in a small voice. "Also, there was the body of a young woman. I'm so sorry you have to learn about it this way, Dr. Frederickson. It's such a terrible tragedy."

After hanging up I sat for a long time, just staring at the phone. I knew I should call Garth immediately, but I just couldn't will myself to pick up the receiver and dial the number of his precinct station house. I felt gutted, incapable of movement or decision. I had become something much worse than a mere stalking horse being used by both sides; I had been transformed into a Judas goat given just enough tether to track Veil and, in the process, target people. Loan Ka and his family and Kathy had survived the war in Southeast Asia; they'd survived Colonel Po, as well as the postwar ravages of the Pathet Lao.

What they hadn't survived was talking to me.

And if and when I found Veil, then Veil, Garth, and I would be killed. There was no longer much subtlety to the plans of Veil's hunters.

Calling Garth wouldn't ease my rage and despair, and I knew that I would continue to feel paralyzed unless I somehow struck back. I couldn't involve Garth in any plans for revenge because he was on the investigation in an official capacity. There was nothing Garth could do but investigate and report, which was not the situation with me. I could kill, and that was precisely what I planned to do.

I checked to make sure that the magazines and the chambers of both the Beretta and Seecamp were fully loaded, then replaced them in my ankle and shoulder holsters. I rummaged around in Garth's closets and cabinets until I found what I wanted—a twelve-foot-long electric extension. Feeling as if I were moving in slow motion at the bottom of a sea of grief and hatred, I put on my parka, dropped the extension cord into one of the pockets, then walked out of the apartment.

Bypassing the main elevators and the stairs, I went into a storage area at one end of the hall and summoned the freight elevator. I

descended to the basement, got out, cut through the laundry room
where a young couple were doing their wash, banged my way out
of the building through a rear delivery entrance. I walked up a
long, sloping concrete ramp to the sidewalk without bothering to
look around to see if my watchers might have this side of the
building covered. I didn't care who might be watching me, because
I didn't think anyone would try to stop me before they realized
what I was up to, and by then it would be too late. I had one big
move left to me, and I was determined to make it regardless of the
consequences.

After going two blocks, I turned left, went down the block and
crossed at the corner, putting me on the same side of the avenue as
the Con Ed van. I waited for a fairly large group of pedestrians to
come my way and fell into step behind them, keeping to the inside
of the sidewalk, away from the street. I took the extension cord
from my pocket, tied a small loop at one end. As the group I was
moving with came abreast of the van I cut across the sidewalk,
ducked under the wooden barricade. New Yorkers are notorious
for ignoring virtually everything that doesn't directly concern
them, so I wasn't too concerned about being challenged by anyone
but a cop as I hopped up on the running board at the back of the
van. I dropped the small loop over the top of one of the handles on
the twin doors, looped the rest of the cord tightly around both
handles. Then I stepped off the running board, went around, and
looked up at the side.

Any concerns I'd had about the van's being nothing more than
what it appeared to be were instantly dispelled when I saw the
small, glass-covered viewing portals cut into the side of the van,
partially disguised in the heavy block lettering of the Con Ed logo.
I'd hit my mark, and now somebody, even if it was just a foot
soldier, was going to pay for the murders in Seattle, after I got the
answers to a number of important questions.

With a grim smile and wave up at the central viewing portal, I
jumped into the cab of the van. I'd been prepared to hot-wire the
vehicle, but somebody had thoughtfully left the keys in the igni-
tion. After pulling up the seat as far as it would go, I turned on the
engine, put the van into gear, and rumbled forward through the
barricade, easing my way out into the traffic.

Checking the rearview mirror on the far side of the van, I could
see that the unlikely sight of me hijacking a Con Ed van had finally

attracted some attention; a knot of fifteen or twenty people were standing beside the broken barricade, some of them excitedly pointing in my direction. What I needed was some privacy and seclusion, things I wasn't likely to find with a stolen van in the middle of Manhattan.

I cut across town to the West Side Highway, headed north. I kept checking in my rearview mirror, but I saw no cops and heard no sirens, and when I made it to the George Washington Bridge I felt I was home free—at least as far as pursuit was concerned. I still had some very dangerous cargo to handle.

I crossed the bridge on the upper level, got off in New Jersey at the Fort Lee exit. I circled on a ramp under the bridge, turned left on a street that led to the entrance to a park on the very edge of the New Jersey Palisades, overlooking the Hudson River. The park was closed for the winter, with a chain blocking off the access road. However, the weight of the van easily snapped the chain, and I rumbled in low gear up the snow-covered road into a tree-shrouded parking area. I turned off the engine and ran, slipping and sliding, back down to the street. There weren't many cars, and I was hoping nobody would notice—or care about—the tire tracks on the access road. I pulled the chain taut, managed to tie the broken links together with my handkerchief, then ran back up into the parking area.

There was no sound from inside the box of the van—no pounding, shouting, or cursing, as might have been expected from a man or men who'd suddenly found themselves trapped and being carted around town to an unknown destination. I certainly hoped I hadn't stolen the van when the owners had been out to lunch.

I went to the edge of the parking area and poked around under the bare trees until I found what I wanted—a long, firm stick. I trimmed one of the ends into a small fork, then returned to the van. I stopped a few feet to the side of the doors, drew my Beretta, and poked with my stick at the wrapping around the handles of the doors. It took some time and doing, but I finally managed to unwind the extension cord, leaving only the small loop over the door handle nearest to me. I threw away the stick and yanked on the extension cord. Both doors flew open, and in the same instant a fusillade of bullets poured out through the opening. I counted about ten shots in four or five seconds, from what sounded like two handguns. I waited until there was a lull in the shooting, then sucked in a deep breath, stepped forward, and peered into the interior of the van through a crack between a door and the side.

Inside the van, banks of electronic equipment lined two of the three walls; the men had not only been watching, but listening, probably by means of a bug somewhere in Garth's apartment; telephone conversations could have been monitored by means of an NSA satellite. There were also cots, a portable toilet, and a small refrigerator—all the comforts of home.

Two men dressed in fur-lined leather coats were crouched toward the rear of the van, their guns pointed toward the opening. They must have caught a glimpse of my head, because suddenly they both turned their guns in my direction and fired simultaneously; one bullet ricocheted off the metal floor, while the other flew through the crack and passed just over my head. I fell to the ground, rolled to the opposite side of the van, came up firing. I caught one man in the chest, and the other in the right eye; both died instantly. I swung my gun up, leveling it on the barrel chest of the big man with the triangular face who was sprawled across the top of a bank of electronic equipment against the right wall, clutching at a ceiling strut for support.

"I'm coming down now, Frederickson," the man said evenly.

"You do that."

Gripping the strut with both hands, the big man swung down to the floor, landing easily on the balls of his feet just in front of the corpses of his two dead companions. Now he was all business, without a trace of the effeminacy he had displayed on the plane. Even standing still, and despite his formidable size, he gave the impression of someone with grace of movement, unexpected speed, and great strength. His face with its broad forehead was impassive, the pale eyes revealing nothing. If he was worried about what I was going to do to him, he didn't show it—and that worried me.

The big man gestured disdainfully with his thumb at the bodies behind him. "I told them that what they wanted to do wasn't such a good idea. You're pretty clever, Frederickson. I believe I've underestimated you. I won't do it again."

"I don't give a shit what you do, pal, as long as you're doing it hopping on one leg," I said as I aimed my Beretta at his right kneecap and fired. It was an accurate shot; the problem was that the big man didn't stay where he was supposed to, and the bullet smashed into a computer console behind him.

With quickness matched in my experience only by Veil Kendry, at the moment I had pulled the trigger the man had grabbed the strut above his head, swung up and out of the bullet's path. As I started to turn the gun on him for a second shot, I saw him release his right hand from the strut and flick his wrist. I knew enough to duck, and the star-shaped *shuriken* whistled through the air just above my head, slashing open my parka across the shoulder blades. I came up ready to fire, then had to fall to the ground as pieces of electronic equipment came hurtling out of the mouth of the van and crashed all around me. Something sharp and heavy hit my right shoulder, sending a spasm of pain up into my neck. I pushed the tape recorder off me and jumped to my feet, firing blindly into the mouth of the van. When I'd emptied the Beretta, I crouched, dropped it into my pocket, and whipped the Seecamp out of my ankle holster. Then I slowly straightened up, peered around the edge of one of the doors into the van.

The big man was gone.

I spun around, gun shoved out in front of me, and looked for footprints leading away from the van. There weren't any. I suddenly realized where he was and started to turn back, but it was too late. There was a soft thud just behind me as the man leaped down from the top of the van. I was halfway around when steel-hard knuckles hit me squarely on the spine, at the base of my neck. All strength and feeling abruptly vanished from my body, and I toppled forward on my face into the snow.

With that single blow the man had snapped my spine, I thought, too much in shock to release the scream that was building in me. The only sensation I had was the cold of the snow on my cheek and in my mouth; in an instant I had become nothing more than a head on a useless body. I didn't know if I had the courage to spend the rest of my life strapped in a wheelchair, and I hoped the man would finish the job and kill me.

"It's true what they say about you, Frederickson," the big man said casually. "You're a real pain in the ass."

I tracked him with my eyes as he walked to the front of the van, climbed up into the cab. The van started up, rumbled forward and over the rocks that served as a border around the parking area. It kept going through a snow fence, across the park toward the edge of the cliffs. The van never slowed as it crashed through the last

barrier separating it from a three-hundred-foot drop and disappeared from sight.

The gunfire might have been muffled by the snow and trees, but
the sight of a van toppling off the Palisades into the Hudson River
was certainly going to attract attention, and probably cause a monumental traffic jam, on the George Washington Bridge, just below.
I wondered how long it was going to be before a squadron of police
cars came screaming into the park.

For a few moments I thought the big man had missed his timing
and fallen into the ice-choked river along with the van. I had not
seen him jump out, but after a few seconds his imposing figure rose
from the ground. Casually brushing snow from his coat, he started
to walk back toward me.

The big man was quite a magician, I thought. One of his tricks
that I particularly appreciated was the one in which he apparently
hadn't crushed my spine after all, but only struck some particularly sensitive nerve cluster to paralyze me temporarily. I still
wasn't ready to do any polkas, but a blessed chill was beginning to
creep along my fingertips and palms, and emanate up into my
groin. Also, like oases in a desert of numbness, there were patches
of what felt like prickly heat over the rest of my body.

The butt end of the Seecamp poked out of the snow a few inches
from the fingertips of my left hand; if feeling continued to return, I
was going to have a trick or two of my own to show the magician.

The big man walked up to me, crouched down, casually resting
his forearms on his knees, so that I could see his face. He seemed
totally unconcerned about the gun, although it was closer to me
than to him. "Where the hell is Kendry?" he said distantly, looking
around him as if he half expected Veil suddenly to materialize from
the snow or surrounding trees—a prospect I found most inviting, if
improbable.

"You're asking me?"

"It was a rhetorical question."

"Who are you?"

"Ah, I don't think I want to tell you that, Frederickson. Knowing my name would only distract you and your brother from your
primary job. In fact, I've already become an unfortunate distraction to you, and I regret that. I want you to find Veil Kendry for
me, and after that matters will take care of themselves. You can
forget about me now, because you probably won't ever see me

again; as I said, I won't repeat the mistake of underestimating you."

"I may not see you, but you'll be around."

"Of course—but there'll be nothing you can do about it. I'm not a threat to you and your brother, unless you again choose to make me so. My only interest is in flushing Kendry, and I believe you have the best chance of doing that. He seems to be leading you along a trail, at the end of which he—through you—will have accomplished whatever it is he wants to accomplish. The sooner you reach the end of that trail, the sooner he'll come out of hiding."

I could feel cold in both arms now, but the rest of me was lagging behind. I knew I wouldn't have more than one chance to get the gun, and I wasn't ready to take it yet. "Why did you have to kill those people in Seattle?"

"I didn't. I was on the plane with you, remember?"

"You ordered it done. It's the same thing."

"I didn't order it done. The fee for my performing that sort of service is far too high to warrant using me for that kind of relatively simple operation. In fact, I didn't even know about the killings until I overheard your conversation with the florist. Those killings were performed by someone else."

"But you reported on where I'd been, and the people I'd talked to."

"Yes. That I did."

Now I could feel cold spreading along my belly and up into my shoulders. I grabbed for the Seecamp. With the speed of a striking snake, the big man's hand shot out and snatched the gun out of the snow a fraction of a second before my hand got there. He ejected the clip, removed the round from the chamber, then flipped the gun back to me. "Here," he said quietly. "Put that in your pocket with the Beretta. I certainly don't want you to be defenseless."

"Fuck you," I said, struggling to work myself up into a sitting position. "If you're so anxious to get to Veil Kendry, and you're using me to do it, maybe I'll just stop looking."

"That would be a mistake, Frederickson, because then you would be pitting yourself against me instead of doing your job." His voice, a soft, almost soothing baritone, suddenly took on sharp edge. "The chances that you and your brother will eventually survive this business are, in my opinion, nil. However, the only chance you *do* have to survive is to keep going. There are others who want to kill you now, so in a very real sense you and your brother are on a rapidly spinning treadmill; try to stop, and you'll be broken. You already know far too much to suit these people, and the only reason you're alive right now is because I've been able to convince them of your usefulness. But I didn't say you were the *only* way to find Kendry. Still, you're obviously the key player in a game Kendry's chosen to play. Therefore, *I* want you to keep playing. If I decide that you're only going through the motions, or are taking steps to protect Kendry from me, then I will retaliate by killing your brother as quickly and easily as I killed Colonel Po."

"An intriguing threat," I said, trying to get to my feet. My nervous system still wasn't ready to handle that, and I slumped back down into the snow. "Why don't the two of us hop into a cab and go down to his station house right now? Then you can deliver that threat in person. Garth will get a big kick out of it."

"I don't deliver idle threats, Frederickson."

I believed him. "You killed Po?"

"Yes. That operation did require my skills."

"Look, if you're so damn anxious to find Veil, why don't you help me? Give me information I can use. Who are you working for?"

"The names of the men who actually hired me and take my reports would mean nothing to you; they're just fronts. For you to try to untangle all the blinds and double blinds in this chain of command would be a monumental waste of time."

"All right, you untangle it for me. You have a very good idea of who's behind the whole thing, don't you?"

The big man's thin lips curled back in a quick, disdainful smile. When he spoke, there was scorn in his voice. "Of course. It's a man I've done special assignments for in the past. He never felt the need to hide his identity then; now he thinks he's being clever. Actually, he's a cretin who's well equipped for certain kinds of work, but not for what he's doing now. He's way out of his depth. A man should know his limitations, and this one doesn't. This man fights best in dark places; in the dark, he's a savage and efficient alley fighter. But he doesn't do well in the light; not well at all. That's why, in the end, his whole strategy was doomed to failure from the beginning."

"Why do you work for a cretin?"

The big man looked genuinely surprised. "For a great deal of money, of course. Also, in this case, I'm looking forward to meeting Mr. Kendry. I've heard a great deal about him."

"I'd love to have you meet him, pal. You may be bigger than he is, but he's better. He'll shove your head up your ass."

The big man laughed. "Spoken like a loyal friend."

"You expect me to play Twenty Questions? Give me the name of the cretin."

"I think not."

"Why the hell not?! Why should *you* play games with me? You say you want to find Veil, fine. You want me to get to the end of the trail, fine. Help me. The name of the man who wants Veil dead is the key to the box of secrets Veil wants me to open."

The big man shook his head. "What you say is probably true, but knowing the name would only be another distraction."

"Let me be the judge of that. Just give me the Goddamn name."

"No."

"Damn it, that's insane!"

"Frederickson, there's absolutely no doubt in my mind that, if I gave you the name, you'd go after *that* man instead of tracking Kendry. That would accomplish nothing, except to quickly get you killed for your efforts. If you're killed, then Kendry will abandon the game and simply do what he could have done in the beginning —hunt the cretin himself. Kendry could get to the man and kill him, but not without being killed, or captured, himself. That scenario is not at all in my interest."

"What the hell are you talking about? You want Veil dead; according to you, that's how he'd end up. What other interests do you have? What the hell difference does it make to you what I do with the information you give me?"

"It's not important, Frederickson. Don't worry about anything but following the trail Kendry has laid out for you."

"Some trail. Why the hell did you kill Po? He could have given me a lot of the information I need."

"I was asked to kill the man, and I was paid my fee."

"You afraid you're not going to get your money if somebody else kills Veil?"

"No. I have already been paid my full fee. But I take pride in my work, and I have a certain reputation to uphold if I expect to continue being paid my customary fees in advance. The kinds of people who hire me listen to reports of how assignments like this are carried out."

"Then it's future earnings you're worried about?"

"Now I think you're beginning to understand. I don't want anyone else doing my job for me."

"All right, if you won't give me the man's name, at least tell me why it's so important to him to have Veil killed. What does Veil have on him?"

"I haven't the slightest idea."

"You're full of shit."

"It's the truth. I really don't know what the man's problem with Kendry is, and I don't care. For me, it would be irrelevant information. My only concern is with finding and killing Mr. Kendry."

"And, I assume, Garth and me when this is over?"

"The cretin doesn't need me for that, Frederickson. He can have the two of you killed any time he pleases—the reason, as I said, why you have to keep moving, so as to demonstrate to him your usefulness to me."

Suddenly there was the sound of sirens, very close. The big man straightened up, then reached down and lifted me to my feet by the back of my parka. The feeling in my legs was returning now, and I was able to shuffle along as the big man guided me firmly across the parking area and into a copse of trees, heading toward the street.

"You're walking on the edge of a razor, Frederickson," the man continued. "Obviously, the cretin will not tolerate you learning too much—the reason he had me kill Po before you could talk to him. I'd much prefer that he continue to let you live, but he could change his mind at any time. Watch yourself."

"Your concern is touching."

"What can I say? I find I rather like you."

"The information I have doesn't *mean* anything unless I get this man's name to go along with it!" I said, thoroughly frustrated.

"Just keep going, Frederickson. And don't forget that I'll kill your brother if I think you're jerking me around."

The big man pushed me into a row of bushes on the edge of the sidewalk just as two Fort Lee police cars, sirens screaming and lights flashing, went speeding up the access road into the park. An officer who had unhooked the chain got into a third car, raced after his colleagues.

"You're just chasing after your own death, pal," I said as I was lifted by the back of my parka out onto the sidewalk. "I'm betting Veil knows you're on his trail, looking for him."

"That may be."

"If and when Veil does choose to come out in the open, the very first thing he'll probably do is kill you."

"Good hunting, Frederickson."

The big man tossed me back into the bushes, and I momentarily lost sight of him. By the time I extricated myself and looked around for him, he was gone.

12

When I came marching into Garth's station house an hour later, a lot of heads turned in my direction. I knew a number of the detectives and uniformed officers, but no one said a word to me; they just stared.

"Well, well, well," Garth said in a dry tone that failed to hide the relief he obviously felt at seeing me alive. His flesh was pale under its greenish pallor, and there were dark rings of weariness and worry— and possibly sickness—under his eyes. His shirt was stained with perspiration. "It seems you're not at the bottom of the Hudson River after all. A minor errand?"

"Ah, you've heard," I said, going directly to the coffeepot on a warmer standing in a corner of his office. I poured myself a cup of the brackish-looking brew, grimaced when I tasted it.

"The NYPD has heard a lot of things, and we're trying to sort out what it means. About three hours ago we got a call from some guy on the street claiming that a dwarf, of all people, wearing a brown parka just like yours, of all things, had just stolen a Con Ed van from in front of the apartment building where you and I currently reside, of all places. How about that?"

"Will wonders never cease? Listen, if that van is really registered to Con Ed, I pledge to personally paddle my way to the bottom of the river and bring it back up." I took a slip of paper out of my pocket, tossed it on the desk. "Here's the plate number."

"What happened to your coat, Mongo? That looks like a knife cut."

"Something like that. While you're checking the registration, see if you can find out which city official or agency issued the work permit for that location; ask for a copy of the papers."

Garth gave a curt nod, picked up his telephone. While my brother spoke with Motor Vehicles, I sipped at my coffee and stared at the front page of the newspaper on Garth's desk. The photograph of Liu Sakh Po, head askew, stared back at me. Again, I had the haunting feeling that there was something important in the picture that I was missing.

"There's no such registration," Garth said as he hung up the phone and tossed the slip of paper into the wastebasket. "Not for Con Ed, or any other vehicle. It doesn't surprise me. I called Con Ed right after we got the report of a stolen van, and they told me all their vehicles were accounted for. Also, there's no record of a work permit being issued for that site."

"That doesn't surprise me."

"In the beginning, before we heard about the van going off the Palisades, a few of the cops around here thought it might be a hoax."

"You knew damn well there was no hoax."

"Sure," Garth said, lowering his voice as he rose, walked around the desk, and closed his door on the staring faces outside his office. "I just wasn't sure what to do about it. Whatever you were doing, you seemed to have the situation under control." He paused, smiled wryly as he sat back down behind his desk. "You were in the driver's seat, so to speak, and nobody called to report *their* van stolen. Then the report came in of the van going into the river. I'll admit that caused just a tad of concern."

"When they bring the van up, they'll find two bodies in the box."

"Nice, Mongo."

"I guarantee they're not Con Ed workers."

"Tell me what happened."

"You want to get a stenographer in here to take my statement?"

Garth thought about it as he stared at me with narrowed lids. "No," he said at last. "I'm not feeling too trusting any more about what outsiders may have access to my written reports, and we already have enough complications. Until somebody steps up to officially report a missing vehicle with a Con Ed logo, we'll keep this between ourselves."

"What about your captain and the rest of the cops around here?"

Garth shrugged. "You see me investigating, don't you? I'll make up a report and put it away someplace. If it looks like the shit is going to hit the fan, I'll produce the report and claim that I misplaced it."

"Whatever you say; that's your department." I took the Seecamp out of my pocket, gripping it by the end of the barrel, placed it on Garth's desk. "In the meantime, you might try to get some prints besides mine off this gun. Also, let's get a police artist in here. I want to see if we can't come up with a name."

"Whose name?"

"A very big fish that got away. He's a man with the best sleeper-move since Mr. Spock, and he's also the man who says he's going to off *you* unless I keep truckin' along to his satisfaction."

I told my brother what had happened. Garth listened in silence, without taking notes.

Garth dusted the butt of the Seecamp himself, came up with two partial prints that weren't mine. An hour later a police artist, under the impression that Garth was looking for a mugger who'd slashed my coat, turned my description into a pretty good rendering of the big man. Garth took the sketch to be copied and the prints to be checked. I sat down in his chair, found myself once again staring at the *New York Post* photograph of the broken Po. Then, suddenly, I knew what was wrong with the picture.

It was the newspaper in Po's hands.

Po, probably at the moment of his death, had crumpled the paper up toward his chest, and the back page was partially exposed. Even though the *Post* reproduction was grainy, I could tell that the paper Po had been reading was a *New York Times*, not a local Albany paper. That, in itself, wasn't unusual. What was strange was the ad on the back page which, even partially obscured and stained with blood, I recognized as one for *Vogue*.

A news addict, I read the *New York Times* every day with something approaching religious passion, every page front to back, including the advertisements. For the past week the back page of the first section—the one Po held in his hands—had been taken up with ads for *Sports Illustrated, Reader's Digest,* and a complaint by the Scientologists that the I.R.S. was harassing them.

The morning newspaper Colonel Po had been reading in the middle of the night when his head had been squashed was at least a week old—maybe more, since I couldn't remember what day or days the ad had run.

I picked up Garth's phone and called the advertising department of the *Times.* Five minutes later I had the information I needed.

The *Vogue* ad had run for three days, the second day being the one when somebody had taken a shot at Veil, the third, the day of the night when I'd almost been burned to death.

Garth must have seen something on my face when he came back into the room. "What's the matter, Mongo?" he asked as he closed the door behind him.

I got out of Garth's chair, leaned against the edge of the desk. "I was just trying to figure out what Po was doing in the middle of the night reading a newspaper that was almost two weeks old."

Garth raised his eyebrows slightly. "Is that what he was doing?"

"Yep." I pointed to the newspaper in the photo. "I recognized this ad and checked with the *Times.* Guess what?"

"The day Kendry was shot at?" Garth said tightly.

"That day, the day before and after. A perfect bracket."

"Damn," Garth said, growing excitement in his voice. "There had to be something in that issue that was keeping Po up nights— even two weeks after it happened. You talk about a worried man!"

"And it has to be connected with Veil's disappearance," I said, pushing off the desk and heading for the door. "I'm going to the library."

Garth moved into the doorway, filling it. "Relax, brother, and finish your coffee. You've run enough minor errands for one day, and I think it's better if you stay off the streets until we see how this latest wrinkle smooths out. The super in our building keeps all the papers for the Boy Scouts, and they're not due to be picked up until next month; we'll find the issues we need down in the basement. According to your own words, somebody could decide to step on you at any time—as if we didn't already know that. From here on out, you don't leave my sight except to go to the bathroom."

"Okay," I said, moving back to lean against the desk.

Garth looked puzzled. "What do you mean, 'okay'?"

"Okay means okay."

"You said okay once before to taking it easy, and the next day you hijacked a van, killed two men, and almost got killed yourself."

"This is a serious okay. I must be getting old. Can you get any kind of make on the big guy with the spooky eyes?"

"I've got people working on it. Don't hold your breath."

"Hey, Garth, self-defense or not, I still killed two men. You sure you don't want to call in someone to take my statement, just to cover your ass?"

"I'm sure," Garth said curtly as he sat back down behind his desk. He opened the top drawer, took out a black felt-tip marker and a yellow legal pad.

"I still don't understand what you're going to tell all the people who are going to be asking you questions."

"You want a lot of cops and reporters asking *you* questions and following you around?"

"No, I can't say that I do."

"Then fuck them," Garth said as he drew a thick, black circle around the newspaper in Po's hands. "It's not their brother who's being watched and hunted."

I didn't like the sound of Garth's voice and words any more than I liked his ghostly pallor. His duties as a police officer had always been something he'd taken very seriously, and he was probably the most honest cop in New York City. Now he seemed to be shrugging off those duties in an almost casual manner, and in a way that could come back to hurt him very badly. But there didn't seem to be anything I could do about it—and I had been the one who first raised suspicion in his mind about possible collusion between the NYPD and our trackers.

"The name of the man who's hunting Veil is in there," I said, pointing to the newspaper Po held.

"Maybe," Garth replied distantly.

"I'm damn sure of it. The guy who did the sleeper number on my spine wouldn't give me the man's name, but he was downright chatty. He may have revealed more than he meant to—or maybe he did it intentionally, and was just covering his own ass, which he didn't have to plop down in the snow for fifteen minutes to do unless he was interested in trying to tell me a few things. This guy's no dummy, and it's hard to tell what he was really up to. He was hired through a series of blinds, but he was certain whom he was really working for, and he ended up drawing me a kind of profile of the man. First, the big guy had worked for this man before."

"Long-term relationship with professional killer," Garth said, and wrote it down on the legal pad.

"Top-rank professional," I added. "But a free-lancer. I think he was brought in after the two men who tried to kill me messed up. He made it clear that he was a professional, private contractor—and a very expensive one."

"A very powerful man with unusual connections," Garth intoned as he wrote on his pad. "Access to extensive funds, and possibly has high-class killers on his payroll."

"The big guy was totally contemptuous of this man—kept calling him a cretin. He described him to me as a night alley fighter who wasn't any good in the light, or the open. It has to mean that our man *used* to fight in the dark, and in secret."

Garth nodded, wrote some more.

"Veil Kendry was involved with this alley fighter a long time ago," I continued. "I was told our man's trying to be cute now by attempting to mask his identity."

"Possibly a public figure," Garth said in a very low voice.

"A murderer, and almost certainly a psychopath—to date, he's responsible for the deaths of twelve people, five of them young people or kids, and an old Hmong grandmother. He's obviously influential, wealthy himself or with access to almost unlimited funds, and by all indications we might very well recognize his name if we knew it. That's who wants Veil Kendry dead, and that's who we're looking for."

"Shit," Garth said quietly as he drew heavy lines through all the notes he had written.

There was a knock, and a uniformed officer I didn't recognize opened the door and stuck his head into the office. "Lieutenant? May I speak to you for a moment?"

Garth nodded, rose, and walked out of the office, closing the door behind him. He came back in fifteen minutes later looking shaken. He slumped down in his chair, tossed a thin yellow folio onto the desk top.

"Bad news?" I asked.

"You could say so."

"Mind if I look at it?"

"Don't bother; there isn't that much to look at."

"But obviously enough to shake you up."

"It's a telex copy of the files Interpol and the F.B.I. have on a man whose real name is probably Henry Kitten—although they're not even sure of that. The information in the file is, as they say, highly speculative."

"Henry *Kitten?*"

"Hey, what can I tell you? Complain to the woman who married his father."

I flipped open the folio, studied the charcoal sketch stapled to the cover page of the file. The man in the sketch did have a vaguely triangular face, but that was just about the only similarity. "Hey, I know this is only a sketch, but I'm not sure this is the guy I tangled with."

"Kitten's a master of disguise, among other things."

"He didn't look disguised to me," I said as I looked at the second page. There was a myriad of dates, times, and places around the world associated with important assassinations Henry Kitten was strongly suspected of having carried out.

"That's why he's a master of disguise," Garth said dryly. "Then again, he may have been using his real face just for you. Apparently, you never can tell with Kitten. It wasn't your physical description or the partial prints that made the computer spit this out; it was your description of his MO—popping up on street corners and out of vans, incredible speed, blows that can paralyze, and so on. Interpol and the F.B.I. say it's Henry Kitten, and they're very much going to want to talk to you and me when they see the file card I had to fill out in order to gain access to their computer files. It won't be long."

"They can wait."

Garth leaned back in his chair and laughed without humor. "Maybe I'll tell them we're out of the country for an indeterminate length of time like our dear friend Mr. Lippitt."

"Why keep harping on Lippitt? What good does it do?"

"He pisses me off. He'd be dead if it weren't for you."

"We'd be dead if it weren't for him. As far as I'm concerned, everything's even. What's the bottom line on this Henry Kitten?"

"The bottom line, brother, is that he's a serious bad-ass."

"American?"

"Nobody knows. There's some thinking that he may have a little

Japanese in him. If you read the whole report, the word *ninja* keeps popping up. The thinking is that he certainly spent a lot of time in Japan, because he's obviously had access to the kind of special training you don't pick up in your friendly neighborhood karate school around here. That's the man you were messing around with up in Fort Lee."

"He did a whole hell of a lot more messing with me than I did with him. How does one go about hiring this Henry Kitten?"

Garth shrugged. "Nobody in law enforcement knows; if Interpol knew that, they'd have trapped him a long time ago. I guess you just have to travel in the wrong circles." Garth paused, tapped his fingertips impatiently on his desk top. "Having that son-of-a-bitch around really complicates matters."

"Why? If he's to be believed, I'd be dead right now if not for him. He certainly could have killed me in the park, and he didn't."

"But he could turn on you. I used to think Kendry was the worst bad-ass I'd ever met or heard of. That was before I read that file on Kitten."

"I'll still put my money on Veil in any *mano a mano* fight. In any case, why worry about it? Veil has to know this guy's on his case, so I don't even feel the need to try and warn him. All you and I have to do is stay alive and on the move."

"Oh, really? Is that all we have to do? I'm thinking maybe it's time you resigned your commission and left it to the cops and the F.B.I. We'll put you in protective custody, keep you on ice until this thing is resolved one way or another."

"No," I said simply. "I don't believe anybody can protect me against Kitten if he wants to get at me, and you're the only cop I trust at the moment. Besides, it's *you* Henry Kitten will kill if I don't keep going. He was very clear on that point, and I don't think for a moment that he was bluffing. Besides, I have no intention of crawling into a hole. I still have a client, remember?" I gestured toward the door. "Let's split."

"Where are we going?"

"The only place left to go; the last bread crumb. Colletville."

Garth nodded, put on his coat, and followed me out the door.

13

We stopped by Garth's apartment to pack overnight bags, picked up the three *New York Times* we wanted from a pile in the basement, then took off. It was a drizzling winter dusk, and I read by the faint illumination of the car's dome light while Garth plowed through rush hour traffic and watched in the rearview mirror for anyone who might be trying to follow us. I started with the newspaper dated the day after Veil disappeared, since it would be the one to carry a report of anything significant that had happened on the day in question.

I had anticipated hours of reading, analysis, discussion with Garth, and lots of guesswork, but we had barely made it across town to the West Side Highway before I had the sinking feeling that I knew exactly who wanted Veil dead. I felt I knew, and wished I didn't, the identity of the man who had ordered up my torture and death, and who was, to date, responsible for the deaths of a dozen people.

Since there was no way I wanted this man, with all the power he represented, for an enemy, I decided to keep looking for a candidate who would present far fewer complications. It was no use. No matter what I read, I kept coming back to the same name, the same set of articles. By the time we crossed the George Washington Bridge, there was no longer any doubt in my mind about the identity of the killer we were hunting.

"Shit," I said with a sigh, dropping the papers on the floor and slumping in the seat.

"What's the matter? You getting eyestrain?"

"I've got heartstrain. I know who our psychopathic killer is."

Garth glanced sideways at me, and even in the dim light I could tell by the expression on his face that he wasn't quite sure whether or not I was joking. "Come on, Mongo; you've only had your nose in those papers for less than an hour, and most of the time you've been skimming."

"I really only had to read one piece, and the follow-up article inside. It leaps right out at you."

"So? Don't keep me in suspense. What did you find out?"

"Garth, what happened on the day Veil disappeared?"

"Lots of things happened," Garth snapped impatiently. He didn't like traffic, and he didn't like to play guessing games; still, I felt I had to come at him from an angle in order to make him feel the same measure of shock I had felt when I'd realized the truth. "Why don't you just get to the point?"

"The president came to town."

Garth laughed harshly. "Kevin Shannon didn't do it, Mongo. His wife would never give him permission to do such nasty things; it's bad politics. Trust me on this one; Shannon's not our man."

"But one of Shannon's key people is."

"Who?"

"Orville Madison."

"Who the hell is Orville Madison?"

I looked quickly at Garth, saw that he was serious. It made me very uneasy. "Did you hear what I said? It's Orville Madison."

"I heard what you said. You tell me this Orville Madison may be the man behind all this; now tell me who Orville Madison is."

"You get the paper every day, Garth. How the hell can you not know who Orville Madison is?"

"I read the sports, metropolitan, and sometimes the entertainment sections, brother," Garth said evenly. "I don't listen to newscasts, and I haven't followed national or international news since Valhalla. I know the name of the president and the mayor of New York; on a good day, I may even remember the name of the governor. It's enough. Since we're all doomed anyway, I don't give a damn what the stupid politicians and generals are up to. In the end, it won't make any difference. I thought you felt the same way."

At one time I had. The words spoken by a madman, and the things he had shown us, had left wounds that would never fully heal. However, time and work had wrought a good deal of healing in me, and I had once again begun to take an interest in things and events around me. Not so, I now realized, with my brother. Garth remained trapped as deeply as ever in the depths of depression and despair.

I wondered if it was killing him.

"Orville Madison is Shannon's nominee for secretary of state," I said quietly, suddenly filled with a great sadness.

"So?" Garth's voice was a kind of shrug. "What does the *Times* have to say about Madison that makes you think he's the guy we're looking for?"

"It doesn't call him a psychopathic killer, if that's what you mean," I replied, countering with a little sarcasm of my own. "But what's there pretty well matches the profile we already have of the man."

"A speculative profile."

"Veil was shot at and disappeared on the eve of the president's announcement of his appointments to the cabinet; Shannon's penchant for secrecy is legendary, and so the public had no inkling of who those men and women were going to be until Shannon made the announcement. It wasn't until the next day that the names and biographical profiles of those people appeared in the papers. It was the next day's *Times* that Po was reading almost two weeks later when he was killed, which has to mean that he was most concerned about what he found in it."

"You don't know which of three papers he was reading, and you don't know if he was reading about the presidential appointments."

"It's easy enough to check the date; all you have to do is call the Albany cops when we stop. They should give you that information. You'll see I'm right."

"You still haven't told me what makes you so suspicious of Madison."

"For openers, he's currently Director of the Central Intelligence Agency, and will remain so until he's confirmed."

There was a long silence. Finally, Garth said: "Go ahead."

"Being Director of the C.I.A. isn't a big deal in itself. The position can be, and usually is, a political appointment made for lots of different reasons, including political payoffs, and the man who gets it usually has a public record a mile long. That's not the case with Madison. He came up through the ranks, and it was a shadowy journey to say the least. He was appointed to the top post two and a half years ago, but before that he was Director of Operations in charge of all the heavy, sneaky stuff the C.I.A. does. You don't even get a published photo of the Director of Operations, much less a public record, and you usually find out damn little about the man even after he leaves the post—which you usually don't find out about."

"There has to be information about him available now."

"Oh, sure. The *Times* bio is filled with all sorts of personal information—but nothing about his record when he was running Operations. That's all classified. He's fifty-eight years old, and he's been with the C.I.A. one hell of a long time. We can't even know how much of the personal stuff is made up. He's a Goddamn pig in a poke."

Garth thought about it. "To the public, yes, but certainly not to Kevin Shannon—and not to the House and Senate members who know him and must have worked with him. Christ, after all the embarrassments caused by cabinet members over the past fifteen years, you have to assume that Shannon and his other people have vetted all those nominees—*especially* this Orville Madison—more thoroughly than any nominees in history. Nobody's ever accused Shannon of being a dummy. Hell, you even like him. Finally, don't forget that all of the nominees will be grilled at the confirmation hearings by senators who've gotten very picky about whom they consent to put into those kinds of positions of power. It won't fly, Mongo. Shannon's not about to nominate some crazy who could sink his administration before it even sets sail."

"Not if he *knew* Madison was crazy. In fact, that may be precisely what's going on here, the key to it all. Sure, Madison's been vetted—but let's assume the investigators missed something, and it's a biggie, something very dark and nasty that's been buried for a long time and which would prevent Madison from being confirmed if people found out about it. Madison knew that once his nomination was made public, there were certain people—Veil Kendry, for one—who could hurt him badly if they ever started talking about what they knew, and they were believed—his link with Po, for example. God knows why Shannon wants a former C.I.A. Operations man for a sensitive, up-front post like secretary of state, but he obviously does. And Madison wants the post. Now, once Madison becomes a public figure he knows he's going to be vulnerable to disclosures to the press, or at the confirmation hearings, and so he decides to launch a preemptive strike against the man he fears most —Veil Kendry."

"If Madison were so afraid of these past associations coming to light, why would he wait two weeks to kill Po?"

"He wasn't concerned about Po saying anything to the press, because Po had enough problems of his own and certainly wouldn't make a very creditable accuser. Po became a danger to

Madison only when *we* discovered a link between Po and Veil Kendry. Madison was worried about what Po might say to *us*. That's how that tune goes. It has to be Orville Madison, Garth."

Garth began drumming his fingers nervously on the steering wheel. "Keep looking, Mongo," he said after a long silence. "Nobody ever said you didn't have a silver tongue, and you make a pretty good hypothetical case for our man being this Madison joker. But it's still all speculation, without a single shred of proof; no matter what you say, I find it damn unlikely that the kind of cold-blooded maniac we're looking for could get through the kind of screening process any cabinet nominee goes through. There must be something else in one of those newspapers."

"Damn it, Garth, there isn't. This is it."

"Keep looking, anyway."

We stayed overnight at a motel just off the Kingston exit of the New York State Thruway, thirty miles from Colletville, to the west. Garth called the Albany police, identified himself as a New York cop, and asked for the date of the newspaper Po had been reading in his study the night he'd been killed.

I was right.

We checked out at dawn in order to get to Colletville early. We ate breakfast at a diner in Veil's hometown, then drove directly to the high school. Given more time and less pressure, we probably could have been a bit more subtle in our approach. Not being blessed with these things, we simply marched into the high school office and introduced ourselves to a secretary. Garth showed his shield and asked if it would be possible for us to see the principal for a few minutes. It was. We were ushered into a nicely appointed office highlighted by a rust-colored rug and a collection of hunting trophies in a display case next to a window looking out over the surrounding Catskills, their forests covered now with early morning mist.

The principal, Matthew Holmes, was a boyish-looking man in his early thirties. Garth introduced me not only as his brother, but as a criminologist working on the matter in question as a paid consultant. The preliminaries over, I sat in a chair to one side of the office, letting Garth, with his police credentials, take the point.

"Lieutenant," the young principal said, "how can I help you?"

"First, we appreciate your agreeing to see us on such short notice," Garth replied.

"I take it this is a police matter?"

"Yes, it is, but I have to tell you that I have no official capacity in this county. I can only ask you to give me certain information, some of which may be confidential, as a courtesy. We're searching for a material witness to the crimes of arson and multiple murder. Other murders may be committed if we don't act quickly, which is why we really don't feel we can afford the time to go through the process of getting a court order to see certain school records."

"I see," Holmes said tightly. Suddenly the man seemed decidedly uncomfortable as he toyed with a heavy glass paperweight and stared out the window at the mountains. "Why don't you tell me what it is you want to know?"

"We have reason to believe that the crimes that have been committed are closely connected to a man by the name of Veil Kendry. Kendry—"

"Who?" the principal asked as he turned quickly and looked at Garth. He had stopped playing with the paperweight, and his discomfort appeared to have gone as quickly as it had come.

"Veil Kendry," Garth repeated slowly. "Do you know of him?"

"Somehow, the name seems familiar . . ." Holmes thought about it, finally shook his head. He looked immensely relieved. "No, sir, I can't say that I do."

The mercurial changes in Matthew Holmes's manner made me wonder who had come to mind when Garth had mentioned arson and murder. I wanted to ask, thought it better not to. Colletville, I was sure, had its own problems, and anything that didn't concern Veil Kendry was irrelevant to our needs.

"According to our information," Garth said, "Kendry went to school here. Your central district office confirmed that. He would have graduated—if he graduated—in nineteen-sixty-three or four. I'd like to look at his school records, if I may."

"Why, Lieutenant?"

"We're looking very hard for Mr. Kendry, not only because he's a material witness, but because he could be in considerable danger. It's a long shot, but those records just could reveal the name of a relative or friend we could contact who might know where he is. Actually, there could be other information in there that could be helpful, but I won't know until I look."

There was a prolonged silence, during which I had the distinct impression that Holmes was thinking about more than Garth's rather straightforward request. "I don't see why not," he said at last. "Obviously, we're a very small district, and if this Veil Kendry did go here, his records could still be kept at this school building. Just a moment, please."

Holmes pressed a button on his intercom, instructed his secretary to search for any records on Veil Kendry, using the approximate dates Garth had given him. He also asked her to bring us coffee.

We sat for the next fifteen minutes sipping coffee and chatting. Holmes, a graduate of a good school, had accepted the post in Colletville because it had afforded him the opportunity of having his own school at a relatively young age. Now, he told us, he was interested in a "change of pace," and had applied for a principal's post in the South Bronx. He wanted to know all we could tell him about New York City, and we assured him that being the principal of a school in the South Bronx would be a change of pace indeed.

Finally Holmes's secretary, a cheerful, gray-haired woman in her fifties, came back into the office. She handed a faded, yellow file to the principal, smiled at us, then turned and left.

"I don't know what's in here," Holmes said to Garth. "Because of the legal implications, I think it might be more correct if I didn't allow you to actually read the file. I'll look at it now, and I'm sure I'll be able to answer any questions you might have."

"That will be fine," Garth said. "We're most interested in the name of a relative—or anyone at all—he might have stayed in contact with over the years, or even visited periodically."

Holmes nodded, opened the file folder, and began to scan the contents of the first page. I watched his eyes move back and forth across the page, saw him frown slightly. "There's an address here, but I know the people living there now, and their name isn't Kendry."

"No. The Kendrys moved away some time ago. I checked that."

"According to this record, he didn't even live with his parents during his high school years. There's another name listed here . . . an aunt by the name of Madeline Jamison. However, the houses in that block were torn down a couple of years ago. That's who he lived with while he went to high school, but that house isn't there anymore."

"May I use your phone book?" I asked, rising from my chair.

Holmes took a thin directory out of his top drawer, handed it to me. There weren't any Jamisons listed. I looked at Garth, shook my head, sat back down in my chair.

"It seems he only lived with his aunt off and on. Twice he was . . . oh, my." Holmes abruptly looked away from the file, once again appeared uncomfortable.

"Mr. Holmes?" Garth prodded gently. "What about the times when he wasn't living with his aunt? Did he go back to live with his parents, or did he live somewhere else?"

"Lieutenant," Holmes said tersely, "I'm afraid I never realized the extremely sensitive nature of some of the material in Mr. Kendry's file. The law says that it must be kept confidential, and I totally agree. I may have made a mistake in agreeing to share this. Frankly, I don't see how the information could help you find this man, and we could all be in legal difficulty if I share it with you. I think it will be in everyone's interests if you go ahead and obtain that court order you mentioned."

Garth bowed his head, sighed heavily, then leaned forward and rested his hands on his knees. "Mr. Holmes," he said softly, "two nights ago three young people just past high school age were murdered in Seattle, along with their parents and grandmother. They were all blown to pieces."

Holmes frowned. "You suspect Veil Kendry?"

"No, sir. But he's definitely connected to it somehow, and more people—young people—may die unless we find him soon. The information you have in that file in front of you could be important."

"But I don't see how."

"That's why you're an educator and I'm a cop. Let me decide if it's important. I give you my word that the information won't be used if it's not necessary; if it is used, nobody will be told where we got it from. Please, Mr. Homes. Lives are at stake."

Holmes considered Garth's words, finally nodded. "According to these records, Veil Kendry was a very disturbed and violent young man, Lieutenant; the reason he was living with his aunt was because he was thrown out of his own home at the age of fourteen by his parents, who could no longer tolerate his bizarre behavior. He was twice committed to a mental hospital, once by his parents and once by the courts."

"What's the name of the facility?"

"At the time it was called Rockland State Hospital. It's down-state, and I'm familiar with it. Now there's a separate facility for kids, called Rockland Children's Psychiatric Center, but it still serves the same purpose. Children usually aren't committed there unless they're homicidal or suicidal—sometimes both. He did attend Colletville High otherwise, but there's no record of his having graduated. That's about it, Lieutenant."

Garth and I looked at each other, and I wondered if disappointment was as clearly etched on my face as it was on his. The trail in Colletville was more than two decades old, and there was nothing left here but the cries of a tormented young man still echoing in a musty, yellowing school file.

"Thanks, Mr. Holmes," Garth said, rising and shaking the other man's hand.

Holmes read my brother's voice and face. "I was right. It isn't any help, is it?"

Garth shrugged. "It sheds light on a few things, but it won't help us find him. We very much appreciate your cooperation."

"Wait," Holmes said as Garth and I headed for the door. We stopped, turned back. "Jan Garvey, one of our social studies teachers, graduated from Colletville High. I don't recall exactly when she graduated, but she's been teaching here for quite a few years. I think there's a good possibility she was a contemporary of this Veil Kendry, or at least may know something about him."

"We'd very much like to talk to her," Garth said quickly.

"I don't want to disturb her during class, but if you'll wait a moment I'll check her schedule and see when she has a preparation period."

"No. We'll wait until after school. I don't want her to feel rushed."

"That will be fine. Naturally, I have to get her permission. School is dismissed at three fifteen. If Ms. Garvey agrees, you can see her then."

Garth nodded. "Thanks, Holmes. When you get your school in New York City, you look me up. Having good contacts with the cops won't hurt you in trying to run a school in the South Bronx. Consider me a good contact."

"Thank you, Lieutenant," Holmes said, smiling. "I appreciate that. I'll see you later. Come here to my office, and I'll introduce you to Jan Garvey."

14

Something had come up to prevent Holmes from meeting with us again after school, but his secretary told us that Jan Garvey was expecting us, and we should go up to her room on the second floor.

The social studies teacher turned out to be an extremely attractive woman, close to six feet tall in her heels. Her hair was auburn-colored, graying nicely at the temples to give her a ripe, sexy look. Her features were accented by dark, soulful eyes. She projected an aura of toughness with dignity, like someone who had known much suffering but come back from it a deeper and better person than she had been before. She was, I suspected, a survivor, and probably an outstanding teacher, one with the sensitivity and intelligence to comfort and counsel those students who needed it, yet at the same time be able to back the biggest bad-ass in class right up against the wall.

At the moment, the woman's dark eyes were shadowed with anxiety, and she looked shaken as she stood in the doorway of her brightly decorated classroom and greeted us. "Hello, Lieutenant," she said to Garth, then looked at me. "I've read a great deal about the colorful Dr. Robert Frederickson, also known as Mongo. It's a pleasure and honor to meet you."

"I'm flattered," I answered with a smile. "I've been called a lot of things, but this is the first time I've ever heard myself described as 'colorful.' I'm going to have to note that in my diary, Ms. Garvey."

"Call me Jan, please."

"I'm Mongo, as you mentioned, and the lieutenant's name is Garth."

"I understand that you want to talk to me about Veil Kendry," the woman said as she ushered us into her room and closed the door behind her. The warmth in her voice had been replaced by wariness and tension.

"Yes," Garth replied.

"What is it you want to know?"

"Anything and everything you can tell us about him."

"How is he?"

"He's in a lot of trouble, Jan."

Again, shadows moved in Jan Garvey's eyes, and she shook her head sadly. "I'm very sorry to hear that. I thought he was doing so well. I've read articles about him and reviews of his work. Once, I made plans to go to New York to see one of his exhibits, but I backed off at the last moment. I . . . I'm not sure why. I guess I was afraid that being that close to Veil would remind me of too many things I don't want to be reminded of."

"Then you did know him well?" Garth said carefully.

The woman's thin laughter was laced with sadness. "Yes, Garth, I'd say so; I'd certainly say so. Can you tell me what he's done?"

"He hasn't done anything, Jan," I said, knowing that Garth would probably take strong exception. "Some other people are trying to do things to him—and us. For your own protection, we can't tell you much more than that. But it's very important that we find him, and soon. Lives could depend on it. We're asking you to trust us. You're the last person we know to speak to, the last hope we have of finding out things about Veil which we need to know."

The woman studied me for some time before speaking. "Then you're not looking for him because of some crime he's committed?"

"No. But he's disappeared, and something in his past is the key to why—and maybe where—he's gone. We're not exaggerating at all when we tell you lives are at stake. We're hoping that something you know might be of help."

Jan Garvey turned away quickly. "It all seems so long ago," she said in a small voice. "I haven't seen Veil in more than twenty years. How could anything I say be of any use to you?"

"Jan," Garth said with more gentleness in his tone than I'd heard from him in a long time, "we're not sure just what it is we're looking for. The only thing we know for sure is that you're the last link to him we know of. We'd like you to tell us everything you know, or have heard, about Veil Kendry, and let Mongo and me filter and weigh the information. It's obvious that you cared deeply about this man at one time, and still care. I give you my word that nothing you say to us will be used to hurt him."

"I believe you," the woman said with a catch in her voice that was close to a sob. "But it hurts me so much to remember." When she turned back to look at us, tears suddenly sprang to her eyes, and she bolted for the door. "Excuse me," she called back over her shoulder. "I'm sorry, but I have to get some coffee. I'll be right back."

"What the hell are we still doing here?" Garth asked almost an hour later as we stood by the classroom windows staring out at the gathering dusk. A storm was on its way, making the sky even darker. There were snow flurries in the air, harbingers of the much heavier flakes that would begin falling soon.

"Just wait," I replied, listening to the rising wind whistling outside the window.

"You keep saying that. She's stiffed us, and for all we know we're locked in here now. She's not coming back."

"We caught her by surprise, and we upset her. I think she'll be back."

"Why is it so damn hard for you to take a hint?"

"Five more minutes, okay?"

Garth glanced at his watch. "Okay. It looks like she loved Kendry, doesn't it?"

"Still does."

"That's one beautiful woman."

"Yep."

"If we didn't already know that Kendry was out of his mind, this would confirm it. Can you imagine having a woman like that still loving you after twenty years and not doing anything about it?"

"Maybe he didn't do anything about it precisely because he loves her. Whatever burden he's been carrying, he didn't want her to have to share it with him. Don't forget the bullet hole in his window. How could he ask someone to share his life if that could also mean sharing his death?"

"Okay," Garth said simply as he continued to stare out the window, where thick flakes had now begun to fall straight down from the sky. "What a schmuck," he added distantly.

"Give the man a break, Garth," I said irritably. "Veil chooses to live the life of a monk so that people he cares about won't be hurt, and you call him a schmuck."

"I wasn't talking about Kendry."

"Then who's a schmuck?"

"Anybody who'd camp out on the side of a mountain in weather like this."

"What are you talking about?"

Garth crouched down to my eye level, pointed toward a mountain in the distance. "About eleven o'clock, near the top of the second mountain. There's a fire up there. See it?"

I looked along the direction of his pointing finger, squinted into the gloom, but could see nothing but snow falling and the barely discernible outline of the mountains. "No. You must be on drugs."

"I don't see it now, but I'm telling you that I did see a fire up there."

"Bullshit."

Our argument about nothing was interrupted by the sound of a door opening and closing behind us, and we spun around. Jan Garvey, looking pale and with melting snow glistening on her face and clothes, stood just inside the doorway. A brown paper bag stuck out of her open purse. "Forgive me," the woman said softly. "I still have so much feeling inside, and there's so much hurt associated with . . . the things you want me to talk about. I got scared. Thank you for understanding, and thank you for waiting. I do want to help in any way I can." She set her purse down on a desk top, took out the bag. Inside was a bottle of bourbon and three plastic glasses. "I can't fool around with the ghost of Veil Kendry without a little booze," she continued with a wry smile. "I hope you two like bourbon."

"I love bourbon," Garth said, "and Mongo will drink anything that has alcohol in it."

"Sorry there's no ice."

"Ice will only ruin good booze," Garth replied, bringing me my drink. We sat down in two of the student desks, watched as the woman downed her drink, immediately poured herself another.

"I feel him in this room," she said with a shudder. "We sat in this classroom together, in those desks back by the window."

"How long did you know him?" Garth asked quietly.

"We grew up in this town together. He was my first lover, and he made me pregnant for the first time. I had to have an abortion. I went to some butcher who damn near killed me."

"Jan," I interrupted, "those aren't the things we need to hear, and you certainly don't have to talk about them."

"Please," she whispered. "You asked me to tell you anything

and everything I remember. There's so much that I just didn't know where to start . . . so I started there."

"Go ahead," Garth said. "You tell us anything you want, any way you want to."

The woman nodded, sighed. "It's all right. I can talk about it now—after a lot of craziness on my part and two broken marriages. There was always a lot of madness in this town. Maybe that's why I decided to come back here to teach; I'd finally defeated it, the madness, and I was proud of that." She paused, passed a hand across her eyes. "He may have come back for the opposite reason—the madness had finally defeated him."

Suddenly I felt the hair rise on the back of my neck. I straightened up in my desk, but it was Garth who asked the question.

"Who are you talking about, Jan? Veil Kendry?"

The teacher shook her head, gazed down into her drink. "No, not Veil. Veil never came back."

We waited for her to tell us whom she'd been referring to, but she resumed where she had left off, and neither Garth nor I wanted to interrupt her.

"I probably wound up with Veil because we were both wild," Jan Garvey continued after a period of silence. "But there was a big difference between the two of us. I was just a bad-ass kid out of control, with no self-discipline. A lot of Veil's craziness wasn't really his fault. He was born brain-damaged, you know."

Garth and I looked at each other. "We didn't know that, Jan," I said. "We'd like to hear about it."

We watched as the woman slowly walked across the room to stand by the window. It had grown too dark in the room to see her features, but I figured she knew where the lights were if she wanted to turn them on.

"He almost died at birth of a very high fever," she said in a low voice. "He wasn't supposed to live more than a few hours. It's how he got his name; his parents gave it to him as a kind of prayer that he would pass safely through the veil separating death and life. Obviously, he did, but the fever damaged a part of his brain and he ended up with a curious affliction. He was—is—what physicians and psychiatrists call a 'vivid dreamer.' To Veil, his dreams have always been as real as everyday life. It was years before anybody realized it. As a child, when Veil would have a nightmare, he wouldn't wake up like a normal child when he had monsters of all sorts chasing him. His first hospitalization in a mental institution came when he was ten years old; he'd drunk gasoline in an attempt to kill himself."

I shuddered, trying to imagine the unspeakable terror of a child when the ogres that chase all of us through dreams always caught him, perhaps did things to him; I wondered if phantom teeth sinking into dream flesh could cause real pain, suspected that they could.

"They kept him there six months during his first stay," the woman continued, "and it was there that they discovered his vivid dreaming. They treated it with medication, stabilized him, and sent him home. But this is a small town, and everyone knew where he'd been. By the age of eleven he'd been permanently branded as crazy, and the other kids constantly teased him.

"The medication helped, but one of its side effects was that it made him sleepy all the time. He had a choice—exist in a drug-fog most of the time and not have terrible nightmares, or do without the drug and suffer the consequences when he went to sleep at night. Veil was always incredibly gutsy, even as a kid. He kept challenging himself, trying to wean himself off the drugs. Then, finally, he found something to replace the medication."

"Violence," I said softly.

The silhouette of the woman's head against the window nodded. "Yes. Without the medication, Veil was in a constant state of tension. He began to fight all the time. He almost always fought older and bigger boys, and—in the beginning—usually got beaten up. But he kept fighting, because he'd discovered that the fighting drained off the psychic poison in him, and he could sleep at night without suffering from the nightmares. Then he got sent back to the mental hospital, after he'd been kicked out of his house and gone to live with his aunt, when he almost killed the captain of the football team, who'd made the mistake of challenging a much smaller and younger Veil Kendry to fight. This time he was referred to the hospital by the courts.

"He spent almost all of his junior year in the hospital. We wrote each other constantly, I went to visit him, and he was sometimes allowed to come back for home visits. He changed a great deal during that year. He was still like a time bomb waiting to go off, but he was far more controlled and self-contained than he had been. He had new medication, which was far better than the stuff he'd been given before. Also, he had something else; someone at the hospital had begun teaching him the martial arts as an outlet for his aggression and a means of obtaining self-control. Veil practiced his martial arts and read about them every free moment. That second stay at the hospital saved him. He had tremendous respect for the teachers and therapists there, and maybe it was the way he talked about them that made me finally get my act together years later, go to college and get a degree in order to become a teacher myself. But that was a long time coming. I still had a lot of wildness to get out of my own system.

"Veil liked to roam at night on his motorcycle—and I roamed with him. By this time he'd gained a very big rep around the area as a fighter, and there was always somebody who wanted to take him on. Veil always obliged all comers, whether it was in the parking lots of bars or in some field where a fight had been prearranged. It wasn't long before a lot of money started changing hands at these matches, with Veil making a lot by betting on himself and giving large odds. Sometimes he'd fight three or four men in one night. I didn't understand something—not then. I thought Veil was fighting for the money, but he wasn't. The others were fighting for money, or a reputation as the man who beat Veil Kendry. Veil was literally fighting for his life, his sanity; fighting was the only way he could keep his demons at bay."

There was a prolonged silence, and once I thought I heard Jan Garvey try to stifle a sob. However, when she spoke again, her voice was clear and strong.

"Then he got in trouble with some local sheriff's deputies. He was only seventeen, but he really was an incredible fighter, what with the karate he'd learned and the moves he was always making up. A lot of macho men around here didn't like the fact that a seventeen-year-old kid should have such a big rep. When one of the deputies got his jaw broken in a challenge match with Veil, he got four of his buddies to go after Veil and try to arrest him. Veil beat up all four of them. Then he was arrested by the State Police. Everyone in three counties, including the State Police, knew about the challenge matches, and the judge had a pretty good idea of what had really happened. He sympathized with Veil, but also— justifiably—considered Veil to be an increasingly dangerous man. The charges were dropped in exchange for Veil's agreeing to enlist in the army. Veil did, and two weeks later he left. I drove him to the bus station. It was the last time I ever saw him."

"Did he ever write to you, Jan?" Garth asked.

"Once, early on while he was still in basic training. It was to say he loved me, but also to say good-bye. He wrote that, for better or worse, the army was the only chance he had for a new life, and he was putting everything in the past behind him. He was setting me free."

Now Jan Garvey abruptly crossed the room and turned on the lights. Her eyes were red-rimmed and puffy, but dry. "I don't know whether all my talking has helped you," she continued in a firm voice as she poured more bourbon into our plastic cups, "but it's certainly helped me. All these years; I guess I never realized how much these memories of Veil have haunted me. There was, and is, nobody like Veil, and I guess it was those memories that broke up my marriages. I had such mixed emotions when I started reading about his growing success as an artist. I hated him for leaving me behind, for forgetting about me, and I realized at the same time that I still loved him. Then I knew I was happy for him. He'd finally found another way to fight his demons; his painting was a new kind of salvation." She paused, sighed, sipped at her bourbon. "Now, you say somebody is trying to kill him."

"Yes," I said. "Jan, Veil was very successful in the army. He was most certainly an outstanding combat soldier, because somewhere along the line he was made an officer—probably a field commission. And he was promoted steadily, to the rank of full colonel. What you've told us helps us to understand better a lot of things about him, but there are still too many important gaps missing. Something happened to him toward the end of his career in the army, and somehow we have to find out what it was. Please think very carefully. You told us he only wrote you that one letter. Can you think of *anyone,* anyone at all, he might have written to regularly over the years?"

"I doubt he wrote to anyone," the woman said distantly, in a voice so low I could hardly hear her, "but Gary probably knows what happened to him."

"Gary?"

Once again there was a prolonged silence, and Jan Garvey seemed cut adrift on a sea of thought and memory. "Forget I mentioned that name," she said at last. "Gary can't help you; he can't even help himself. All Gary will do is kill you."

Suddenly I thought I had a pretty good idea what had upset Matthew Holmes when we'd first mentioned that we were looking for someone in connection with arson and murder. There also seemed a good possibility that Garth really had seen a fire in the storm. "Jan," I said, "earlier you talked about the madness in Colletville. You were talking about Veil, of course, and yourself. Then you said that you'd come back here because you'd defeated the madness, but that somebody else may have come back because he was defeated by it. Did you mean Gary?"

"Yes," the woman replied softly. "I shouldn't have said that; I had no right. I have a big mouth."

"Why don't you have the right? Why is it wrong to talk about Gary?"

"I told you he can't help you."

"I don't understand. You said that he may know what happened to Veil. Why wouldn't he want to help?"

"It's not that he won't; he can't. I mean that literally. Gary Worde is quite insane, and very, very dangerous."

"Jan," Garth said, rising to his feet and setting down his cup, "where can we find this Gary Worde?"

"You can't," the teacher answered softly. "Nobody knows where to find him, and you mustn't try. It can only bring harm to you, and perhaps to Gary. Leave him alone."

"We have to try, Jan," Garth said, a slight edge to his voice. "Remember that there are lives at stake here."

I rose, went to a window and stared out into the darkness. A cold draft blew in my face. "Jan," I said, "all over America there are so-called 'hidden veterans'—men who came home from the war with very deep emotional wounds they found they just couldn't handle. They can't, or won't, function any longer in our society, and so they go off to live by themselves wherever they can find solitude. They go into wilderness areas where they can live off the land, with as little contact with other people as possible. Is Gary Worde this county's hidden veteran? Is he up in those mountains?"

Turning away from the window, I saw Jan Garvey nod. "Gary has no contact with anyone at all," she said quietly. "At least none that anyone around here has heard of, and we would hear."

"How does he get food and clothing?" Garth asked.

"Nobody knows. I suppose he could get food by trapping, but clothing and other things . . . ?" She finished with a shrug.

"How long has he been up there?"

"Almost nine years. Sometimes you'll see a campfire up there at night, and then you won't see another one for a long time. You think maybe he's dead, but then one night you'll see another fire, in a different place. I think he must move around a lot; there's a great deal of wilderness around here."

"How do you know the campfires aren't set by hikers or hunters?"

"In summer, maybe. But not in winter—not in those mountains."

I asked, "Why would this man know what happened to Veil in the war? Southeast Asia's a big place."

"He *might* know. Gary was Veil's closest friend, besides me. They enlisted together. Gary had his problems, too, and so he decided to go off with Veil. I know they went through basic training together, in the same unit. Gary used to write home fairly regularly, and his family shared the news with everyone."

"When Gary came home, did he talk about the war?"

Jan Garvey shook her head. "Never. Everyone knew right away that Gary was in a lot of trouble. Later, we found out that he'd spent six months in a V.A. mental hospital before he'd been discharged to come home. He'd gone away an overweight kid, and he came back looking like an old man who'd been in a concentration camp. Everyone tried to help as much as they could, and for a while he lived in a little converted room over his parents' garage. He suffered from night terrors; sometimes, you could hear him clear across town screaming in the middle of the night. Then, after a time, I guess he started suffering from the same terrors during the day. He couldn't work, because he'd just drift off in the middle of doing something, squat down, and cover his head. Then he'd start screaming."

"It sounds like classic postcombat stress syndrome," Garth said to me, raising his eyebrows slightly. "Severe."

I nodded in agreement, looked at the woman. "Jan, why didn't his family, or the authorities, have him committed to a V.A. hospital?"

"His parents were going to. Gary had begun to fantasize that the

Viet Cong were waiting just outside town and were going to come in after him. Everyone knew he was psychotic, and people were afraid he was going to explode and kill himself, or somebody else. The problem was that Gary was as terrified of going back to the mental hospital as he was of his phantom Viet Cong; apparently, his experiences there were as much a nightmare for him as whatever happened to him in the war. We all felt a responsibility toward him. This is a close-knit community. The feeling was that we'd sent him off to war as a kid of seventeen, and he'd come back . . . worse than dead. Nobody wanted to cause him any more suffering. We wanted to take care of him, but we just didn't know how. Finally, Gary solved the problem for all of us. One day in August just before sundown, nine years ago, he came out of the room over his parents' garage, walked down the middle of the street to the edge of town, and just kept going up into the mountains. That's where he's been ever since."

Garth shook his head. "Hasn't anyone from around here ever gone up to look for him?"

Jan Garvey nodded. "Yes; once. And one of the men in the search party almost had to have a leg amputated after he walked into some kind of mantrap Gary had set. After that, everyone has just left Gary alone. There may be a lot of traps like that up there; Gary's still fighting the war in his mind."

"I'd think he'd be a danger to hunters and hikers," Garth said, still visibly upset.

"Oh, he most certainly is. The county has posted the entire area, and everyone around here stays well away from any of the sites where fires have been spotted. Also, we try as best we can to warn away strangers; a few years ago, one man came back with a story about how a wild man had almost killed him. So far, obviously, we've been lucky. Don't expect help from anyone, state troopers included, if you do decide to go up there looking for him." The woman paused, smiled thinly. "Colletville and the surrounding towns really don't want it known that we're running a kind of huge, open-air insane asylum for one maniac on public lands."

Garth grunted, walked across the room, and stopped directly in front of the woman. "Whatever happens, we won't make trouble for Gary, or this town." Garth paused, reached out and gently gripped Jan Garvey's shoulder. "I don't mean to frighten you, but there are a few things you have to know. I very much wish that

Mongo and I could walk out of here with you now and take you to dinner, but we can't. We can't even be seen together. Mongo and I have been very careful. As far as we know, we weren't followed up the Thruway; nobody who shouldn't know is aware that we're in Colletville, or that we've talked to you. But we can't be absolutely certain. Now, just in case we're wrong and men come to talk to you, you simply tell them about this conversation—all of it except for the part about Gary Worde. That's very important. Nothing that you know is a threat to these people, but Gary Worde may very well be a threat. If you can follow these directions, everyone—including your friend in the mountains—should be safe."

"I understand," the woman said evenly. "I know you're going to look for him. Please be very careful. Remember that he's crazy."

Garth smiled, jerked a thumb in my direction. "So's Mongo. The two of them will get along just fine."

After leaving the school by a back entrance, we went through our usual ritual of driving slowly and watching in our rearview mirrors for lights. There were none.

Despite the storm, we found a place where we were able to pick up a pizza and a six-pack of beer for our dinner. Back at our motel, before sitting down to eat, Garth called his precinct station house.

There was news.

The NYPD had kept in touch with the Seattle Police Department regarding the deaths of Loan Ka and his family, and Kathy. The Seattle police, at Garth's urging, were treating the deaths as murders, but still had no leads in the case. However, something curious had happened within hours of the explosion, and the police there were wondering if Garth thought there might be a connection. Three local Hmong, men with criminal records for extortion and illegal use of explosives, had been found murdered, their corpses dumped in an alley near a station house. The men's bodies had been mutilated, skinned from the necks almost down to the waists; the coroner's report indicated that they had been alive when the skinning had been done, and it was the torture that had killed them. Furthermore, the right thumb of each man had been severed, and the missing digits had not been found.

Garth suggested that Seattle be advised not to waste any more time or manpower on the case.

15

The next day we outfitted ourselves with camping and survival gear, and supplies. We bought small-bore rifles and ammunition, then used another chunk of Veil's ten thousand dollars to rent a large, heavy Jeep with four-wheel drive. With our gear and a half dozen ten-gallon cans of gasoline strapped down in the back of the Jeep, we headed up into the mountains.

We knew we were going to have to get lucky; we could drive for weeks through the Catskills without seeing any sign of our quarry, and the problem was further complicated by the fact that our hidden veteran certainly wasn't going to be hanging out near any main road. After all his years in the mountains, Gary Worde would almost certainly have built at least one semipermanent shelter, but it would be far away from roads, people, and towns. Besides the extra gasoline, Garth and I had purchased sturdy hiking boots.

The starting point for our search would be the mountain where Garth thought he had spotted a campfire the night before, and that was the general direction—south by southwest—in which we headed, constantly keeping our eyes on the Jeep's dashboard compass. Occasionally we veered off the main road to explore ice- and snow-covered side roads. While Garth drove, I scanned the surrounding countryside with high-powered binoculars, looking for signs of—anything. What I saw were a lot of deer, a few hearty winter hikers exploring the foothills, and a group of brightly clad cross-country skiers. That was it.

The mountain where Garth thought he had seen the fire turned out to be ten miles away—which probably meant that he hadn't seen anything more than some random reflection of light in the window glass. It made no difference; we had to start somewhere, and that mountain seemed as good a place as any. Without some glimpse of fire or smoke, our chances of finding Gary Worde were a good deal less than minuscule.

For lunch we ate sandwiches from our large, well-stocked ice locker, then turned on gas-powered space heaters and waited in the Jeep until nightfall. We took turns sleeping and searching the tapestry of night for the tiniest speck of fire on the mountain, but sighted nothing. At dawn we crossed that mountain off one of the five topological maps we had brought with us, started up the Jeep, and headed for the next mountain.

We spent three days and nights driving through the mountains in a twenty-five-mile radius around the town of Colletville and were about to give up when, near midnight of the third night, I glanced to my right through the binoculars and clearly saw wisps of smoke rising in the distance into a sky brightly illuminated by a full moon. I quickly checked the map, saw that we were ten miles away from the nearest town. We parked the Jeep off the road, slept for a few hours, and at dawn loaded and hitched on our backpacks. We checked our pocket compasses, then headed off in the direction where I had seen the smoke.

After a day of hiking west, we both began to suspect that my sighting of smoke might have been as phantasmagorical as Garth's sighting of fire in the schoolhouse window back in Colletville. By nightfall, two city boys were thoroughly exhausted from tramping over hill and dale. We pitched camp, built a huge fire to cheer ourselves up, but didn't have the energy to cook. We ate cold cuts washed down with beer, then talked strategy—or lack of it. Just before sundown we had spotted, far in the distance, the top of what appeared to be a fire-lookout tower, close to the top of yet another mountain. Before going to sleep, we decided that we would try to make it as far as that tower the next day, and then turn back if there was no sign of Gary Worde; there seemed no sense in throwing away good time after that we would have already wasted in a futile search.

Over the river and through the woods . . .

We were again up at dawn at the beginning of what looked to be a fine, bright day. Refreshed, we cooked ourselves a big breakfast of eggs and Canadian bacon, cleaned up the campsite, and started off again in the direction of the lookout tower. After a half hour of walking we reached the top of a rise and were relieved to see below us a dry streambed which looked like easy walking and which appeared to meander off in the general direction of the tower. I led the way down the hill, entering a thick outcropping of fir trees. I was the first to see the streambed again when we emerged from the trees, and it was almost enough to give me a heart attack; thoroughly startled, I yelped in astonishment and jumped backward, bumping into Garth.

In the few minutes that it had taken us to walk down the forested hillside, something had appeared in the streambed that definitely hadn't been there when we'd started down; sitting on a huge boulder not ten yards away from us was a fairly large man. He was wearing a blue, fur-lined parka, faded jeans tucked into high-top laced hiking boots. His thinning brown hair looked clean but was very long, pulled back from his face and tied in a pony tail, and he had a full beard which reached the center of his broad chest. His eyes were large and brown, perhaps a bit too bright. Large hands were wrapped around a sturdy walking stick which he had laid across his knees. Powerful field binoculars hung on a leather strap around his neck.

"You've got to be Mongo Frederickson," the man said, pointing a stubby index finger in my direction. He looked more than a bit bemused.

Garth and I glanced at each other, then back at the man. Our rifles were stuck in sleeves in our backpacks, not easily accessible. "Who the hell are you?!" I snapped.

"My name's Gary Worde," the man said easily in a deep, rather pleasing baritone. "If you are Mongo, then the sour-looking big guy with you is your brother, the cop. Are you two looking for me?"

"How the hell do you know who we are, and what makes you think we're looking for you?" I asked, feeling rather foolish.

The bearded man shrugged his broad shoulders, touched the binoculars slung around his neck. "I've been tracking you for the past two hours from the top of the lookout tower back there. From the way the two of you trip over your own feet, you're sure as hell not hikers—and there are no hiking trails in this area, anyway. So I asked myself, what would an odd pair like you two be doing around here? A mutual friend, Veil Kendry, talks about you a lot. Let's just say I put one big guy and one little guy together and came up with your names. Did Veil send you with a message for me? Is he all right?"

Garth unhurriedly unzipped his parka, reached inside, and withdrew his service revolver. He cocked the hammer, walked out into the streambed, and put the gun to the man's head. It wasn't a very friendly thing to do, but I definitely agreed with his next point. "For some reason I don't believe you, pal," Garth said in a quiet voice that carried clearly in the sharp, cold air. "I try to put you together, and I don't come up with any answer at all. Now, what's your real name, and what are *you* doing here?"

The gun bore touching his forehead didn't seem to bother the man. His expression didn't change at all as he rolled his eyes in my direction and raised his eyebrows slightly. "Mongo? Tell me why I shouldn't be who I say I am."

"You don't match up with the report we got. Gary Worde's supposed to be the wild man of these mountains, and nobody's even seen him for nine years. You don't look or sound very crazy to us, but you do look too Goddamn well fed and well dressed to be the man we're looking for."

"Who told you all this?"

"A friend of Worde's in Colletville."

The man frowned slightly. "Then Veil didn't send you?"

"No. As a matter of fact, you might say we're looking for him."

"Why are you looking for him?"

Confused and uncertain of what to say, I said nothing. While it was certainly true that this man casually sitting on a boulder in the middle of a dry streambed didn't match up with anything Jan Garvey had told us about Gary Worde, it was also true that it wouldn't make any sense for our trackers—assuming they knew about Gary Worde, which was a big assumption—to sit this man down in our path to try to trick us. It bothered me, as did the man's seeming indifference to Garth's gun at his head.

"You'd best answer my question," the man cautioned in a tone of voice that sounded oddly like a threat.

"When was the last time you saw Veil Kendry?"

"I don't measure time the way you do. It was three seasons ago."

Spring. Veil had pulled one of his disappearing acts in the spring, for about three weeks. "He came here?"

"Yeah. He visits me at least once, sometimes twice, a year."

"Why does he visit you?"

"Because he's my friend," the man said with a slight shrug of his shoulders. "We practice together in these mountains."

"Practice what? Martial arts?"

His answer was to execute a series of maneuvers so fast I

couldn't follow them. The bearded man ducked forward and to his left beneath Garth's gun, which clattered to the rocks as the side of the man's hand hit Garth's wrist. In what seemed less than the flicker of an eyelid, Garth had been disarmed and turned around, with one of his arms held in a tight hammerlock. The bearded man's right forearm was across my brother's windpipe.

Feeling like nothing so much as a winded commuter who has just seen his train pull out of the station, I drew my Beretta and started to circle around to where I might get a clear shot at the man who called himself Gary Worde. "Let go of my brother, or I'm going to put a bullet through your head."

"Put the gun away, Mongo," the man said easily. "You're lucky I recognized you as the Frederickson brothers, or you'd both have been dead a few seconds after your brother here pulled his gun on me. Put yours away."

"Let go of Garth first."

"No."

Garth was turning blue. I released the hammer on the Beretta, flipped it in my hand, and offered it to the bearded man butt first.

"I didn't say I wanted the gun," the man continued. "I just asked you to put it away." I dropped the gun into the pocket of my parka. The man immediately took his forearm away from my brother's throat—but he didn't release the hammerlock. "You still haven't answered my question, Mongo. If Veil didn't send you, what are you doing here?"

"We think you've got some answers we need to know."

"What are the questions?"

"What was Veil doing in Saigon near the end of the war, just after he'd been pulled out of Laos? Do you know?"

Shadows moved in the man's eyes, and his jaw muscles clenched and unclenched. "Why do you need to know?" he asked softly.

"It's a long and complicated story. The bottom line is that Veil's in big trouble; somebody wants him dead, along with us. We believe that the key to who's hunting Veil, and why, lies in something that Veil was involved in during the war. It's Veil's past we're hunting, and that's why we're here."

"Oh, shit," the man said as he abruptly released Garth and half turned away. He waved one hand in front of his face, as if trying to chase away invisible gnats—or something else. "So that's finally going down."

Garth and I glanced at each other in surprise as the bearded man suddenly started walking away. Garth picked up his gun, then ran after the man and grabbed his arm.

"Gary, I'm sorry! We don't understand. What's going down?"

Gary Worde shoved Garth's hand away, kept walking. His shoulders were hunched now, as if against the cold. Without looking back he motioned for us to follow him.

Garth and I walked in silence on either side of Gary Worde as he walked west in the dry streambed. His hands were thrust deep into his pockets, and his shoulders remained hunched. After a half mile or so he turned to his right and climbed up out of the bed. We found ourselves on a cleared path running up the face of the mountain on which the lookout tower stood. Panting and sweating from the quick pace Worde had set, Garth and I stopped to adjust our backpacks. Still silent, Worde helped us by removing some of the heavier articles from both our packs. He wrapped the articles inside my sleeping bag, hoisted it over his shoulder. Then we started off again.

"What you heard about me in Colletville is true," Gary Worde suddenly said in a quiet voice so low that Garth and I had to strain to hear him. "At least it was true back then. I couldn't—can't—make it anywhere there are people just going through their regular routines day in and day out. The fact that they don't know or think about the things that happened in the war only makes me think about them more; if you will, my memories are like air rushing into the vacuum of other people's forgetfulness or indifference. That's when I get . . . crazy. It's when the bad dreams come."

Worde shuddered, cast an anxious look at Garth and me. We returned his gaze and nodded, but remained silent. Garth reached out, squeezed his shoulder.

"Some people would say that the army let me out of their nuthouse too soon," the hidden veteran continued as we reached the top of the mountain and walked along its crest. Around us was nothing but forest, rolling hills, more mountains. "That isn't true; I never would have gotten better there. They had me doped up with chlorpromazine, and all I did was sleep all the time. But I still dreamed. I would have died there, and I guess they finally came to realize that. They gave me a permanently refillable prescription for lithium, the name of a shrink at a V.A. hospital in the Albany area, and let me go. I came home to Colletville."

We started down the opposite side of the mountain. Halfway down, beside a swiftly moving stream, was a log cabin which looked sturdily built and came complete with glass windows. Perhaps three-quarters of an acre of forest had been cleared around the cabin, and there were a number of patches of broken ground where I assumed vegetables were grown in the spring and summer. Pelts of raccoon, fox, muskrat, beaver, and deer were curing on stretch racks in the cold air and sunlight. A skinned deer carcass, half butchered and covered with a muslin cloth, hung from an eave of the cabin, and on a chopping block next to the stream lay an ax and a rifle. Cords of firewood were stacked around the sides of the cabin, and smoke drifted up from a stone chimney.

Gary Worde had again lapsed into silence for some time before we'd approached his cabin, and Garth and I sensed that he was trying to center and gird himself for the psychological turmoil talking about the war would entail. Garth and I helped him prepare a meal of venison and vegetables, served on skewers, which we ate sitting on wooden stools around the huge, open hearth in the center of what served as the cabin's living room. Afterward, he brewed coffee and served it to us in carved wooden cups. It was almost sundown before he spoke again.

"Nobody knew how to react to me when I came home," Worde said quietly as he sipped at his coffee. "A lot of people were downright hostile, as if they considered me responsible for getting us into the war in the first place, or for losing it. Most of the people were kind; they tried to understand and help. But others asked the strangest questions; one guy wanted to know how many women and children I'd killed. Pretty soon I stopped answering any questions. I never did fill the prescription for lithium, because I knew it wouldn't help. I began to drink heavily, but that didn't help either. During the day, I couldn't forget all the horrors I'd seen, and every night I'd have nightmares and relive them. I'd wake up in the middle of the night, screaming. After a while I started . . . screaming during the day. I'm sure you were told that I started to believe there were Viet Cong surrounding the town, waiting to come in and get me."

Without warning, Gary Worde suddenly set down his cup on a corner of the hearth, slipped off his stool, and crouched with his hands over his head. Garth started to go toward him, but he sat back down when I shook my head, signaling danger.

Slowly, like a cobra rising from a basket, Gary Worde straightened up and began to dance to the deadly music he heard in his head. His eyes glowed in the firelight as he flung one arm out, then the other, spun and kicked high into the air. He continued these graceful but deadly karate moves, a series of *kata*, for close to fifteen minutes, spinning, lunging, punching, and kicking his way around the cabin as he did battle with the demons in his mind, his imaginary enemies marching out at him from twenty years in the past. When he had finished, he wiped the sweat from his forehead with the back of his hand, sighed heavily, and sat back down on his stool.

"There was nobody to talk to who could understand," the man continued in an even tone, as if nothing had happened. "Nobody except Veil."

"You were in touch with Veil back then?" I asked quietly.

"Yes. The war was over, and Veil had just arrived in New York. Somehow, he'd heard—or guessed—that I was back in Colletville, and he called me. He called a number of times; usually he'd call me from a pay phone, and I'd call him back. We'd talk for hours. He asked me to keep everything a secret—where he was, and even that we were in touch. I did as he asked, even though at the time I didn't understand his reasons."

"You do now?" Garth asked.

The question had come too soon, and once again we were treated to a prolonged period of silence. Garth and I looked at each other inquiringly, but neither of us spoke. Gary Worde's strange and violent dance had convinced us that the man was, indeed, dangerous, and could not be pressed. If he was going to tell us anything, it would have to be in his own time, in his own way, at his own pace.

"Once, I went to New York to visit Veil, without telling anyone where I was going," Worde said at last. "Veil thought that coming to New York and staying with him might be good for me. Fuck, it didn't take me long to see that he was crazier than I was, although for different reasons. Also, he handled his craziness differently; he was always brawling, and he could kind of hold things together in his head as long as he was fighting. I'd had enough fighting and seen enough blood and broken bodies to last me a lifetime. I had no way of freeing myself the way Veil did. I figured there was no sense in my going to hell in his handbasket, so I came back to Colletville. Still, that visit to New York helped me in one way; it helped me to realize that the only time I really ever felt good was when I was by myself, up in these mountains.

"Still, for some reason I thought I just had to learn to live my life like everyone else—work, and have a family, and be a part of society. I'd come up to these mountains on weekends, but during the week I'd try to be . . . like them. It didn't work; everything got worse. I was rapidly becoming an alcoholic, and I started to get DT's to go along with my nightmares. Once, I nearly killed a man because I thought he was a VC sneaking up on me; he was just a businessman in a blue suit walking down the sidewalk in the middle of the day.

"I knew I was going to have to be sent back to the V.A. mental hospital, and I knew I'd die there. Then I realized what I had to do. I made one phone call—to Veil, telling him what I planned to do. Then I walked up into these mountains, and I've been here ever since. It was a good decision; I can only survive where there's solitude."

Gary Worde refilled our coffee cups, and for a time we sat quietly, watching through a window as a huge moon rose into the night sky.

Finally Worde continued: "When I walked into the woods, I had nothing but the clothes on my back and a hunting knife. Fortunately, it was summer, so I had time to build a crude shelter for the winter. I'd been in . . . Special Forces. I was well trained in survival craft, and that helped. But that first winter was rough. I don't know how I survived, but I did, literally living in caves, like an animal. I built snares, ate the flesh of whatever I caught, and used the pelts for warmth. As strange as it may seem, in the middle of all that physical misery I was happy. And I was so exhausted every night just from doing what I had to do to stay alive that I slept without dreams. I didn't miss booze; in fact, I didn't miss anything. For the first time in as long as I could remember, my mind was clear.

"I moved around a lot in that first year, and I looked pretty ragged, to say the least. I know I scared the shit out of a couple of hunters who came across me. Also, some people may have been caught in large snares I set for deer. After that, I think people became afraid of running into me because the hunters and hikers stayed away.

"Some time later, Veil—who's one hell of a tracker, in case you didn't know—found me up here. He'd changed, mellowed; he'd found a new way to fight off his own nightmares. I'd found peace in isolation, and he'd begun to find it in art. I think we must have talked for two days straight, without sleeping. He'd brought me things—canned food, tools, medicine, clothing—that he'd lugged all over creation while he was looking for me. He hadn't come to ask me to go back with him, because he understood why I had to be where I was. He just wanted to see me, and do what he could to make things more comfortable for me.

"He came back four more times that year when he found me, bringing me more things and helping me to build this cabin. After that, his visits became routine things, and I looked forward to them very much. He'd brought me steel traps, and I was able to set up good traplines. I cured the pelts of the animals I caught, gave them to Veil on his visits to sell back in New York to pay for the supplies he brought me. While he was here we'd talk and work on certain martial arts techniques that are difficult to describe, but are best practiced in places like these mountains."

I thought I had a pretty good idea what Gary Worde was talking about; I remembered the silent walking technique Veil had taught me, and which I had used to sneak up on Loan Ka's sons in Seattle. I wondered what other deadly arts the two men had practiced here, but did not ask.

Garth and I helped the man wash the dishes and cooking utensils, using water drawn from a spigot in a rain barrel suspended near the open hearth to keep the water from freezing. When we had finished, Worde removed one of four carved pipes from a rack, filled it with a mixture, and lit it. Almost immediately, the air inside the cabin was filled with the sickly-sweet smell of marijuana. He offered the pipe to us, and we declined. And we waited. As Gary Worde had told us, and as he had made abundantly clear, his sense of time was not ours. He would tell us what we wanted to know, assuming he possessed the information, when he was ready, and not before.

"Veil told me certain things which you'd probably like to know about," the hidden veteran continued at last in a flat, matter-of-fact tone as he stared out the window into the moonlight-washed night.

"There were two reasons why he felt he could talk to me about these matters. First, I'm up here where nobody can find me; second, he knew he could trust me to keep my mouth shut even if people could find me. It's very dangerous information—dangerous to Veil, and dangerous to anyone else who shares it."

"We're well aware of that, Gary," I said quietly. "But now that information may be the only thing that can save Veil, and us. A lot of innocent people have already died because of Veil's secrets."

"Veil's not responsible for that."

"I didn't say he was, although it's difficult to understand why he's done certain things the way he has. All we want to do is stop the killing, and nail whoever is responsible. Do you know who that is?"

Now Gary Worde slowly turned toward us; half his face glowed in the flickering orange light from the fireplace, the other half remained hidden in shadow. "Maybe now is the time to talk about those things, maybe it isn't. I hear you when you say Veil's in trouble, and that you need this information to help him. That's heavy. But what I know about Veil is heavy, too, and I'm not at all sure I'm going to share it with you unless you can convince me that you have a very good reason for wanting to know it."

"We believe Veil wants us to have the information, Gary."

"Then why didn't he tell you himself?"

"Because we live in the city, not in the mountains, and that made us too vulnerable. We believe Veil wanted, rightly or wrongly, for us to discover things this way, bit by bit. This is a guess, but I think that in Veil's mind he believed this was the best —maybe the only—way to get the truth out with any chance for his survival, and ours."

"Convince me of that," Worde said, sitting back down on his stool by the hearth. "We have all the time in the world."

"Veil doesn't."

"Tell me what's happened."

I did, starting at the beginning when I had walked into an unlocked, brightly lighted—and empty—loft.

16

Apparently, I was convincing.

"Lieutenant General Lester Bean," Gary Worde said without hesitation when I had finished talking. "That was the name and rank of the officer in the helicopter that brought Colonel Po into Laos and took Veil out."

"Not Robert Warren?" I asked. "That was the name of the general that signed Veil's discharge papers."

Worde shook his head. "No; I never heard of any General Warren. Bean was Veil's army C.O. The man in the civilian clothes was a guy by the name of Orville Madison. A real fuck."

I looked at Garth and even in the dim firelight could see him stiffen on his stool. I felt absolutely no satisfaction over the fact that I had picked Orville Madison's name out of a newspaper five days before. There was nothing for me in Worde's confirmation but a cold, empty feeling in the pit of my stomach. There was something almost anticlimactic in hearing Gary Worde link Orville Madison to Veil; now that we virtually knew for certain that Madison was the killer hunting Veil and us, I didn't have the slightest idea what we were going to do with the information. I was afraid— not only for Veil, Garth, and myself, but for the country.

Kevin Shannon, I thought, must have been on drugs when he dreamed up the nomination of Orville Madison as secretary of state. Or, an even more ominous thought, Madison could have something on Kevin Shannon. It was just what the United States needed; I tried to imagine what the reaction of Americans, and other people and governments around the world, would be when the media began trumpeting the news that the charismatic and dashing newly elected president of the United States had nominated an active, busy-beaver murderer to the top post in his cabinet.

If the fact became known and was believed.

Despite everything that had happened, we still had no evidence that Orville Madison had ever even received a parking ticket, much less ordered the murders of men, women, and children from his office in Langley. The only people left alive who had firsthand knowledge of the connection between Veil Kendry and Orville Madison were two certified loonies, one of whom nobody but the other loony had seen in nine years. That left only the two Frederickson brothers to tell what could be described as wild, unsubstantiated tales, and Orville Madison would be doing his best to rectify that situation once he found out about our latest stop.

"Madison was Veil's C.I.A. controller, wasn't he?" I said.

"Yes," Worde replied.

I shook my head in an attempt to clear it. I was getting a contact high from the marijuana smoke, and I assumed Garth was experiencing the same sensation. The firelight and shadow inside the cabin shimmered and danced before my eyes, and I had to hold on to the edge of my stool in order to steady myself. "Why was Veil taken out of Laos?" My voice had a metallic ring to it, and it echoed inside my head.

"To play toy soldier," Worde answered dryly, sucking on his pipe.

"I don't understand."

Worde grunted, set aside his pipe. "It was near the end of the war, when everyone but the generals and a few politicians knew it was lost. Back in the United States, it was all coming apart almost as fast as it was in Southeast Asia. Every day you had demonstrations in a dozen different cities; you had the march on Washington, the revelations about the Pentagon Papers—all of it. You'll recall that a lot of politicians and military people were blaming the fact that we were losing the war on the media. A few of those people decided to do something about it."

"What did they decide to do about it?" Garth asked quietly. "And who did the deciding?"

Worde shrugged. "Veil didn't know who made the decisions at the top level, so I don't know. But their reasoning went that, since newspapers and television were responsible for an anti-American, defeatist attitude and our failure to win the war, a way had to be found to manipulate newspapers and television in order to get the people to support the war effort. Just about every military and political spokesman had been discredited; nobody believed anything they said. Then some genius decided that it could all be turned around if only we found the right spokesman—a bona fide hero, like Sergeant York in the First World War, or Audie Murphy in the Second. The genius decided that what was needed was a John Wayne type who'd actually fought in the war, and who could fight what was perceived as a publicity battle on the home front."

"They wanted to give that job to *Veil Kendry?*" I asked in disbelief.

The hidden veteran nodded brusquely. "In fact, at one point the notion had reached a stage where the plan was given a name—Operation Archangel, from Veil's C.I.A. code name."

"Excuse me, Gary," I said, still holding on to the edge of my stool for fear that I would float away if I didn't, "but I can't quite see Veil Kendry as a likely candidate for media hero; too independent, too unpredictable, and too downright violent. I can see Veil punching out some reporter's lights if he didn't like a question. I'm talking about the way he was back then."

"You're right, of course—but only the people who'd actually met or dealt with Veil knew that. As a matter of fact, there had to be dozens of candidates better suited for that kind of assignment than Veil. But then, Veil was the highest decorated soldier of that war; Veil *was* the Sergeant York and Audie Murphy of Viet Nam. The man had a bagful of bronze and silver stars, and had been awarded the Congressional Medal of Honor twice for bravery in the face of the enemy. This was *before* he was sent into Laos, and it was how he got promoted to the rank of colonel. Because of his C.I.A. connection and the nature of some of his duties, his awards were kept secret. When Operation Archangel went into effect, everything—or almost everything—he had done would be made public. People might argue about the war, but they wouldn't be able to dispute the fact that Veil was a man of incredible valor, a hero."

"Damn," Garth said hoarsely, in a tone of respect. "You wouldn't be able to even guess at any of that if you looked at his record now."

"I don't know what record you've seen," Worde replied, "or what's been put on it. But what I've told you is the truth of the matter. Of course, the reason he'd done all those things and won all those medals was because he was crazy as a loon; Veil would be the first to tell you that. Veil reveled in the sights and sounds and feelings that destroyed me and so many others; he'd be swimming in blood up to his neck, wading through a field of beheaded and castrated corpses, and barely even notice. In this sense, he was a kind of 'ultimate warrior'; he needed the kind of action for which soldiers are decorated. It was this war record that finally swayed what Veil believed was a small Senate select committee, sitting in secret session, in his favor. Orville Madison, so I'm told, was a master of that kind of political intrigue and maneuvering. It was Madison who'd been pushing hard for Veil's selection, and when the dust finally cleared from all the Washington infighting, Madison had won. The plan became officially known as Operation Archangel."

I asked, "Why was it so important to Orville Madison that Veil be selected?"

"There were two reasons. The first, and the most obvious to everyone, was that Veil's selection for so exalted an honor would reflect very favorably on Madison, since Veil was *his* man; regular army, yes, but also a C.I.A. operative whose most important work had been done under Madison's control and orders. All of the other candidates had men championing their selection for the very same motive. Veil's selection would be a very large feather in Madison's career cap."

"The second reason?"

"Orville Madison hated Veil's guts."

Garth started to ask a question, but I raised my hand to silence him, leaned forward on my stool. "I think I've got it," I said with an eerie feeling of both sickness and growing excitement. "This was an honor virtually any other soldier would have given anything for, what with its honor, glory, and a full pass home, away from the fighting; but it was something Veil would find intolerable, and quite possibly humiliating."

"That's correct," Worde said. "Combat was something Veil performed as well as—and possibly better than—any soldier who's ever lived, and he desperately needed it, as well, to keep his head straight. He wanted no part of being what he called a 'cardboard hero.' He hated the very idea of the assignment. Madison had known precisely what Veil's reaction would be, and he was probably more than a little concerned that Veil might just say fuck it, tear off Madison's head, and shove it up his ass. It's why Madison brought General Bean along with him into Laos—to back him up, and to make certain that Veil understood that the only alternative to accepting the assignment was a court-martial and the loss of his career. Bean was there to make certain Veil understood he had no choice, and to make him think twice before simply punching out

Madison." Worde paused, shrugged. "Veil did what he had to do; he got into the helicopter."

"Why did Madison hate Veil so much?"

"Because he couldn't control him, and because he feared him. I was in Special Forces with C.I.A. responsibilities myself, and word about career C.I.A. personnel got around. Madison was a soul crusher, a sadist who liked to burn out his operatives; he'd find a man's breaking point, then push him past it. He must have been very good at what he did as far as the agency was concerned, but, to a man, his operatives hated and feared him. Except for Veil. To Veil, Madison was just an obnoxious son-of-a-bitch he ignored whenever possible. Veil always knew what had to be done, and he did it—with or without Madison's blessing. He considered Madison irrelevant to his mission, and this drove Madison up the wall. Because of his combat record, Veil had power too, so the personal battle between Veil and Madison was kind of a standoff. Veil often told Madison to fuck off, and he got away with it. But Madison finally beat him on the Operation Archangel thing because so much preliminary planning had been done and high-level decisions already made, behind Veil's back. By the time Veil found out about it, Operation Archangel had virtually already been put in place. Veil would have had to buck a good part of the military and political establishment, and he didn't have the juice to do that."

Garth said, "Putting Colonel Po in charge of Veil's village was an added twist of the knife."

"Right—a delayed twist, because Veil wasn't aware of Po's reputation at the time. If he had known . . . well, I'm not sure what would have happened. Anyway, he was shipped off to Tokyo for six weeks of R and R, and special training for his new assignment."

"What kind of training?" I asked.

"Public relations bullshit—what he was supposed to say, and when he was supposed to say it; what he was *not* supposed to say. That sort of thing. Meanwhile, the White House PR staff was gearing up for the media blitz that would kick off with the president, the joint chiefs of staff, and a whole load of important congressmen meeting Veil at Dulles Airport when he flew back to the States. There would be a Washington parade in his honor, and another one the next day in New York, complete with ticker tape. The president would issue a proclamation of sorts honoring Veil as a national hero, and the fact that he was the most highly decorated soldier of the war would be made public. Literally overnight, Veil was scheduled to become the most publicized hero since Charles Lindbergh.

"The presidential proclamation and parades were just for openers. Among other things, Veil was scheduled for a year-long cross-country tour with hundreds of personal appearances. Biographies and other books about Veil would begin to appear in bookstores. Hollywood would make films about him—starring Veil himself, of course, if it was discovered that he had any acting ability at all. His face was going to appear on armed forces recruiting posters, and there'd even be a comic book featuring him. The message would be very simple: Veil, a kind of god of war, had given everything he had to fight against our enemies, and it would be virtually sacrilegious for the American public to betray his efforts and sacrifices; it was time for those misguided Americans who had opposed the war to rally behind this savior of American will and values. Veil's mission was to rally public support for an all-out, last-ditch effort to win the war by any means necessary, including the possible use of tactical nuclear weapons. Veil was to be the personification of everything most Americans want to see in themselves, and the idea was for him to lead us away from the brink of defeat to final victory. That was the scenario.

"I think Veil realized early on, in Tokyo, that he wasn't going to make it. Deprived of combat, faced with an assignment he couldn't stand even to think about, an old problem reappeared. Do you know about . . . ?"

"Yes," I said. "We were told about his brain damage and the vivid dreaming by the same person who told us about you."

Gary Worde nodded. "He finished his training. It was thought best for Veil to disembark to the United States from Viet Nam, so he was sent back to Saigon. You already know some of what happened there. When he met that pimp and the Hmong children on the street, there were only two hours left before he was supposed to be at the airport and on the plane for the VIP flight that would take him home to the presidential greeting party. It was when he saw the pimp and the children that Veil felt the final twist of the knife and realized the lengths Madison had gone to in order to try to break his spirit.

"Veil went crazy. You know how he rescued the rest of the children and took them to the relief agency. Then, instead of going to the airport, Veil went to the safe house where Madison lived and had offices, and he beat the shit out of him. It was while Veil was busting up Madison that he found out about the joint commando force that was on its way to wipe out the Hmong village. Veil forced Madison to order him up an armed helicopter. You know what happened when he flew into Laos, and you know that he survived the crash of his helicopter. He managed to hike out of the jungle, back into Viet Nam. He turned himself in to the first American unit he ran into, and they turned him over to General Bean. Veil assumed he'd be executed, and he accepted that. He was put in the stockade, and plans were made for a summary court-martial. It never came off.

"Somebody in the army pointed out that they had a problem with Veil, and neither of the options they were considering—Veil's execution or imprisonment—was going to solve it. Veil had left some of the most important and powerful people in the country—including no less than the president of the United States—standing around on the tarmac at Dulles Airport with their thumbs up their asses while he flew off to commit a treasonous act by firing rockets and bullets at his own countrymen and our allies. It would have been an absolute public relations and enemy propaganda disaster if that fact was made public. The media would be talking about nothing else for months, and a super-soldier's desertion in the face of C.I.A. treachery would become the issue, not the necessity of winning the war. The story of Operation Archangel would have had exactly the opposite impact on the nation of what was intended.

"The fact that Veil had turned himself in was already an official matter of U.S. Army record; he was in General Bean's personal custody, and—after the episode with Po and the Hmong—Bean was no friend of Orville Madison's. So it was too late for the C.I.A. simply to take Veil out behind some tree and shoot him. If the army tried and shot him, the event would attract all sorts of reporters with dangerous questions. Imprisoning Veil might attract less attention, but then Veil would be free to communicate. Obviously, nobody wanted Veil sitting around writing his memoirs."

"Gary," I said, "Operation Archangel, according to you, was not only in place, it was already moving. It takes hundreds of people to plan and orchestrate that kind of media campaign, so those hundreds of people—including a lot of reporters—must already have known what was supposed to happen."

"They knew what was supposed to happen, but not whom it was supposed to happen to; they didn't know who was supposed to be at the center of it. It was thought that keeping Archangel's identity a secret until the last moment would heighten dramatic impact, so Veil's name had never been announced; only a handful of people knew that Veil was Archangel. So it was possible to *cancel* Operation Archangel, for whatever reason they might think up, and then classify the information and restrict it to the few people who already knew the whole thing, and who wouldn't talk in any case. It just wasn't possible to contain the damage that would result if Veil's name and activities ever became connected to it. His cooperation was needed."

"So they let him go," Garth said. "He must have had one hell of a lawyer."

"He didn't need a lawyer," Worde replied as he refilled his pipe with more homegrown marijuana and lit it. "He had Orville Madison."

"Come again?" I said, concerned that the marijuana smoke might be making me hear—or Gary Worde say—absurd things.

The hidden veteran puffed on his pipe, blew a thick, night-blue smoke ring. "Although Veil didn't know it at the time, it was Orville Madison who argued for Veil's release in exchange for his promise to remain silent about everything that had happened."

"That doesn't make any sense," Garth said.

Gary Worde threw back his head and laughed loudly. "It does when you know Madison."

"Why the hell would Madison do anything to help Kendry?" Garth persisted.

The laughter abruptly stopped, and Worde leaned forward on his stool. "Madison had been beaten up, both physically and professionally; finally, Veil had defeated him. More than anything else, Madison wanted to exact revenge—and he thought he'd figured out a way to do it. He understood Veil as well as anyone, and it was this understanding that he hoped to use. At this time Veil probably preferred death to imprisonment, because he knew that he would lose his mind behind bars. But Madison couldn't exact the kind of personal revenge he wanted if Veil were dead or in prison. Madison wanted Veil out, where he could get at him. And he managed it. Veil's records were to be completely altered, with all mention of his combat record and medals erased; in effect, Veil was to be erased, made a nonperson. In exchange for his freedom, Veil was to promise never to discuss anything concerning his war record or Operation Archangel."

Garth shook his head. "This was Madison's idea of revenge?"

"It was the foundation of it. Madison didn't think Veil could survive for very long outside the army, where his need for violent behavior was not only sanctioned but rewarded. In fact, he had himself wheeled into Veil's stockade cell to tell him just that. Madison told Veil that, in his opinion, Veil would self-destruct within six months, either from drugs, booze, or getting himself stabbed in some back alley."

"It almost happened," I said quietly, remembering Garth's description of Veil's first years in New York City.

"I know that better than you," Worde said. "But there's more. Madison thought he was being clever, and he was, but he wanted to make absolutely certain that he had all the bases covered. He informed Veil of the fact that, in the event Veil didn't self-destruct, he would kill him anyway."

"Madison *told* Veil this?"

Worde nodded. "It had already been agreed upon that the C.I.A. would keep Veil under constant surveillance to make certain he kept to his part of the bargain, and Veil would do nothing to hinder this surveillance. Madison guessed—correctly—that Veil had probably never known a day of real peace or happiness in his life. Madison said that if and when a moment, a day, came when Veil did find peace and happiness, that would be the time when Madison would have a bullet shot through his brain. In effect, Veil was put under a kind of life sentence of death, and he would never know at what moment that sentence might be carried out." Gary Worde paused, drew himself up straight, and passed a hand over his eyes. "That's all Veil told me," he continued in a voice like a sigh. "It's all I know."

"Gary," I said, "I didn't mention this before, because Garth and I wanted to hear what you had to say first, but Orville Madison is alive and doing very well, thank you. This isn't the first time we've come across his name in connection with this business."

"In that case, you know who had somebody wing a shot at Veil," Gary Worde said without hesitation. "You also know who's hunting Veil, and you."

"Agreed. But there are complications. Gary, do you have any idea of what's going on in the country or the world?"

"Not a thing."

"We have a new president, a man by the name of Kevin Shannon. Shannon seems like a pretty straight arrow, except for the fact that his choice for secretary of state is Orville Madison."

Gary Worde stared at me for some time, then slowly shook his head. "That's a good one," he said in a soft voice. "And they call me crazy."

Garth rose from his stool, stretched, and glanced over at me inquiringly. I was fairly certain I knew what he was thinking, and I had a lot of the same questions.

"Gary," I said, "you're the only person Veil has ever spoken to about Orville Madison, so we'd like to know your thoughts on a few things. Madison's career not only survived the fiasco of Operation Archangel, it bloomed. Who knows? That could have been the price he exacted for *his* silence. We know that he's been the C.I.A.'s Director of Operations for the past few years. Now he gets to leap right out on center stage in the diplomatic community as top dog in the State Department and probably in the cabinet. Now comes the question. For all these years, Veil has kept to his part of the bargain; even if he had decided to say something, nobody would have believed him. All of his damaging records—real and phony—would have been mysteriously leaked, and he would have been dismissed as a psychotic crank. The one thing Veil cares about, his painting career, could have been seriously damaged. Finally, it's highly arguable whether anyone would really have *cared* about Operation Archangel—an incident that happened a long time ago in a war everyone wants to forget anyway. I can't understand how Madison could perceive that he had anything to worry about. Why, then, should this very successful man risk losing everything by sending an assassin after Veil?"

"You want my opinion?"

"Yes."

"I think you're missing the point by trying to figure out what Madison might have been worried about. I don't think he was worried about anything. I don't think he planned to kill Veil because he thought he had to; I think he did it because he *wanted* to. Finally, he would take his revenge, and it would be a very satisfying way of capping off his other triumphs. He saw it as finally evening a score. After all, he certainly didn't plan on having his man miss Veil."

Garth grunted. "It could be, Mongo," he said to me in the tone of voice of a newly converted true believer. "Once his man missed and Kendry disappeared, Madison suddenly really did have a problem, and he knew it. The truce had been broken, and now all bets were off. Now he *had* to kill Kendry, because—from his past experience—he would necessarily assume that Kendry would stalk and kill him, regardless of the consequences. Then you came on the scene, and Madison realized that what Kendry planned was far worse; Kendry planned to expose him in a way that couldn't be ignored, and *then*—maybe—kill him. Madison panicked, and by torturing and trying to kill you proceeded to dig himself an even deeper hole. I'll damn well see the bastard buried in this one."

"*If* we can get some kind of proof, which we still don't have, and if he doesn't bury us first." I turned to the hidden veteran. "Gary, will you come out with us and tell what you know to a Senate committee? If you do, I think Veil might be ready to come out of hiding. He's accomplished one of his goals, to let Garth and me discover the story bit by bit, so that we'd believe and fully understand the enormity of the power he's up against. If you'll come out, I think he'll surface. You're the only person, besides Veil, who has anything more than secondhand knowledge about any of this. I realize that we're asking you to willingly make yourself a target, and I know—"

I stopped speaking when Gary Worde abruptly threw his pipe to the floor and sprang to his feet. Startled, uncertain of what Worde intended to do, both Garth and I started to draw our guns. We stopped when we saw Worde reach over his head, grab the rim of the bottom of the rain barrel and tip it. Water splashed over the flames in the hearth, sending up clouds of hissing steam. The cabin went dark, and when the steam cleared all we could see was the silhouette of Worde's head and shoulders against the window.

"Gary?" I said in a low voice. "What's the matter?"

"Come here."

Garth and I walked across the cabin until we were standing next to the bearded man.

"Do you hear it?" Worde continued.

I listened, heard nothing but the almost palpable silence of the mountains. I even held my breath, but still heard nothing. "No," I said, and looked at my brother. Garth merely shrugged his shoulders.

"You've been living in noisy places for too long," Worde said. "Keep listening."

Slowly, like an aural mirage arising from a desert of quiet, there came a sound. But this was no mirage. A plane was approaching from the west.

"There are no airports around here set up for night takeoffs and landings," Worde said quietly, "and no one would use them if there were. Also, I recognize the sound; it's a big, two-engine job, and one of the engines is pitched slightly lower than the other. It's the same plane that's been flying around here for four days—since about the time when you say you showed up in Colletville."

"Goddamn," I breathed, fighting back the panic I could feel rising in my chest like a hot tide. All the time Garth and I had been traveling up the Thruway and looking back over our shoulders, we hadn't once thought of looking in the right direction—up; and we probably wouldn't have thought anything of it if we had seen a plane. Orville Madison's men had known where we were all the time.

Garth and I picked up our backpacks, slipped the rifles from their sleeves, then followed Gary Worde outside and stood in the moon shadows beside the cabin. The plane finally came into view, flying low on the horizon, and the sound of its twin prop engines grew louder. It was a good-sized cargo plane, and as it passed over the top of a mountain in the distance it began to bank and turn, heading straight for us. Putting out the fire hadn't helped; the pilot obviously knew exactly where to find us, and his instruments would have allowed him to pinpoint our location even if there wasn't a full moon.

The plane gained altitude, then started to bank in a circle around us. The first figure dropped from its cargo bay as it flew aross the moon. A few seconds later the man's black chute billowed open and he started to drift toward the ground. Clearly silhouetted against the moonlit sky, the figure looked decidedly lumpy; our guest dropping into the night forest was a serious commando with some serious equipment.

Orville Madison had decided to end the waiting game; whether or not Madison knew about Gary Worde and what the hidden veteran had to tell, he had decided that Garth's and my taking the time to find a man living in total isolation could bode him no good. Henry Kitten would undoubtedly be very angry and disappointed, and we would be very dead.

Soon the first commando had company. As the plane continued to describe a large, high-altitude circle around our position, five more lumpy figures leaped out into the night, opened their chutes, and began to float to the earth. We were caught in a deadly circle perhaps two or three miles in diameter, and the circle would begin to close on us as soon as the men landed.

"Brother," I said, "I do believe it's time we split."

"Outstanding idea, Mongo. Gary—?"

We both turned around to find that Gary Worde had disappeared. Garth and I were alone.

17

Our first thought was that Gary Worde had panicked at the sight of the commandos and abandoned us—but he was gone only long enough for Garth and me to work up a little panic of our own. When he reappeared, he had a huge bowie knife in a metal scabbard strapped around his waist. *Nunchaku* sticks, their polished mahogany gleaming in the bright moonlight, hung around his neck by their connecting chain. In his right hand he carried a packet about the size of a paperback book wrapped in dirt-encrusted, heavy-duty yellow oilskin. He squatted down, set the oilskin packet to one side, and started to rub dirt over his hands and face, indicating that we should do the same.

"Gary, I can't tell you how sorry I am that we drew these people here," I said as Garth and I quickly smeared dirt over our exposed flesh. "We thought we'd been careful to make certain no one was following us, and we wouldn't have come here otherwise."

"Don't worry about it, Mongo," Worde replied in a low, breathless voice. I could only guess at the nightmares that were going through his head at the moment; he was clearly frightened, but controlling it. His reaction was called courage. "Veil made clear to me from the very first time he came up here that any kind of association with him was extremely dangerous and that something like this could happen. It was one reason he told me the whole story of what had happened to him. I accepted the risk because Veil was the one person whose company I enjoyed—and needed." He straightened up, hefted the packet. "I also accepted this."

"What's in it?" Garth asked.

"I don't know," the bearded veteran replied as he slipped the packet inside his coat.

"When did he give it to you?"

Worde thought about it. "It's hard for me to say. It was quite a few years ago; I don't know how many. I remember that it was in the fall. He brought it to me on one of his visits. He asked me just to bury it someplace and keep it for him; he said he might need it someday. I'm thinking now may be that time."

I glanced at the luminous dial on my wristwatch, saw that four minutes had passed since the figures had begun to drop from the sky. "Gary, do you think you can get us out of here through that ring of commandos?"

"You just follow me," Worde replied in a low voice that trembled with both fear and anger. "I don't care how well trained or equipped those jokers are; they don't know these mountains, and I do. They don't know we're on the move, so don't do any shooting except as an absolute last resort. If we can break through the circle without being detected, I think we'll be home free. We'll walk in single file, and you should try to step exactly where I step. Okay?"

Garth and I nodded.

"Then let's do it."

Garth and I followed Gary Worde as he walked down to the stream. He picked up his rifle from the chopping block, then started back the way we had come. After a hundred yards or so he cut to his right and headed up a fairly steep embankment. As we had been instructed, Garth and I tried to step exactly where he stepped, and as a result found ourselves avoiding dead sticks and loose stones. Worde obviously had excellent night vision, for we were moving at a fairly brisk pace through a densely wooded patch of hillside where little moonlight filtered through the trees. We tried as best we could to imitate his silent walking—a curious, rolling gait that Veil had showed me and which enabled Worde to move silent as a ghost through the night forest.

Suddenly Worde stopped, and I almost bumped into him. He motioned for us to be silent, then cupped both hands to his ears. I listened, but could hear nothing but the sound of our own raspy breathing. After a few moments we moved off again, but we had gone less than a hundred feet when Worde stopped again and listened. After watching him pluck from silence the sound of the approaching plane, I had a great deal of respect for Worde's hearing; still, judging from the positions of the commandos when they had dropped from the sky, I didn't think any one of them would yet be close enough for us to hear his passing.

"Veil?" Gary Worde called in a low voice that was just above a whisper, and which sounded curiously like the soughing of the wind.

Veil?!

Suddenly, behind us, there was an explosion that shook the ground. We spun around in time to see a column of white and orange flame shoot up into the sky from the site where Gary Worde's cabin had been.

"Shit," Garth said. "One of those sons-of-bitches moves fast."

"Satchel charge," Worde murmured. "Whoever made it to the cabin knows we're not there. Now we'll see what kind of communications they have."

As if in response to Worde's thought, the cargo plane came flying in low from the south, gained altitude, and then banked into a tight circling pattern with the flaming cabin as its epicenter. Then flares began to fall, incandescent balls of fire that stripped the cloak of night from us.

We were in trouble; although the hillside was covered with trees, there was no foliage. There would be a spotter up in the plane equipped with high-powered binoculars to search for us, or signs of our passing. We threw ourselves to the ground next to the trunks of trees and froze as the plane flew off into the distance. Finally the flares winked out, and night rushed back in over the mountain. We waited, listening, but could hear nothing but the drone of the airplane circling somewhere out of our line of sight. After more than two minutes passed, I began to dare hope that we hadn't been spotted.

Then the plane came into view; it banked against the moon, then began to descend rapidly, coming directly at us.

"Oh, no," Worde moaned in a barely recognizable voice as the first black canister dropped from the belly of the plane and began to turn lazily end over end as it angled down toward us. "Oh God, no."

We sprang to our feet. Worde threw his *nunchaku* away and we half-ran, half-fell down the hillside as fast as we could. There was an explosion, and I didn't have to look back to know that the spot where we had been was erupting with napalm flame. We were flushed, and there was nothing left to do but run.

We'd become separated in the scramble down the hillside, but Garth and I found each other just inside the tree line by a small, open glen. Ten yards to our left, just beyond the tree line and bathed in moonlight, a trembling Gary Worde was kneeling on the ground with his hands crossed over his head.

"Gary!" I shouted as Garth and I ran to him and grabbed his arms. "Gary, get up!"

We managed to pull Worde to his feet and drag him back into the minimal shelter of the trees as another canister dropped from the sky and splashed a river of flame through the forest on the opposite side of the glen. Still holding Worde, Garth and I started to run back through the trees. We had gone perhaps fifty yards when Worde suddenly broke free from our grasp, spun around, and screaming, ran back through the trees. Garth and I sprinted after him, but stopped at the edge of the tree line and stared in horror at the figure kneeling in the very center of the clearing. This time his head was neither bowed nor covered, but back; his rifle was in his hands, and he was pumping bullets at the fast-approaching plane.

"Gary!" I screamed. "Get up! Get the hell back here!"

But the hidden veteran was beyond the sound of any human voice; the spiritual barbed wire that had been holding him together for so many years had finally snapped and was flailing at him. He was back in Viet Nam, and this time he didn't intend to come back.

I started to run toward the hopeless rifleman in the clearing, then felt my feet fly out from under me as Garth grabbed the hood of my parka and yanked me backward. It was Garth who darted forward as I scrambled to my feet—and then we both dropped to our bellies as automatic weapons fire suddenly erupted from the top of a rise a hundred and fifty yards to our left. Bullets raked through the bare, skeletal trees, snapping off branches which rained down all around and over us. When I turned my head, I could see the figure of the commando standing straight and with his legs braced to either side of him as the submachine gun he held against his hip bucked and chattered. Gary Worde's lifeless body jerked spasmodically under the impact of the bullets, while above us the plane banked and reversed course for another napalm run.

If Gary Worde's corpse went up in flame, so would the oilskin packet he carried. The only piece of evidence—if it was evidence—against Orville Madison would be destroyed.

"Cover me, Garth; throw some fire in that prick's direction. We need that packet."

"What—?!"

Garth lunged and grabbed for me, but I was already on my feet and scrambling through the snow in the clearing. Bullets kicked up little white fountains around me as I ran, rolled, and crawled toward Gary Worde's bloody corpse. I heard Garth's rifle shots—three, four, five. But a rifle in the darkness against a man equipped with a submachine gun wasn't much of a match.

Out of the corner of my eye I saw the cargo plane coming in low over the treetops, on a direct line with me. Another black canister dropped from its belly; if I wasn't ventilated by bullets, I was soon likely to get roasted.

"Mongo!"

"I see it!"

Worde's corpse was on its belly. I rolled it over, then put my hand inside his coat and groped through the gore I found there. My fingers closed around the packet. I pulled it out, jumped to my feet, and started back toward the trees just as the canister landed behind me. I leaped and rolled, clawing my way through the ice and snow as a great *whoosh* rolled over me in a tidal wave of sound. The odor of gasoline stung my nostrils as thick, billowing clouds of suffocating black smoke swirled over and around me. Flames slapped at my face—and then I was out of it, and into Garth's grasp.

"Jesus!" Garth shouted as he lifted me up, then slammed me back down into the snow. He rolled me back and forth a few times to smother my burning clothing, rubbed snow through my hair, over my face and neck. Finally, apparently satisfied with the fruits of his labors, he sighed and sat down hard in the snow.

"How am I?" I asked loudly in order to be heard over the roar of the fire in the meadow and the forest beyond.

Garth frowned and shook his head in disgust, even as tears welled in his eyes. "Only slightly singed."

"I'm glad to hear it." I held up the packet. "Look what I've got."

Garth, a strange expression on his face, didn't even glance at the packet. "Why did you do a dumb-ass thing like that?"

"Huh?"

"Why did you run out and risk your life like that? Trying to save somebody's life is one thing, but Worde was already dead. That package wasn't that important, Mongo. None of this shit is."

"I don't understand what you're saying."

"Who gives a shit if Orville Madison becomes secretary of state or not?"

"I thought you were beginning to."

"Wrong. I'd break the man's spine if I could get my hands on him, but I don't give a shit if he becomes secretary of state. I give a shit about trying to keep you in one piece. Then you go and do a damn fool thing like that and almost get yourself killed for a lousy package which could contain dirty laundry, for all you know. What do you think would happen to me, Mongo, if you died?"

I had no answer for a question I'd never expected to hear. I was trying to think of something to say when I suddenly realized that the shooting from the ridge had stopped. Startled, I glanced toward the ridge; the silhouette of the commando was gone.

"I think I got the son-of-a-bitch," Garth continued quietly.

"Then what the hell are we doing sitting here?!" I shouted, jumping to my feet. "Let's go!"

A dead commando meant a hole in the ever-tightening cordon, and so we began climbing the ridge directly toward the spot where the gunman had been standing. However, we had to take into account the possibility that the man was just playing possum and hoping we would do exactly what we were doing, and so we proceeded with a good deal of caution. Halfway up the ridge we split up, with Garth going to the left and me to the right. With my Beretta out, I darted from tree to tree, listening for any sound from the top of the ridge, looking for any movement. I'd made it all the way to the crest of the ridge when I heard Garth's voice.

"Here, Mongo," my brother called softly. "I've got him."

Moving in the direction of Garth's voice, I found him standing over a large man dressed in a camouflage uniform of brown and white. The man had night-vision goggles draped around his neck, a large pack strapped to his back, and his lifeless hands held an Uzi submachine gun. He made a formidable-looking corpse, but it hadn't been Garth who'd killed him; the commando's throat had been deeply slashed from ear to ear, and the thumb on his right hand had been amputated.

"Goddamn," I said when I'd recovered from my initial shock. Gary Worde had been right on target when he'd called out Veil's name.

"Yeah," Garth murmured as he reached down and picked up the Uzi. He took two ammunition clips from the man's belt, dropped them into his pocket. "If Kendry had really wanted to make me feel good, he'd have hung around just a few minutes longer. Which way is the truck?"

Taking out my compass, I held it in the palm of my hand and squinted at the needle in the moonlight. "That way," I said, pointing to my left. "But we can't cut over that way until we're sure we're outside the ring. For now, I think we should keep on going straight."

"Right," Garth said curtly, and we started down the opposite side of the rise at a trot.

Our thoughts with the man who had died of the disease called Orville Madison which we'd brought with us into his place of solitude, we walked due north in silence for better than three hours, until the sun began to rise over the horizon to signal a cold, white dawn. We'd paused often to listen and watch, but we had detected no sounds of pursuit. Now we stopped at the top of a mountain and scanned the surrounding landscape through our binoculars, saw absolutely nothing except distant plumes of smoke rising from the forest fires started by the canisters of napalm.

There was no cargo plane, no sign of the five surviving commandos. There was also no sign of Veil, although we knew he had to be out there someplace.

Puzzled but relieved at the absence of any kind of pursuit, we checked our compasses, then started off to the east. With a little luck, I thought, the Jeep would be where we'd left it, and it would start.

A half hour later two New York State Police helicopters appeared in the distance, heading toward the fires.

"Do we want to be rescued?" Garth asked as we stood inside a shadowy copse of fir trees and watched as a third helicopter passed almost directly overhead.

After some consideration, I shook my head. "I don't think so."

"It could save us a long hike, and a very cold night in the mountains; we can't risk a fire."

"We need time to think about what we're going to do next and who we're going to see. I think we're better off if we keep our options open. If the State Police get hold of us, they'll have an awful lot of questions I'm not sure we want to answer yet—at least not to them."

"You're right. Why don't you open the packet and see what the hell's in there?"

"I was thinking it might be better to open it in the presence of at least one official witness. It's sealed pretty good, and as long as we leave it that way there are tests that can establish the fact that it's been sealed and underground for a few years. That could be important."

Garth nodded his agreement. "You sure the Jeep is in this direction?"

"Ask me in a day or two," I said, and started down the side of the mountain.

We'd headed in the right direction, and the Jeep was where we'd left it; unfortunately, we never got a chance to see if it would start. New York State troopers were waiting for us—in force—when we emerged from the forest on a ridge just above the place on the highway where we had parked the Jeep almost a week before. Suddenly, grim-faced men in blue and gray uniforms seemed to be popping up or out all over the place, surrounding us with their guns drawn.

"Freeze!" a tall, burly state trooper standing fifteen yards ahead of us shouted as he leveled a shotgun between Garth and me.

We froze, slowly raised our arms in the air.

"Where's the other one?!"

"What other one?" I asked. "Look, Officer, we were just out for a little hiking."

"With a submachine gun?"

He had a point. Almost as an afterthought, Garth relaxed his fingers and the Uzi clattered to the frozen ground. One of the troopers quickly stepped forward and snatched it up. Then we were grabbed, hustled down to the road, slammed up against a car, and roughly frisked.

"You're making a mistake, Trooper," Garth said in his most reasonable tone of voice. "Look in my wallet; you'll find a detective's gold shield. My name's Lieutenant Garth Frederickson, and I'm on special assignment for the NYPD. This is my brother, the criminologist Dr. Robert Frederickson."

"We know who you are, Frederickson," a big, black trooper growled from somewhere behind and above my right ear. The man found my Beretta and Seecamp, relieved me of both. "But you're no longer on assignment for anyone, and it's likely that both you and your brother are going to be learning a lot more about criminology from the inside of a prison. Both of you are under arrest for violation of the Federal Espionage Act. Now, where's your buddy?"

"We don't know who you're talking about," Garth replied in a low, rasping snarl that no longer sounded quite so reasonable.

"Veil Kendry. When and where did you split up?"

Garth and I both started to turn around, stopped when a rifle barrel knifed down between us and smashed against the hood of the car.

"Who's Veil Kendry?" I asked, and heard Garth softly grunt his approval. These were definitely not the right people to talk to or show anything.

"Shut up, you little bastard," the trooper behind me said as he prodded me hard between the shoulder blades with his rifle butt. "He's the man you and your brother have been selling our country's secrets to for the past five years, and he works for the Goddamn Russians. Don't bother trying to deny it, because the government people have you cold. All three of you are fucking spies."

It seemed the rope I thought Orville Madison was supposed to be hanging himself with still had a few kinks left in it.

18

Garth and I were handcuffed, bundled separately into the backs of two State Police cars, and given a speedy ride—complete with wailing sirens—to a headquarters building just off the Thruway, near Albany. We were strip-searched and all our possessions taken away. We were placed in separate cells in a small lockup facility at the rear of the building, given a meal, and allowed to sleep under the supervision of a trooper sitting in a chair in the corridor just outside our cells.

In the morning we were served a breakfast that was surprisingly good for jail food. A few minutes after the dishes were taken away, I heard the cell door on the opposite side of a tile partition open and close, and then two sets of footsteps walking away down the corridor, toward the front of the building.

Garth was brought back about an hour later, and a young, attractive female trooper came through a door to my right, opened my cell, and motioned for me to come out. I was led down the corridor to a pale green door which the woman opened for, and then closed behind, me.

The small interrogation room was bare except for a metal desk and chair set back against the far wall, and a second folding metal chair placed in the middle of the room. A heavyset trooper in a uniform with a captain's insignia sat very erect behind the desk. To his right was a tape recorder, which he turned on as I entered the room, and on the desk top in front of him was a yellow legal pad and felt-tipped pen. The man had close-cropped brown hair, and dark, expressive eyes. I went to the chair and sat down, crossed my legs and smiled at the trooper. He didn't smile back. We sat and stared at each other for close to five minutes, while the recorder kept running.

"I know," I ventured at last. "I just don't look like a spy. That's why I'm so good at it; people don't take me seriously. Garth is the one who looks like a spy, and that's always been a problem. I insisted that the Russians hire him, too, as kind of a package deal. He needed the money."

"You think this is a joke?" the trooper asked in a low voice that was surprisingly lilting. His nameplate said McGarvey. Irish.

"I think the idea of Garth and me being spies is a joke."

"I take you very seriously, Frederickson. I won't bullshit you if you don't bullshit me."

"Somebody's already bullshitting you, Captain, and it isn't me."

"What the hell's going on?"

"Didn't my brother tell you?" I asked with more than passing interest.

"You tell me. What happened up in those mountains? We found seven corpses up there; one was really just a pile of burned bones. Six of those men were dressed in uniforms and armed to the teeth; they'd all had their throats slashed and their right thumbs severed. It also looks like somebody was dropping firebombs from a plane; I've seen burn patterns like that before, in Viet Nam. It looked like a Goddamn war zone up there."

It appeared that Garth hadn't told the man anything, which didn't surprise me. "That's because there was a war, Captain."

"Will you tell me what's going on, Frederickson?"

"I'm the one who should ask you that. Your men said that Garth and I are wanted on espionage charges. Somebody's pulling your chain, not to mention a lot of strings. I think you know that, or at least suspect it strongly."

"Nobody pulls my chain, Frederickson," McGarvey said evenly. "Maybe that's why I'm sitting here asking you to tell me what's going on."

"I think I hear what you're saying. But I notice that you didn't say anything about strings. If you'd done even an itty-bitty check on Garth and me before your men jumped our asses, you'd have known that the charges were ridiculous—maybe something dreamed up on the spur of the moment by somebody in a panic and very desperate to get us locked up where he can get at us. The New York State Police are being used as baby-sitters, and *that's* what this is all about. In fact, I might even venture a wild guess that you were pointedly requested *not* to interrogate us. How am I doing, Captain? Do I win a prize?"

McGarvey's heavy eyebrows raised slightly. "Like I said, Frederickson, nobody pulls my chain. But now you're trying to; you still haven't told me anything."

"I'm working on it."

"Work harder."

"What person or government agency asked you to pick us up? F.B.I.? I mean, the charges against us would fall into their jurisdiction, right?"

"I'll ask the questions, Frederickson," McGarvey replied dryly. "You may be the smaller of the Frederickson brothers, but you've certainly got the biggest mouth and smoothest tongue."

"Garth gets disgusted easily, Captain. When he gets disgusted, he either takes a swing at you or gives you the silent treatment. I'm more patient."

The captain's response was both unexpected and disturbing. "Your brother's a dangerous man, Frederickson," he said in an odd tone of voice.

"Indeed," I replied, feeling uneasy. The expression on the other man's face was one of genuine concern, and I wasn't sure I liked that.

"I don't think you understand what I mean. He's not living on the edge; he's hanging over it by his fingertips. I've seen men in that condition before. He's going to explode one of these days, maybe when you least expect it."

"Is this knock-the-brother business some new kind of interrogation technique?"

"No. It's an observation. He has a drug pallor, you know. Is he on anything?"

"Garth doesn't even do aspirin."

"Well, my suggestion is that you two get this business behind you as quickly as you can. In my opinion, he needs professional help—and quickly."

"What did he say to you?" I asked, feeling genuinely alarmed, yet not certain that I wasn't being manipulated. Captain Mc-Garvey knew his business; he could play both good guy and bad guy at the same time.

"It's not what he said; it's the way he looks."

"Garth's just cranky this morning," I said, trying to get my mind off Garth and back to the business at hand. "Being shot at and having napalm dropped on your head does that to some people; it puts them off their feed."

"He's very protective of you."

"Yeah, well, I'm his brother and he doesn't like it when people shoot at me and drop napalm on my head, either."

"Who shot at you and dropped the napalm?"

"Just maybe the same people who called you and asked that we be picked up. I'm sure it's occurred to you that there just might be a very direct connection. What about it, Captain? Does that give you pause?"

The answer was clearly yes. McGarvey was silent for some time, and then he abruptly reached over and turned off the tape recorder. A few things might be bothering Garth, but something was also bothering this New York State trooper a great deal. He obviously smelled a whole barrelful of dead fish—but then, it wouldn't take a genius to do that. What McGarvey also smelled was tremendous power, power to, at the least, destroy his career; despite his confident, almost defiant, demeanor, the smell of that power had to frighten him. He had pride in his person and his job, but—exactly like Garth and me—he had to be wondering what kinds of wheels were furiously turning in Washington and how he was going to avoid being crushed under them.

"I'd heard of you a long time before this, Frederickson," McGarvey said at last. "And I've done my own checking on the report I got."

"What report?"

"I told you I'll ask the questions."

"We're not very likely spies, are we?"

"You still haven't told me what happened up in the mountains."

"I'm not sure you want to know," I said carefully.

"Why not?"

"Because then the same people who want Garth and me dead might want to kill you. Remember that you didn't get a request to pick us up until *after* the bullets and napalm had missed."

McGarvey rewarded me with a brief nod of his head. "An interesting observation, Frederickson, and it's noted," he said in a flat voice. "But you let me worry about my safety."

"Captain, let us ponder this problem together. Why don't you tell me what government agency told you that we're wanted on espionage charges?"

"Frederickson, why do you want to play games with me?"

"Is that what I'm doing? Maybe I just want the two of us to reach some unpleasant conclusions together. And whatever happened to the Miranda rule? Aren't Garth and I entitled to the services of a lawyer?"

"We have a right to hold you for forty-eight hours; this is a special case. Do you want a lawyer?"

"It's a moot question. There's no way Garth and I are going to be allowed to talk to a lawyer, and you know it."

"If you're innocent, it's in your interests to talk to me, Frederickson."

"Okay, let me ponder the problem by myself. First, let me assure you that Garth and I are perfectly happy to be sitting here in your lockup. We're a hell of a lot safer here than we would be out on the streets. In fact, I'm surprised that we're still here; I wouldn't be surprised to find out that you're stepping on some very big toes right now, because you were under pressure to turn us over to the other interested party yesterday, right after you arrested us. Am I right?"

Captain McGarvey said nothing, but the trooper's face now revealed a great deal; he was a commanding officer who feared that his organization and men were being used, and didn't like it.

"Now I think we may be getting somewhere," I continued quietly. "Captain, if you had turned us over, Garth and I would be dead right now. Up to this point, we probably owe you our lives. If I'm right, you were perfectly willing to cooperate fully with the people who called you—except for one thing. You didn't believe the story they told you, and that stuck in your craw. There were too many unanswered questions, and you figured that the New York State Police have a right to know what's going on in their own state—especially when it involves firebombing in the Catskills and seven dead men. That's really what this interrogation is all about, isn't it? It's personal."

McGarvey stared at me for some time, then nodded slightly. "All right, Frederickson, I'll give you that," he said simply. "I am asking these questions for myself; I don't like being jerked around. Even if you were to say something incriminating, it wouldn't be admissible precisely because you don't have a lawyer."

"In that case, I do believe I want to tell you what's going on."

McGarvey reached over to turn on the tape recorder, which gave me a little time to think. I needed it; I knew where I wanted to go with the trooper, but wasn't at all sure how I wanted to get there. I wasn't about to lay out everything I knew or suspected just for McGarvey, and there was no way I was going to implicate Veil in the killings of the commandos or anyone else. At the same time,

I had to present a good enough case so that McGarvey would continue to act as a buffer between Garth and me, and Madison's men. I was going to have to do a lot of improvising and hope I didn't get tripped up.

"You say you've heard of me, so you know I hire out as a private investigator," I continued. "A month ago I was given a rather large retainer by the Senate committee charged with investigating the president's cabinet nominees."

"Why hire you, Frederickson? Why wouldn't the committee use its own staff investigators?"

"Because the specific matter the senators wanted investigated was extremely sensitive, and they were afraid of leaks if their own people did it. There were persistent rumors that the nominee for secretary of state—"

"Orville Madison, the C.I.A. guy?" I'd gotten McGarvey's undivided attention.

"Right. The rumors were to the effect that Madison has, or had, a long-standing connection with people in organized crime, specifically with one of your local boys—Liu Sakh Po."

McGarvey frowned, leaned forward, and placed his forearms on his desk. "Po was murdered a few days ago. We'd been trying for the better part of a year to put together a case against the bastard that would stick."

"I'm aware of that, Captain, and so was the Senate. One of the rumors was to the effect that Madison had been receiving money for years from Po, in payment for Madison's having helped him enter this country secretly—and probably illegally—after the war, and then helping him to get back into business. In other words, it looked like the nominee for secretary of state might have been getting a piece of the action from Po's whorehouses and drug rings. On the other hand, the president had made clear that he was committed to Madison's nomination unless and until any of the rumors were proved to be true. I think you can understand why the committee wanted to bring in an outsider with a reputation for both fair-mindedness and discretion. Anyway, I got the gig. At the time, I thought it was because I must have been living right; that is no longer my thought."

"That's a very heavy tale, Frederickson."

"Yeah. Now I think it might be a good idea if you turned off the tape recorder."

He did. "Where does your brother come into it? He's a cop, not a P.I."

"Soon after I got started on the case, two men tried to kill me. Obviously, they missed, but they did manage to burn down the apartment building where I live. Five people died in the fire, which made it a case of arson and murder. Garth was assigned to the case; since it was connected with my investigation, we decided to tag along together."

"Who do you think was trying to kill you?"

"At first, I assumed it was Po overreacting to the fact that I wanted to investigate his business operations and political connections."

"Po's dead," McGarvey said curtly. "And those weren't Albany mobsters we found dead up in the mountains—not with camouflage fatigues, night-vision goggles, and Uzi submachine guns. They were equipped like combat soldiers."

"Indeed."

"What were you and your brother doing up there in the first place?"

"We'd received a tip that there was an emotionally disturbed veteran living by himself up there, a man by the name of Gary Worde. We were told that Worde might have invaluable information on the connection between Po and Madison."

"Who gave you the tip?"

"It was an anonymous caller. Still, Garth and I figured it was worth our time to go looking for him."

"Did you find him?"

"No; it was a wild goose chase. If there is somebody living up there, we sure as hell couldn't find him; however, as you've noticed, somebody certainly managed to find us. The phone call had to be part of a trap; we were set up. We were wandering around up there, and the next thing we knew there was a plane dropping napalm and people shooting at us."

"I don't believe the two of you killed all those men."

"You believe right."

"Who did kill them?"

"I don't know. We never saw six of the seven men you mentioned, except when they parachuted from the airplane, and the guy we took the Uzi off was dead when we found him."

"Who's Veil Kendry?"

"Never heard of him; the name doesn't mean anything to me."

"What about the two Con Ed men you killed?"

An unpleasant surprise, always a danger in improvisation. Some very nasty, fanged chickens were coming home to roost; Madison was pulling out all the stops. "It's true that I killed two men who were inside a Consolidated Edison van, but they were assassins, not utility workers, and they were trying very hard to kill me. As far as I know, the matter's under routine investigation. Naturally, I made a complete statement, and a report was filed."

"Strange; nobody seems able to find the report."

"It'll turn up. You know how bogged down the police can get with paperwork; things get misplaced."

McGarvey grunted noncommittally. "You and your brother disappeared a few years ago, Frederickson, and you didn't surface for better than a year. You want to tell me where you were?"

A huge, ice-cold fist clenched around my heart and began to squeeze, making it difficult for me to breathe. "No, Captain," I replied simply, "I do not."

That raised McGarvey's eyebrows again. "Oh? Why not?"

"Because where we were, and what happened to us, has absolutely nothing to do with this matter. I can't speak about it."

"You mean you won't speak about it."

"As you wish."

"Were you in Russia?"

"I love it!" I said, and laughed. Laughter was the next best thing to whistling through this particular potential graveyard. Garth and I were in a lot of trouble, and I knew it. Madison had been doing his homework, and he'd concocted quite a dossier on us. "That must be some report you got. The problem is that it's fiction; with any kind of promotion, it should make the best-seller list."

"Answer the question," McGarvey said in a considerably sharper tone of voice than he'd been using up to this point. He had the look of a man who thought he was about to close the books on a matter that was important to him. "Were you and your brother in Russia for that year?"

"Not likely, Captain."

"I think you were, Frederickson. I think you were with Veil Kendry, and you were being trained as agents."

"To do what?"

"You were trained to train others to become experts in urban guerrilla warfare."

I sighed, shook my head. Madison had carefully crafted a pastiche of facts and lies, sense and nonsense, that could keep Garth and me answering questions for a very long time—time we didn't have. I had no idea what McGarvey had told Madison's people to explain why he was refusing to turn us over to them, but the excuse wasn't going to last much longer. The trooper was almost convinced that we were guilty of whatever we'd been charged with, which meant that I had to find a way of bringing the game with McGarvey to an end, and in the process somehow get us sprung. I really had nothing to play with, and so I decided to play one card that had already proved valueless once, and follow it with another that was only a joker. After that, there would be nothing left to do but sit quietly at the table and see what might happen.

"Captain," I said, uncrossing my legs and leaning forward in my chair, "let's cut through this. I was hired by the Senate committee because of my reputation for discretion, but enough is enough. I'm going to give you a telephone number known by perhaps only a dozen people in the world. It's a private, direct line to the office of a man by the name of Lippitt."

"Never heard of him."

"You're not supposed to have heard of him, any more than you were supposed to have heard of Orville Madison before he was nominated as secretary of state. Lippitt is the Director of the Defense Intelligence Agency, and he'll tell you that most of what you've read in that report you received is bullshit. You might also mention the trouble we're in, and tell him we'd appreciate a personal visit from him as soon as possible."

"Will this Lippitt tell me where the two of you were for that year?"

"I doubt it strongly."

"But he knows?"

"He'll assure you that we weren't in Russia," I replied, and gave him Lippitt's number. "After you call him, place a call to Senator Kathleen Wyndham. She's—"

"I know who Senator Wyndham is, Frederickson."

"Good. She's the head of the Senate committee investigating the nominees, which makes her my boss. You make sure you talk to her, not anybody else; tell her everything that's happened here."

"You have a number for a direct line to her?" McGarvey sounded impressed.

"I had it, but I lost the slip of paper somewhere up in the mountains. Make sure you tell her that I've been digging very deeply into Orville Madison's background and have found some very disturbing things." I paused, took a deep breath. "Tell her I said there's an Archangel looking over her shoulder."

The trooper frowned. "What the hell does that mean?"

"It's just a code, so that she'll know the message comes from me. Tell the senator that I'd like to see *her* personally just as soon as possible. Tell her there's a great deal at stake, and that it's a matter of life and death—literally. Would you like me to make the calls myself?"

McGarvey shook his head, as I'd known he would. "Do you really believe that a United States senator is going to drop everything she's doing in order to hop aboard a plane and fly here to see you?"

"If you say everything I've asked you to say, and if you tell her there's an Archangel looking over her shoulder, I certainly hope so."

"Who do you think sent those men after you up in those mountains, Frederickson?"

"Captain, earlier I said that I wanted us to arrive at some unpleasant truths together. We've arrived. After everything I've just told you, you know damn well who tried to kill us up in the mountains; it's the same man who tried to kill me earlier and ended up burning five people to death; it's the same man who blew up an entire family in Seattle simply because they knew the truth about him. It also happens to be the same man who's demanding that you turn Garth and me over to his people, so that they can kill us. We're talking about Orville Madison himself."

"You're full of shit, Frederickson," McGarvey said; but the blood had drained from his face.

"Am I? I'm sorry to put you between a rock and a hard place, Captain, but the decisions you make in the next few hours will determine whether Garth and I live or die. The request to pick us up and turn us over came from the C.I.A., didn't it?"

"Frederickson, I—"

"Don't bother denying it, McGarvey, because I know it's true. Now, it's the F.B.I. that's responsible for counterintelligence, not the C.I.A., and the F.B.I. gets very touchy about incursions into its territory. You know that too. Orville Madison was head of the dirtiest department in the agency, and he'll remain with the C.I.A. pending his confirmation. What he's been doing isn't exactly standard operating procedure, and so he's had to use a string of operatives who are absolutely loyal to him personally. He's running out of those kinds of operatives; if he weren't, he never would have involved the New York State Police. He never counted on you having the guts to hold us and ask a few questions for yourself."

McGarvey, still very pale, was silent for a long time. "Do you realize what you're saying?" he asked at last.

"That President Shannon's nominee for secretary of state is a cold-blooded, psychotic killer who'll do anything to cover up certain things in his past? Of course I realize what I'm saying."

"Why didn't you tell me all this at the beginning?"

"Would you have believed me, before I had a chance to point out certain things you could think over?"

"What makes you think I believe you now?"

"Madison is counting on you not believing Garth and me. I'm counting on you continuing to do the right thing; if you do, I think there's a good chance we can nail this guy. Oh, and by the way: it was Madison who had Po killed. For that job, he used a kind of super-assassin he'd hired from outside the C.I.A."

"That's crazy, Frederickson."

"It's the truth."

"What kind of hard evidence do you have to back up any of this?"

"Let's get Mr. Lippitt or Senator Wyndham here. Or you can set up a conference call where we can all talk and listen."

"You're holding something back on me, Frederickson," McGarvey said in a low, slightly menacing voice. "That isn't a very good idea."

"Captain, why don't you go make those calls?"

19

Waiting; trying to remember all the lies I had told so that I could repeat them if I had to, hoping I'd done the right thing in offering up a decidedly bent version of the truth. Garth, whose cell I now shared, wasn't so sure.

"If you were going to talk to him at all, why didn't you just tell him all of it, straight?"

I winced at the loudness of Garth's voice. Putting my finger to my lips, I walked around the cell, checking the walls, ceiling, and under the cots for anything that might be a listening device. I didn't find any—which didn't mean there weren't any there. I motioned him toward the sink, where I turned on the faucet. "Where would you have had me start?" I asked in a low voice. "With a newly elected president coming to town? A bullet hole in a window? A painting and ten thousand dollars in a hidden compartment? How about a white-eyed *ninja* who seems to be able to appear and disappear at will? Come on. If I'd started trying to explain how and why Veil is the center of gravity in this particular universe, I'd have had to talk about all the killing *he's* done up to this point, and then get into the whole Archangel business."

Garth shrugged. "So?"

"So the way I handled it seemed like a good idea at the time," I replied, making no effort to hide my irritation and impatience. "My version played a whole hell of a lot better than the truth would have. Besides, Veil's the only ally we have at the moment, and he doesn't need a horde of state troopers and F.B.I. agents looking for him in addition to Henry Kitten and Madison's people. Veil's discredited, remember? Bringing him into it would only have made a bad situation worse."

"Ally? You've always had a weird way of looking at the world. He's responsible for this shit."

"Funny, I thought Orville Madison was responsible."

"Kendry's responsible for *you* being in the situation you're in."

"What, are you visiting this cell as a tourist?"

"I don't give a shit about myself, and you know it. Besides, I ended up here working in an official capacity."

"We've been through this before, Garth, and there's no sense in playing it all through again. I took his money, didn't I?"

"To put it in the bank for him. He sandbagged you. The trap he set may have been subtle, but it was still a trap."

"Asking a friend for help isn't setting a trap."

"He knew what would happen."

"Drop it, Garth. What's done is done."

" 'Dropped' is what we're going to be when Lippitt won't talk to McGarvey, and your Senator Wyndham—*if* he can even get hold of her—tells him that your story about being hired by her committee is a fairy tale."

"Don't be such a Goddamn pessimist. Besides, what difference would it have made if I *had* told McGarvey about Veil, Gary Worde, and the Archangel plan? We'd still have had to run some kind of game on McGarvey if we hoped to get somebody from Washington to bring us in. Lippitt was worth another try, and gambling on Wyndham having some brains and suspicions didn't seem like a bad bet. I couldn't think of anything else."

"You'll never pull this one off, Mongo. I'm not saying you were wrong; I'm just saying it won't work."

It wasn't going to take long to discover whether or not Garth had a gift for prophecy. Approaching footsteps echoed in the corridor. I didn't like their sound, staccato-quick, like drumbeats of anger.

McGarvey's face, when he appeared in front of our cell, was pale with fury. "I gave you the benefit of the doubt, you bastard," he said to me in a trembling voice. He clenched, unclenched his fists. "That's a mistake I'm happy to say I won't ever have the opportunity to make again. What the *hell* did you think you'd accomplish by shoveling all that bullshit at me? Did you think I was a fool? Didn't you think I'd actually make the calls? Did you think that because of your reputation I'd just open the doors and let you walk out if you pitched me just any old story? I take what you did as a personal insult, Frederickson."

"Captain, I—"

"Shut up! I don't want to hear any more lies! That first number you gave me isn't even working. There is no 'Mr. Lippitt,' is there?"

So Mr. Lippitt was still out to lunch, and apparently intended to stay there until the Archangel matter was resolved, one way or another. The old man who had played such an important part in our lives, the irascible and tenacious fighter whom even Garth had come to consider a friend, had even unplugged his phone. Perhaps, I thought, it was understandable. Lippitt and Madison were, after all, colleagues in the close-knit covert intelligence community, and had been for years. Lippitt had probably known Madison longer than he had known Garth and me, and the two men could well be drinking buddies. Mr. Lippitt just didn't want to get involved.

Strike one.

"Senator Wyndham says you're trying to make a fool out of me," McGarvey continued. "She just laughed when I asked if her committee had hired you to investigate Madison."

"Did you mention the Archangel?"

"She didn't know what I was talking about."

So much for what I'd dared hope might be a thorough Senate investigation.

Strike two.

McGarvey continued, "The fact that Orville Madison was confirmed as secretary of state this morning made it seem even funnier to the senator, Frederickson. She didn't ask how I felt. Now I'm going to do what I should have done in the first place, which is to turn you over to the people who know how to deal with spies."

Orville Madison's men must have been camped out in the parking lot all night, because it wasn't ten minutes after we'd received the bad news from the captain when a trooper came into our cell, cuffed our hands behind our backs, and led us out of the lockup area to the front of the building where four big, unshaven men in business suits were waiting. The exchange was short and simple. Nothing was said. Papers were signed, and Garth and I were led outside to separate cars, both late-model Chevrolets.

Madison's men were apparently not interested in our personal belongings or the contents of our backpacks, for there was no sign of them. There was always the possibility that the packs had already been placed in the trunk of one of the cars, but I doubted it; the men had gotten what they'd come for. Whatever was in the yellow oilskin packet I'd taken off Gary Worde's body, I was glad I hadn't told McGarvey about it. Someday, in some way, the truth about Orville Madison might still come out.

There was also some consolation, if not a great deal, in the knowledge that the men who killed us would almost certainly die themselves, in a most unpleasant fashion. Veil was still free. I suspected that Orville Madison's tenure as secretary of state was going to be a short one, which made me happy. What made me unhappy was the thought that he would almost certainly be honored as a martyr after Veil killed him.

As we approached the cars, I turned to look at Garth, to say good-bye, but I was rudely shoved forward, slammed into the back seat of the first car. One of the two men accompanying me slid onto the seat beside me, while the other got behind the wheel. The driver started up the car, pulled out of the parking lot. I looked back, saw the car with Garth in it following close behind.

"I take it we're finally going to meet Secretary Madison," I said carefully. "I assume he wants to know all we have to tell him about where to find Veil Kendry."

Fat chance. The man beside me, who was red-eyed from lack of sleep and smelled slightly of body odor, just kept staring straight ahead. We pulled onto the southbound lanes of the Thruway and drove along at exactly fifty-five miles per hour, as silent as the funeral cortege we were. Orville Madison would know that we didn't have the slightest idea where Veil was, and so it was only a question of where, and in what manner, they intended to kill us.

As we drove along, I found myself looking out the window at the passing landscape, savoring the sight of trees and grass and sky for what I assumed would be the last time. It was an exceptionally bright day for February, and I was sorry I would not see spring.

It seemed an excellent time for the cavalry to arrive, but there wasn't even a car in sight, much less a horse. There was the sound of sirens far in the distance, behind us, but that didn't seem important; it wouldn't make much sense for the State Police to turn us over to the bad guys only to try and get us back a few minutes later.

But the sirens kept coming closer, and no car that the State Police might be pursuing sped past us. In the rearview mirror, I could see the driver glance up nervously, while the man beside me turned around in his seat and looked back.

"Something's gone wrong," my seat partner said tensely. "They're after us."

"Kill him," the driver said in a flat voice.

"We can't! What excuse can we give?"

"Not our problem; Madison will get us out, probably on some national security angle. But we have our orders. We don't want bullet holes or blood; use your hands."

He used his hands, leaning over in the seat and wrapping them around my neck. I used my foot, or more precisely the toe of my shoe, kicking up hard into the man's groin. His eyes bulged, his breath exploded from his lungs in a kind of whoop, and his hands came away from my throat and went to his crotch. As he bent forward, his throat was exposed. I lunged forward and sank my teeth into his jugular.

"What the hell—?!"

I heard the driver's startled shout over the strangled cries of the man whose throat I was biting. He clawed at my back and head, but I stayed fastened to his throat and bit down hard. I felt my teeth sink through his flesh, then into the tough walls of the carotid artery. Working my head back and forth like a terrier, I kept gnawing. Then blood spurted, filling my mouth and splashing over my face. I jerked my head back and ducked away just as the driver, struggling to control the speeding car with one hand, reached over the back seat with his gun and fired off a shot. The bullet missed me, hit the shoulder of the man whose life was gushing out through the tear in his throat.

I could hear two distinct sets of sirens now, two trooper cars continuing to gain on us. I had no way of knowing what was going on in the car behind, but I had to assume that those men had made a similar decision, to kill Garth. Considering my brother's size, I didn't think they'd be overly concerned about blood or bullet holes; they'd simply shoot him, if they hadn't already. Sooner or later the driver of the car I was in was going to put a bullet in me, unless I could find a way of putting him out of commission. With my hands cuffed behind my back, I had no choice but to use my whole body as a weapon and shoot for the moon.

I stood up on the back seat, then, as the driver's revolver again swung around in my direction, bounced up and over into the front seat, landing head first in the driver's lap and stripping his hand from the wheel. The car immediately went out of control, into a shrieking power slide. I rolled over into the passenger's seat, slid down onto the base of my spine, and planted both feet on the dashboard just as the car hit the shoulder, abruptly stopped skidding, and began to roll. Pushing with all my might against the dashboard, I closed my eyes and held my breath as the car bounced and rolled in a bone-jarring, kaleidoscopic cascade of nauseating motion and a cacophony of shattering glass, snapping plastic, and tearing metal. Through it all, I somehow managed to stay braced in my position.

Finally, what was left of the car came to a rest. Glass tinkled, metal groaned, steam hissed. Slowly, I opened my eyes, saw the reason why my back felt ready to break and the muscles in my legs ready to tear loose from their joints; I was upside down. I couldn't see the man who had been in the back seat with me, but I thought it quite safe to assume he was dead. I also found it immensely satisfying to see that, while the driver's seat belt had kept him securely fastened in his seat, the steering column had collapsed in on him and crushed his chest. Powdered safety glass was everywhere, covering the interior of the car—and me—like sharp, scratchy snow. There was pain in every muscle and bone in my body, but it was welcome pain; it meant my back hadn't been broken. Indeed, I doubted that anything major was broken; if it were, I wouldn't have been able to remain braced. I accepted the pain as a celebration of life.

From somewhere outside my disoriented, upside-down universe, I heard the sound of gunfire and felt sick at the thought that my brother might be dead. At the same time I smelled gasoline, and knew I was likely to be dead very soon myself if I didn't get out of the wreck fast. I relaxed the tension in my legs and dropped the short distance to the inverted roof of the car, landing on my left shoulder and crumpling into a heap.

I'd always had excellent control of my body, and years in the circus combined with the training Veil and other martial artists had given me had allowed me to expand and refine that control to a high degree. I used that control now to arch my back and drop my right shoulder almost to the point of dislocation; that allowed me to draw my cuffed hands under my hips and down the length of my legs, putting them in front of me. I searched through the glass and twisted metal, got lucky and found one of the men's guns. I made a quick, rolling exit out through the gaping hole left by the shattered windshield, got to my feet, and ran as fast as I could away from the car just seconds before it exploded, knocking me to the ground. I rolled over onto my belly, ducked, and hunched my shoulders against the flaming debris and black smoke that rained and swirled around me, pointed the gun in what I hoped was the general direction of the highway.

What I saw when the smoke cleared didn't look good. The second Chevrolet had skidded to a stop at a sharp angle off the side of the highway, and Madison's men were behind it, their backs to me, trading gunfire with four troopers who were shielded by their own cars, forty or fifty yards away.

There was no sign of Garth.

I raised the gun with my cuffed hands, carefully sighted down the barrel on the back of one of the men, and shot him between the shoulder blades. His arms flew up in the air as he arched and fell stiffly backward. Startled, the second man ducked away from the trooper's fire, turned, and saw me at the same time as I squeezed off two shots; one bullet caught him in the face, the other in the chest. I was up and running even before he hit the ground.

Fortunately for me, the troopers had stopped firing when the two men had disappeared from sight. My muscles fueled by fear at what I might find inside the Chevrolet, I sprinted up the slight incline, yanked open a rear door on the bullet-scarred car. To my immense relief, I found Garth huddled on the floor, where he had rolled in order to avoid the hail of bullets. He appeared unhurt, and his eyes went wide with both joy and concern when he saw me.

"Mongo! You're shot!"

At first I didn't understand, until I looked down and realized that I was covered with blood. "I had to take a little nip out of a guy," I said as I dropped the gun and grabbed two handfuls of Garth's parka and helped him out of the car. "It's his blood, not mine."

The four troopers, with Captain McGarvey in the lead, came running toward us, guns drawn, along the shoulder of the highway. When McGarvey saw us walk out from behind the car, he abruptly stopped and holstered his gun, motioning for the others to do the same. Then McGarvey walked slowly toward us, disbelief written all over his face as he stared at me.

"Frederickson," the captain said, "how the hell did you survive that car crash?"

"Oh, that? Surviving flaming car crashes is just a routine part of Russian spy training. You'd be amazed how many candidates they mash or burn up before they get somebody like me who can do it right."

McGarvey didn't smile. "Are you all right? You're covered with blood."

"Like I was telling Garth, most of it doesn't belong to me. How about getting our cuffs off?"

"Sorry, Frederickson," McGarvey mumbled as he produced a set of keys from his pocket and freed my hands, then Garth's. "I still don't understand what's going on, but you were certainly on target when you said I shouldn't turn you over to those men."

"Don't worry about being sorry," I said as a trooper brushed past me and walked to join one of his colleagues, who was angrily waving on rubbernecking drivers. "I'm just happy you changed your mind and came after us."

"I wish I could take credit for changing my mind, but that's not what happened. We got a call five minutes after those guys drove off with you. There's someone who wants to talk to you."

"Who?"

"Come on," McGarvey said, motioning for us to follow him to the trooper cars. "There's a good motel a few miles back where you can clean up and get some rest. The rooms will be courtesy of New York State."

"We need our backpacks."

"No. Everything we have stays with us for the time being. If you'll give me your sizes, I'll see that you get fresh clothes—also courtesy of New York State."

"Hold on a minute," I said, stopping, then taking a step backward to stand beside Garth. "Your concern is touching, Captain, and I mean no disrespect to you when I say that you must have received one whopper of a phone call. Who was on the other end *this* time, and who wants to talk to us?"

"You'll see."

"What the hell does that mean?"

"It means I can't tell you, Frederickson," McGarvey said in a slightly embarrassed tone. "Give me a break."

"Give *you* a break?! Damn, Captain, I love your material. Are we still under arrest?"

"No . . . uh, not technically."

"Still, if it's all the same to you, we'll pass on the motel and save the state some money. We're safer in your lockup; you can leave the cell doors open if it makes you feel better."

McGarvey shook his head. "They want you in a hotel or motel —the best. We'll put a guard on you."

"How long will it be before we get to meet this person?"

"I don't know."

"What do you know?"

"Whoever it is has to come from Washington. Besides that, all I've been told is that you're to be well taken care of."

The thought of a hot shower, a good meal, clean sheets and a soft bed was certainly inviting—but I couldn't help but remember what had happened to Colonel Po when Orville Madison had decided to pay Henry Kitten's fee for an "extra assignment." If Henry Kitten were to be sicced on us, the assassin would also find the thought of us in a hotel or motel inviting.

"We still prefer the lockup," I said.

"No."

"Remember what happened when you didn't listen to me before?"

"This is different. I have my orders. I told you we'll put a guard on you."

"One guard won't do. We'll need one outside our door, one on the roof, and one outside the window on the ground. Our room will have to be on the top floor. When you hear what I have to tell you—"

"Hold it right there, Frederickson," McGarvey said, putting up his hand. "You can have anything you want, including as many guards as you think you need. But I don't want to hear what you have to tell me—not now. I'm not even supposed to talk to you, beyond what I've already said, and I'm not supposed to listen to anything you have to say."

20

We were taken to a motel just off the Thruway, no more than a mile or two from the trooper substation. Caked with blood and mud and sprinkled liberally with powdered glass, I looked like nothing so much as a grisly variation on some Wednesday night special at the local ice cream parlor; we were taken to our suite of rooms through a back entrance so as not to shock any early guests who might be a tad taken aback by my appearance. The captain was a fast shopper, because he was back with new clothes by the time we'd pulled ourselves out of our hot tubs. He'd also brought our wallets and the rest of our personal belongings, but not our guns or backpacks. We ordered a pitcher of martinis and lunch to be brought to our suite. We ate, checked—rather blearily, to be sure—to make sure our guards were in place, then lay down to take a nap. We had barely fallen asleep when the phone rang. A driver was waiting for us downstairs.

We were taken back to the substation, ushered into McGarvey's small but nicely appointed office in an administrative wing of the substation, and left alone. Garth paced while I eased myself down into the captain's red leather swivel chair and propped my feet up on the edge of his desk.

"Well, looky here," Garth said dryly as he stopped by a window that looked out over a small auxiliary parking lot adjacent to the administrative wing.

"I'm comfortable. Describe it to me."

"One long, black limousine with smoked windows, one uniformed chauffeur, two trim, mean-looking guys with walkie-talkies."

"Sounds like Secret Service."

"Could be. The door to the limousine is open, and the help look like they're just hanging out. I wonder where our esteemed visitor is."

"Probably talking to McGarvey, finding out what we said to him and precisely what happened."

"What's our strategy with this guy, brother?" Garth asked quietly.

"A good question; I'm not sure of the answer. We're still a long way from home, and I'm pretty sure we still have miles to go before we sleep. The administration has finally gotten a whiff of what Orville Madison really smells like, but that doesn't mean we're going to be awarded any medals. On the contrary; there are going to be a lot of people rushing to cover their own asses, while at the same time they do everything in their power to protect Kevin Shannon. This guy's here to assess how much damage we could inflict if we wanted to, and to try to gauge our attitudes. I think we'll just have to wait and hear what he has to say, and play it by ear."

"Agreed."

Fifteen minutes later the female trooper opened the door and ushered in a youngish-looking man in his mid or late thirties. He was lean, with a full head of razor-cut brown hair and large brown eyes. Elegantly dressed in a three-piece black pinstripe suit, he wore highly polished Gucci shoes that matched his black leather attaché case. He looked decidedly uncomfortable as the trooper closed the door behind him, leaving him alone with us.

I immediately recognized the man as Burton Andrews, a baby-faced troubleshooter whose star had rapidly risen because of his ability to bash state committees into line during the campaign and bash delegates into line during the convention. He had a reputation for single-minded loyalty to Kevin Shannon, and now carried the title of Personal Aide to the President. There was no doubt in my mind that the aide had been dispatched to a trooper substation near Albany to try to bash us into line, regardless of what we had to say, or what we might think.

Andrews kept switching his attaché case from one hand to the other as he glanced back and forth between Garth and me. I suspected he was waiting for me to get up and offer him the swivel chair; he would have a very long wait. Garth had settled down into the second most comfortable chair in the office, and it was obvious that he wasn't moving either. Andrews, a man used to power and its accoutrements, as well as the deference of others, was going to have to sit in a metal folding chair, which he did after a few more moments of case and foot shuffling. He placed both feet flat on the floor, rested the attaché case on his knees, and folded his hands on top of the case.

The presidential aide coughed nervously, cleared his throat. "My name is Burton Andrews. I've . . . uh, I've heard a great deal about the two of you."

Garth and I looked at each other, then back at Andrews. We said nothing, but Andrews must have seen something in our faces, because his own face reddened. "Forgive me, gentlemen," he continued. "I know that we have a great deal to discuss, and that you're certainly not in the mood for chitchat. It's just that it's very difficult knowing how or where to begin."

"Begin by cutting out the bullshit," Garth said in a voice that was a low rumble from his chest. "The first thing we want to know is what your boss has done about that fucking madman Orville Madison. He damn well better be locked up someplace."

Andrews' face grew even redder, and he began to fumble nervously with the handle of his attaché case. "Gentlemen, obviously all of us in the administration are aware that we have a serious crisis on our hands. I wouldn't be here otherwise, would I?"

"Crisis?" Garth said in a voice that I knew was deceptively mild, like the eye of a hurricane. "What fucking crisis? We're not talking about any crisis. Are we talking about a crisis, Mongo?"

"No, Garth, we're not talking about any crisis."

"Andrews, what have you done about Madison? *That's* what we're talking about. Try to pay attention."

"I don't think I care for your tone of voice, Lieutenant," Andrews said to my brother, his own tone slightly petulant.

"You're not listening, Andrews," I said, waggling my feet at the aide. Slouched in the swivel chair, I could just see over the desk into Andrews' face. I felt shielded from all the power Andrews had brought with him into the room, and I liked it that way; I made no effort to sit up straighter. "Garth's point, which I believe he has been most patient in trying to make, is that we don't care pigshit about the administration's political problems as a result of this business, which is what *you* mean when you talk about a crisis. A lot of innocent people are dead, and Orville Madison's men, acting under his direct orders, killed them. Since Orville Madison is the president's responsibility, we would like to know what Kevin Shannon is doing about it. In short, we would like to know where Orville Madison *is* at this moment."

"I'm not your enemy, Dr. Frederickson," Andrews said in the same slightly petulant tone.

"We never said you were, Andrews. But you're certainly not our friend, either. You're the president's man, and I think you'd do just about anything to protect him—which leads me to point out that you haven't answered the question. Madison's trying very hard to kill us, you know."

"This is a very complicated matter, Dr. Frederickson."

"Answer the question, or you won't get what you came here for."

"What did I come here for?"

"To find out exactly how much we know about a number of things, and what we intend to do with the information. Now, can you guarantee our safety?"

"Yes," Andrews replied curtly. "I might point out that neither of you would be alive at this moment if it weren't for the president."

"That's who called McGarvey?"

"I called; the president authorized the call."

"How did he find out where we were and what was going on?"

"I think we may be getting ahead of ourselves," Andrews said in a low, strained voice, averting his gaze. "I'm not certain we yet know exactly what's been going on."

"Bullshit," Garth said evenly.

I asked, "How did you find out we were here?"

"We . . . received word."

"From whom?"

"We just received word."

"You've spoken to Captain McGarvey. You know what's happened here, and you must certainly understand that Orville Madison's men intended to kill us."

"I understand that the two of you have made a lot of allegations and may be prepared to make more."

"Allegations," Garth murmured, looking up at the ceiling. "Great word."

"I can prove those were Orville Madison's men who came to get us," I said to the presidential aide as I swung my feet to the floor, sat up in the chair, and leaned forward on the desk. "I can prove Madison's involvement in thirteen murders, and I can demonstrate his reasons for ordering them to be carried out."

"Can you, really?" Burton Andrews' eyebrows lifted ever so slightly.

"Beyond a reasonable doubt, yes—to reasonable men who care about the truth and want to see justice done, regardless of the consequences. I'm not sure you fit into that category, which is why I see no reason for trying to prove it to you; a Senate hearing would be a more proper forum. You have no legal status, Andrews. You're just a high-powered errand boy sent here to assess what measures have to be taken to assure optimum damage control. Maybe we'll help you contain that damage, maybe we won't. We don't like your attitude. We've been through a gauntlet of death and destruction set up by Shannon's secretary of state, and we've watched a lot of good people—men, women, and children—die because of that maniac. Then, a couple of hours after Madison almost kills us, you show up and want to play games. You'd be well advised to play straight with us. Otherwise, Garth and I take a hike—maybe to the newspapers."

"We should have you negotiating with the Russians, Frederickson," Andrews said wryly.

"Fuck you. What do you want from us?"

"You'd go to the newspapers with your so-called proof?"

"There's nothing 'so-called' about it. Is that what we're doing? Negotiating?"

"See what I mean? You'd be a tough man to bargain with—if we were bargaining. Tell me what your proof is. Show it to me."

"First admit that the president knows that Orville Madison is a murderer, and then tell me what's being done about it. Is Madison under arrest?"

Andrews' answer was to snap open the case in his lap. A vein pulsed in his temple as he took out a sheet of paper, which he did not offer to show to either Garth or me. "Dr. Frederickson," the baby-faced man said stiffly, "you filed a petition under the Freedom of Information Act for certain documents concerning any and all operations in the Viet Nam war under the general code name Archangel. You also requested the 'true and original'—your words —service records of one Veil Kendry. Is that correct?"

"If you know that, am I to assume that the materials I requested are waiting for me at home in my mailbox?"

"I would doubt it very much, Frederickson. First of all, it often takes months—sometimes years—to process petitions like yours.

In addition, as you may or may not know, the information you request is highly classified. Your petition will eventually be denied."

"Then why bring it up?"

"Because even a request for such information could make some people question your motives."

"My motives were to shake up certain people and get their attention; it seems to have worked. In any case, I don't need any of your documents; Garth and I already know all we need to know about Archangel."

"Do you, really?"

"Yes. Do you know about Archangel, Andrews?"

"How did you get mixed up with this man, Veil Kendry?"

"Am I mixed up with him?"

"You asked for his service records."

"He's a friend of mine."

"What do you know—or think you know—about Kendry?"

"Let me tell you something about Veil Kendry, Andrews," I said softly. "He is, or was, Archangel, and there are two songs this Archangel sings. One song is of gentle, almost aching beauty; the other is of savagery, violence, and death." I paused, then—curious as to what his reaction might be—raised my right hand and waggled my thumb at him. "You know what I mean?"

He knew what I meant. The presidential aide's face went pale, and he quickly looked away. For a moment I thought he was going to be sick, but he contented himself with taking a series of deep breaths. It meant that, while the first five thumbs had almost certainly gone to Orville Madison, the last batch, from the commandos in the mountains, had gone directly to the Oval Office along with a detailed report on everything that had happened since the night of the president's speech at the Waldorf, and perhaps with a list of certain demands. It explained the president's quick action in having Andrews call the trooper substation. Veil had saved our lives once again, this time through the mails.

"If your boss got the thumbs," I continued, "it means he also got a report on what Madison has been up to. What does the president think of his secretary of state now?"

"Please," Andrews said, a pained expression on his face. "He's not going to remain as secretary of state, Frederickson. Certainly, I don't have to tell you that."

"Well, that's the first piece of good news we've had since you walked in here; but it's not *that* good. What *else* is going to happen to him? Sending him off to Martha's Vineyard with a fat pension isn't quite going to do the trick. The party's over, and it's time for you to stop playing hide and seek. We've got the goods on Madison, and you know it. Are we going to work together, or not?"

Andrews' pained expression hadn't changed; if anything, it had grown more pained. "Frederickson, surely you're sophisticated enough to know that we—"

"We?"

"The administration. We have to keep our options open. This mess could cause a great deal of trouble for a lot of innocent people."

"You mean it could cause a great deal of trouble for Kevin Shannon."

"Of course it could. But I also include the citizens of the United States of America, and our allies. This matter must be handled with discretion. Kevin Shannon is the president of our country, which makes him a symbol as well as a man."

"Not to us. Shannon's just a man with a big job. If he can't handle it, he shouldn't have run. Or he should resign."

"Have Madison killed," Garth said matter-of-factly. "Blow the son-of-a-bitch away."

They were the first words my brother had spoken in some time; he'd been staring out the window during most of my conversation with Andrews, and I hadn't even been sure he was listening. Now his words hung in the air like dark, soaring birds of prey. I thought it was a rather good suggestion, providing a full and satisfying measure of poetic justice, and I waited to see what Andrews' reaction would be.

"I'll pretend I didn't hear that, Lieutenant," the aide said after a long pause. "Making casual statements like that could get you a long term in a federal prison."

"First of all, you heard me wrong if you thought I was being casual," Garth said in the same flat tone. "Second, you have too many conflicting loyalties and interests for me to give a shit what you do, pal. You don't want this story to come out because it would embarrass your boss, which means you don't want a trial. But I guarantee you that Mongo and I aren't about to let Madison have a pass on this. So, you have him killed. Madison has made a whole career of that type of thing, so there's no reason why the favor shouldn't be returned. If you don't want to bite that bullet, hand him over to me; I'll do the job for you."

"Well, Lieutenant, let's look at some alternatives. What if I were to assure you that—"

"You can't assure us of anything, Andrews," I interrupted. "You have to *do* something. We couldn't negotiate with you over what to do with Madison, even if we wanted to. We're not the final arbiters of his fate. There's still an avenging Archangel out there, remember? And he'll stay out until this business is taken care of to *his* satisfaction, not ours. Garth's suggestion is a good one."

"Please don't mention the possibility of killing anyone again," the aide said tightly.

"What the hell was Kevin Shannon thinking of when he nominated this guy?" I asked.

"I'm really not at liberty to discuss the president or his decisions."

"Does Madison have something on him?"

Andrews stiffened. "President Shannon is his own man."

"That would make him a unique politician. Did he know about Madison's involvement in Operation Archangel before he nominated him?"

Andrews frowned. "You really do know about the Archangel plan, don't you?"

"You're damn right, I do. Want me to go through it with you?"

"No," Andrews said after a pause. "I believe you. Frankly, I've just found out the details. That, along with the statement Veil Kendry submitted to the president, was my reading material on the flight here. The Archangel plan may have been tacky, but I don't really see anything sinister in it."

"That's your opinion. But the Archangel plan itself really isn't the point, is it? It's the sequence of events that led up to Veil's defection, and then what happened after the plan fell apart; it's the death sentence Orville Madison personally imposed on Veil, and his subsequent attempt to carry it out on the eve of his nomination; it's all the carnage that's resulted from Madison's botching the assassination and then striking out in all directions in a panic because of his fear of both Veil and the truth coming out. The issue here is the punishment of a murderer. We're not saying that the president should have known about, or even guessed at, the dark side of Madison's character. Paranoid schizophrenics are usually intelligent, and they're very good at concealing their illness, especially from powerful people the paranoid schizophrenic thinks can help him."

"Oh? You're a psychiatrist in addition to all your other accomplishments, Dr. Frederickson?"

"No, Andrews, but I do happen to be a recognized authority on paranoid schizophrenia. Check it out."

"I'll take your word for it," Andrews replied dryly.

"Another characteristic of paranoid schizophrenics is that they never know enough to quit while they're ahead. Also, they love to gloat in victory over their enemies—real or imagined. Orville Madison blew it all when he decided to celebrate his nomination to one of the most powerful positions in the world by making good on a threat he'd made almost twenty years before. In effect, he engineered his own destruction. Now bury him."

"Perhaps we're trying to. But what we know, or suspect, may be very difficult to prove in a court of law. And for you two to start making what some might call wild accusations could only make matters worse. Do you see what I mean?"

"I see that you're a slippery son-of-a-bitch," Garth said. "You know we're telling the truth."

"Not the point, Lieutenant," Andrews replied without looking at Garth. "There's still not a shred of physical evidence linking Orville Madison to your troubles. There is only your word, and Veil Kendry's statement. Bear in mind that most people would brand Veil Kendry as a madman for the things *he's* done."

"Whatever he's done, Andrews, the fact is that he's given your boss ample time to clean his own house. Veil's already been betrayed once by this country. Now he has, in effect, done the work of Congress and the administration by exposing Madison for what he is. If you don't act against Madison, you'll be betraying Veil again."

"That's preposterous, Frederickson. You can't even link Madison to this Archangel plan, let alone to Veil Kendry. All the people you talked to who were supposed eyewitnesses to the events Kendry describes are dead."

"Killed by Madison."

"Proof, Frederickson. Where's the proof?"

"Damn it, there are *records*. The government has them. What the hell were you reading on the plane?"

"What I read on the plane was a brief overview of the Archangel plan, and its objectives. There were no names, no dates. The actual records are classified. As I'm sure you're aware, you can't cite classified records for reasons to subpoena classified records. You must have other evidence which the classified material may amplify."

"Find a man by the name of Lester Bean. He was a lieutenant general in the war, and he was Veil's C.O. He'll testify to the link between Orville Madison and Veil Kendry."

"Bean's name was mentioned in Kendry's statement. I made some inquiries before I came here to see you. Bean is in retirement, and nobody seems to know where he is."

Which might or might not be the truth. It didn't make any difference; the clear message was that we were not going to get any help from the administration. Dealing with Burton Andrews was growing tiresome and depressing.

"Veil Kendry *was* the Archangel plan, Andrews."

"Proof, Frederickson."

"What does Madison have to say about all this?"

Andrews shrugged. "What would you expect him to say? He claims to vaguely remember a plan for a minor public relations project that was eventually aborted, but that's all. He denies knowing anybody by the name of Veil Kendry, and says he was never involved in anything called Operation Archangel."

"You believe that?"

"What you and your brother, the president or I, believe—or even know to be true—is irrelevant. Bear in mind that Mr. Madison has occupied the highest echelons of power for a very long time and has had almost unlimited access to the files you keep talking about. I wouldn't be a bit surprised if all *those* files have been tampered with, altered; otherwise, he would have made up some kind of a cover story instead of simply denying everything."

"Your point is well taken," I said quietly.

"You said you had proof of these allegations, but it's become obvious to me that you're bluffing. Still, proof or no proof, we're left with a most serious problem which must be dealt with. It's why I've given you the assurance that Orville Madison will soon be resigning as secretary of state. Considering our position, that may be the most we can hope for. It's going to be a very delicate thing—the almost immediate resignation of a newly appointed secretary of state—to handle with the news media, and we would like *your* assurance that neither of you will be feeding the media sensational stories that could have serious repercussions on everything from the value of the dollar to our relations with our allies—not to mention the morale of our citizens. Will I be able to give the president that assurance, gentlemen?"

"Forcing Madison out of office isn't enough, Andrews," I said, wearily shaking my head. "Not nearly enough."

"Personally, the president and I might well agree with you. But even if it were in everybody's interests to do so, you couldn't go into a court of law with what you have—which is nothing."

"It won't be nearly enough for Veil Kendry, Andrews."

"But he's not here, is he?"

"He's out there someplace, very close by, waiting to see what happens. If he doesn't like what he sees, I'm sure he'll kill Orville Madison himself."

"So be it," Andrews said with a kind of verbal shrug. "But if and when this Veil Kendry ever shows his face, he's going to have plenty of his own problems to deal with. The statement he sent to the president amounts to a signed confession to murder. The man's a self-confessed multiple murderer—and a barbaric one, at that. He *admits* to killing two men in New York City, three in Seattle, and six up in the mountains."

"Veil killed the killers Madison sent. Madison is responsible for the deaths of five people in New York, and six in Seattle."

"But Mr. Madison hasn't submitted a signed confession, has he? I'd say Mr. Kendry is finished."

Andrews was probably right, I thought; Veil would be destroyed. Even if Veil killed him, Orville Madison would still have defeated Veil Kendry. And the Frederickson brothers. I'd been beaten, burned, and jerked around a lot, but as things now stood it would all have been for nothing; Veil could have gone after Madison from day one, without involving me. I wasn't earning my ten thousand dollars.

Andrews nervously cleared his throat, continued: "We both agree that you can't negotiate for Veil Kendry, Dr. Frederickson. What about negotiating for yourselves?"

"Meaning what, Andrews?"

"It's my understanding that the two of you now have some legal difficulties of your own. Even if you manage to get these problems behind you, it's quite possible that your careers could suffer irreparable damage. On the other hand, if you and the lieutenant could be counted on to continue to exercise the caution and discretion you have so admirably displayed up to this point, I wouldn't be surprised if ways could be found to extricate you from this situation without penalty so that you can get on with your careers and your lives."

A curious offer, spoken, combined with a clear threat, unspoken, of lots and lots of additional problems if we didn't go along quietly. I had a serious urge to get up, walk around the desk, and punch the other man. Instead, I said: "I wasn't bluffing before, Andrews. I can prove a solid, very personal connection between Orville Madison and Veil Kendry."

"Oh, really? And how will you do that?"

I pressed the call button on the captain's desk intercom.

"What is it, Frederickson?" It was McGarvey himself, and he sounded a bit bemused. His trooper had obviously told him that I was sitting at his desk.

"Captain, would you be kind enough to bring in my backpack? It's the smaller, brown one."

"I know which one it is, Frederickson." Suddenly the captain's voice sounded strained, unnatural.

The three of us sat in silence, waiting. Five minutes later, Mc-Garvey entered the office carrying my backpack. The burly trooper captain looked decidedly uncomfortable; his face was set in a kind of stiff mask as he walked across the room and set the backpack down on the desk in front of me. "Here you are, Frederickson," he said in a flat voice, and immediately turned away.

"Stay, if you will, Captain," I said as I repositioned the pack and snapped open the top. "I'd like you to witness this."

I dug my hand into the pack, pushed it down through dirty clothes into the middle of my bedroll, where I had stuffed the yellow oilskin packet. "Captain," I continued, "I have something here that I want you and Mr. Andrews to see. It's something that Veil Kendry had a friend bury for him up in the mountains a lot of years ago; a good forensic chemist will be able to tell us exactly how many. It will prove a link between Kendry and Madison that goes back to the war. Andrews, at the very least it will prove that Madison is lying through his teeth when he denies knowing Veil."

Wriggling my fingers, I continued to search for the feel of the oilskin, but found nothing where I thought I had put it. Fighting a growing sense of panic, I upended the pack and spread the contents out over the surface of the desk. I sifted through the dirty clothes, unrolled the sleeping bag. The packet was not there.

"There was a small package sealed in yellow oilskin inside this backpack," I said to McGarvey as I walked around the desk to stand directly in front of him. "I know it was there when you brought us in. What the hell did you do with it?"

McGarvey said nothing, but he did not avert his eyes. There was a curious expression on his face, a mixture of sympathy, embarrassment, and not a little anger. He was a man of integrity and honor, his eyes and expression said, but there was only so much he could do for us. He'd already bent far under heavy pressure once, but he was afraid he would be broken if he tried to do it this time; he could not buck the wishes—or actions—of an official presidential emissary, especially when, as had almost certainly happened, the spectral issue of national security had been raised.

Burton Andrews had been allowed to search our belongings. He had found the packet, opened it, and examined its contents. Whatever had been in the packet must have proved all I'd said it would, because the presidential aide had felt compelled to steal it.

"Dirty pool, Andrews," I said, turning to the baby-faced man with the large brown eyes who was sitting stiffly in his chair, steadfastly staring out the window. His hands were clenched tightly together on top of his briefcase. "Tough bargaining is one thing, but stealing and concealing crucial evidence in a series of crimes including murder is something else again. Now, you get your skinny ass out to the car and bring that packet back in here so that Captain McGarvey can see what's in it."

Andrews didn't move. Garth did. Deliberately, with disarming casualness, my brother rose from his chair and walked over to where the presidential aide was sitting. Sensing Garth's presence, Andrews turned his head back just in time to catch the full force of Garth's fist smashing into his face. Andrews' head snapped back as a crimson geyser of blood spewed from his shattered nose. Andrews and his chair flipped over backwards, while his attaché case and the papers it contained went flying through the air.

"My brother almost died getting that package," Garth said to the fallen man in a voice that was all the more chilling for its lack of passion, its cool, measured tone. "Maybe you should die for taking it away from him."

McGarvey and I reached Garth at about the same time, and while the trooper wrapped his arm around Garth's neck in a choke hold I went for my brother's legs, trying to trip him up. But an aroused Garth is something—or not something—to see. My brother swatted me to one side and, with McGarvey lifted off the floor and hanging on his back, bent over and cocked his fist in preparation for another blow that would really put Andrews' lights out, and possibly even kill him. I wished McGarvey would hit Garth over the head with his gun butt, but it was very obvious where the trooper's sympathies lay, and it was too late for that anyway.

"Garth, stop it!" I screamed as I pulled at my brother's belt. "Don't hit him again! You'll kill him! It doesn't make any difference that he took the packet! *I know what's in it! Nothing is lost!"*

Garth's fist stopped in midair, and his arm dropped back to his side. McGarvey took his arm away from Garth's throat, stepped back and—like my brother—stared at me quizzically.

"You do?" Garth asked softly.

I looked down at Andrews. The presidential aide was holding both hands cupped over his broken nose, but in his eyes, plainer than either shock or pain, was the same question.

"I do," I said defiantly, staring hard at Andrews. "After the Operation Archangel abort and Veil's banishment from the army by Madison, he eventually learned to control his madness through painting. From the beginning, Veil's style and technique had been to compose massive, realistic murals comprised of smaller, surrealistic canvases that appeared abstract when viewed singly. I've seen many of those murals myself—surreal landscapes, peaceful, and without people. But I realize now that his work wasn't always like that. When he first started, his *style*—but not his technique—was different.

"When I spoke to Viktor Raskolnikov, Veil's dealer, he told me that Veil's style had been different when he first started to paint; the colors were richer, more vivid, and many of the shapes in the individual canvases more pronounced. Those first shapes were fragments of portraits of people, and the subject of his first mural, or murals, was the story of what had happened to him—his assignment in Laos, his conflicts with Orville Madison, his replacement by Colonel Po, the Archangel plan, the incident with the pimp in Saigon, his defection, and, finally, his banishment and the sentence of death imposed by his ex-C.I.A. controller. All of it was included in his first work, in fine detail. You can bet that Orville Madison's face is all over the place, along with Colonel Po's, and Veil's.

"What had happened to him had to have been eating up Veil inside, but he couldn't talk about it to anyone. What he did was to *paint* it, after almost self-destructing, and that got it out of his system. Eventually he began to sell his work, but before he sold any painting he would photograph it, number the photograph, and probably record the name of the person or institution that had purchased the painting. The packet contained a photographic record—probably slides—of all the Archangel paintings, along with a number key for putting all the individual canvases back into their original sequence to form the larger mural. There would also be a list of people and museums that had the paintings. In fact, I had number one, the very first painting in the first sequence. I had it hanging on my bedroom wall, but it was lost in the fire that Madison's men started when they tried to kill me. But the rest of the paintings still exist, scattered all over the country." I paused, smiled thinly at Andrews. "How am I doing, you amoral son-of-a-bitch?"

Andrews, dripping blood all over the front of his shirt and vest, rolled over on his side, took a handkerchief from his pocket, and pressed it to his nose. "How could you know?" he said, defeat in his voice as well as his body. "The package was sealed."

McGarvey's breath came out of him in a small explosion, and the big trooper reached over and gripped my shoulder. "Goddamn," he said, a huge grin on his face.

"I'm tired of you, sleazeball," I said, leaning over Andrews and fairly spitting the words at him. "I'm also tired of your sleazeball boss, the president of the United States. I can't believe I voted for the bastard. Damn, you're small men."

"Frederickson, listen—"

"Shut up. I've already listened to everything I want to hear from you, or anybody else in this administration. All the people Madison has killed and the lives he's destroyed . . . and you treat *us* like criminals. You didn't think that Garth and I were concerned

over the impact this information might have?! You didn't think Veil
was concerned?! Yet, you would have destroyed Veil Kendry and
us, and sent Madison into a cushy retirement someplace, just so
that your administration wouldn't be embarrassed. You helped to
save our lives, and we appreciate that, but it's not enough; nothing
you seem able to do or propose is enough. Too many other people
have died at the hands of your secretary of state. All we ever
wanted and want, all Veil wants, is *justice.* You knew what we'd
been through, and still you couldn't come here and deal with us in
good faith." I paused, sucked in a deep breath to try to tamp down
my rage, turned to McGarvey. "Are Garth and I free to go, Captain?"

"You certainly are, Frederickson. The sergeant out at the front
desk has your guns. Tell me where you want to go; one of my men
will drive you, or we'll get you plane tickets—courtesy of New
York State, of course."

Garth walked over to me, put his arm around my shoulders, and
gave me an appreciative pat. "Is it the *Times* or the *Post,* brother?"

"Let's start with the *New York Times.* Captain, may we use your
telephone?"

"Certainly," McGarvey said, picking up the telephone on his
desk and moving it to the edge closest to me.

"I know a few reporters on the *Times,* Andrews, and I'm going
to begin by talking to one on the phone; that's just in case something happens to us after we leave here. Once the story gets going,
our deaths won't make a difference; the reporters will have Veil's
paintings to look for and piece together to verify that story. You
may have the sequence key and catalog of owners, but that's fine.
Keep them. Even if you've destroyed them it won't make a difference. Viktor Raskolnikov has slides of every painting Veil has ever
sold; with his eye, sorting out the early slides and piecing them
together into the Archangel mural or murals shouldn't be too great
a trick. Raskolnikov also has a list of the original owners, so reporters across the country will not only know what to look for, but
where to look. It won't prove Madison's a murderer, but it will
make a great story, and it will reveal what kind of a man Madison
really is. *That* may be all we can hope for. Then, when Veil kills
him, at least people will know why. It will be a great media event—
an entire nation, through newspapers and television, putting together one huge jigsaw puzzle with themes of treachery, betrayal,

and death by Kevin Shannon's secretary of state. Every time another piece of that puzzle is found, a big, bloody chunk of this
administration goes down the toilet. And, who knows? Maybe, as
the process goes on, something *will* be found to prove that Madison's a murderer, and Veil won't have to do your dirty work for
you. It's certainly going to be interesting, don't you think?"

Andrews looked up at me, fear in his eyes. "If you do this,
Frederickson, you'll be a traitor," he said hoarsely. "The damage
you'll do to this country will be unimaginable."

"Bullshit. The damage we'll do to the Shannon administration
will be unimaginable, but you're the one, acting on orders from
Shannon, who decided he wanted to play what you politicians love
to call hardball. People like you and your boss are the ones who do
unimaginable damage to this country when you lie, and when you
use your power to twist or circumvent laws for your own convenience. You have no soul. This country doesn't need sleazeballs like
you in power. The bad taste this story leaves in people's mouths
will be more than offset by the tale of one unbelievably courageous
man, a fierce patriot and the greatest soldier this country has ever
produced, fighting against impossible odds, not only with his combat skills, but with his art. And he wins when the truth finally
comes out. The image Veil projects will be what Americans are
attracted to, and what they will identify with. Your whole sleazy
crew will soon be forgotten, but not Archangel. Maybe Veil will
give Americans new respect for themselves, and help us finally to
get the Viet Nam war behind us once and for all. In fact, I think it
might be jolly good fun if we dubbed this whole process Operation
Son of Archangel. You like that idea, Mr. Andrews?"

Garth smiled crookedly, said: "I like it, Mongo."

McGarvey said: "I don't understand half of what the hell you're
talking about, but I like it too."

Andrews said: "Captain, I need to use your phone."

"Just as long as you call collect, creep," McGarvey said, then
turned and walked to the door. "I'll get a medical kit for His
Highness."

Garth and I followed McGarvey out of the office, and I closed
the door behind us. Five minutes later the door opened and Andrews, his face still covered with his bloody handkerchief and fear
in his eyes, stood and stared at us for some time without speaking.
McGarvey, Garth, and I stared back.

"Would you two come with me, please?" Andrews said at last.

"Sure," I replied. "Right after I make my call to my reporter friend. I'm a little anxious to get Son of Archangel rolling."

"Please, Frederickson; no calls yet. You've won, and you are in a position to destroy this administration. I . . . mishandled this situation badly. Perhaps you'll be more gracious than I was, and give this administration and this country just a bit more time."

"Give me back the package of slides, the list of owners, and the sequence key. We'll give it all to Captain McGarvey for safekeeping."

Andrews lowered his eyes. "I'm sorry. I destroyed the package after I saw what it contained."

"He's telling the truth," McGarvey said, the disgust in his voice directed at himself as well as Andrews. "He had me start a fire in a trash can in the back. For your information, it looked like there were four pieces of paper along with the slides. One had names and numbers on it, and the other three looked like sketches."

I grunted. "Three murals to piece together."

"There are still the slides belonging to the art dealer," Andrews said. "You have nothing to lose by holding off just a little longer. Will you come with me? There's a plane waiting for us at Albany Airport."

"Where are we going?"

"Washington. The president of the United States would very much like to speak to the two of you."

21

"How the hell did you know what was in that packet?" Garth asked me when, hours later, we were finally alone.

"What else could it have been?" I replied as I stretched out on a monster bed in a monster suite in the most monstrously expensive hotel in Washington. In the bedroom there was a spectacular view through a huge picture window out over the Ellipse. In the distance, the sun was going down behind the Washington Monument; the last, blood-red rays were split and scattered by the tip of the spire, making it appear as if the concrete spear had pierced the ball of fire in its heart. There were two Secret Service agents in the hallway outside the suite—whether to guard us or keep us from leaving, we weren't sure, but at the moment it didn't seem to make much difference.

"Whatever was in the packet almost certainly had to relate to the Archangel business," I continued. "Otherwise, Veil wouldn't have gone to so much trouble to make sure it was in a safe place, with Gary Worde in the mountains; a safe deposit box was no good, because Madison could have gained access to that. He put the record into a kind of time capsule without knowing if, or how, he would ever use it. But what kind of record? Veil certainly didn't walk out of any army stockade with secret documents in his pocket, and he would have had no access to any kind of documentation after he was out. So whatever was in the packet had to have been *created* by him. When I realized that, everything else fell into place. Vivid reds, browns, and greens combined with flesh tones are the colors he used when he first began to paint. Those are also the colors he'd used in the painting he left for me in the secret compartment in his loft, the colors of men, blood, and jungle."

"Kendry could have gone up there and gotten the slides himself, at the beginning," Garth said, unrelieved bitterness in his voice. "Instead, he let you and me roam around on a Goddamn scavenger hunt."

"It's arguable whether he could have gone himself, Garth. Remember that he'd been under constant surveillance from the time he'd been kicked out of the army. Madison must have known about his visits to Worde, and after the botched assassination attempt Madison's men were almost certainly watching those mountains; they could have been waiting for him to try to go to Worde long before we ever went up there. We provided the necessary distraction for Madison's forces. It's also arguable whether he could have done anything with the slides himself even if he had been able to get them out without being ambushed. Without someone else to bear witness to the truth, he would have been just a discredited man peddling a bizarre slide show while constantly having to look over his shoulder."

"So now we're the ones who constantly have to look over our shoulders."

"He couldn't have done it alone, Garth. He needed us."

It was obvious from the expression on Garth's face that he didn't agree, but he let it go. "A hell of a piece of quick thinking under pressure, brother," Garth said, putting a huge hand affectionately on my shoulder.

Garth sat down on the edge of the bed, and we remained silent for some time, staring out the window as the wounded sun continued to sink down behind the monument.

"I should have killed that fuck, Andrews," Garth continued at last in a matter-of-fact tone that startled me and sent a little chill up my spine.

I eased myself up into a sitting position, next to Garth, and looked into his face in the gathering darkness. What I saw, I didn't like. "I'm glad you didn't, brother. I don't think we could have gotten clear of that, and I like happy endings."

"We're never going to get clear of this, Mongo. Madison's been trying to kill us with bullets; these guys are trying to do the same thing, in a different way. There isn't going to be any happy ending."

"Why not? You said the same thing when we were caught up in Valhalla, and we were in one hell of a lot worse shape then. I think we're in a pretty good position right now."

"I just wish I'd killed him when I had the chance," Garth said distantly, after a long pause.

I couldn't think of anything to say, and we again lapsed into silence. After a few minutes I stood up and groped my way around the suite until I found a light switch.

We had been asked to be patient and wait. We were patient, and we waited. At six thirty there was a knock at the door. It was one of the Secret Service agents asking if it was a convenient time for us to be taken to dinner. It was a most convenient time, and if our attire —jeans, denim shirts, and hiking boots—did not seem quite appropriate for going out to dinner in Washington, nothing in the demeanor of the agent indicated that he thought so, or that there would be any problem.

There wasn't. We were taken to one of Washington's better restaurants. Arrangements had obviously been made beforehand, for the maître d' nodded to the two agents as we entered, and we were ushered through a velvet-roped gate, past a number of startled diners, to a candle-lit table in a private booth at the rear of the main dining room.

"Shannon's laying it on a bit thick, isn't he?" Garth said to one of the agents sitting across from us.

"The captain has been asked to order for us, Lieutenant," the stern-faced man replied evenly. "I hope you approve. You won't be disappointed."

We weren't. An hour and a half later, stuffed with French cuisine and fine wine, Garth and I followed the agents out of the restaurant to the waiting limousine that had brought us.

Followed by a second car with four Secret Service agents in it, we rode slowly through the night streets of Washington. I had assumed we were going to be driven to the White House, but that wasn't the direction in which we were headed. Finally the car pulled up to the entrance of a park, and I knew where we were. Up and down the street, spaced twenty yards or so apart, were police cars, with their lights off. The officers standing on the sidewalk were alert and watchful.

"The president will meet you at the war memorial," one of the agents said as he opened the car door for us. "Just follow the sidewalk."

Garth and I ducked under the wooden barricade that had been placed across the entrance and headed down the sidewalk into the park. There were lights over the walk, but they had been dimmed to the point where they were not much brighter than the dappled moonlight. We walked in silence, for there seemed nothing left to say to each other. We had "come in from the cold" only to end in an even colder place, and now we were on our way to meet the supreme commander of what was beginning to look like just one more enemy army.

We came around a bend in the path and suddenly found ourselves confronted by the startling sight of the Viet Nam War Memorial, its long slab of polished black stone faintly glowing in the moonlight like a sacred obelisk left behind by some ancient, extinct tribe of warriors.

Suddenly a man with a walkie-talkie stepped out from behind a clump of bushes to our left. "The lieutenant has to say here," the Secret Service agent said, blocking Garth's path.

"Bullshit!" I snapped, moving closer to Garth. "My brother and I go down there together, or we don't go at all."

"Then you don't go at all," the agent said evenly, looking directly at me. "You won't get around us on this one. We didn't approve of meeting here in the first place. We lost the battle on choosing the meeting site, but we won't budge on choosing who goes down there. We're responsible for the safety of the president. The lieutenant is dangerous; he attacked a presidential aide."

"Fuck you, thank you, and good night." I said, and turned around. I started to walk away, but was stopped when Garth gripped my shoulder and turned me around again.

"Go ahead, Mongo," Garth murmured. "This man's just doing his job, and he happens to be right. You go ahead and see what Shannon has to say. I'm feeling very spooky, and I really don't care to meet with the son-of-a-bitch anyway."

"Okay, brother. You all right?"

"I'm all right. Go take care of business, and don't give him shit."

I squeezed Garth's hand, then walked ahead, across a short open expanse, to the lip of the recess in which, like a monster shard in a great, rectangular bomb crater, the Viet Nam War Memorial stood. Again, I found myself profoundly moved by the stark simplicity and awesome power of the sculpture. As had been intended, the black stone slab cut not only through space, but also through all the pretensions and desperate, muddled rationales all sides offered to try to explain the most complex and ultimately futile war the United States of America had ever fought.

I slowly descended a ramp into the magnificent hole in the ground, walked up to the granite, and touched my fingertips to the sharp lines of the stonecutter's art in the center of the wall of names. Keeping my left hand on the wall, I moved to my right until I finally came to the last of the names. The rest of the wall was naked black stone awaiting more bad news about bones unearthed from unmarked graves halfway around the world.

There were some names that should be added, I thought—the victims, including two children, who had died in the fire that had destroyed my apartment building; Loan Ka and his family, and Kathy; Gary Worde, and the six fighting men of America's armed forces sent to die in shame on a madman's murderous errand.

I was most impressed by the monument—and angry that Kevin Shannon should use the mystery of the site in an embarrassingly obvious effort to manipulate my feelings. I resented the banality and predictability of his action and found it depressing.

I heard footsteps behind me, and I turned as Kevin Shannon,

casually dressed in charcoal slacks, black loafers, black turtleneck, and a heavy white cardigan sweater, came down the ramp and walked toward me at a brisk pace. He was shorter in person than he appeared on television or in photographs. His thick, gray-streaked black hair was cut sharply in the swept-back style that was his trademark. His craggy, fifty-seven-year-old face could not be described as handsome, but his features were nonetheless striking, with a square jaw, pronounced cheekbones, and bright, black eyes. He looked like a man who could control himself as well as situations, and it was this bearing—along with his political views—that had first attracted me to him. I had believed in Shannon, believed he was somehow different from the mangled politicians who usually survive the internecine warfare that is our political system to gain election to high office. Now I felt like a fool.

His grip, when he shook my hand, was firm. "Good evening, Dr. Frederickson," Kevin Shannon said in his pleasing baritone.

"Good evening, sir." Courtesy costs nothing.

Shannon motioned for me to sit down on the stone bench behind us. I did, and he sat beside me. He crossed his legs, reached into a pocket of his cardigan, and to my surprise, brought out a small silver flask emblazoned with the presidential seal. He unscrewed the silver cap, drew a shot glass out of the same pocket, set them both down on the bench between us.

"Your rather extensive dossier indicates you like Scotch, Frederickson. I thought you might like to share a drink with me. The flask is for you."

I hoped that the offer of a presidential souvenir at the beginning of our discussion was an attempt at humor, but I had the most disquieting feeling that it wasn't. Like Burton Andrews, probably like most people who crave for and exercise power, Kevin Shannon seemed to have had his soul, as well as a good deal of common sense, displaced by a preoccupation with symbols. It was at once fascinating and unnerving, and I wondered how much of this presidential stroking I was going to have to put up with before we got down to business.

"No, thank you," I said.

Shannon shrugged, set down the flask next to the shot glass and cap. "What do you want, Frederickson?" he asked, leaning toward me and resting his forearms across his knees.

"I thought Burton Andrews might have told you."

"You tell me."

"Justice."

"We might disagree over what constitutes justice."

"Let the courts decide. That's what they're there for."

Shannon leaned back, drew a pack of cigarettes from his pocket. He offered me one, which I declined. He lit one, inhaled deeply, exhaled slowly. "What, in your opinion, would constitute justice in this matter?"

"At the very least, Orville Madison should be sent to prison for the rest of his life."

"What about Veil Kendry?"

"He should be left alone."

"Ah. That might or might not be just, but it would certainly be a circumvention of the law. No?"

"No. Not if he received a presidential pardon in advance—something on the order of what Gerald Ford provided for Richard Nixon would seem appropriate. There were extenuating circumstances for everything he's done. He's killed, yes—but only in self-defense, or in defense of others."

"He's killed for revenge."

"That, too—which is why a presidential pardon is needed. But we know, and I'm sure Veil knows, that things aren't going to work out that way. I can't speak for Veil, but I'm certain that when he sees Orville Madison being dealt with appropriately, he'll come in peacefully and surrender himself to the authorities."

"Oh, good," Shannon said, lighting a second cigarette from the butt of his first. "That's just what I need. With a little luck, Madison's trial will be over in a year or so, and then Kendry's trial can begin. Are you serious? My entire term would be dominated by headlines about Archangel and a defrocked, murderous secretary of state. Do you think I intend to allow myself to be mortally crippled by events before my tenure in office has barely begun?"

"I'm sure I don't know what you intend, sir."

"Do you think I wanted to become president so that my administration could be blown out of the water before it had even set sail?" Shannon continued like a man whose carefully prepared speech had been interrupted. "Do you think I will jeopardize this administration's place in history because of one man's mistake?"

"Mistake? You're talking about a man who's killed—"

"I know what I'm talking about, Frederickson. I'm talking about an entire administration imperiled because of a long-standing personal grudge between two men. I won't have it. What you propose is patently ridiculous. Frankly, I'm surprised at your naiveté."

"I wouldn't presume to try and guess why you wanted to become president," I replied curtly, trying to suppress my anger. "And if you'll pardon my continuing naiveté, I don't understand what you mean when you say that *you* won't have it. You're responsible for Orville Madison—not for his actions, because you couldn't have known he was a lunatic, but for making certain he's sufficiently punished for those actions."

"Mr. Madison has been totally neutralized, Frederickson."

"What the hell does that mean?"

"It means he's lost all vestiges of power already. If you knew Orville Madison as well as I do—"

"How well *do* you know him?"

"Well, enough. As a matter of fact, our relationship goes back a good many years; I'm sure you'll be interested to know that it goes back to the war in Southeast Asia. I was a congressman then, without a great deal of seniority, but I was rewarded for certain good political deeds by being named to a very prestigious, select, secret Senate-House committee that monitored intelligence activities in Southeast Asia. That's how I met Madison, and he deeply impressed me. I knew he was ruthless, but certain kinds of jobs require ruthlessness; his was one of them. I respected him for his ability to get things done, and for his ability consistently to win skirmishes against other men who were every bit as ruthless as he was. I was one of the people who first heard about—and approved —the Archangel plan. I was also instrumental in cutting through about a thousand miles of red tape in order to get Colonel Po secretly into this country after the collapse of Saigon. I didn't know about the affair with the Hmong village, or about Madison's bit of business with Kendry. I never even knew why the plan had been abandoned. I'd like you to believe that."

"I do believe you, Mr. President, and I appreciate your candor." It was the truth; indeed, I considered it a remarkable admission.

"I thought you would. I'm telling you all this so that you can appreciate that I'm even more vulnerable to certain revelations that you thought I was. I might barely survive as a badly crippled president after the business about Orville Madison came out, but I would never survive being named as the man who helped bring Po into this country. I'd be forced to resign, and I don't intend to let that happen. For Mr. Madison, complete loss of power is a punishment worse than death. I suspect Veil Kendry might even agree with me."

"Somehow, I doubt it. Madison has killed too many innocent people."

"Madison is now secretary of state in name only. At the moment, he can't even get back into his office at Langley; they won't let him through the gate. Very soon, he is going to announce his immediate resignation, for reasons of health. Orville Madison is going to retire from public life, and I can assure you that he'll never be heard of—or bother anyone—again."

"Where's he retiring to?"

"That will be a secret; after all, Madison wants assurances that he'll be protected from Veil Kendry in the future. Also, we don't want the Russians nibbling at him; he knows too much, obviously. Now *he'll* be under constant surveillance for the rest of his life, and he understands that."

"It's not enough, sir. Why don't you just tell the whole story yourself, before anyone else has a chance to?"

"By 'anyone else,' you're referring to yourself and your brother?"

"I'm referring to anyone else. Just get it out in the open and behind you, and trust the American people to give you the chance to begin again."

Kevin Shannon crossed his arms over his chest and sighed deeply. Somewhere in the darkness behind us, walkie-talkies crackled. "Thank you very much, but I just won an election, and I don't feel like going through another campaign. There are too many other matters to which I want to devote my energies. Do you have any idea how many kinks a prolonged matter like this could put in the lives of you and your brother, Dr. Frederickson?"

It was time for yet another game of hardball, with a high slider aimed right at my head. I found I was more depressed than angry, and I said nothing.

"If you try to pursue this matter in the media or the courts," Kevin Shannon continued evenly, "you two could be tied up in knots for years. On the other hand, if we can find a way to work together to resolve our differences, I believe I can assure you that the two of you will be free of any further entanglements."

"We've heard the same offer before," I said tightly.

"Well, now you're hearing it from me," Shannon replied, unperturbed. "You can go back to your lives as they were before, resume your careers. The same general amnesty will apply to Veil Kendry."

"You have that kind of power? You can just erase everything that's happened?"

"Not everything," Shannon replied evenly. "I have the power to make *your* troubles, and the troubles of Veil Kendry, go away. But you have the power to make *my* troubles go away in this Orville Madison affair. In effect, I'm saying that I'll wave my magic wand if you'll wave yours. Forget about going anywhere with what you know about Orville Madison, Operation Archangel, and Veil Kendry's most ingenious artwork. Just go home to New York City and go back to work. Nobody will bother you. In addition, I'll arrange for the two of you to receive the Congressional Medal of Honor; that should certainly enhance your respective careers."

Suddenly I felt light-headed and slightly nauseated. *"What* did you say?"

"The Congressional Medal of Honor; I'm prepared to nominate you and your brother."

"For what?"

"Certainly not for your exploits of the past few weeks," the president said with a nervous laugh. "The medals will be awarded for heroic acts you and your brother performed in the service of your country a few years ago."

Suddenly everything in the night seemed very still, except for the pounding of my heart inside my chest. "What heroic acts would those be?" I asked in a voice that sounded like that of a stranger.

"What? You don't think that, as a member of the Senate, I had a review on what happened? Furthermore, when I became president-elect I was fully briefed by my Director of the Defense Intelligence Agency. Mr. Lippitt told me how instrumental the Fredericksons were in breaking up that global spy network."

I hadn't realized I'd been holding my breath until my chest began to hurt. I slowly exhaled. Mr. Lippitt, I thought, had told Kevin Shannon a fairy tale, probably the same fairy tale he'd told to a great many other men in power since Valhalla. The three of us, with some unusual help, had managed to break up a global conspiracy, all right, but that conspiracy had been much more terrible than anything as tame as a spy network. Ironically, the horror that had been Valhalla was directly related to the kind of thinking Kevin Shannon was displaying. It made me feel even more nauseated and angry. For thousands of years, men like Kevin Shannon had been killing the world as fast as men of vision could breathe life back into it. The process went on.

"Sir, I most certainly mean to be disrespectful—and I know I'm speaking for Garth—when I suggest that you take your Congressional Medals of Honor and shove them up your presidential ass."

Kevin Shannon didn't much like that. He flushed angrily, quickly turned his face away. "There's no need to be rude, Frederickson," he said tightly.

"If you don't want me to be rude, then stop being insulting."

"I didn't mean to be insulting."

"But you were. You'll force Madison to resign anyway, so that much will be accomplished no matter what Garth and I do or don't do." I paused, rose to my feet. "When you see that bastard Madison, tell him he'd better stock up on telegenic blue shirts, because he's going to be seeing a lot of himself on television."

"No, Frederickson; I won't."

I'd started to walk away. I stopped, turned back to face the other man. "You won't what?"

"I won't force Madison to resign," Shannon said, his dark eyes suddenly seeming to glow with passion in the moonlight.

"I don't understand. You'd keep a madman and a murderer in the most important post in your cabinet out of *spite?!*"

There was a long silence. Finally, Shannon said: "Sit down and listen, Frederickson. You may yet hear something that pleases you."

"I doubt it very much," I said, remaining on my feet. "But I'm listening."

Shannon lit his third cigarette. "Has it occurred to you to ask why I nominated Orville Madison?" he asked quietly.

"You've already answered that question. You've known him a long time, and he impressed you with his ruthless efficiency. You're buddies."

"There are many men I've known for a long time, Frederickson, and many men I respect for their efficiency. I am not Mr. Madison's 'buddy'; we've known each other for years, yes, but we've never really been friends. Frankly, I've never much cared for the man personally. Yet, he is the man I chose to be my secretary of state. Would you like to know why?"

"Not nearly as much as I'd like to know how you could even *consider* keeping him on."

"Because Madison has also known Arkady Ilyich Benko for more than twenty years, and they *are* 'buddies.' "

That got a good two or three blinks out of me. Arkady Ilyich Benko was the mint-new Soviet premier, a warrior, bloodied but unbowed, who had emerged as premier after serving in the Directorate of the K.G.B. Orville Madison's blood brother.

"I managed to surprise you, didn't I, Frederickson?" Shannon continued in the same soft voice.

"It's true?" I asked, feeling short of breath.

Shannon dismissed my question with a wave of his hand. "Like Madison, Benko was very active during the war in Viet Nam. They butted heads a number of times while they were there, and they continued to do so as each ascended to the top of his profession; but the confrontations began growing more symbolic, less vicious, as the years passed. Madison speaks fluent Russian, which I think you will agree would be an admirable achievement for any diplomat, but especially for a secretary of state; admirable and highly desirable. The two men genuinely like—and, even more important, genuinely respect—each other. They also trust each other; indeed, each trusts the other probably more than he trusts a good many of his compatriots. Arkady Ilyich Benko will release a thousand political prisoners from the Gulag, or allow a thousand Soviet Jews to emigrate, *tomorrow*, simply as a gesture of good will, if Orville Madison asks him to. I mean that literally, and I am absolutely certain of the truth of the statement. *Now* talk to me about 'justice.' Which is more just? Should I use Orville Madison, and his unique personal relationship with the Soviet premier, to free thousands of political prisoners and perhaps create the best relations we've had with the Soviet Union since World War Two? Or should I destroy this tool—and with it the opportunity for real and lasting peace— because he went a little crazy and killed thirteen people? Surely, that many people die in automobile accidents every day; many times that number. Which should it be, Frederickson? Justice for thirteen people, or the very real possibility of a better world for five billion? Tell me what you would do."

"All right, Mr. President, I will." I paused, swallowed. My

mouth was dry. I had no reason to doubt a word Kevin Shannon had said regarding the relationship between Madison and the Soviet premier, and he had painted an awesome and seductive picture of a world in which tensions between Russia and the United States were markedly reduced. But it was still only a picture, a dream, and the trail of death behind me was all too real. And Orville Madison was still a homicidal maniac, which made him, in the final analysis, beyond the control of anyone. "First, I'd take steps to provide justice in my own backyard before I worried about saving the world. Second, anyone who likes, respects, and trusts Orville Madison can't be all good. Madison isn't ultimately responsible for foreign policy, *you* are. I wouldn't trust *Benko,* who helped put all those Gulag prisoners there in the first place. I'd clean house, prosecute Madison, and start over. That would make Benko respect *me.*"

"Which is why you're not president, and I am," Shannon said with another disdainful gesture of his hand. "If I'm going to have to put up with a media circus no matter what I do, then I might as well fight to keep the man I wanted in the first place, and try to head Veil Kendry and the Fredericksons off at the pass. The hell with you, Frederickson. Do your worst. I still believe Orville Madison will be the best secretary of state this nation has ever had, and that the world will be a much better place in four years than it is now."

"We'll demand a Senate hearing, Shannon."

The president's response was to laugh. "You'll *demand* a Senate hearing? How far do you think you'll get?"

"I guess we'll just have to find out. Believe it or not, I really don't want to go to the newspapers with this—not yet. Regardless of what I said to Andrews, I don't think the media is the proper forum for this to be brought out; I don't believe that would be in the best interests of the country."

"I know you believe that," Shannon said mildly, "because it's so obviously true. I thought you'd back off on that."

"Which makes you a good poker player—on the first hand. Now you're forcing us to it."

"No. You want a congressional hearing, you've got it. Indeed, I insist. It's in the administration's interests to have it on the record that you were invited to present your allegations in a proper, congressional forum before peddling them to the newspapers."

"You know they're not allegations."

"What I know isn't the point, is it? You can't subpoena me, and I'm not about to help you sabotage what I believe to be a singular, once-in-a-generation opportunity to rechannel the world's riches and energies from preparing for war to reaping the benefits of peace. But I still challenge you to do your worst. As a matter of fact, you and your brother will find an invitation waiting for you when you get back to your hotel room; I took the liberty of arranging a congressional hearing for you before I came here. I was hoping that the outcome of our meeting would be that you'd decline the invitation."

"We're not about to accept an invitation to any hearing which you've arranged."

"Suit yourself. The fact that you received an invitation will still be a matter of record, and it's the only invitation you'll get. You can bet your pension on that."

"Jesus Christ," I said in a hollow voice. "You're as mad as Madison. Americans have another Goddamn megalomaniac for their president."

"Listen to me, you stubborn, sanctimonious, naive troublemaker!" Shannon snapped in a voice that suddenly vibrated with rage. He abruptly rose to his feet, and his right arm shot out, index finger pointing at the black wall. "You see that monument?! On it are the names of thousands of men who died in an *insane* war that was the most *incredibly* stupid act of political blindness, cultural ignorance, arrogance, and paranoia any country in the West has ever committed! It damn near gutted us, and it may *still* gut us if we can't, finally, find a way to get it behind us! *That* is our legacy from Viet Nam—in the eyes of the world, and in our own hearts! *I will not become just one more casualty of that stupid war!* Do you hear me?! What I can accomplish is too important!"

President of the United States Kevin Shannon took a deep breath and slowly lowered his arm. When he spoke again, his voice was calmer. "I can rebuild America's cities, which is precisely what I intend to do. You may be registered as an Independent, Frederickson, but I'm well aware of your political inclinations. You'll love what you see, be proud of the accomplishments of the Shannon administration. You'll see massive amounts of aid flowing to *every* area of this country that needs it—aid to farmers and migrant workers, to inner-city families and Appalachian families;

you will see an economic policy that is fair to every segment of this society; you will see a tremendous easing of international tensions because the United States will take the lead in initiating a *rational* and *consistent* foreign policy based upon reality, not ideology; you will see the promotion of human rights and aspirations instead of corporate profits. You will see this nation literally rebuilt, Frederickson—physically and spiritually. America will become the kind of nation you and I know it can, and should, be. Like it or not, I am counting on the relationship between Madison and Benko to give me the freedom, and release the necessary funds that would otherwise go into the defense budget, to do these things. Do in me and my administration, and you know what you're going to get?—precisely what you've had. Is that what you want, Frederickson? What action should you take that will provide the greatest good for the greatest number of people? Give me the freedom to deal with, and use, Orville Madison in my own way, and I believe I can give you a much better world. You can help me to build a truly moral nation. Take some time to think about it."

"I don't have to think about it," I said, feeling a great wave of sadness wash across my heart. "I don't believe nations are moral or immoral, responsible or irresponsible. Only human beings are those things. Populations that make up the tribal groups we call nations only follow the examples set by their tribal leaders—political, religious, and cultural. You will make a good political tribal leader only if *you* are moral and act in a moral manner. You're a fool, Shannon, if you believe for an instant that you can build some kind of Golden Age for America on a rotten tin can of an idea—Orville Madison as secretary of state, for whatever reason—that is not only immoral, but reeks of death. You won't be another casualty of the war if you do the right thing. Cut Madison loose, and stop obstructing justice. Be moral, Mr. President; be responsible. *That* will send one hell of a message to the Russians, and to the rest of the world, a message that we are a responsible nation of laws made up of basically moral people who care deeply about justice, no matter the short-term inconvenience and cost."

Kevin Shannon said nothing. He stood staring at me for some time, the expression on his face stony and unreadable, almost blank. Then he deliberately reached down, picked up the silver flask with the emblazoned presidential seal, and slipped it back into the pocket of his cardigan sweater. He walked past me without a glance, went up the ramp, and disappeared from sight. Instantly, walkie-talkies crackled, and disembodied, electronic voices could be heard all over the park.

Feeling exhausted and lost, I slowly followed after him, trudged up the ramp. I felt light-headed, and there was a sour, bitter taste at the back of my throat, as if I had been breathing poison air. I started back the way I had come, through a park that was already empty. After about twenty steps I turned off into some bushes, bent over, and was sick.

22

As advertised, an invitation to present our testimony to a closed joint House-Senate committee was waiting for us when we got back to our hotel. There was also an ominous message for me to the effect that I should call the head of my department as soon as possible—ominous because I couldn't understand how anyone at the university had known where to reach me. The invitation and the message had been placed on top of our backpacks, which had been set outside the locked doors of our hotel suite. We moved into a YMCA a few blocks away.

When I called the university the next morning to touch base with the head of my department, I learned that I had been summarily suspended from all teaching duties, without pay. The university couldn't fire me outright, because I had tenure, and so there would be a hearing at some indeterminate time in the future. However, it was strongly hinted that I might consider resigning, since the charges of incompetence, unprofessionalism, and moral turpitude could prove to be very embarrassing to me.

When Garth called his precinct, he found that he too had been suspended without pay. Although he had been specifically assigned to the arson and murder cases connected with the burning of my apartment building, and had been authorized to accompany me to Albany as part of his investigation, he was now told that he had greatly exceeded his authority when he had accompanied me into the mountains to search for Gary Worde. Also, an NYPD investigation was under way to determine whether he might have aided and abetted me in certain criminal acts by suppressing evidence.

Kevin Shannon had wasted no time in displaying for us his own brand of "ruthless efficiency."

The committee hearing was three days off, and it turned out to be a very long three days; the hammer blows of raw political power continued to fall.

My P.I. license, along with my carry permits, was lifted pending investigation of my "moral character and commission of certain criminal acts." I declined the invitation to turn my handguns in to the nearest police station.

Also, Viktor Raskolnikov and his gallery had suddenly become the target of an I.R.S. investigation; all of his files, including slides of paintings that had been sold and a list of their owners, had been seized. Now we had nothing but the knots in our lives Kevin Shannon had promised us, nothing left to do but play out a string that had already unraveled.

It was all very depressing.

"First, I would like to thank the committee for allowing this statement to be read into the record," I intoned in a flat, dry voice, reading from the paper in front of me. "Regardless of the outcome of your deliberations, I believe this statement will bring into sharper focus certain events of mutual interest which have happened in the past, are happening now, and which may happen in the future."

Beside me, Garth sat very straight, stiff and still, hands folded on the bare, warped wooden surface of the ancient witness table at which we sat. The expression on his face was blank, and he seemed to be lost in his own thoughts, a long way away. Wherever he was, I thought, it would have been just as well if I were with him. I felt like a lonely blackjack player in a near-empty casino waiting for a dealer to show up. Except that this game had been rigged before we'd ever sat down at the table in the well of a cavernous, dusty meeting hall in an otherwise unused section of the Old Senate Office Building. The choice of setting was at once meant to be intimidating, while at the same time underscoring the futility of our appearance there. It was a perfect example of overkill.

"It is important for you to know that I love the United States of America—not because it is the country where I was born and grew

up, but because it is the country it is. Indeed, it is only within the
past fifteen years that I have come to feel at home here, and to
appreciate how much I owe to it. Before that, I had no love of
anything; I did not know what the word 'love' meant. I had only
drives and needs. The institutions and traditions of this society
literally saved my life, allowing me to discover talents and
strengths within myself in a way I would never have thought possible."

I estimated that the hall could hold upwards of five or six hundred people. There was even an overhanging balcony, but it was
cloaked in darkness now, like the entire rear of the hall which
spread out beneath it. In fact, the "hearing" could just as well have
been held in a cloakroom. There was a stenographer in the well
with us, situated between the table and a long, raised dais where
five senators, all men in their late fifties or early sixties, sat behind
a table covered with green felt. Senator Kathleen Wyndham, head
of the committee charged with investigating Orville Madison in the
first place, was conspicuous by her absence.

Orville Madison also sat up on the dais itself, albeit apart from
the senators, near one end of the table. He was flanked by two
black-suited aides who sat stiffly in their chairs, felt-tipped pens
poised over white legal pads, glaring at Garth and me. Madison
had a microphone placed in front of him, and it appeared that he
would be given the opportunity to ask questions or make a statement if he so chose.

In person, Orville Madison was a rather unimposing figure—
probably a good part of the reason he had been so successful in his
career as a master spy. He had thinning gray hair and a head that
seemed slightly too large for the rest of his body. His black suit,
although obviously expensive and well cut, did not fit well, and I
suspected he might have lost a lot of weight recently; the collar of
his white shirt was loose around his neck, and his tie was crooked.
His face was puffy, and there were angry red, broken veins in his
nose. He had not glanced at us once, preferring to stare straight
ahead of him out into the darkness beneath the balcony. His dark
eyes seemed curiously lifeless, like buttons sewn into the face of a
rag doll. There was no sign of guilt, regret, or any other emotion
registered on the doughy features.

The burly, armed marshal standing next to the side door a few
feet in front of Madison looked bored.

I continued: "During the time frame covering incidents in the past that are the basis of this investigation, it would be fair to say that I was quite mad."

"Dr. Frederickson?"

"What is it, Senator?" I asked, looking up from the paper I'd been reading.

John Lefferton, the senior senator from Oklahoma and the man who appeared to be chairing the hearing, peered down at me through his thick bifocals. "I'm not sure I understand what's happening here. You said that you wanted to read a statement."

"I am reading a statement."

"You're telling us that you are, or have been, mentally ill?"

"A lot of people who know me think that, but I never admit to it. No, that's not what I'm telling you."

"But your statement—?"

"I said I wanted to read a statement; I didn't say it was *my* statement. This was written by Veil Kendry."

After some exchanging of startled glances, there was a hurried conference, with the microphones shut off. Finally, the microphones were switched back on.

"How did you come by this document, Dr. Frederickson?" Lefferton asked.

"It was left in my room at the YMCA last night."

"You've *seen* Veil Kendry?"

"No. The letter was in an envelope on the table next to my bed when I woke up this morning. It's from Veil; I recognize the signature."

"Uh, didn't you lock your room?"

"Sure. Veil Kendry's a very sneaky fellow, when he wants—or has—to be."

Suddenly the senators and the marshal seemed decidedly nervous; the senators looked at each other, while the marshal stiffened and squinted into the darkness of the balcony and at the rear of the hall. The marshal unsnapped the flap over his holster, put his hand on the butt of his gun.

Fred Mares, the senator from Michigan, turned in his chair. "Marshal, are the doors to this meeting hall locked, as directed?"

"Yes, sir," the marshal replied with a firm nod. "I locked them all myself, and checked them again just a few minutes before you all arrived."

John Lefferton turned his attention back to me. "Dr. Frederick-son, I'm sorry, but I'm afraid we can't permit you to finish reading a statement that is not your own. We've heard—and suffered—quite enough from Mr. Kendry, *in absentia*. If he has more to say, he should be here. This hearing is being held as a courtesy to you and your brother, but we will not allow a killer at large to dictate what this committee will or will not hear."

"Suit yourself," I said as I shrugged and dropped the paper on the table in front of me.

"Pardon me?"

"I said, suit yourself, Senator. If you don't want to hear Veil's statement, I won't read it."

Arlen Smith, the senior senator from Texas, leaned his rail-thin frame forward on the table and looked down at Garth. "Lieuten-ant, is there anything you wish to say to this committee?"

"My brother speaks for both of us," Garth said in a flat voice, without looking up. He hadn't even bothered to turn on his micro-phone.

"What is it that you wish to say to this committee, Dr. Freder-ickson?"

"Nothing."

"I don't understand. Why are you here?"

"I came to read the statement Veil Kendry wanted read, Senator, and—originally—to bear witness to the events he describes. When he wrote this, he couldn't have known what a waste of time this hearing would be. Well, I'm not about to waste my time with you. The fact that Senator Wyndham has been excluded from this little gathering tells me who you are; you're all original members of the committee that heard details of, and passed on, Operation Archan-gel. Of active members of government involved in the plan, the only person missing here is Kevin Shannon. This has got to be the ultimate in ad hoc committees, and I say you can all go to hell."

That produced some startled glances, a few flushed faces, and another hurried, whispered conference.

"Dr. Frederickson," Lefferton said, "we must caution you to maintain an attitude of respect here. Otherwise, you will be held in contempt."

"Suit yourselves."

"How did you first become involved with Veil Kendry in this matter?"

"It's all explained in Veil's statement. Do you want to hear the rest of it?"

"No, sir, we do not. We want you to answer the question."

"Veil's my friend."

"That's not an answer."

"You know the answer, Senator; you've all been briefed."

"Why do you say that?"

"Because you're United States senators, from both parties, and you wouldn't have agreed so quickly to what amounts to a most unusual procedure unless Kevin Shannon told you a few things. You may not know the whole Archangel story, or all of what that man sitting to your right has done, but you've been told enough to become convinced that a great deal is at stake here."

Lefferton cleared his throat. "We'd like to hear your version of events."

"No. I pass, Senator. What you want is for me to make certain statements on record, so that you can shoot me down later. Expect to hear from me again in five years or so—or however long it takes me to find the proof to back up what I have to say. When I do put it together, you'll be able to read all about it in the newspapers—along with an account of this hearing."

"Ah," Smith, the senator from Texas, said as he leaned forward and peered down at the stenographer, whose fingers were flying over her keyboard. "Are you telling the committee that you have no proof of the allegations you came here prepared to make against Secretary Madison?"

"I *had* proof, Senator. What I strongly suspect you *weren't* told at your presidential briefing is that Kevin Shannon, through his aides, has either destroyed or confiscated all of my evidence. In fact, I.R.S. investigation or not, *all* of it has probably been destroyed by now."

"That's an outrageous accusation, Dr. Frederickson," John Lefferton said in his most reproving tone of voice.

"Yeah? Well, I thought snatching and destroying the evidence was pretty outrageous."

"Dr. Frederickson—"

"My brother and I would like to be excused, Senator. We have nothing further to say at this time."

"You may *not* be excused, Frederickson! And if you try to leave before you are excused, the two of you will find yourselves escorted directly to jail for contempt of Congress!"

"You do what you want, Senator."

"Do you know where Veil Kendry is?"

"It looks like he's in Washington, doesn't it?"

"Do you know *where* in Washington? Do you know where he is staying?"

"No."

"When did Secretary Madison's name first become linked in your mind with the events under review?"

"When I read it in the newspapers."

"Excuse me?"

"You heard me."

"Are you trying to have fun at the expense of this committee?"

"I wouldn't think of it, Senator."

"You're saying that before you read Secretary Madison's name in the newspapers, you had no indication of any wrongdoing on his part?"

"You've got it."

Lefferton, allowing himself a small self-congratulatory smile, removed his bifocals and cleaned them with a linen handkerchief. "That's really quite an incredible admission, Dr. Frederickson," he said at last.

"I'm glad I'm holding your interest."

"Now, you say that we may hear from you in five years or so, and at that time you may have some kind of incriminating evidence against Secretary Madison. Would you be so kind as to share with this committee how you plan to gather this proof? Will you be reading more newspapers?"

I waited for the laughter on the dais to die down, said, "For openers, I plan to kind of go into the art business."

"What does that mean?"

"The man sitting to your right is a murderer—"

"Dr. Frederickson!" Arlen Smith shouted, pounding his fist on the table. "How *dare* you make such a statement without anything whatsoever to back you up?"

"Come off it, Senator," I said wearily. "You love it; the whole purpose of this hearing is to get me to make statements like I just did, so that you can make comments like you just did. It looks great in a transcript. You asked me a question, and I'm trying to answer you. I happen to know that Orville Madison is responsible for the murders of thirteen people. That may never be proved, but what can be proved—with time—is that Madison is a liar when he says he's never heard of Veil Kendry. Once that link is established, other bits and pieces of evidence may well surface. You see, when you passed on Operation Archangel, Madison never told you who Archangel, the centerpiece of the plan, was. Veil Kendry was Archangel."

The aide sitting on Madison's right tapped his microphone with the tip of his pen. "That's preposterous, Frederickson."

"Are you speaking for yourself, pal, or your boss?"

The aide glanced at Orville Madison, who gave an almost imperceptible nod of his head. "Secretary Madison continues to deny any knowledge of Veil Kendry, aside from what he has heard in the past few days."

"No kidding? Then, perhaps the good secretary would care to tell us just who Archangel was."

"That information is classified," the aide said stiffly.

"It doesn't make any difference, pal. As far as I'm concerned, what you just said is the first worthwhile thing that's gone into this record. I trust the stenographer will make a note of the fact that Madison nodded his head when I asked if you were speaking for him. In fact, some years ago Veil executed a series of paintings—"

"Paintings," Lefferton interrupted, peering over the top of his bifocals at a paper in front of him. "There is something here about paintings. Would you care to tell us what it is these paintings purport to show?"

"They paint a picture of a liar."

"But you don't know where to find these paintings. Is that correct?"

"You know it's correct, Senator. Thanks to the I.R.S., acting on behalf of the president, the records of the whereabouts of these paintings have been seized. The paintings are scattered all over the country, maybe all over the world. But I'll eventually find them—and if I end up in prison as a result of all this, then I'll hire somebody to find them for me. That's something you're now betting your reputations and reelection campaigns on, gentlemen."

"And they lose, Mongo," a very familiar voice said from somewhere above and behind me. In the vast, nearly empty chamber, the voice echoed. *"I know where the paintings are."*

Veil Kendry's words were punctuated by an ominous *schlish-clack* of metal sliding over metal—an ammunition magazine being slipped into the stock of an automatic weapon, the safety being released.

The faces of the marshal, aides, stenographer, and the senators drained of blood and their eyes went wide as they stared up at the balcony above our heads. Garth and I slowly turned in our chairs, glanced up.

Veil, dressed in jeans and a faded denim jacket over a green plaid flannel shirt, was standing on a seat in the balcony, one booted foot resting on the protective brass rail. His gray-streaked, yellow hair fell to his shoulders, and he was unshaven. Even in the dim light that just reached the first row of the balcony, his pale blue eyes glinted with anger as his gaze swept over the men on the dais below him; even without the Uzi submachine gun he held in his hands, he would have made a most imposing, spectral figure, and I felt a chill run through me.

The anger left Veil's eyes as he looked down at me, and he flashed a crooked, bittersweet smile. "It looks like you've found the dark at the end of the tunnel, my friend. A hell of a job, Mongo; a hell of a job."

"Yeah," I replied dryly. "Thanks, Veil; it's always nice to hear from satisfied clients."

"I'm sorry."

"For what?"

"For all the pain, and for placing you in such bad company."

"You don't have to apologize for anything, not to me. I know you never really wanted to involve me in the first place; I just about had to ransack your place to find my retainer. I'm honored that I was the one you chose to ask for help."

"I'd be long dead by now if it weren't for you, my friend."

"Somehow, I doubt that."

"It's true. You distracted the bastard, and made him split his forces. I needed you and you were there—as I knew you would be."

"Yeah, well, wait'll you see my itemized bill."

"This wasn't the way I thought it would go, Mongo."

"I know. You made the mistake of giving some of our elected representatives too much credit for integrity and guts. They don't want to hear what you have to tell them."

"So I've noticed. Well, maybe we can still salvage something from this mess."

"Go for it."

The marshal had taken advantage of the chitchat between Veil and me to start to draw his gun out of his holster. Now his hand froze in midair as the Uzi abruptly swung in his direction.

"Unless you want to be carried out of here in halves," Veil said calmly to the man, "take the gun out of its holster with your fingertips, then carry it over and put it on the witness table."

The marshal hesitated just a moment, and Veil squeezed off a burst of fire that cut a line of holes in the wall barely six inches above the man's head. The marshal ducked, covered his head with his hands, and fell to the floor. Veil waited for the terrified man to look up, then waved toward the witness table with the Uzi. The marshal rose to his feet, walked quickly down into the well, and placed his .45 on the table in front of Garth and me, then went back to where he had been standing.

Everyone but Madison had reacted sharply to Veil's unexpected appearance, and everyone but Garth and Orville Madison had jumped to their feet when Veil had fired the Uzi. Now I glanced at Madison, saw that his previously impassive face was twisted with hate. His button eyes had come alive and were glowing with hatred and rage. Both of his aides had dropped out of their chairs and crawled in the direction of the senators, leaving their boss alone and isolated at the far end of the table. I found myself grinning, immensely enjoying the show. I nudged Garth, but he did not respond.

John Lefferton took a deep breath, adjusted his bifocals, then stabbed a trembling forefinger at the figure in the balcony. "Sir, we are United States senators! You—!"

Veil silenced the man with a second burst of gunfire that raked the wall above and behind the senators' heads; wood splinters and chunks of plaster erupted in a spray that fell over the men as they ducked under the table.

Welcome to the war.

In a single motion, Veil pushed off the balcony railing, leaping out into space and sailing over our heads fully fifteen feet in the air. Flexing his knees at the last moment like a ski jumper preparing for a landing, he crashed down directly in the middle of the table on the dais. There was a sharp, resounding crack, and the table split, collapsing down its length. Veil, who had never lost his balance, casually stepped from the rubble, brushing plaster and wood splinters off his front, walked down into the well, around the table, and up to stand next to me.

"How'm I doing?" Veil asked in a low voice.

"Not bad. Damned if I don't think they're ready now to listen to your statement."

"We'll see," Veil said, placing the Uzi on the table in front of him, pulling up a chair, and sitting down next to me. He pulled the microphone over, tapped it with his fingernail to test if it was live. It was a somewhat eerie sensation watching Veil preparing to testify in a hall that was filled with suspended plaster dust particles, pocked with bullet holes, and reeked of cordite. My ears still rang from the thunderous gunfire.

Through it all, Orville Madison had barely moved, except to pull his chair back from the collapsed table. The marshal had backed up to the wall, and was staring wide-eyed at Veil. The senators and Madison's two aides, brushing debris off their suits and out of their hair, slowly emerged from beneath the table and glanced tentatively at the man with the Uzi seated at the witness table. Veil could easily have killed them all, and they knew it; but he hadn't, and now they were waiting anxiously to see what he was going to do.

"Seats, everybody," Veil said dryly. "You wanted me here in person, so here I am. Now here's my statement."

The marshal slowly reached out for the doorknob a few inches from his left hand. Veil merely grabbed the metal stock of the Uzi, looked at the man, and slowly shook his head. The marshal dropped his hand back to his side and moved away from the door.

"Ma'am?" Veil said to the stenographer, who was still slumped in her straight-backed chair with her hands over her head. After a few moments, she slowly peered out from under one arm, and Veil gestured toward the machine in front of her. "I won't hurt you, ma'am. Would you please continue to take a record?"

The woman sucked in a deep breath, lowered her arms, placed her hands out over the machine. Slowly, one by one, the senators began to sit back down. The aides remained on their feet, halfway between Madison and the senators, as if sensing they were trapped in a kind of no-man's-land.

"First of all, gentlemen," Veil continued, speaking quietly into the microphone, "it's a fact that the president of the United States has chosen to keep a sadist and a murderer as his secretary of state, even after the facts were made known to him—by both Dr. Frederickson and myself. For some inexplicable reason, Mr. Shannon has chosen to play a bizarre game rather than take advantage of the opportunity—an opportunity paid for with much pain, great risk, and the blood of innocent people—my friend and I have afforded him. I suggest to you that Mr. Shannon is badly in need of your advice and strong guidance, to say the least.

"On the afternoon of the day when President Shannon was to announce his choices for his cabinet, Madison called to inform me that he was shortly to be nominated to become secretary of state. The purpose of the call was twofold; to enable Madison to personally gloat over me in what he had reason to believe would be the last moments of my life, and to position me by the telephone, in the center of my loft, where I would presumably make an easy target for his sniper, who had been waiting for Madison to make the call. Unfortunately for Mr. Madison, I had taken the precaution of installing thick, optically distorting glass in all the windows of my loft; the sniper missed—and I made sure he didn't get a second chance.

"Now that Mr. Madison had attempted to make good on a threat he had made to me many years ago, I considered simply hunting him down and killing him. I chose not to, although he certainly deserved it, for a simple reason. In a few hours, Mr. Madison would be nominated to a lofty and very public position, and this country, which has given me so much, has seen and suffered far too many assassinations of its public officials. Also, I had absolutely no desire to make a martyr of this piece of latrine slime. As astounded as I was by the nomination, and knowing that it had triggered the attempt on my life, I assumed at the time that a new president had simply been duped by a very clever criminal who was out of control. I thought I owed it to my country to expose the man for what he was, while at the same time trying to limit the damage to the country. It was to this end that I enlisted Mongo's help. My friend was tortured and almost killed because I could not be close enough to prevent it; I was fortunate to get to him in time to save his life, but not the lives of the five people who died in the fire that Madison's men started. For those deaths, I am, in a way, as responsible as Madison, as guilty, because I was the one who'd purposely sought to panic the man. If I had foreseen the deaths of those people, perhaps I wouldn't ever have begun. But once having begun, and with five people—including two children—dead, I felt I had no choice but to continue, and to rely on Mongo's—Dr. Frederickson's—investigative skills to uncover the truth and to put together a case that the right powerful people would listen to.

"At no time did I foresee, or possibly could have conceived, that the president of the United States would not only turn his back on the truth and continue to protect the man, but actually try to keep him in his post; at no time could I have imagined that members of the United States Congress would turn their eyes from the truth and allow themselves to be manipulated by a president. Truly, politics must carry a danger of its own kind of madness. Had I to do it over again, I would certainly proceed in a different way. But, to my regret, I can't do that—any more than I can restore the lives of the thirteen people Madison has killed while pursuing me. But I'm still not going to kill Orville Madison, gentlemen; that would be far too easy on all of you. Instead, I leave him with you; he's your problem now, not mine. And while you and this wretched administration are pondering what finally to do about him, I think it's time for me to pursue justice in the third branch of the government. I'm curious to see what my own trial for murder will bring out, and what the reaction of the public will be to my testimony and that of the brave men sitting beside me. As of this moment, I am surrendering myself into the custody of Detective Lieutenant Garth Frederickson."

Veil clicked on the Uzi's safety catch, then abruptly slid the weapon across the table to Garth. This done, he leaned back in his chair, crossed his legs, and casually folded his arms across his chest as he stared back at the dust-covered senators sitting on the debris-littered dais.

"Well done, Colonel," came another very familiar voice, this time from the back of the meeting hall. *"Your trial would certainly be interesting, but I think there may be a better solution."*

It was beginning to feel like Homecoming Week in the Old Senate Office Building, and it wasn't a bad feeling at all. This time even Garth reacted, grunting with surprise and turning around with me in time to see Mr. Lippitt, looking rather odd—at least to us—in a finely tailored three-piece suit, come ambling down an aisle out of the darkness into the light. Veil, it seemed, was not the only uninvited guest who knew how to pick locks.

Mr. Lippitt, a head shorter than the man who walked beside him, hadn't changed at all since I'd last seen him; he never seemed to change. I had no idea how old the Director of the Defense Intelligence Agency was, and I didn't think anyone else did, either. Mr. Lippitt, with his totally bald head, piercing brown eyes, and electrifying, commanding presence, seemed to be forever. I knew only that he had fought in World War Two, which would put him well past the age when most men his age would have retired. But Mr. Lippitt was neither retired nor retiring; from the moment he had made his presence known, there had been no question about who was in charge in this meeting hall.

Veil slowly rose as the men approached, pushed back his chair, stood very straight, and saluted.

"Well done, Colonel," the tall, stiff-backed, gray-haired man with Lippitt said, returning Veil's salute. "Very well done."

It had to be General Lester Bean, I thought. Our old friend had brought quite a surprise with him, and it explained a lot of things —if not everything. Lippitt hadn't turned his back on us after all; he simply hadn't been able to help us, or even communicate, without tipping off Madison that he was baby-sitting Veil's ex-commanding officer, waiting for—now.

Lippitt came over to Garth and me, squeezed our shoulders. "It's good to see you, my friends," the old man said, smiling warmly. "I'm deeply sorry I wasn't able to respond to your calls; I thought it best to keep our point of attack completely hidden. Orville Madison is a formidable opponent."

Indeed. "I think we understand, Mr. Lippitt," I replied. "Better late than never."

Lippitt nodded slightly. "Somehow, I knew you'd say that. Also, you know what faith I have in your ability, and Garth's, to handle any situation. I was never really worried about you."

"Funny, Lippitt; somehow I knew you'd say that."

Mr. Lippitt turned toward the dais. "Gentlemen, may I be permitted to address this gathering?"

"Of course, Mr. Lippitt," John Lefferton said, shaking his head slightly as he used a handkerchief to wipe perspiration from his neck. "Would you care to join us up here?"

"I certainly would not," Lippitt answered curtly. "What I have to say won't take that long. It's past time—long past time—that this unfortunate business was wrapped up."

An ashen-faced Orville Madison slowly rose to his feet. "Lippitt," he said in a low voice, "I want to talk to you. In private. You owe me that much."

Lippitt ignored him, spoke directly to the senators. "The man with me, in case you don't know him, is Lieutenant General Lester Bean, U.S. Army, retired. I believe you will be interested in what he has to say, since he was Colonel Kendry's commanding officer in Viet Nam, and both men have had extensive dealings with Mr. Madison. General Bean will testify to the fact that Orville Madison was Colonel Kendry's C.I.A. controller—something which I believe Mr. Madison has denied. He also has a great many other things to tell you about Mr. Madison, and is prepared to present certain U.S. Army documents which will shed a great deal of light on an incident that occurred in and around a Hmong village in Laos many years ago, Colonel Kendry's surrender to the authorities for what we might call a breach of military discipline, and Mr. Madison's key involvement in the disposition of that case. It was soon after this disposition that this committee was informed of the cancellation of the so-called Archangel plan."

Lippitt paused, and for almost half a minute there was not a sound in the chamber. Then, moving almost as one, the five senators, marshal, and two aides turned to stare at the man sitting at the far end of the broken table. Suddenly Orville Madison began to tremble, almost imperceptibly at first, then with tremors that moved in waves up and down his entire body.

"Lippitt," Madison said in a hoarse voice as he leaned forward on his knuckles, "stop this. You're making a big mistake. The president needs me."

Lippitt continued to ignore him. "General Bean came to me some weeks ago," he said to the senators. "It was the same evening that President Shannon announced the choices for his cabinet. General Bean told me that he feared for his life, and that he wished to share with me certain classified documents he had secretly photocopied and taken with him when he retired from the military. Frankly, I did not take the general's fears seriously, and I refused to look at documents which were, in effect, stolen. What I did do, out of courtesy, was invite the general to spend the night in my home. In the morning, we learned that his home had burned to the ground during the night, and that the police strongly suspected arson."

"Lippitt!" Madison screamed.

"After making arrangements for General Bean to stay in one of our own safe houses, I began my own investigation into just what —and how big—the problem was. It quickly became apparent that the problem was a big one indeed. In order to keep Mr. Madison off my trail, and the general's, I deemed it necessary to cut off all communications with everyone—including my dear friends the Fredericksons, to whom I owe my life, even when I knew they desperately needed my help. All of us, gentlemen—Colonel Kendry, Mongo and Garth, General Bean and myself—have sacrificed a great deal to come to this juncture; we have risked our own lives, and the lives of beloved friends, and we have had friends die, all so that, finally, the elected representatives of this great nation would be given an opportunity to do what they are supposed to do, namely, show that we are a nation of laws. This, gentlemen, is the moment of truth, and none of us is leaving this room until the evidence is read into the record, and until you have decided how to deal with a president who appears to be as out of control as the man he wants for his secretary of state."

"Tell Mom and Dad I love them," Garth whispered in my ear as Lester Bean sat down at the witness table and pulled the microphone over in front of him. "Try to explain, and ask them to forgive me."

Intent on Lippitt and Bean, and the reactions of Madison and the senators, I wasn't certain I'd heard Garth right. I turned toward him, was startled by the glazed look in his eyes and the almost blank expression on his face.

"What?!"

"I'm dying, Mongo," my brother whispered, "so what I do doesn't matter. I'm still not sure these people are going to get it right."

"Garth, what the hell are you talking about?"

Garth's answer was suddenly to grab the marshal's .45, click off the safety catch, raise it, and without hesitation fire two bullets into Orville Madison's head. Madison died instantly, collapsing over the table and rolling down into the well, leaving blood and brains smeared on the wall behind where he had been standing.

It happened so quickly and without warning that everything,

including the roar of the gun, had some of the quality of a dream; there were no shouts, no scrambling, and even as the echo of the gunshots faded away everyone remained still—except Garth, who swept the Uzi off the table and then backed away a few steps. I watched in horror as the .45 in Garth's hand slowly turned, stopped when it was pointed at Veil.

"Garth, please put the gun away," I said quietly, terrified by the expression—or lack of it—on my brother's face. In the dusty light Garth's flesh was a pasty, pale green, and suddenly the man with the gun in front of me became a stranger who had somehow been able to invade the body, and was lurking behind the glassy eyes, of my brother.

"My brother could have been killed because of you," the stranger said in a stranger's voice to Veil.

I half expected Veil, with his incredible speed and reflexes, somehow to take command of the situation—duck away out of the line of fire, perhaps even get to Garth and disarm him.

Instead Veil, his arms at his sides, merely stepped slowly and deliberately back from the table, away from Lippitt, Bean, and me, presenting himself as a clear target. "I'm sorry, Lieutenant," Veil said evenly. "You're absolutely right; I had no right to do what I did."

"Sorry isn't good enough," the stranger said.

I knew Garth was going to pull the trigger of the .45, just as I knew that Veil wasn't going to do anything to defend himself. I pushed my chair out of the way and lunged for Garth, trying to put myself between him and Veil. I failed at that, but did manage to spoil Garth's aim. The gun went off a few inches from my left ear, and out of the corner of my eye I saw Veil grab for his right shoulder as he was spun around by the impact of the slug.

Then Lippitt, the marshal, Bean, myself, and even a couple of the senators were on Garth, dragging him to the floor. I ended up on the bottom of the pile, both hands gripping the gun. I was expecting a fierce struggle, but there wasn't any. Garth was lying very still, his joints apparently locked, his muscles rigid and hard as stone.

"Get off!" I screamed, shoving and kicking at the bodies covering Garth and me. "Get the hell off!"

The shouting and kicking weren't necessary. The others, reacting to Garth's sudden catatonic stiffness, had already begun to back off. I was left alone, kneeling beside Garth with tears flooding my eyes and rolling down my cheeks.

The signs had been there all along, I thought; I'd seen them, but had simply refused to do anything about it. McGarvey, the trooper, had seen them and pointedly warned me that Garth was ready to explode and shatter. I'd ignored the warning.

Now even the stranger was gone, and I was left with a stiff, empty-faced, and empty-eyed figure whose hoarse, labored breathing was the only indication that he was alive.

Orville Madison was finally dead, but it meant nothing to me; I had lost my brother with him. Garth was gone, hiding in some lonely, cold, hideous place in his mind where I feared I would never be able to find him.

23

Mr. Lippitt arranged for Garth to be taken to the C.I.A.'s psychiatric clinic on the agency's grounds at Langley, Virginia. It was, Lippitt had assured me, not only the most secret but the best facility in the country for psychiatric diagnosis and short-term care. Garth's ending up in a C.I.A. psychiatric clinic was a bitter irony I did not care to dwell on.

Indeed, I did not care to dwell on much of anything. As much as possible, I tried to keep my mind a blank as, hour after hour, I sat beside my brother's bed and stared at his unseeing eyes staring at the beige ceiling. Doctors came and went, Garth was wheeled out for tests and brought back, and still I sat, lost in my own dark world of despair, remorse, and self-recrimination. Finally I fell asleep in my chair, and when I awoke I found Veil and Lippitt in the room.

Lippitt, a physician himself, was studying the thick ream of charts and test reports secured to a clipboard tied to the railing at the foot of Garth's bed. Veil, his injured right arm in a sling, saw that I was awake, offered me a thermos filled with hot coffee. I nodded my thanks, poured myself a cup.

"I've got a pint of Irish Mist hidden up my sling, Mongo. You want some?"

I shook my head. "How's your arm?"

"I was lucky; the collarbone's cracked, but not broken. It should heal fairly quickly." He nodded toward Garth. "No change?"

"No change."

"Does he show any signs of recognizing you, or hearing anything anybody says?"

"See for yourself," I said, trying to keep the bitterness I felt out of my voice. "He reminds me of your loft; the lights are on, but there's nobody home. It's just a shell, fed and drained by tubes. He told me he was dying."

"He's not," Lippitt said as he circled something on one of the sheets with a red felt-tip pen, then turned the page. "But it's understandable that he thought so."

"What does that mean, Lippitt? What's the matter with him?"

"Just give me a chance to finish checking these," the Director of the Defense Intelligence Agency said, holding up one hand.

"Sorry about your arm," I said to Veil.

"I'm sorry for what's happened, Mongo. I feel responsible."

"No, I'm responsible. Garth and I went through some bad times a couple of years ago, and I guess Garth just never recovered from it. He came out not caring about anything but me; all my life, from the time I was a child, Garth was my protector. It's why . . . what happened happened. I should have paid more attention to certain symptoms."

Veil reached out and gripped my shoulder. "I don't know how to thank you, Mongo. If you ever need me, I'll be there."

"I know that, and it wasn't necessary to tell me. Incidentally, I think you might want to move out of your loft and lie low for a while, at least until your shoulder heals."

Veil raised his eyebrows slightly. "Why?"

"You could have a *ninja* biding his time, waiting to off you. His name is Henry Kitten, and he's the real McCoy. The man has talent."

Veil shrugged his good shoulder. "Never heard of him, and word of real talent usually gets around to me sooner or later."

I told Veil about Henry Kitten, the incident in the Fort Lee Historical Park, what the pale-eyed *ninja* had told me. Veil listened with keen interest, but absolutely no sign of concern.

"I hope he got some money up front," Veil said with a thin smile when I had finished.

"He did; all of it. But—"

"Then he's long gone, Mongo. Don't worry about it."

"But—"

"Mongo," Lippitt said, abruptly dropping the chart on its connecting cord, turning and walking toward me, "with your permission, I'd like to place Garth in the Rockland Psychiatric Center, up in Rockland County. All expenses will be covered by the D.I.A."

"No thanks, Lippitt," I replied curtly, offended when I knew I shouldn't be. "Garth has good insurance coverage; what that doesn't cover, I'll pay for. It's because of me that he's here, so I'll damn well take care of him until . . . I'll just damn well take care of him."

"I don't care for the self-pity in your voice, Mongo," Lippitt said with an impatient shake of his head. "It's most unbecoming in a man with your courage and usual good sense; there are better ways to spend your wits and emotions. I heard what you said to the colonel a few minutes ago about Garth's never recovering from the unfortunate events in which we were involved. Interesting. You and I seem to have bounced back quite nicely. Do you consider Garth the weakest of the three of us?"

"I didn't say that, Lippitt, and I don't appreciate your putting words in my mouth or thoughts in my head. But I'm looking at my brother. *You* look at him. If it weren't for me, he wouldn't be here."

"If it weren't for your willingness to help Colonel Kendry, I'm quite sure that your brother would be dead right now. This Archangel business saved his life. Now, it's up to the doctors—and perhaps you and me—to save his mind."

I could think of nothing to say, so I said nothing; I simply sat and, with Veil, stared dumbfounded at the old man. Lippitt sat down on the edge of the bed, took Garth's limp hand in his. When he spoke again, all traces of harshness were gone from his voice.

"Have you ever heard of a chemical called nitrophenylpentadienal?" Mr. Lippitt continued quietly, looking inquiringly back and forth between Veil and me.

Veil immediately shook his head. I thought about it for some time, thinking the name sounded familiar, and finally found the answer in memories of a brief flurry of newspaper articles that had appeared in connection with the expulsion of a number of exposed K.G.B. agents from the United States.

"Spy dust," I said.

Lippitt nodded. "Right. NPPD, so-called spy dust, is a rather unusual chemical in that it has extreme tenacity when bonded to human flesh; once picked up from an object, it will remain on a person for a very long period of time, through repeated washings, and will in turn leave traces on any object the person touches." Lippitt paused, smiled thinly. "It's the Silly Putty of the spy trade, great fun to play with. Even infinitesimal traces will show up under fluoroscopic light, so it's a very useful chemical for keeping track of the movements of certain people whose movements you want to keep track of. The C.I.A. uses it, the K.G.B. uses it, we use it—and we all deny it, because the long-term health effects of the drug aren't known.

"In fact, aside from its tenacity in clinging to human flesh, very little is known about NPPD. You won't even find it listed in any standard chemical reference book. Virtually all information to date about NPPD has been discovered by government scientists, and that information is classified. Would either of you care to venture a guess as to *why* it's classified?"

"Because they really haven't found out that much," Veil replied dryly. "In government circles, incomplete information usually ends up classified information."

"Correct, Colonel. Now, Mongo, there are certain laboratories around the country, staffed by government scientists, authorized to produce and conduct research on NPPD. They are trying to determine whether the chemical can be absorbed through the skin and, if so, what its short- and long-term effects might be."

"The case of industrial espionage Garth was working on," I said, looking at my brother's still form and feeling short of breath.

"That's right," Mr. Lippitt said. "Somebody was—is—stealing secrets from such a laboratory in New York City. Although neither the NYPD nor Garth was aware of it at the time, I was the one who arranged for Garth to be assigned to that case, precisely because I had such faith in his honesty and his ability to get the job done. I wasn't aware that he'd been transferred, or why, until your calls started coming in. We believe he was being slowly poisoned, and the only thing that saved his life was being transferred away from whoever was poisoning him. However . . ." Lippitt finished by holding up Garth's lifeless hand.

"NPPD?" I asked, still feeling short of breath and having difficulty absorbing what Lippitt was telling me.

"Presumably. But more tests have to be made. That's why we want him at RPC; they're the best, and we do have a secret affiliation with a highly specialized clinic there. He'll receive the best possible care, and you'll have unlimited access to him; Rockland County isn't that far away. Also, I will personally make certain you are kept up to date on all developments concerning his condition." Lippitt paused, turned to Veil. "What I've just discussed is strictly between us, Colonel."

"Of course, sir," Veil said evenly. "And both of you will know where to find me in case I'm needed."

There was a large lump in my throat; I swallowed hard, but it wouldn't go away. "Thanks, Lippitt. Thanks for what you just told me, and . . . just thanks."

"You're quite welcome," Lippitt said, putting Garth's hand back beneath the sheet. The old man rose, gently squeezed my shoulders. "Now, no more self-indulgence; no self-blame. All right?"

"All right."

"Let me take you to a hotel. There's nothing more to be done here."

I shook my head. "Thanks, Lippitt, but I'd like to stay just a bit longer."

"Just let me know when you're ready to leave. A car will take you to the airport, and the driver will have a ticket for you. We'll transfer Garth to RPC as soon as you sign authorization papers."

"Have somebody bring in the papers. I'll sign them now."

"You want company, Mongo?" Veil asked.

"No, thanks. I'll see you back in New York."

Veil and Lippitt were almost out the door when, drifting up from the psychological rubble in my own mind left by Garth's breakdown, I suddenly remembered another small matter that would have definite impact on all our futures. "Hey!" I called after the men. "What's being done about Madison?"

Veil and Lippitt turned back, and it seemed to me that there was just a trace of a smile on both men's faces. "Done?" Lippitt said. "Just what is it you think should be 'done' about the secretary of state?"

"Come on, Lippitt. What's been going on? How are the newspapers treating the whole thing?"

"Colonel, have you seen anything in the newspapers about Mr. Madison?"

Veil shook his head. "I haven't seen anything in the papers, but I believe the White House issued some kind of statement to the effect that he'd planned to take a short vacation. I think he's off on a hunting trip."

"Jesus, you'll never get away with it," I said. "You've got five senators, a United States marshal, two legal aides, and a stenographer who saw Garth blow out Madison's brains."

"Ah, yes," Lippitt said mildly. "Five old politicians worried about their place in state and national history, two young men who'd very much like to work for the D.I.A., and two career civil servants."

"You'll still never get away with it."

"No?" The old man's lips pulled back slightly in what was, for him, the equivalent of a broad grin. "Obviously, you're not one of those people who believe in conspiracy theories of history."

24

The Rockland Psychiatric Center, located in Orangeburg, New York, was a small city, complete with its own police and fire departments. As I drove back out through its tree-lined streets after seeing Garth settled in and conferring with his doctors, it struck me that the vast complex more closely resembled a college campus than a mental health facility—except, of course, for the thick steel bars on the windows of many of the buildings and the vacant stares of many of the patients wandering about the grounds on the arms of nurses or volunteers.

I wondered if I would ever again see my brother up and walking around.

As I neared the eastern exit from the complex, I caught a glimpse of a separate, newer complex of buildings off a hundred yards to my left. There were swings, a baseball field. It would, I thought, be the Children's Hospital, a separate facility where Veil would have been treated when he was here, if it had existed.

Veil's service record had been corrected, and all of his honors restored to him.

A much chastened and humbled Kevin Shannon had issued an invitation to me—through Mr. Lippitt, of course, who had undoubtedly planted the notion in the man's head—to come to the White House to receive a personal apology. I'd declined. Lippitt had told me he thought Shannon could turn out to be a fine president. I didn't care what he turned out to be.

My P.I. license had been restored, along with my carry permits, and all pending criminal charges against me had been dropped.

The university had likewise dropped its charges against me and had offered me a hefty raise. In my letter of resignation to my ex-department head, I had suggested that she consult with Kevin Shannon as to what she could do with my raise. I didn't feel like teaching anymore, couldn't see the point. After what I considered the university's betrayal of me, I felt I had nothing left to teach anyone that was of any value—at least nothing that would be accepted in a curriculum guide.

From now on, I thought, my life belonged to my brother.

But first, there was another bit of business to be taken care of before I could consider the Archangel affair over. I was not nearly as sanguine as Veil concerning the threat posed by Henry Kitten; indeed, it had occurred to me that Veil might know a great deal about Henry Kitten and had professed ignorance and indifference simply to keep me out of further harm's way. In any case, I considered Henry Kitten to be nothing less than a walking, talking doomsday machine. The sudden death of his employer would make no difference at all to the assassin, who had made it clear to me that he took great pride in his work, played for an international audience of potential future employers, and always finished an assignment. There was no doubt in my mind that Henry Kitten would keep coming until either he or Veil was dead. I planned to do all I could to see that it was Henry Kitten who ended up dead. Veil, with his injured arm, would certainly need help.

It was dark by the time I reached the East Village, and the streets were crowded with people of all ages, types, colors, and dress out enjoying an unusually balmy early spring evening.

The crowds thinned out and finally disappeared by the time I reached Veil's street. I parked my car in front of his loft, smiled when I looked up and saw the white light spilling out all the windows; injured arm or not, Veil was back to work, painting. It would be interesting, I thought, to see what changes, if any, would now show up in his style.

And then the lights in the loft, and all along the block, winked out. The rest of the neighborhood appeared to be unaffected, and I could see the lights of the skyscrapers in midtown continuing to glow, but I was left sitting in a car in the middle of a rectangular piece of unrelieved night. I quickly ducked down behind the dashboard and drew out my Beretta. I pushed open the door on the passenger's side and sucked in a deep breath. Then I rolled out of the car and, keeping low, sprinted across the sidewalk toward the steel door below Veil's loft, which I somehow knew would be open.

George C. Chesbro was born in Washington, D.C., and is a graduate of Syracuse University. A resident of Rockland County, New York, Mr. Chesbro was a teacher of Special Education until 1979, when he resigned his position to write full time. In addition to his novels, he has published numerous short stories, poems, and articles and is the author of an educational sound-filmstrip series for handicapped children and adults which is widely used in Special Education classrooms across the country. His far-ranging interests include chess, music, and the infinite variety of human belief systems. *Two Songs This Archangel Sings* is his seventh novel, the fifth featuring Mongo.